Sleeping Dogs:
The Awakening

JOHN WAYNE FALBEY

ISBN-13: 978-0-9855187-1-4

Library of Congress Control Number: 2012909065

DEDICATION

To Annie, my best friend, my partner, my playmate, my biggest fan and most ardent supporter. Thank you for your love, patience, encouragement and trust. No one has ever had a better life companion than you are. All my love, Hans.

CONTENTS

PART ONE

THE ALPHA DOG

"It is nought good a slepying hound to wake"
Chaucer, *Troilus and Criseyde*

1 GEORGETOWN: THE ACCIDENT

The windshield wipers on the Grand Cherokee swept intermittently across the glass, creating an almost hypnotic rhythm. It was a soft rain; little more than a heavy mist that partially obscured the surrounding landscape and created a halo effect around the occasional streetlight. The driver had the radio on. Phil Collins' "In the Air Tonight" was playing.

'I can feel it comin' in the air tonight, O Lord. And, I've been waiting for this moment for all my life, O Lord*"*

It was in the early morning hours only a few days following the advent of a new year. The Jeep's sole occupant, fatigued by the long day of travel, was relieved to be to be nearing the end of his journey. A feeling of apprehension had grown steadily stronger as he neared his destination, the Georgetown section of Washington, D.C. He had remained in self-imposed exile for many years. Now an old friend and mentor, a man to whom he owed so much, had insisted on seeing him.

'I've seen your face before my friend, but I don't know if you know who I am*"*

The weary driver thought back to an earlier time when he was a younger man and his friend had been middle aged. He had learned so much about himself from this man, Clifford Levell. There had been others like the driver there too. All of them had been young and gifted in ways other people were not. The driver remembered every one of them, even the ones who had died. He often wondered what had become of each of the survivors.

'Well, I was there and I saw what you did, saw it with my own two eyes*"*

Only Levell, whom they affectionately had called the Old Man, would know the answer to that question. Levell had maintained communications with each of them – separately for their own safety. The

1

driver wondered briefly if the Old Man had summoned any of the others to this meeting. Probably not, he thought. It would be too dangerous for them. He had been the closest to Levell and probably was the only one who had been invited.

"How could I ever forget? It's the first time; the last time we ever met"

He was driving through a quiet residential section of Georgetown only a few blocks from Levell's home. Usually very attentive to his surroundings, he was tired and lost in his thoughts in the dark, mist-shrouded night. He failed to notice another car approaching on his right from a side street until it was too late to avoid the collision. He yanked the steering wheel hard left trying to spin the Jeep on the wet road. He wanted to impact the large black limousine with the right side of his car against the left side of the limo rather than take its direct force head-on against the side of the Jeep.

It didn't work. Instead, the Jeep was only partially angled to the left when the collision occurred. The limo driver instinctively had yanked his steering wheel hard to the right. The result created a point of impact with the limo's left front fender striking the Jeep's right front fender. The airbags deployed and prevented serious harm to the driver. The force of the impact spun the Jeep 180 degrees so that its left side bounced off the left side of the limo then spun back almost 180 degrees and rolled forward across the intersection ultimately ramming a light pole and knocking it askew. The limo had sloughed part way around and stopped in the middle of the intersection facing toward the direction from which it had come.

The driver sat in the shattered Jeep for a few moments with his mind racing. This was one of the worst things that could have happened to him. He couldn't get involved with police or emergency medical personnel. The urge to climb out of the car and bolt into the night was powerful. The Old Man's house was only a couple of blocks away. As he calmed himself with a series of slow, deep breaths, the driver stared through a side window, the glass now crazed by the impact. The limo was illuminated by the tilting streetlight. The limo driver and another man were getting out. Both were very large men. Both were dressed in dark suits, white shirts and dark, solid color ties. Each had an earpiece. And each held a sidearm in one hand. There was something vaguely sinister about them. If his suspicions were correct, these were among the last people with whom he wanted any contact.

Knowing what had to be done, the driver waited calmly as the two men approached the Jeep. They were careful not to point their weapons directly at him, but it was clear to the driver that they were well trained, and capable of using deadly force if they deemed it appropriate. He waited with both hands on the steering wheel where the men could see them. They approached on the driver's side, and one of them moved around behind the driver's door.

2

The limo driver leaned his six foot five inch frame down and peered carefully at the man behind the Jeep's steering wheel. Other than a day's growth of beard, the driver's skin was smooth and unlined. His features were even with a strong chin and patrician nose. He had light brown hair, parted on the right. But it was his eyes that caught the limo driver's attention. They were an icy blue, like the color of a glacial crevasse. They were locked onto the limo driver's eyes without any sign of emotion. It unnerved the limo driver. As a very large and rough looking man, he was used to people being intimidated by his presence.

"You are alright, yes?" the limo driver said. He spoke with a distinct Eastern European accent, confirming the Jeep driver's initial suspicions.

"Yes".

"You are please showing identification." He held his hand out for emphasis.

With his right hand, the Jeep's driver reached slowly into his right front pocket and pulled out his wallet. He removed a driver's license and handed it to the man. As the limo driver took it from him, the man in the Jeep noticed that the back of the other man's hand was heavily tattooed, even his fingers.

The limo driver squinted at the ID in the poor light and said, "Valter Bailey. From Omaha, Nebraska." He pronounced each word slowly. English was his second language. Barely.

"That's right," Bailey said.

The limo driver glanced briefly at his companion, then, turning back to Bailey, said, "You are long way from Omaha, yes? Is late. Vhat you are doing in Georgetown?"

"I'm here to attend a college reunion. Flew into Dulles, rented this vehicle, and was trying to find my hotel. It's been a long time since I was here, and I may have gotten a bit lost," he said, trying to feign sheepishness.

The limo driver said, "You are please to step out of car slowly...and keeping hands vhere vee can zee dem."

Bailey, who was wearing thin glove liners, presumably to counter the cold January weather, kept his right hand on the steering wheel and slowly reached down and opened the door. In the process, he nicked the little finger of his left hand on a piece of glass from the broken windshield. A small trickle of blood began to ooze from the cut.

He swung his legs over the rocker panel and stepped carefully out of the truck. He knew the situation was bad and probably about to get worse. He needed just the right moment in order to act.

The limo driver studied him for a moment. There was something about Bailey's muscularity and efficiency of movement that suggested an ability to handle himself when physically challenged. The large man motioned Bailey toward the rear of the Jeep. The three men stepped around the truck and under the tilting streetlight. The limo driver paused momentarily and held his hand to his earpiece.

As he did, Bailey noticed the additional tattoos on the man's neck. He glanced at the other man. He had similar body graffiti. He recognized the markings as gang symbols for a ruthless Eastern European crime syndicate.

The limo driver listened for a few moments to a voice coming through the earpiece then glanced quickly at the other man for a brief moment. Each took a step or two backward and the limo driver said, "Vee are thinking you are not ziss man, Bailey, und vee are thinking you lie about college reunion."

Bailey, trying to look intimidated, smiled weakly and said, "Wh...what do you want me to do? The accident wasn't my fault. You ran the stop sign." He made an effort to put a whine in his voice.

The limo driver stepped closer and raised the weapon in his right hand so that it was about 45 degrees with the ground and pointing just to the outside of the Bailey's left kneecap. It reinforced his observation that the two men were well trained.

"I have good nose for bullshit," said the limo driver. "I am thinking you are one of Levell's peoples. I think you are on way to see him." He turned slightly to his right to smirk at his companion. When he did, the muzzle of the weapon edged farther away from Bailey's knee. That was his moment of opportunity.

Moving swiftly forward, he gripped the limo driver's thick right wrist with his left hand. Half turning to his left, he wrapped his right arm over and around the big man's right arm with his forearm just above the elbow joint. At the same time he raised his right leg and drove the heel of his shoe into the outside rear portion of the man's right knee, buckling it and tugging him around into his companion's line of fire. It was all part of a technique Bailey had practiced countless times over the years, and had used on more than one occasion.

Seamlessly, as a flowing part of the technique, Bailey pressed down with force on the big man's wrist while simultaneously driving the upper part of his arm upward with pressure from Bailey's right wrist. It dislocated the limo driver's elbow and the weapon fell from his hand. As the man screamed in pain, he shoved him at the other armed man then sprinted up his massive falling body like a running back scaling his offensive linemen at the goal line and launched himself in a flying kick. His right heel smashed the other man's nose and he staggered backward.

Before he could recover and focus his weapon at his attacker, Bailey had closed the gap and drove his right knee very forcefully into the man's groin. The injured man grunted loudly and bent forward, his knees buckling, grabbing at his assailant. But Bailey was too quick. He had both hands on the victim's right arm and swung it up and around, careful to keep the weapon in the man's hand pointing away from him. He continued to sweep the arm backward and up, no mean task with a man that large. But Bailey was not a small man himself at six feet two inches and two hundred twenty-five pounds with no perceivable body fat.

He tugged the big man off balance toward him so that he was forced to shift his weight to his right foot then swept that base leg from under him. The big man did a forward somersault and landed on the back of his neck. Before he could recover, Bailey drove the heel of his right shoe deep onto the soft tissue of his throat, destroying his windpipe, larynx, and the scream that tried to rise from it. Unable to breathe, he would be unconscious in a minute or so and dead within a few more.

Bailey turned back to the limo driver, who was writhing in pain on the street. He picked up both men's weapons, Glock 23C models, one in each hand. He bent over the limo driver for an instant and brought the butt of one of the Glocks down with great force crushing the man's forehead and driving bone splinters into his frontal lobe. It may not have been a kill shot, but at the very least it would permanently destroy motor skills, libido, and problem-solving and creative thought processes. The man, if he survived, would be vegetative for his remaining years.

He shifted his attention to the black limo, knowing that time was running very short. By now, neighbors undoubtedly had heard the crash and called the authorities. He walked swiftly, but cautiously, toward the car keeping one Glock focused on the middle of the windshield and the other on the left rear window. When he was still fifteen feet away, the right rear door opened and another large man climbed out. He was dressed similarly to the first two. He tried to bring his weapon up to brace his arms on the limo's roof for stability when Bailey open fire with both of the .40 caliber Glocks. One round pierced the big man's left eye and exited the back of his skull taking much of his brain matter with it. His head snapped backward, and his body toppled forward. The corpse slid down the side of the limo leaving a bloody streak all the way to the pavement.

As Bailey drew close to the limo, the left rear window began to lower. He aimed both Glocks into the darkness behind it. A face slowly emerged from the dark. He kept both weapons trained on it and made a quick scan of the car. The passenger was alone now. It was an older man's face, but the years had been kind to him and Bailey recognized him immediately. His face had collected more wrinkles and his hair, still parted in the same style, was much grayer and thinner, but there was no doubt about his identity. He was wearing a dark brown double-breasted Burberry trench coat and clutching a cordovan leather attaché case in his hands. It took a few more moments for the other man to get a good look at the person now training the two Glocks on him.

"Jesus Christ! I was right. It really is you, Whelan!" he said as he recognized the man's real identity. "But...you're dead!" And then it was he who was dead; shot in the middle of the forehead by a slug from one of the Glocks.

2 GEORGETOWN: LEVELL

Whelan could hear the sounds of sirens approaching from the distance. He glanced around and saw lights on in the upper stories of the old houses around the intersection. A few neighbors were peering out of bedroom windows in their homes. He squeezed off a couple of rounds shattering the windows, but not otherwise harming the occupants. It had the desired effect. They ducked quickly out of sight and didn't return

He wasn't concerned that he had been seen. He wasn't planning to be captured, and he doubted anyone could positively identify him given the poor light in the intersection and the overcast, moonless night. He shoved a Glock into each of his windbreaker's side pockets, reached through the open window, grabbed the attaché case from the dead man's hands and moved swiftly across the intersection, purposely heading in a direction away from Levell's house. At the end of the next block, he turned right and ran effortlessly for three blocks before turning right again. The old man's house was at the end of the block.

He quickly climbed the steps to the front door and rang the bell, glancing around to make certain no one was watching. It seemed as if an eternity passed while he waited for a response. By now the police would have interpreted the excited babble of the residents and begun fanning out through the neighborhood, knowing he couldn't have gone far on foot.

At last, the door opened and an Asian man of indeterminate age faced him. He was about five feet seven inches tall with closely cropped black hair and finely chiseled features on an expressionless face. The man wore baggy black trousers and a black form fitting tee shirt. He was lean and very wiry with no discernible body fat. Whelan guessed him to be Korean, and knowing Levell as he did, assumed he was a master of the martial arts.

"May I help you?" the man said. He had a high-pitched voice and a noticeable accent.

"Mr. Levell is expecting me. I'm running late."

The Asian man eyed him for a moment then said, "Wait here", and started to close the door.

Whelan said, "I need to wait inside…with the door closed."

The man, aware of the sirens, quickly connected the dots and stepped aside. Whelan was prepared to wait by the door until the other man returned, but Levell's voice broke in from somewhere in the house. "Mr. Rhee, is that him?"

"Yes, Mr. Levell, he here now."

"Well, for Christ's sake bring the man in here!"

The Korean man motioned to Whelan to follow him as he led the way across a large living room toward a hallway on the other side. The living room was dimly lighted by a single ornate lamp on a small table in one corner. The dark woods and Victorian-style furnishings contributed to the gloomy pall of the room. Several paintings, which he took to be Gainsboroughs or very good imitations, hung on the walls. The windows were blocked by heavy velvet drapes. The tray ceiling had a slight dome effect and supported a large glass chandelier. A big, expensive looking rectangular rug, probably very old and valuable, covered the middle of the room. It was underlain by a dark hardwood floor. The house had a musty odor about it. Whelan shifted the handle of the attaché case to his left hand and followed Rhee.

He was led down a wide, poorly lit hallway to a room that obviously was a den. Tall wooden bookshelves lined three walls including the one through which they entered the room. One of the walls contained a large stone mantled fireplace in which several logs were burning nicely. The fourth wall was decorated with framed photographs from Levell's life experiences and was bisected by another set of dark, heavy velvet drapes that blocked a window. There was a large paneled wooden desk in the middle of the room. Papers were strewn all across its surface. A small lamp on one corner of the desk provided the only light in the room.

An old man with closely cropped iron gray hair, bushy eyebrows and strong jaw line sat in a wheelchair in front of the desk, a heavy robe across his lap. Despite his obvious disability, he displayed a military bearing. Whelan was saddened to see his old friend and mentor, Clifford Levell, in this state. He knew the man, now only in his mid-seventies, before the accident had robbed him of his mobility. He remembered Levell as a strong, vigorous, hard-living man.

The two men looked at each other for a moment. Rhee stood quietly in the background, prepared for any exigency. After a moment, Levell spoke.

"I'll be goddamned! Brendan Whelan, the Prince of Wolves!" Levell said, making reference to the translation from Irish Gaelic of Whelan's given and surnames. His voice was clear and strong, although it retained a familiar raspiness. "Son, you are a sight for these failing eyes of mine. Give me a big-ass hug."

Whelan leaned over and hugged the old man, surprised by how strong the man he remembered as a warrior's warrior remained in spite of his handicap. "It's been a long time. How are you, Cliff?"

"How the hell do you think I am? I'm confined to this damn baby buggy. Isn't that a bitch?"

Whelan wasn't sure what to say. "I'm sorry, sir. Is there anything I can do?"

"Look, Brendan, sooner or later life kicks the shit out of all of us. But I have no regrets; it's been a very good life. And it remains so." He paused, then said, "You ask if there's anything you can do? Yes, hell, we've got work to do. And quickly. We're running short of time."

He motioned Whelan to sit in one of the large, overstuffed leather desk chairs. "You're probably famished. When's the last time you ate?"

"On the flight this morning, I think," Whelan said.

Levell turned to the Asian man and said, "Mr. Rhee, please bring our guest something to eat." He held up his hand indicating that he had more to say to Rhee, and turned back to Whelan. "Will you join me in a nightcap?" He glanced at his watch and said, "Make that an early morning cap."

"A cold beer would hit the spot," Whelan said. "It's been a long day. The flight from Shannon seems like a week ago."

"I heard sirens. That have anything to do with you?"

"Yes. As luck would have it, I literally ran into an 'old friend' of ours on the way here. I was blindsided in an intersection a few blocks away. Bottom line, I killed three bodyguards and the man they were supposed to be protecting." Whelan paused for a moment then said, "It was Case."

Levell sat forward suddenly in his wheelchair. "Harold Case?"

"The same."

"He's a part of the reason I called you back from Ireland. Actually, I suspect he may have been on his way here to speak with me. Did he know it was you?"

"Yes, that's why I killed him. It's long been my understanding that the world thought the others and I had died years ago. Case would have blown that cover."

Levell rubbed his hand together in satisfaction. "Harold Case, that miserable sonofabitch. His departure was long overdue. Wish I had done it myself." He paused for a moment then said, "The Agency was supposed to have destroyed all files twenty years ago when the plug was pulled on the operation. Somehow, not all files were purged. Case was working for someone who wants to expose the operation to further discredit this country and enhance his own political ambitions. "

"And that would be?"

"The senior senator from New York, Howard Morris."

Whelan nodded in recognition of the name. He had been living in Ireland for almost twenty years, but he had stayed current on America's foreign and domestic issues.

Levell said, "He's bankrolled, of course, by a certain multibillionaire with a one-world socialist view. The funds originate with a specific foreign power that has sought the destruction of this country for the better part of a century. Once laundered through the supposed business machinations of the billionaire, the funds are used in America and abroad to support organizations whose purposes are to undermine the U.S. economy, political system, and stature in global affairs. The end game is the destruction of our democratic republic based on capitalism, to be replaced by a socialist society, or worse. This effort has been underway for decades in the United States, infiltrating the political system, the news media, unions, the system of education and other institutions, including, no doubt, members of our military's junior officer corps.

"The foreign power and its domestic allies are on the verge of realizing the fruits of their long labors. That's why I called you back. Those of us...we refer to ourselves as the Team, who are dedicated to preventing that destruction desperately need the services of you and your former colleagues."

"So who is this Team?" Whelan said.

"We are individuals who are highly placed in the senior ranks of the military, the intelligence community and private industry. We are all of one mind when it comes to preserving the freedoms and opportunities inherent in a democratic capitalist society. For now, that's all you really need to know."

"You said Case was on his way here. Why?"

"I suspect he thought I could be persuaded or bribed to help him corroborate the files he discovered."

Aware that Rhee was still waiting, Levell turned to him and said, "Mr. Rhee, please bring our guest a sandwich and a cold beer. And while you're at it, I'll have a glass of that very old, single malt scotch I've been saving. This is an occasion for a celebration."

Rhee nodded impassively and left the room.

Levell looked at Whelan and asked, "Any witnesses to the scene with Case? Anyone who could identify you?"

"None that are alive or capable of rational thought processes."

"Fingerprints?"

Whelan held up his hands. "Glove liners."

Levell looked at Whelan's left hand. "Is that a cut on your little finger?"

Whelan looked at the injury. "It's nothing. I don't even remember getting it."

"Nothing my ass," said Levell. "Even the slightest trace of body fluid can be unlocked with today's DNA analysis. Let's just hope the part of your records that included your vital statistics was destroyed, as ordered, twenty years ago." He paused and shook his head. "With these goddamn government bureaucrats, though, nothing ever seems to get destroyed, burned, erased, or deleted as it's supposed to be."

Whelan nodded in agreement, rose from his chair, peeled off the glove liners, strode to the fireplace and threw them into the flames. They were consumed quickly.

"Weapons?" said Levell.

Whelan patted his windbreaker. "Two Glock forties I took off the bodyguards. Can Mr. Rhee dispose of them?"

Levell nodded. "Case was a motherfucker, but he was well connected in government. His demise will set off a shit storm. Add to that the number you did on three very highly trained security people and the absence of suspects." His eyed narrowed in thought and he said, "The Feds will be combing through this neighborhood for days leaving no stone unturned. We've got to get you out of here, and fast before it's too late."

"There are a couple of other items," Whelan said. "For one thing, from their accents, Case's muscle may have been Ukrainian."

"That figures," Levell said. "This mess I've been forced to drag you into revolves around a billionaire, Chaim Laski. That name ring a bell?"

Whelan nodded. "Yes," he said.

"Sonofabitch surrounds himself with big, nasty Ukrainian thugs. Senator Morris is Laski's bitch, and Case was working for Morris. What else do you have?"

"Harold had an attaché case, so I brought it along. Might be worth looking into." He held it out toward Levell.

Levell nodded. "Good. Let's have a look at its contents."

3 J. EDGAR HOOVER BUILDING

The J. Edgar Hoover Building houses the headquarters operations of the Federal Bureau of Investigation. It's a massive, multistoried structure on the north side of Pennsylvania Avenue between 9th and 10th Streets Northwest in Washington, D.C. Deep in its bowels, eighteen people were crammed into a small conference facility designed for a maximum of ten occupants. All were beginning to perspire as their collective body heat dissipated throughout the room that already was overheated by the building's HVAC system. Some sat flipping through messages on their smart phones; others were engaged in animated conversations or phone calls. A few were watching a very large black man, the district commander of the Metropolitan Police Department's Second District. He was leaning over the conference table and bellowing at the Bureau's Supervisory Special Agent, Mitchel Christie.

Ordinarily, Christie was officed in the Bureau's separate Washington Field Office at 601 4th Street Northwest. To compensate for overcrowding in the field office, some agents recently had been relocated to the Hoover Building. In Christie's case the move had been sudden and very recent. When he had left his office last evening it had been in the field office. The Harold Case affair changed that. He received a call at his home before four o'clock in the morning. His boss told him he was being assigned to head up the investigation, and would be relocated to the Hoover Building. He didn't like surprises and he didn't like change. But he was a company man and did as he was told.

Christie, the SSA, sat calmly at the head of the table, his eyes focused on the large man's angry face. The only outward sign of tension was the soft drumbeat as the fingers of his left hand slowly tapped in unison on the tabletop. He was working very hard to keep his temper under control despite the steady shower of spittle flying in his direction as the big man bellowed in rage. It mixed with the perspiration beginning to roll slowly down his face. Finally, as he neared the end of his patience, he held up his right hand, palm outward, and said, "Steve." That didn't seem to have any effect. He paused for a moment and raised his voice a notch and said, "District Commander Williams, screaming and shouting isn't going to accomplish anything. It's seven o'clock in the morning and the event happened only four hours ago. Everybody here was yanked out of bed to come in and work on this thing. Let's not waste any of their time."

"Waste time? Waste time?" Williams yelled. "You're not the Commander of the MPD's Second District. This massacre occurred on my turf!"

"I'm very much aware of that," Christie said. "And, while we'll work closely with your people, the Bureau has been assigned primary jurisdiction of this investigation."

Williams' eyes seemed to bulge in their sockets as he struggled to control his rage. "You have no fuckin' idea what my office is like right now. Phones ringin' off the fuckin' hooks, citizens crapping their drawers in fear, media hammering away at me for details I don't have. And my boss calling me every fifteen minutes expecting answers when I'm not even sure what the fuckin' questions are yet. What I do know is I got three innocent dead people and one vegetable on my hands. This fuckin' meeting should be happening in my office instead of me having to drive over here to watch you clowns having a circle jerk." He stood up and took a deep breath.

The SSA continued to lock eyes with Williams. "Three of those men were in this country illegally, on expired visas. They each have extensive police records in Europe. And if they were 'innocent' citizens, as you seem to want us to believe, Harold Case might still be alive."

The district commander slammed a very large palm down on the table sending a shock wave all the way to its far end. "You cheeky bastard! Any of my people could eat any of your candy-assed little Bureau twinkies for lunch." When he lifted his palm, it left a large wet mark on the tabletop.

All other activities in the room ceased as the SSA rose to his feet. He was a tall, lean man, but at six feet three inches he was a good three inches shorter than the district commander, and spotted him almost one hundred pounds in body weight. The tense moment was interrupted as a small, fortyish woman with short blonde hair and wire rim glasses approached the SSA and whispered to him, "One of our forensics people is on the line, sir. I think you're going to want to hear this." She handed him her cell phone.

"Christie", he said. "What have you got?"

The voice on the other end said, "It's Billingsley, sir. We may have uncovered an anomaly that could be relevant."

"Yeah?"

13

"It's a very small blood sample, but it doesn't appear – preliminarily anyway – that it came from any of the victims."

"Where did you find it?" said the SSA.

"Actually, sir, we found two samples. Oddly, one on the right wrist of each of the two victims found near the Jeep. But their skin wasn't broken in those areas."

The SSA's eyes narrowed in thought. "On their wrists?" He paused for a moment then said, "Any theories yet?"

"Not really," Billingsley said. "Might be that one of the assailants was injured and the blood was transferred in close quarters combat. Judging from the injuries suffered by those two victims, it was hand-to-hand at some point."

"Has the sample been sent to the lab for DNA testing yet?"

"Yes, sir."

"Good work. Keep me posted." The SSA pressed the disconnect button and handed the phone back to the woman, his assistant. "Charlotte, I wanna know the minute the DNA results are available." She nodded and returned to her seat near the other end of the table.

Christie turned toward the others gathered around the table and raised his hands signaling for them to pay attention. "Alright, people, let's get focused." The room suddenly quieted. Only the district commander remained standing, glaring at Christie, who said, "It's only been a short while since the event and we still don't have much to go on, but let's recap what we do know one more time."

The SSA sat down, purposely ignoring the smoldering gaze from the district commander, who, with an undisguised snort, finally lowered his massive frame into a chair.

"At approximately three a.m. this morning, an event involving fatalities occurred in a residential section of Georgetown. It appears to have involved a collision between a late model Jeep Grand Cherokee and a limousine. The Jeep was rented earlier this morning at Dulles by a man identified as Walter Bailey of Omaha, Nebraska. The limousine was under lease by a Delaware corporation that's in that line of business. It was hired for the evening by a retired CIA employee named Harold Case. Mr. Case was seventy-two years old and was working as a private contractor for a senate investigative subcommittee. There were three fatalities and a potentially fatal injury. The men accompanying Mr. Case all were Ukrainian nationals who were in this country illegally. They apparently were working for a private security firm organized and headquartered in the Cayman Islands."

The SSA glanced at some sheets of paper on the table in front of him. "Mr. Bailey appears to be an assumed name. There's certainly no trace of such an individual in Omaha. Agents from our Atlanta office are checking into it, but it appears that the real Walter Bailey, on whom the identity is based, died at the age of twenty-eight while undergoing heart surgery in Georgia in 1998."

A chubby man with glasses and thinning hair, who was sitting next to Charlotte, raised his hand. "Excuse me, sir, but can the car rental people at Dulles identify the man who rented the Jeep?"

"Unfortunately, no, Chuck," Christie said. "The car was rented from Hertz over the Internet from a public access computer in a library in Palo Alto, California. It was rented under the Walter Bailey name on a Hertz Number One Gold account. That means the car was waiting for him in the company's lot with no check-in required. He just got in and drove it off. It was late and raining. No one saw him. The Hertz account was bogus; a dead end."

"But didn't Hertz's surveillance cameras pick him up?" Chuck said.

"Yes, but the conditions were poor. He was wearing a cheap-looking raincoat with the collar turned up and a hat pulled low on his face. All we know is that he had longish hair, wore glasses, and was somewhat pudgy. We're putting together a sketch of what we think he probably looks like and will get a copy to everyone here."

"What about ballistics at the crime scene?" Chuck said.

"Nothing. Shell casings appear to be from side arms carried by the Ukrainians. It appears that one of them was used to kill one of the Ukrainians as well as Mr. Case. Case, incidentally, was shot execution style. Head shot. Close range. There are severe powder burns around the entry wound. No fingerprints, fibers or body fluids in or on the Jeep that haven't otherwise been accounted for. No credible eyewitnesses. No anything at this point." He purposely chose not to reveal the blood samples Billingsley had told him about.

The district commander intervened. "Do we know what Case was working on for that senate subcommittee?"

Christie closed his eyes for a moment and rubbed his right temple. He knew from his years of experience with the Bureau that there would be little rest for him in the foreseeable future. "We're trying to gather that information now, Steve. Apparently it's a matter of considerable national security. The only person who appears to know much about it is the committee's chair."

"And that would be?" the district commander said.

"Senator Morris."

"Howard Morris?"

"Yes. The senior senator from New York."

"Shit!" the district commander said. "That political hack is the biggest self-serving prick in a town full of them. He's a left wing loony. Always looking for ways to embarrass this country in the eyes of the rest of the world."

Christie nodded. "And generally succeeding at it."

"He won't tell us shit unless he somehow stands to gain from it," Williams said.

Christie nodded again. He'd had several cups of coffee on an empty stomach since the first call had come through at about three thirty that morning. The burning sensation in his stomach was turning into something much sharper. He wondered how much liquid remained in the bottle of Mylanta in his office and when he would have an opportunity to get to it.

4 GEORGETOWN

They were still in Levell's study. Whelan had finished a large turkey and Swiss sandwich on multigrain bread that had been prepared and served by Rhee, who since had withdrawn from the room. Whelan was nursing the second cold Dogfish Head 60 Minute IPA. "You still keep your beer at an icy 40 degrees, Cliff," he said with satisfaction.

"Anything warmer and you might as well drink piss like the Brits do."

Whelan smiled. Levell had aged outwardly since he had last seen him, but it didn't appear that he had changed in any other way.

Levell glanced at a large antique grandfather clock and said, "Given the unexpected difficulties you ran into earlier this morning, we need to be more cautious than ever. Debrief your trip up to the time you arrived here. Leave nothing out."

Whelan took another pull from his beer. "As you know, the plane and car reservations were made by one of your contacts. I flew into Dulles from Shannon using a fake British national ID."

"Luggage?"

"Just a small carry-on."

"Did you disguise your appearance for the flight?"

"Yeah, three piece business suit, cordovan lace-ups, goatee and mustache, Julius Caesar bangs, glasses. Pretty much kept my face buried in a newspaper or head turned toward the cabin hull, 'sleeping'," he held his fingers up to indicate quotation marks. "Being in First Class, everyone pretty much minded their own business. I enhanced that with a certain aloofness that complimented the businessman image."

"What about Dulles?" Levell said.

"Put a cap on as I deplaned and went into the first head I came to. Changed into the clothes I'm wearing now, added a cheap raincoat, shaggy wig, rain hat, different glasses, glove liners and used the three piece suit for extra padding around my waist. Packed everything else, including the glasses and fake whiskers in the carry-on."

"The car pick up?"

"Took the Hertz shuttle from the airport."

"Driver notice you?"

"Yeah, but given the hour and the fact that no one else was onboard, there wasn't much I could do. I was careful to keep my head down and touch nothing, even with the glove liners on. Made no conversation with him. I sat behind the luggage rack that's immediately behind the driver. Gave him two bucks when he dropped me off. That's pretty standard. Any more or less can get you noticed."

"Surveillance at the car lot?"

"Sure, there are cameras everywhere today. But I took care not to give them much to record."

"And the carry-on and extra clothes?"

"Followed your instructions and dropped the clothes in one Goodwill drop-box, the carry-on, raincoat and hat in another. Tossed the wig and glasses out the window in two different places."

Levell nodded in approval. "That should have the boys and girls at the Bureau chasing their tails." He glanced at the attaché case that had belonged to the late Harold Case. He was anxious to examine its contents. "Let's take a minute or two and go over the incident with Case again," he said. "Then we'll see what ol' Harold's attaché has to offer up."

Whelan drank the last of the Dogfish Head and nodded. "Sure." He set the empty bottle on a small soapstone coaster on a side table near his chair.

Levell ran a strong looking hand across a cheek. His face was lined by age and the stress of the life he had led, but he still had a full head of hair, gray and close cropped, every bit the Marine officer he once had been. "Isn't it the height of irony that, after all these years, you and that sonofabitch run into each other when you're on your way to see me." He shook his head. "Do you think his ramming your vehicle was a deliberate act?"

Whelan thought about the question for a moment or two. "I don't think so," he said. "As much as neither of us believes in coincidences, I think that's what this was; just one incredibly unfortunate coincidence."

"Like I said earlier, I suspect he was on his way here."

"My gut told me he was," Whelan said. "Want to tell me why?"

"It's part of the reason you're here. I'll fill you in later. Run the whole sequence by me again," Levell said.

"Sure. Case's limo approached me from a side street on the right. The driver either ignored or didn't see the stop sign. I admit I wasn't as focused as I should have been and didn't see 'em until a moment before impact."

Levell shrugged. "It was a long day for you. You were tired."

"Even so, you trained me to be ever vigilant as a way of life."

The older man nodded and made a motion with his hand for Whelan to continue.

"When the dust settled, the limo driver and another man riding shotgun got out and approached the Jeep. Both were armed and made no real effort to hide it." Whelan said.

"Were they pointing the weapons at you?" Levell said.

"Not at first. But I've been trained too well not to have gotten a sense about it. They were both big men and I could tell from the way they conducted themselves that they were not your average Little League dads."

"What did they do?" Levell said.

"Asked me to get out of the truck and kept the weapons – Glock forties, aimed pretty much at my knees. They were all very large men, including the one who stayed behind with Case."

"Glock forties. Exceptionally large men." Levell said. "That does sound like the Ukrainians Laski surrounds himself with. Based on what I told you earlier about the Laski connection, it makes sense they would be escorting Case."

"Why Ukrainians? There's a lot of muscle available on the street." Whelan said.

"These guys are criminals, thugs, the lowest form of vermin in an otherwise decent Ukrainian society. Under the Soviets, most Ukrainians were treated as third class citizens, something less than human. Abusing them made the Ruskies feel better about their own sorry asses. After they left, most Ukrainians were able to move on with their lives and better themselves in honest work.

"These guys who work for Laski are something else entirely. They did the Ruskies' dirty work, and don't give a flying fuck for an honest day's effort. They're ruthless, conscience-free, and cheap. Exactly what a scum-sucking pig like Laski would need."

Whelan shrugged. "I think you're right bout them being on their way here," he said.

"Why did you think that?"

"Right after I got out of the truck, the two men appeared to get some kind of information on their earpieces. Where I was standing, Case might have gotten a look at me and alerted them." Whelan said.

Levell drew in a long, slow breath. "After twenty years, you think he recognized you? In the rain and poor lighting?"

"I think he must have, because right after that things got interesting."

"How so?"

"After they got the communication, the driver of the limo said something along the lines of me being 'one of Levell's people', and being on my way here. That confirmed the need to neutralize them as well as anyone else in the limo."

Levell rubbed his cheek again and his eyes narrowed as he looked at Whelan. "Case, that old sonofabitch, must still have had decent eyesight in spite of his decadent lifestyle. What happened next?"

A little smile played at the corners of Whelan' mouth. "Typical of men that large, powerful, and well trained, they underestimated the smaller man. They won't make that mistake again."

A much broader smile of satisfaction lit up the older man's craggy face. "Good to know you haven't wasted all the time and money that went into training you and the others."

"It's been twenty years. How many of us are left, Cliff?" Whelan said.

"Six including you, but there'll be time for that discussion later. Go on."

"I took their weapons and approached the limo," Whelan said. "As I did, a third man exited from the right rear door. I shot him. It was a kill shot."

Levell nodded approvingly.

"When I reached the limo, Case lowered the window. He ID'ed me for sure about the same time I did him. I shot him, took his attaché case, and made my way here on foot."

"You were smart to grab the case," Levell said, "especially given the probability that he was coming here. We'll have a look at it in a minute. But first, do you know if there were any witnesses? Anything left in the truck?"

"A few neighbors were aroused by the noise and were peering out their windows. I scattered a few rounds in their respective directions. That sent them crawling back under their beds," Whelan said. "As for the Jeep, it was clean."

"Good," Levell said. "We'll just have to see if anything develops from the cut on your finger. Now, let's have a look in Harold's attaché case."

5 HART SENATE OFFICE BUILDING

The United States Capitol Complex in Washington, D.C. is about one mile east of the J. Edgar Hoover Building. In the shadows of the Capitol is another massive, multistoried structure, the Hart Senate Office Building. Named for the late Senator Phillip Hart of Michigan, it is home to the offices of a number of United States senators, including the senior senator from New York, Howard Morris. The nine-story structure provides offices for fifty senators, three committees and several subcommittees. It is the farthest from the Capitol and features a ninety-foot high sky-lit central atrium. The atrium is bridged by walkways on every floor. The second through the eighth floors have balconies that overlook the first floor. In the center of the first floor is an atrium area with a massive statue that reaches upward fifty-one feet into the open space of the atrium. The abstract artwork is Alexander Calder's mobile-stabile, Mountains and Clouds. The towering piece combines black aluminum clouds suspended above black steel mountains. It was one of late artist's final efforts.

Serving his fourth term in the senate, Morris was the chair of the select committee on intelligence. He also chaired a special subcommittee probing Central Intelligence Agency covert operations. The subcommittee's existence was considered a matter of national security and its existence wasn't known by many people.

Morris enjoyed a large, seventh floor corner office with a view of Capitol Hill. Despite the view, he had arranged his desk facing the door that opened from the office of his assistant, Janine, leaving his back to the windows. He liked to see who was entering his presence. The office was tastefully furnished by one of the most expensive and sought-after interior designers in the city. Although members of Congress had certain budget constraints on the furnishing of their offices, Morris was savvy in the ways of the federal bureaucracy. He had spared no taxpayer dollars in establishing an oasis of comfort and luxury for himself.

He had come to the office early this morning, expecting Harold Case to provide him with the elements of a huge story that would further endear him to his constituents on the far left and garner more substance in his planned, but as yet unannounced, bid for his party's nomination for president. As he discovered to his mounting dismay, Case indeed had produced the elements of a huge story, but it wasn't the one Morris had expected.

He felt his anger and frustration rising. He stood and strode over to the full-length mirror on the wall to the left of his desk. Morris stared at his reflection. He was a few inches short of average height. The very expensive, tailored suit coat he wore disguised his narrow shoulders. It was made of charcoal gray silk, and he had paired it with a pale pink shirt and pink and gray rep tie. Although he had gained more than a few extra pounds in recent years, it was largely disguised by the work of a talented tailor. He ran a hand through the long gray hair that he wore brushed straight back, and leaned closer to the mirror to inspect his artificial tan. Morris made a mental note to apply a new coat of the tanning gel that evening.

The buzzing of the intercom on his desk phone interrupted his preening. "Senator Morris," his assistant said. "Mr. Jenkins is here."

"Good, send him in." He walked back to his desk and stood behind it. A moment later, the door opened and a tall, lanky black man walked into his office. Shepard Jenkins, wearing a long-sleeved yellow cotton shirt with a navy blue tie and navy trousers and carrying a heavy overcoat, nodded to Morris. "Senator," he said.

Morris waved his chief political strategist toward one of the overstuffed leather client chairs. "Shep."

"You heard about Case, I presume," Jenkins said.

"Shit, by now, everyone's heard about him. You know anything that's not already been on the news?"

"Not yet, Senator. My concern right now is how anyone could have known what he was up to. We've kept this strictly on a need to know basis. Besides the two of us, who the hell else could have known?"

"Maybe the sonofabitch had a loose lip. He was a self-aggrandizing bastard," Morris said. "My biggest concern is the loss of the information he was gathering. Now what do we do? Give up on this project?"

"Dunno, but we should at least consider doing that."

Morris didn't like the sound of that. He tugged nervously at the collar of his shirt and stepped away from the windows. "Jesus, it was supposed to be so simple. Case was tasked with just digging up some old, supposedly nonexistent, records he knew about from his days with the Agency and bringing them to us. This morning!"

"I'm guessing that's what got him killed," Jenkins said.

"Of course that's what got him killed!" Morris said, growing agitated. "If only I could have gotten my hands on those fucking files and released them to my contacts in the news media. The ensuing shit storm would have enhanced my stature with the rest of the world and likely elevated me as the party's frontrunner in next year's presidential campaign. Assuming that pompous, arrogant fuck-up of an incumbent doesn't try to stand for reelection. Laski keeps assuring me that he won't, but I'm not so sure."

He walked around the desk and sat in the other client chair. "You're my fucking strategist. What do we do now?"

"First, we stay calm. Then we figure out whether anyone else knows about what Case was doing and whether they might be able to trace it back to us."

Morris shook his head in despair. "They assassinated the sonofabitch. Fucking assassinated him. Laid in wait and ambushed him."

"Along with three very capable bodyguards," Jenkins said. "We should assume that whoever is behind this is pretty damned good. Those guys were part of Chaim Laski's private army of Ukrainians. Did you know that two of the bodyguards were killed in hand-to-hand combat?"

Slamming his fist down on the desktop, Morris said, "I don't give a flying fuck how they died. They clearly weren't worth a shit at protecting anyone."

The intercom on his desk buzzed, startling him. He shouted angrily at it. "What is it, Janine?"

"A courier is here with a small package of some kind," she said. "Should I sign for it?"

Morris stiffened in fear. Was it a bomb? Were the same people who had killed Harold Case going to assassinate him next? The day had barely started and already it seemed to be worsening rapidly.

"Senator?" Janine said.

"Who sent it?" he said at last.

Janine said, "A Mr. Case."

6 GEORGETOWN

In the hours following the early morning incident in a residential section of Georgetown, SWAT teams of FBI and local law enforcement officers began conducting a house-to-house campaign. Branching out concentrically from the scene of the incident, they searched each house and surrounding property. Farther out, police cars patrolled the neighborhoods looking for anything or any person of a suspicious nature.

A few minutes after eight o'clock, a twenty-foot brown delivery truck pulled up in front of Levell's home. Its marking indicated that it was a delivery vehicle for a chain of appliance stores. The name on the side of the truck in yellow letters said Custom Appliances of McLean. Two men wearing brown work uniforms and jackets, and brown ball caps climbed out on either side of the cab. There were logos on the jackets and ball caps that matched the logo on the truck. They went to the front door of the home and spoke to Rhee for a moment then returned to the truck, where they raised the roll-up gate in the rear of the vehicle. One of the men climbed into the cab and backed the truck into the driveway. Rhee opened the garage door from inside the house.

A few minutes later they had wrestled a Frigidaire 19.7 cubic foot commercial deep freezer from the back of the truck to the hydraulic liftgate. Using it, they lowered the freezer to the street and placed it on a heavy-duty four-wheeled dolly. Both men then rolled the dolly into Levell's garage. Rhee closed the garage door behind them.

Approximately ten minutes later the garage door reopened and the deliverymen rolled an older looking deep freeze out to the truck. As they were about to load it onto the hydraulic liftgate, a police cruiser with two cops in it rolled to a stop in front of the truck. The deliverymen each glanced quickly at each other.

The officer driving the car rolled his window down and said, "Morning, men. Looks like you're working mighty hard this early in the day."

"Yeah, well a job's a job. We got no say in what gets done or when," the truck's driver said.

"You guys seen anything that don't look right to you in the neighborhood this morning?" the cop said.

"Like what?" said the truck driver.

"Well, like any fuckin' thing that don't look right."

The truck driver looked at his partner. "I ain't seen nothin'. What about you. You seen anything?"

"Nah, I ain't seen nothin' either. But I wasn't exactly lookin' for nothin'. It's fuckin' early, it's cold, and I ain't exactly wide awake yet."

The cop turned and looked at his partner, who shrugged. He turned back to the deliverymen. "Well, you see somethin'," he said, "you flag down the first unit you see and tell 'em about it."

"Yeah, sure, we'll do that," the truck driver said.

The cruiser slowly moved off to continue the assigned search pattern. Both deliverymen, sweating profusely in the cool morning air, looked at each other again. "Jesus H. Christ!" the driver said, "Let's get out of here."

Working as fast as they could, they maneuvered the freezer onto the hydraulic liftgate, hoisted it into the back of the truck, and secured it. They lowered the roll-up gate, climbed back into the truck's cab, and drove off.

7 J. EDGAR HOOVER BUILDING

Supervisory Special Agent Christie stood in one corner of his small office space looking out the single, narrow window. Actually, the other half of the window was on the other side of the partition that separated his space from the office of the special agent next door. His office was furnished in what he called Government Gothic; standard issue even at his pay grade.

He looked out at the midmorning bleakness of a cold, wet, January day in Washington and thought about the current case he was working. Was it a terrorist act? Or was it a random act of violence in a city where violence was not unusual? Or was it something else? He needed a lot more information in order to get to a solution.

He shook the bottle of Mylanta in his right hand, and then slowly unscrewed the cap. Raising it to his lips, he emptied the contents in a single gulp. Hurry, he thought as though the medicine could hear him. Subconsciously, his left hand was rubbing and digging at his abdomen as if trying to reach the pain and pull it from his body.

There was a soft knock at his open door and he turned to see the CIA's liaison to the Bureau, Jim Franconia, standing in the doorway. "You wanted to see me?" Franconia said.

"Yeah, Jim. Come in, please. Have a seat." Christie nodded toward the two chairs in front of his desk.

"What's up? Let me guess. This have something to do with Harold Case's death?" Franconia said as he dropped into the chair. He was a shade less than six feet with close-cropped brown hair and a long, angular face. Christie had known him for several years and had worked with him in the past. He knew him to be very competent and instinctively liked the man.

Franconia spotted the empty Mylanta bottle in Christie's hand, smiled and said, "Are things that bad?"

Christie shook his head wearily and said, "It's a long story, and not worth the telling. My wife says I need to retire. Maybe get some cushy office job with a security company in the private sector. She's probably right."

He lowered his lanky frame into his desk chair and tossed the empty bottle into the trash basket beneath his desk. "What can you tell me about Case?" he said.

"He was considered something of a pain in the ass at the Agency, a lifer who rose to mid-senior level by convincing anyone who would listen that he was the best thing since sliced bread."

"Was he?"

"Not as far as I can tell, but in the government, ass-kissing and non-stop self-promotion can do wonders for a career. You've seen that at the Bureau."

"Boy, have I," Christie said. "So what was Case doing in Georgetown at three o'clock this morning in a limo escorted by three private-hire muscle-heads working for a Caymanian company?"

"The limo and the beef brothers were supplied by a senate special subcommittee. He was working on an assignment for them."

"Nice to know the subcommittee has taxpayer money to burn."

"We both know that their budgets aren't a matter of public record," Franconia said. "Maybe you should take your wife's advice and resign. Run for the senate. Get the cushiest office job on the planet and throw away the Mylanta for good."

"Christ! I couldn't stand it," said Christie. "I'd end up strangling one or more of my fellow senators; those posturing, self-important, overpaid, underachieving bastards."

"That would be the patriotic thing", said Franconia.

Christie could feel his stomach beginning to burn again. He took a long, deep breath then said, "What was Case doing for this special subcommittee."

"Why? You think maybe there's a tie between that and his murder?"

"Hell, I don't know, but I'm willing to look at any angle at this point."

Franconia leaned back in his chair and stretched his legs out in front of him, crossing his ankles. He admired his shiny wingtip lace-ups for a moment then said, "As you know, Case had retired from the Agency. He was working as a private consultant to the subcommittee. Because the subcommittee's chair is that asshole from New York, who also happens to chair the Senate Select Committee on Intelligence, Case had authorization to review certain records at Langley."

"Any idea what was in those records?"

"We're looking into it now. Should know something pretty quick, if at all."

"You'll let me know as soon as you learn anything?" Christie said.

"Sure. In the meantime, what do you have to share with me?"

Christie looked at his desktop for a long minute then in a tired voice related what he knew of the case to Franconia, mentioning the blood samples last.

"Shit, Mitch, without prints, reliable eye witnesses, or any other traceable evidence, the blood work is all we've got. What's the lab status on the DNA analysis?"

"Dunno. The lab is still working on it." Christie reached for the phone on his desk. "I'll ask what the status is."

He punched a couple of buttons. After a moment his assistant answered. "Charlotte," he said, "see if you can get the forensics lab for me. I want to talk to whoever is doing the DNA analysis from this morning's event in Georgetown." He hung up and looked at Franconia.

The CIA man looked at his wristwatch. "How long before we get a response?"

"Couple of minutes. While we're waiting, why don't you see if your guys have anything new to add to Harold Case's involvement."

Franconia fished his cell phone out of his trousers pocket and tapped a speed dial key. After a moment, he said into the phone, "Hey, Gary, it's Jim Franconia. I'm with the Bureau's SSA on the Harold Case affair. Anything new on that from our end?"

While Franconia was listening to the update from his contact, Christie's desk phone rang. "Yeah, Charlotte," he said. He listened for a moment then punched a button on the left side of the phone base to access the call holding on an outside line.

"This is Christie," he said.

The voice on the other end of the line had a definite nasal twang. "Special Agent Christie, this is John Deutch in the forensics lab. Tom Billingsley, who works for me, spoke to you earlier this morning."

"Right. What cha' got for me, John?"

Deutch hesitated. "Well,…the metabolites in the samples taken from the decedents' wrists were badly contaminated by microorganisms in the oils and perspiration on the decedents' skin. Basically, they're useless."

"Goddammit," Christie said. "You're telling me we're at a dead end?"

"Not exactly, Special Agent." Deutch's voice sounded like it had a slight quaver in it, as if he was extremely nervous talking to the SSA.

"Well, what then?" Christie said.

Deutch hesitated then said, "We found an additional blood spot on the jacket sleeve of one of the decedents. It's in much better shape than the others."

"What's its status?"

"It's undergoing analysis right now."

28

"Estimated turnaround time?" Christie said.

"The FRV we're using from our LIMS gives pretty rapid profile results. The system amplifies the CODIS 13 core loci. It's the latest iteration of PCR analysis using STRs."

Christie felt his blood pressure rising. "Dammit, John, speak to me in English. I don't give a big rat's ass how the fuckin' process works, just tell me when I can expect results."

Deutch stammered when he said, "A couple of hours, I think."

"You think? Look, it's about ten now. I'll expect to hear from you by noon. One o'clock at the latest."

He hung up and looked over at Franconia, who had ended his own call, and shook his head. "Fuckin' scientists, they're so over-educated they can't speak a recognizable language. God help them if they ever have to place their own order at Starbuck's."

Franconia smiled. "Well, I just learned something that could brighten up your morning."

Christie leaned forward with his elbows on his desk, hands folded in front of him and said, "I'm all ears."

8 TYSONS CORNER

The brown delivery truck rolled down Wisconsin Avenue, turned west onto M Street and exited Georgetown by way of the Francis Scott Key Bridge into Arlington, Virginia. It merged with the traffic on Interstate 66, the Custis Memorial Parkway, and proceeded in a westerly direction. Eventually, it exited on the Leesburg Pike and drove into the commercial heart of Tysons Corner. It was a trip of about eleven miles, and took twenty-three minutes.

The driver pulled into the vast parking area of a regional mall and found a place to stop in a mostly empty part of the lot. The other deliveryman climbed out of the door on the passenger's side of the cab and hurried to the back of the truck. He rolled up the tailgate and scrambled in, closing the tailgate behind him. Using a flashlight, he quickly located the deep freeze, which was in an upright position, unhooked the straps securing it to the wall immediately behind the cab, and opened the door to the freezer. Brendan Whelan stepped out. He was beginning to perspire heavily.

He took a deep breath, looked at the deliveryman and said, "Good timing. It was getting a little close in there."

The other man walked to a corner of the truck, picked up a small suitcase and handed it to Whelan. "Clothes," he said.

Whelan set about changing into the contents from the suitcase. He donned a dark suit, a white, long-sleeve dress shirt, solid color dark tie, and dark lace-ups. Moments after he finished dressing there was a knock on the rear door of the truck. The deliveryman walked to the rear of the truck and rolled up the tailgate. The driver stood there, looking up at Whelan. He said, "Your ride's here," and motioned with his head toward a black Cadillac Escalade parked behind the truck. There was a column of vapor rising into the chilly air from its tailpipe.

Whelan watched as the driver's window on the Escalade slid smoothly down. Rhee stuck his left arm out and motioned for him to get in the car.

He slid onto the front seat on the passenger's side and buckled his seatbelt. Rhee pointed to a small briefcase on the backseat. "Your papers," he said.

Whelan leaned over and reached into the back seat, pulling the briefcase around to his lap. He opened it. Inside were several items including a plane ticket to Tampa, Florida. It also contained a new black leather wallet with two thousand dollars cash in fifty and one hundred-dollar bills and his new identification. It consisted of a driver's license, a few credit cards, business cards, a photo of a bogus wife and two children, a boy about six and a girl about four, and an ATM card. He now was Michael F. Murkowski, a pharmaceutical representative from suburban Chicago.

There was a note in the briefcase advising that Murkowski was a graduate of the University of Illinois, a Rotarian, former member of the Illinois National Guard with service in Operation Desert Storm, and member of the parish of St. Agnes Catholic Church. There also was another note in a code Whelan knew well and could easily decipher. It identified the remaining members of his old unit, the Sleeping Dogs, and where he could find them.

Whelan smiled in appreciation. Levell's people had moved very quickly. He knew without asking that Levell was an integral part of a shadow organization within the government, known simply as the Team. It had access to virtually unlimited resources and information. It was an organization of men and women joined in their dedication to reversing the course of America's drift into socialism or worse.

As he sorted through the contents of the briefcase, he also found a pair of full frame, black nylon eyeglasses. He was relieved that the lenses had no correction. There also was a neatly trimmed, fake mustache, a pair of thin leather gloves, and sunglasses in the briefcase. Finally, there was a phone card as well as a new Smartphone. Whelan knew it would be untraceable as long as he didn't use it to call numbers that utilized incoming call monitors, such as government lines, or those that might be under surveillance such as Levell's.

Levell and other members of the Team, disaffected military brass, senior members of the intelligence community and certain very wealthy individuals of a strong Libertarian bent, had spent years and huge sums of money developing a Voice over Internet Protocol or VoIP communications system that was untraceable and untappable. It utilized strong cryptographic algorithms to negotiate cryptographic keys, or strings of bits, between two parties. Without them, the conversation can't be decrypted. They are created automatically at the start of the call and destroyed at the end. The algorithms, which were enhanced versions of the Diffie-Hellman algorithm, made it virtually impossible for a third party to reconstruct the keys by intercepting the key negotiations. That would require nearly infinite computing resources and an eternity of time to develop it.

It was what the intelligence and law enforcement communities called "Going Dark" in reference to the all but immeasurable space of the Internet where activity defies monitoring.

Whelan placed the cash in the wallet with the driver's license and cards, slipping it into the right front pocket of his trousers. He had stopped carrying a wallet in a rear pocket years ago after a chiropractor had told him that doing so eventually could cause spinal issues. Whelan believed his survival depended on his being in the best physical shape possible. He slid the ticket into the left inside pocket of his jacket. Using the makeup mirror on the back of the passenger side sun visor, he applied the self-adhesive moustache and adjusted the eyeglasses on his face.

Rhee looked at him closely and nodded his approval. It was the only break in his impassivity Whelan had seen. "You need more money, use ATM card," he said with a thick accent. "Not use phone to call Mr. Levell. You want him, you use pay phone. Call this number." He held up a small card with a telephone number written on it. Whelan read it and committed it to memory. Rhee then placed the card in his own mouth, chewed it up and swallowed it. "You call number, let ring three times. Hang up. He call back soon. Question?"

Whelan, with a slight look of bemusement on his face, shook his head and said, "No."

Rhee shifted into drive and the Cadillac began pulling away from the truck. The deliverymen watched it for a moment then walked back around the truck and climbed into the cab. They made a U-turn in the parking lot and drove off in the direction from which they had come.

Rhee exited the parking area on International Drive and took it to the on-ramp for Route 267, which he followed to the entrance to Dulles International Airport. At the airport, he pulled up to the curb in front of the Delta sign. "Plane leave one hour," he said. There was no expression on his face or in his voice.

Whelan got out with his briefcase and closed the door behind him. A moment later the Cadillac pulled away. He entered the terminal, bought a Wall Street Journal, and checked his ticket against the bank of monitors to determine his gate. A few minutes later he picked up his boarding pass and found the appropriate shuttle to take him to the departure terminal.

Once aboard the plane, he settled into his business class seat, on the aisle, as he preferred. On the long flight from Ireland, he had sat in a window seat to better shield his face, but it had been uncomfortable for him. It's much easier to take action from an aisle seat than one on the window. The views from 30,000-plus feet didn't interest him.

He politely declined the comely flight attendant's offer of a beverage and opened his paper. Whelan took note of her well-coifed blonde hair, excessive eye makeup and lip-gloss, and deep cleavage well displayed in a too-tight blouse. She wore an equally tight-fitting skirt. He assumed she either had had cosmetic augmentation since buying the clothes or purposely had purchased them in sizes too small.

To anyone who noticed, his attention seemed focused on the Wall Street Journal. The reality was the opposite. Whelan had scanned the currently open cockpit and cabin area when he boarded, looking for any anomalies. Now, he carefully, but quickly, sized up each of the economy class passengers who were boarding – height, weight, appearance, dress, carry-ons. It was an indelible legacy of his very special training and almost twenty years of living life on the run since that time.

Eventually, the plane was filled to maximum capacity and began taxiing toward the runway. Whelan reflected on the cramped passenger cargo and wondered what it was like today to fly crammed into the economy class section of a plane. He hadn't had occasion to fly much in recent years, after going to ground in Ireland. He preferred to stay there.

The plane roared down the runway and soared easily into the cold, dry wintry air. He stared unseeingly at the newspaper and thought about what lay ahead at his destination. It had been almost two decades since he'd seen his closest friend, the Man With No Neck.

9 J. EDGAR HOOVER BUILDING

Supervisory Special Agent Christie had patched MPD District Commander Williams in on the speakerphone in his office. He looked across his desk at Jim Franconia and said, "Steve, you know this is a Bureau affair even though the incident occurred in your district. As a courtesy, though, we're keeping you in the loop as things develop."

"Yeah, I appreciate that," Williams said. There was a tone of sarcasm in his deep, rumbling voice.

Christie paused a moment and looked at the speakerphone with a look of distaste on his face. He said, "We'll continue to keep you in the loop as long as this doesn't escalate to a higher level of confidentiality. I trust you understand that."

"Yeah."

"For Steve's benefit, repeat what you just told me, Jim."

Franconia cleared his throat, looked at the phone, and said, "We've got a lead on what Harold Case was working on."

"Let's hear it," Williams said.

"Turns out he had one of our people in the Archives section helping him locate some old files."

"Let me guess," Williams said. "It was a broad and she's decent looking."

Franconia looked at Christie and shrugged. "Yeah, right on both counts."

"Figures. Case was a renowned skirt-chaser, even at his age. Go on."

"We're still digging through the details, but it seems old Harold was compiling information on a project that was terminated almost two decades ago."

"What kind of project?" Williams said.

Franconia hesitated for a moment or two and looked at Christie then said, "From what we've been able to gather so far, it looks like it was a very sensitive black ops situation. All materials relating to it were supposed to have been destroyed, leaving no trace whatsoever."

"And were they completely destroyed?" Williams said.

"Apparently not."

"Why not?"

"I'm only guessing, but I would say it probably was one of two things. Either some bureaucrat balked at the idea of destroying government records – which, incidentally, may constitute a crime under certain circumstances."

"Hell, I know that," Williams said angrily. "So what. You telling me that shit doesn't happen?"

"Sure it does. The other possibility would seem to be that whoever was charged with destroying the files didn't understand the order or was incompetent."

"Yeah? If so, I'm glad it was your guys and not mine." Williams said. "So you're telling me there's some kind of connection between a gang of murderers, who waylaid and assassinated three men and left another one with a permanent drool, and one of your black ops projects that got shit-canned twenty years ago?"

"More like eighteen years ago," Franconia said.

"Eighteen, twenty, who gives a fuck. What's the connection?"

"Maybe Case awoke a sleeping dog."

"What?" Williams' voice was laden with impatience.

"It's an old expression," Franconia said. "I think it's from Chaucer, 'It is nought good a slepyng hound to wake'...."

"Fuck Chaucer. What's it supposed to mean?"

Franconia looked at Christie for a second or two then thrust the middle finger of his right hand in the direction of the speakerphone. He looked at Christie and both men grinned. Turning back to the phone, Franconia said, "I think it's kind of like 'be careful what you ask for'. You know, you wake a sleeping dog, the sonofabitch might bite you."

Sensing that the conversation was digressing, Christie said, "It appears that Case was digging up these old records in the employ of Senator Morris. The assumption is that Morris had some sort of interest in this black operation."

"And whatever it was," Williams said, "it resulted in a gang-style killing of the old fart, as well as three of the nastiest guys in this whole fuckin' town."

"For the record," Christie said, "the Bureau does not yet consider this to be an ambush or a planned assassination. There is no evidence to

35

indicate this did not start out as anything other than a collision. One that appears to have been caused by whoever was driving the limo."

"Horseshit!" Williams said.

"Also for the record," Christie said, "the evidence, including testimony of witnesses, such as it is, places only one perp at the scene."

"So now you're telling me there's some kind of fuckin' super ninja running loose in the city who kills people because they run a fuckin' stop sign. Christie, you been watchin' too many fuckin' Jet Li movies."

Franconia involuntarily held his hands up, palms out, as if signaling a stop, and said, "Before we jump to any conclusions, we need to find out what was in the files Case was digging up, and what Morris's involvement in it is."

"Morris has built his career on humiliating the country in order to pander after his leftwing constituency," Christie said. "Probably has something to do with that."

"Wouldn't be the first time the Agency shit itself and some half-assed politician rubbed your noses in it to further his career," Williams said. There was a certain element of satisfaction in his voice.

Franconia let out a long breath and looked at Christie. He made a motion across his throat with a finger, indicating he was ready to terminate the call.

Christie nodded. "We'll let you know what we learn going forward, Steve." He pushed the button and disconnected the call, leaned back in his chair and looked at Franconia.

"The guy is such a prick," said Franconia. "How do you deal with people like him?"

Christie looked wistfully at the empty bottle of Mylanta in the trash basket and said, "I have my methods."

10 HART SENATE OFFICE BUILDING

Howard Morris and Shepard Jenkins were in the small conference room just off Morris's office. There was an open laptop on the table and the remains of the small package that had been delivered earlier that morning. The flash drive it had contained was plugged into the laptop. The two men sat in conference chairs and were hunched over the table staring at the small screen.

After awhile, Morris sat back in his chair and stretched his back. "Jesus Christ," he said. "Turns out there was truth in the rumors after all."

"'Pears so", said Jenkins. "Have to give ol' Harold credit. Though I must admit, I didn't believe him when he first approached us with the story. Sounded like a load of crap."

Morris leaned back over the table and continued to scroll through the documents on the screen. "This is incredible. It's exactly what I've been hoping to find."

"Should give your campaign efforts a big boost once we release it to the media." Jenkins paused then said, "Too bad Case isn't around to enjoy it with us."

Without taking his eyes off the screen, Morris said, "At least he had the foresight to download the materials onto a thumb drive and send it to us separately by courier. Otherwise, all this shit would have died with him when he was killed."

"Sad truth is, it's what got him killed."

Morris's head snapped around and he stared at Jenkins. "Shit! He's dead. Fuck him. What about us? Now that we've seen the files, are we gonna to be murdered, too?"

Jenkins pursed his lips thoughtfully and rubbed the small soul patch beneath the bottom one. "Let's think our way through this. Case originally approached me because he knew you'd be interested in evidence that implicated the government in an embarrassing clandestine matter."

"Yeah, and he was right about that." Despite the efficiency of the HVAC system in the building, Morris was beginning to perspire. "And you did bring it to me and I gave Case the go-ahead."

"So, he used his position as a retired operative and sometime lobbyist for the Agency to access their archives. It was common knowledge inside the Beltway that you were chairing the special subcommittee investigating…shall we say 'government indiscretions', and that Case was working for the subcommittee."

A small trickle of sweat ran down Morris brow and continued slowly down his ample jowl.

Jenkins continued. "So, there's a connection between us and Case, but not necessarily with the work he was doing at the Agency."

"Bullshit! That's easy enough to figure out if the spooks know what he was digging through at Langley." Morris moved the cursor to a document in the tray at the bottom of the computer screen and clicked on it. A typed memo popped up. "Worse yet, according to this note that Case sent with the other stuff, the damn fool was going to pop in unannounced on his old CIA chum, Levell, before coming here."

"Really?" Jenkins said. "Did he think Levell would be interested in providing corroborative testimony? Against a project that was Levell's baby from day one?"

"I don't know what the dumb bastard was thinking. If he *was* thinking. I just know he's dead, and I don't want to be next." A few more trickles of sweat had joined the first one tracking down Morris's face.

"If Levell didn't know Case was coming over, then who killed him…a couple blocks from Levell's house, and why?"

"Must have been the Agency. They're the ones who stand to lose the most when this story comes out."

"That's true, as far as we know. But it seems to me that the Agency is better at fuckin' up a one car parade than pulling off an operation like the one this morning." Jenkins gave Morris a questioning look, as if seeking confirmation.

Morris just shook his head. Beads of sweat flew off.

"Besides, why Georgetown? Why three o'clock in the morning? The Agency could have whacked Case anywhere, anytime," Jenkins said.

Morris just kept shaking his head. "I don't know. I don't know. So what are you saying? That there's someone or something other than the Agency involved in this?"

"I'm not sure what I'm saying. It just doesn't add up. If the Agency didn't whack him, who did? Levell is no longer physically capable of those acts."

"What about that fuckin' Chinaman that works for him?"

"He's Korean," Jenkins said, "and, even though he's supposed to be a skillful martial artist, I don't see this as something one man could have accomplished."

"So? Maybe he brought a whole gang of his slant-eyed buddies to help him."

Jenkins shifted uncomfortably in his seat. As a black man, he had experienced racial bigotry and he found any form of it unsettling and objectionable. He held his tongue, however. He had known Morris for a long time and was well aware of the man's shortcomings including racial prejudices and worse. Nevertheless, Jenkins had hitched his career to Morris's in the belief that the senator had a good chance to become president. Jenkins believed he would become White House Chief of Staff in a Morris presidency.

Still, the behavior seemed odd to Jenkins. The senator himself was no stranger to bias in the form of anti-Semitism. He was the only child of Russian Jews who had immigrated to this country before Morris was born. He had grown up as Haim Moskowitz in Brooklyn, where his father had owned a small tailor shop. Somewhere between college and law school at NYU Morris had determined that he wanted to build a career in politics, and Anglicized his name to Howard Morris.

Starting as a ward heeler in his law school days, Morris had risen through the ranks of the Democrat party to a seat in the United States Senate. And now, with the financial and political backing of one of the wealthiest and most powerful men in the country, he was a legitimate prospect for his party's nomination for president.

Morris was staring blankly at the computer screen. "Harold had an attaché case that he took with him everywhere. He must have had it with him when he was killed." He looked at Jenkins. "I wonder if he had a copy of these files in it, digital or otherwise."

"Bureau's been all over that scene like flies on shit," Jenkins said, happy to be on a subject other than race. "If Harold had the attaché case with him, the Bureau has it now."

"And when the FBI examines the contents and finds these documents, how will that affect me?"

"For God's sake, man," Jenkins said, "you're a United States senator. Head of a select subcommittee investigating government behavior. You had every right to hire Case as an investigator as part of your job. If he broke some laws along the way, that doesn't implicate you. Just deny that you gave him any encouragement or even knew how he was proceeding to get the information. You have the information and that's what's important."

Both men stared at each other for a few moments. The only sounds were the low whirring sound of the HVAC system and the barely perceptible traffic sounds from outside the building.

After awhile, Jenkins said, "Look, you've been handpicked to run for the party's presidential nomination by Chaim Laski, the multibillionaire. He's spent years and who knows how many hundreds of millions of dollars building his political organization to reach this point. He's a fuckin' kingmaker. And you're his guy."

"Yeah, you're right about that," Morris said. "We've done what he asked us to do; found evidence of a black op project that should effectively humiliate the government."

"Right. And it leverages you up with Laski and his loonies. With the backing of Laski and his organization, you should have no real problems getting the nomination and winning the election."

Morris shrugged and said, "I still need a corroborating witness or there will be substantive issues whether this information came from Agency files. Case was supposed to be that witness. Now he's gone. What do I do?"

Jenkins thought about the question for a moment then said, "Cut a deal with Levell. He was a much bigger part of this black op than Case ever was anyway."

"You've gotta be shittin' me. Levell fancies himself a patriot. Old school. This project was his baby. He'd never agree to testify."

"Everybody's got a price, Senator. Even Levell. Just figure out what it is and cut a deal."

Morris sat forward in his chair, elbows on its arms, hands folded over his belly and stared at the table top in front of him. "Levell's price is always in blood," he said in a soft voice.

11 WASHINGTON, D.C.: RESTAURANT

Rhee pulled the black Cadillac Escalade to the curb in front of the venerable Washington restaurant. He left the engine running and stepped out of the car with the grace and effortlessness of a skilled ballet dancer. A valet quickly ran up to him. Rhee handed the valet a generous sum and said, "You not move car. I back soon." The valet nodded appreciatively and returned to his stand.

Rhee easily assisted Levell from the car into his wheelchair and pushed him through a small entranceway that opened into a heavily landscaped courtyard. Despite the chilly temperature, a few clusters of people sat in wrought iron chairs beneath gas operated patio heaters. Some chatted casually, and some appeared to be engaged in more serious conversations.

The restaurant was housed in a structure that originally had been two separate townhouses. The main entrance was several steps up from the sidewalk level with the hostess desk positioned just inside the front door. From there, a wide, elegant staircase led up to the main dining area, or alternatively, a patron could descend a few steps into the bar area that was at the same level as the courtyard behind the restaurant.

Despite the early dining hour the lounge already was crowded as politicians, lobbyists, and assorted bureaucrats of all pay grades began the latest installment of the Beltway cocktail circuit. From the sounds of conversation and the clattering of dinnerware, the main dining area also was filling up with early diners.

Rhee rolled Levell through the courtyard area in his wheelchair and into an entrance to the cocktail lounge. With some difficulty, he managed to get the patrons in the crowded bar to make room for the wheelchair's passage. Eventually, he was able to reach the elevator and took Levell upstairs to the main dining area on the second floor.

As Rhee pushed Levell through the thicket of food service employees and diners coming and going, many of the wait staff recognized the old man as a frequent patron and smiled. Levell, in turn, nodded to each of them and smiled in return. He considered this to be Washington's finest restaurant and couldn't recall ever having been disappointed in the food or the service. The smell of the meals being prepared and cooked in the open kitchen area, the sounds of conversations and clinking of wine glasses, and the tables and booths filled with affluent looking patrons brought back fond memories of past meals he had enjoyed here.

Levell and Rhee crossed the main dining area and entered a much smaller room that seemed designed for more intimate or confidential conversations. They crossed the room to a corner booth, Levell's favorite spot. It was isolated from the other booths and afforded less opportunity for conversations to be overheard. Banquette seats stretched outward from the corner booth along the walls in both directions. Major General Roscoe C. McCoy, a man about Levell's age, with very closely cropped grey hair and a military bearing similar to Levell's, already occupied one of the banquettes. Though seated, it was obvious he was more than six feet tall, broad shouldered and lean with the leathery skin of someone who had spent a lifetime in the outdoors. He wore a dark blue three-button suit with a pale blue dress shirt and red, white and blue rep tie. He rose when he saw Levell approaching and extended his hand. "Cliff, for an ancient version of Ironside, you're looking pretty damned good," he said and smiled broadly.

Levell returned the warmth and sincerity with his own smile. "Sit, sit," he said, motioning with his right hand. "You're not looking so bad yourself, Buster, for a washed up old Jarhead."

With Rhee's assistance, Levell moved from the wheelchair to the unoccupied banquette. When he was comfortably seated at the table, Levell turned his head toward his aide and said, "That'll be all for now, Mr. Rhee." He tapped the cell phone in the left breast pocket of his caramel colored silk and mohair sport coat and said, "I'll call you when we're finished."

Rhee nodded and left the two men to their discussion.

Almost immediately, a waiter arrived to ask for their drink orders. "Good evening General and Mr. Levell. Nice to see both of you again," he said. "May I start you off with something to drink?"

"Good to see you, Samuel," Levell said.

He looked at the glass in front of the other man. Except for ice cubes, it had been drained. "Bring my colleague another of whatever he's having, and I'll have an Arran Single Malt with ice."

The waiter nodded and hurried away.

"So, is the Corps ever going to get around to awarding you the third star you so richly deserve?"

McCoy's leathery face formed a sneer. "Fuck the star," he said. "At this point in my career, I harbor no illusions about making Lieutenant General. Particularly given the current political environment."

"With any luck, that environment will soon be changed."

"Yes, and since the electorate can't…or won't do it, then it's time for true patriots to step forward."

Levell smiled. "Yes it is. And fortunately, as we both know, those the people do exist." Both men nodded and smiled.

"The Team has been a long time getting to this point, my friend," McCoy said.

"Given what's at stake, vetting the right people and getting them into position has required a long time and a great deal of caution."

"But clearly now is the time. It may be too late as it is," McCoy said. "The enemy controls one of the two major political parties as well as the news media, the education system, the unions, and the government bureaucracy. They even have a grip on the Supreme Court. All that remains of the foundations of this country are a number of senior military personnel, several professionals from the intelligence community and some influential and well-heeled patriots from private industry."

"The Russians knew years ago they couldn't go head-to-head with us economically or militarily," Levell said. "They played along about as far as they could, then appeared to cave. But for nine or more decades they have been infiltrating and destroying this country from the inside, twisting reality and molding public perception. And, naïve bastards that we are, most of us went along with it. Hell, some of the weak-kneed, free-loading bastards welcomed and assisted them."

"It's all part of a long-term strategy," McCoy said, "to bring down this country from within by destroying our norms and standards that were the structure on which our society and nation were built, destroying the economy by creating such enormous debt that our currency and credit are rapidly becoming worthless, driving small businesses - the nation's job incubator, into bankruptcy and financial failure, causing massive job losses, the reduction of wealth and standards of living in this country, and weakening our military to the point where we couldn't mount a decent defense against a legitimate threat. And all the while patriotic Americans and conservatives are systematically discredited and defamed."

Levell nodded vigorously. "And from the outside by supporting our enemies, including jihadists and leftist governments throughout Latin America, Asia and Africa, with weapons and technology and money that stretch our defenses. They run up the price of oil, all while Russia is afloat in carbon fuels."

"Thought they'd struck pay dirt with Carter only to watch him inflame patriotism and usher in Ronald Reagan and a brief retaking of the direction of the country," McCoy said. "Probably thought they got a second chance with Clinton, but overestimated his dedication to leftist dogma and underestimated the size of his ego that drove him to the center for the acceptance he craved."

Levell's eyes narrowed and the corners of his mouth turned down in a grimace as if he had just tasted something rancid. "The Reds must have thought they'd hit the jackpot with the current president. Mother and father both Marxists, as were his mentors throughout college and beyond. He runs the government by a series of executive orders, skirting the Constitution by appointing czars who bypass cabinet offices and report only to him without benefit of congressional vetting. Essentially, they're unaccountable for whatever actions they take. He ignores laws he doesn't like or sues states if they are forced to pass such laws themselves. He abuses power through executive orders and a tsunami of regulations that strangle capitalism and entrepreneurship. This democratic republic and the freedoms most of us have taken for granted are in grave danger, my friend."

"And," McCoy said, "although he's so unpopular that his own party doesn't want him to run for reelection, they already have a replacement puppet in the wings."

"Howard Morris," Levell said. "We can't let that happen."

McCoy smiled and said, "Agreed. And with the work we have at hand, isn't it ironic that the enemy has reawakened the Sleeping Dogs."

Samuel returned with their cocktails, and both men lapsed into silence until he left.

Levell spoke first. He raised his cocktail glass and said, "Here's to the success of the venture, my old friend." McCoy raised his glass too and each man took a large swig.

"The Dogs," McCoy said. "It's good you've kept in communication with them all these years since they went to ground."

"I couldn't let them fend for themselves entirely. I always feared that program or one of its operations might resurface someday. The original edict to terminate them with extreme prejudice has no expiration date, even though it's believed they died years ago."

"You created the Dogs with help from me and a handful of others. Speaking of which, whatever happened to those two egghead scientists whose research and theories gave rise to the project?"

"Jacob Horowitz died some years back, but Bill Nishioki is still alive. Lives in a retirement community in a town down the coast from San Francisco. Place called Santa Cruz, I believe."

"Then, except for him, it looks like we're the only ones left from that operation, Cliff."

"I assume you heard about Case?"

"Sure. It's all over the news. It happened near your house. You know anything about it?" McCoy arched one shaggy gray eyebrow questioningly.

Levell looked down at the table for a moment and smiled, then he raised his head and said, "It was pure coincidence. Of all the people for Harold to encounter, he ran smack dab into Whelan, literally."

McCoy let that sink in for a moment. "I know why Whelan was there. You got wind of what Case was digging up, and asked him to meet with you. But what the hell was Case doing in your neighborhood at that hour?"

"Case, as you'll recall, was the bastard who provided the testimony that got the program shut down and the termination notice issued on the Dogs."

McCoy nodded. "Yeah, I know that."

"Apparently, he was on his way to ask me, as one of the few left who had a role in the operation, to provide some corroborative evidence for his work with Senator More-Ass."

"What an asshole." McCoy shook his head in disgust.

"I suspect Case recognized Brendan at the crash scene and ordered his bodyguards to take him into custody. He probably couldn't believe his luck in finding one of the Dogs alive. Under the circumstances, Brendan had no option but to take out the hired muscle, and, when he recognized Case in the limo, kill him, too." Levell paused to take another sip of his cocktail. "He grabbed Harold's attaché case and brought it with him to my house."

"What was in the briefcase?"

"Photocopies of materials from the files on Operation Sleeping Dogs. Pretty damn clear and convincing evidence for Senator Morris's purposes."

McCoy made a snarling sound and said, "That sonofabitch." Then he seemed to brighten and said, "Three bodyguards and Case. Sounds like the Prince of Wolves still has those remarkable skills."

"Why wouldn't he? After all," Levell said with obvious pride, "it was the two of us who trained him and the other Dogs. Did you forget they were the ones who modified your nickname to Buster the Ball-buster?"

McCoy roared with laughter, then in a moment of self-consciousness looked quickly around the small dining area to see if he had disturbed any of the other patrons. "I damn well earned that name, the shit I put those boys through," he said.

Levell had a look on his face that was as close to wistfulness as his innate toughness would allow. "We were a hell of a team, Buster. You with the Corps and me with the Agency. We created something very special with the Dogs."

"Hell, Cliff, you're an old Jarhead too, from before the Agency signed you on. Once a Marine, always a Marine."

"Semper Fi," Levell said, as the waiter returned for their dinner orders.

"Gentlemen, are you ready to order?"

Levell nodded.

"Will you be having the salmon done the usual way, Mr. Levell?"

Levell nodded again. "Start me off with the seafood chowder."

"And General?"

"What's the special tonight, Samuel?" McCoy said.

"Pan seared sea scallops with lime butter and truffle raviolis."

McCoy didn't hesitate. "That'll be fine."

"Anything to start?" the waiter said.

This time, McCoy thought about it for a few moments. "A dozen on the half shell. Mix 'em up," he said.

"Will you be enjoying wine tonight, gentlemen?" Samuel said.

The two men looked at each other. "Sure, what the hell," Levell said.

"A Chard', Cakebread Cellars?" McCoy said.

"Suits me."

"Thank you, gentlemen. I'll be back shortly with your appetizers." The waiter collected the menus and left.

"So," McCoy said, "Whelan's alive and in rare form apparently. Where has he been all these years?"

"Ireland."

"Ireland? Why Ireland?"

"He was born there, remember. Parents immigrated to the U.S. when he was an infant. He speaks Gaelic, has close relatives there, and blends in extremely well. It was a safe place for him to be."

"Do you remember when we first found him? He was in high school. They all were."

"Yeah, I remember. Standout athletes, all of them.

McCoy got a faraway look in his eyes, and said, "First time I saw Brendan, he was playing high school football. Played linebacker on defense and running back on offense. I'll never forget how hard he hit a kid who played for a rival team. Other kid was a fullback, about two thirty or so. He had taunted Whelan before the game started. Said he was a candy-ass, and he was going to splatter him all over the field. Whelan asked his defensive line mates to let the kid through untouched first chance they got. In the first quarter, he came busting through a hole in the middle. That's where Brendan nailed him. Knocked him back a good ten yards. In the air. Knocked the kid clean out of his shoes and helmet."

"Jesus."

"Game was delayed for maybe thirty minutes while medical people tended to the kid. Ultimately, they drove the ambulance right onto the field, loaded him up and hauled him directly to the hospital. Broken ribs,

46

concussion, ruptured spleen, internal bleeding, and assorted other injuries. Kid recovered, but I don't think he ever played football again."

"Can't blame him," said McCoy.

Levell smiled. "Should have seen him on offense. Over two thousand yards and more than thirty touchdowns his senior year. And he was valedictorian of his class."

"I recall that he had college recruiters drooling all over him."

"He did. Every major college team in the country wanted him. Larsen and Thomas, too. But we won the recruiting battle. Same thing with the others."

"As I recall, we started with a decent sized pool of candidates and winnowed it down to what, fifteen or so?"

"Yeah, fifteen. Lost some along the way."

Both men shook their heads at similar distant memories.

"Let's see how well you remember those boys," Levell said.

"What'd you have in mind?"

Levell smiled and said, " In your words, describe Whelan."

Without hesitating, McCoy said, "The alpha wolf among alpha wolves."

Levell nodded. "Larsen."

"The man with no neck," McCoy said. "Freakishly strong and quick."

"Thomas."

"Best pure athlete of the bunch. Deep thinker, too. Didn't he have some of the other guys reading Carlos Castaneda's books, as well as *Zen and the Art of Motorcycle Maintenance* and other arcane stuff?"

Levell smiled and nodded. "I never understood any of that crap but Whelan and Stensen seemed to. What about Kirkland."

"Most disciplined."

"Palmero."

McCoy smiled and shook his head. "Least disciplined."

"Stensen."

"Stensen?" McCoy said, "He's the crazy one, right?"

"Certifiable," Levell said. "Hell, for that matter, they're all a little crazy."

"You've kept track of each one of them over the years. Where are they?" McCoy said.

"Larsen, aka the Man With No Neck, is in Tampa, Kirkland is in the Louisiana Bayou Country, Almeida's in San Diego…"

McCoy interrupted. "Almeida, he's the one they called Colonel Sanders?"

"Yeah, the kid loved fried chicken. Could've had it at every meal."

"What about the other two?"

"Thomas is a college professor in the Nashville, Tennessee area, and Stensen is somewhere in the Hawaiian Islands."

McCoy's eyes narrowed and he stared into space, recalling earlier days. "God, those boys were special," he said.

McCoy nodded. "There's never been anything like them."

SLEEPING DOGS: THE AWAKENING

12 J. EDGAR HOOVER BUILDING

The wintry sky had gone dark outside, and it was well past mealtime. Christie had called his wife to let her know he wouldn't be home for dinner with her and their two children. In fact, he had no idea when he would have the opportunity to go home. A very long day was becoming even longer.

He looked around the short conference table and assessed the condition of his team members. He imagined he looked as exhausted as they did, maybe worse. There were five of them, not counting Jim Franconia, the CIA liaison to the Bureau, who looked surprisingly fresh. Must take a special breed to be a spook, Christie thought. But then, this wasn't an Agency gig. It was the Bureau's, and he was the SSA, the Supervisory Special Agent. The buck stopped on his desk.

There was tremendous pressure to resolve the killings that had occurred in Georgetown early that morning. Christie had been deluged with calls from the White House, Senator Morris's office, the District Commander of the Metropolitan Police Department's Second District, and every sonofabitch that thought he or she had a right to know what the Bureau, and Christie in particular, was doing to catch the perpetrator or perpetrators.

He sighed softly and looked at his crew. Like Christie, the three men on the team had shaved so early that morning that their beards were beginning to show, particularly Antonelli, who had a natural five o'clock shadow anyway. Rickover, fresh out of law school, looked the best. He was barely able to grow facial hair.

The two women were showing the signs of the day's wear and tear also. Though reapplied regularly, their makeup was beginning to smear, and the hairspray was losing its battle with gravity. All five of them, as well as

49

Christie, looked like they had slept in their clothes. He knew it still might come to that. Franconia was the exception. His shirt was still crisp, his slacks creased. He sat in a chair against a wall and separate from the table. It was a matter of interagency protocol. This was a Bureau matter. The Agency was in an advisory capacity on this one.

Christie cleared his throat. "People, I...the Bureau appreciates the strain you're all under. But we are making progress." He paused and looked over at Franconia. "If you were not already aware of it, Mr. Franconia is with the Central Intelligence Agency. He is the Agency's liaison, working with us on this matter." He nodded at Franconia. "Jim, bring us up to date on what you've learned through your people?"

The liaison officer sat comfortably in his chair, legs crossed, hands resting in his lap. "Happy to," he said. "Here's what we know so far."

He got up and walked to a flip chart resting on an easel in a corner of the cramped conference room and picked up a magic marker from the tray on the easel.

"Harold Case, a retired CIA officer, worked unofficially on retainer as a sort of lobbyist for the Agency on Capitol Hill. Over the years, he had developed good connections and seemed a natural for the position." He paused and made notes on the flip chart of what he'd said.

"After retirement, Case developed...ah...how to say this...appetites for the ladies and the ponies and needed extra sources of income. He accepted work with a senate subcommittee chaired by Senator Howard Morris of New York." He paused again and added to his notes on the flip chart.

Rickover raised his hand tentatively and said, "What kind of work was he doing for the subcommittee?"

"Ah, 'therein lies the rub'," said Franconia. "Apparently, the subcommittee is investigating possible transgressions by the Agency in years past." He looked around the room.

"Because of his position with the subcommittee, Case had access to Agency files. With his long career at Langley, he also knew where the bodies were buried, so to speak. It was not a good combination for us."

"So, are you saying the CIA may have killed Case to protect itself from scandal or worse?" said Rickover.

"That's an interesting thought," said Franconia, "but it wasn't our work. Besides," he said with mock seriousness, "we don't have authorization to carry out such operations on our own soil."

Christie was becoming impatient. He glanced at his watch and said, "Okay, Jim, tell us about the files Mr. Case was reviewing."

Franconia nodded. "Fortunately, Case fancied himself a ladies man. He flirted pretty heavily with one of our people in the Archives Section. She

SLEEPING DOGS: THE AWAKENING

wasn't impressed, but she did make note of the files he was interested in." He paused to add more notes to the chart.

"So what was in those files?" Christie said.

"They related to a project, a series of black ops, the Agency undertook maybe twenty years ago, give or take. The project ultimately was scrubbed on direct orders from the White House and all traces, including the files, were supposed to have been destroyed."

Antonelli said, "Wait a minute. It's my understanding that a black operation is of such a covert, highly clandestine nature that it is carried out with great secrecy; and no records of the operation are kept anyway."

"That's generally true," Franconia said, "but some records were maintained in this instance. Probably because it collaterally involved genetic research that I'm about to describe. So, in addition to records relating to their specific missions, apparently there also were records concerning the individual members of the unit."

In an effort to expedite the discussion, Christie said, "But something happened and they weren't destroyed. Let's get on with it."

"So it appears," said Franconia. "Our Archives contact says Case, under a warrant issued by the senate subcommittee, photocopied the files, or salient parts of them anyway, with a small camera-like device. But the files themselves are still in the Archives."

"Have you examined them?" said Rickover.

"Well, I personally haven't," Franconia said with a slight smile. "But the Agency has had people on it since we learned about Case's activities."

"And?" said Christie, motioning with his hands for Franconia to continue.

"The project was the blackest of black ops. It was based on genetic research conducted in the 'seventies by two scientists, Jacob Horowitz and William Nishioki, at a university in California."

"Genetics?" said Rickover. He shifted uneasily in his chair and glanced nervously around the table.

"Yes. Seems the good doctors theorized that evolution of the human species, any species really, is based on continuing advancements at a genetic level. In other words, in every generation, a few people are born who represent what humans will become in future generations. Kind of like God's," he paused and for political correctness added, "or nature's betas of future humans. Over the years, so the theory goes, succeeding generations will develop into improved models."

Rickover's eyes were open very wide. "What would such people look like? Are they mutants?"

Franconia laughed. "Not mutants in the classic sci-fi sense. But they are stronger, faster, smarter, than us current models, so to speak."

"How did the Agency get involved in this?" Christie said.

"As you may know, we scan everything, and I do mean everything. Someone came across an article these scientists had published in one of those unfathomable academic journals – you know, articles that are sure-fire cures for insomnia. It also came to the attention of USSOCOM, the United States Special Operations Command. Those guys are not authorized to conduct covert action operations. Only we, the Agency, can do that. However, we've always maintained a very good relationship with them through our Special Activities Division, or SAD"

"Is that how the Agency got involved?" said Christie.

"Yes. USSOCOM asked SAD's Special Operations Group to help identify individuals who possessed this genetic mutation. They wanted to create a black ops unit that was beyond anything they had in Delta Force, the SEALs, or anything else."

"What's the Special Operations Group?" Rickover said.

"SOG is responsible for all high threat military or intelligence operations with which the U.S. government does not wish to be overtly associated. We funded Horowitz and Nishioki's research…heavily. In time they discovered something like a blood or genetic marker that enabled us to identify people who had this 'beta' distinction."

"So, how did the Agency go about the process of trying to identify these people?" Christie said.

Franconia paused as if uncertain or unwilling to respond. After a moment or two, he said, "Actually, it wasn't that difficult. After all, we knew what to look for. We set up a large screening operation and started poring through records involving every kid who displayed superior intelligence combined with unusual athletic ability. In time, the list was winnowed down through the presence or absence of the marker. Ultimately, fifteen young men were identified."

"How did you test them?" Rickover said. He looked as if he feared the answer.

"Easy. We were interested only in superior athletes. They produced plenty of sweat, saliva, blood, etcetera. Samples were easy to swab up and take back to the lab."

"What was the purpose of all this?" said Antonelli.

Franconia thought about the question for a moment, then said, "If you could go some generations into the future, recruit somewhat more advanced human specimens, and bring them back to the present, wouldn't you have the makings of a superior fighting force, a competitive advantage, so to speak, over your enemies?"

Antonelli nodded. He slowly rubbed the knuckles of his right fist with the palm of his left hand. "So is that what happened to these guys, they became soldiers?"

"More than just soldiers," Franconia said. "They became the most efficient and effective special ops unit this world has ever seen. After 2 years of intensive training in weaponry, martial arts techniques, technology, languages and other disciplines they were deployed on the blackest of black ops. These are highly clandestine activities outside the standards of military protocol, generally unlawful, and include espionage, assassinations, terrorist activities and the support of revolutionary or counter-revolutionary forces, kidnapping, sabotage, torture, false flag activities, and other actions of a similar nature."

"So these guys were supposed to be the baddest of the bad?" Antonelli said.

A smile spread slowly across Franconia's tanned face. "And then some," he said. "The Sleeping Dogs, or Dogs as they came to be known, were specifically trained to be the most effective and lethal of special ops, specializing in quick, covert, deadly strikes in extremely hostile environments. Extreme prejudice was the standing order for all of their operations. Far more formidable than the Russian Spetsnaz, Israeli Sayeret Matkal, British SAS and SBS, or any other special ops outfit, they were authorized to kill anyone and everyone, even civilians, who got in the way of an operation's success, innocently or otherwise."

"Who authorized these guys to take such actions?" Antonelli said.

"There is only one source for that kind of authority," Franconia said. "It came directly from the White House in the form of a Presidential Finding. Following Operation Desert Storm, there was a change of philosophy in the executive branch. Authorization was given to shut down the entire operation. The authorization included instructions to terminate the remaining Dogs with extreme prejudice and destroy all records pertaining to the unit and its activities."

Rickover glanced nervously over his right shoulder and said, "Where are these people? What happened to them when the operation was terminated?"

Franconia shrugged. "Supposedly, they all died in a plane crash."

"Sup...supposedly?" Rickover said. A bead of perspiration had formed on his brow.

"That's the official version." He paused then added, "But no body parts or wreckage were found."

13 WASHINGTON, D.C. - RESTAURANT

Levell was trying to catch Samuel's eye to signal that he and McCoy were ready for another round of drinks. "Do you remember the Dogs' first mission?" he said.

"Of course, we designed it." McCoy said. "It was during the first Gulf war, Operation Desert Storm. They actually infiltrated one of Sadaam's palaces with that sonofabitch in it and surrounded by his elite Republican Guard."

"The Dogs were seconds away from assassinating the little bastard when the order came to stand down." Levell said.

McCoy shook his head in amazement. "How the fuck did they get in? Shit, how the fuck did they get out?"

"You forget," Levell said. "We lost three of the original Dogs in that mission."

"Yeah, and they left behind over two hundred dead elite Guards. But, still, think of it. Seconds away. What would the world be like today if the pussies in the administration and the Pentagon brass had allowed them to proceed?"

"A far better place, no doubt," Levell said, as Samuel arrived with their first courses. Levell held up his empty glass and impatiently made a circular motion with his hand, signaling for a refill of the cocktails.

When the waiter left, he said, "For one thing, this great nation of ours wouldn't be on a short trajectory to becoming an irrelevant, pissant third rate power, in hock up to its ass to support the entitlement dreams of a generation of pussies, groveling and begging for alms at the feet of the fucking Chicoms, Arabs, and others for Chrissake."

Almost shaking with rage, Levell looked around the small room and said under his breath, "Where the hell are those drinks?"

McCoy leaned across the table toward Levell and said, "We know how it happened and who's responsible. And with any luck we'll soon have the pieces put together to change the course of this country's history once and for all. Lord knows, we've certainly been working on it for a long time."

"It's good the Team has decided that it's time to take action. The Dogs really are the final piece," Levell said. "It's ironic that Case and that sorry-assed senator, Morris, were the cause of the Dogs being brought back together. Their meddling and nosing around caused me to have to alert the surviving Dogs." He paused and drained the last of the scotch from his glass. As if by plan, Samuel arrived with the next round. He placed them in front of the two men and again withdrew.

"In retrospect, it may have been a mistake to bring Whelan in for a face-to-face discussion given the unplanned event that happened this morning. It may not take long for the Bureau and the Agency to connect the dots. Although they don't know that any of the boys survived the bogus plane crash, I'm sure we'll be persons of interest. We'll have to be a bit more circumspect where and how we hold our dinners together in the future."

"You think the Feds are that smart?" McCoy had a disdainful expression on his face.

"That attaché case of Harold's? In it were copies of the old files from Langley. Comprehensive enough that not much is left for conjecture."

"I thought those files had been destroyed," McCoy said.

"Apparently not. Also in the attaché case was a receipt from a local courier company, indicating that Harold had something, probably copies of the documents, delivered to that rat-faced senator from New York."

"Morris?"

"Yeah."

McCoy rubbed his chin thoughtfully. "What exactly was in the documents?"

"Everything. Names, dates, places. The genetic research. The missions. Everything."

"Then you're probably right. Things could get a little crispy for awhile, but worth it, ultimately," McCoy said.

Levell nodded and said, "Nevertheless, it's taken the Team many years to get to this point where we can take overt action to redirect the political course of this great country. All those years of carefully recruiting the right individuals in the right positions, vetting the wrong ones, sniffing out the moles who tried to infiltrate the Team, assembling the necessary assets, all while the leftists spread more and more of their poison. Now, at last, it's time for all that hard effort to pay some dividends."

McCoy raised his glass to Levell, and said, "You're familiar with Shakespeare, aren't you?"

"Somewhat."

"Antony's speech near the end of Julius Caesar, Act 3, Scene 1?"

A wry smile slowly creased Levell's face. He said, "Cry 'Havoc!' and let slip the dogs of war."

14 J. EDGAR HOOVER BUILDING

Rickover reflected on what Franconia had said about the genetic research. "Doesn't this...ah...rogue gene, or whatever it is, occur in people in other countries, too?"

Franconia's chin bobbed up and down. "Sure, but apparently no one else knows about it...yet. We very carefully squelched all traces of the research. Sent people to all university and research center libraries and ripped out Horowitz and Nishioki's article. Went into the offices of the journal that published it and removed the file. Hell, we even appropriated all their prior work product and notes."

"What about research centers in other countries?" Rickover said. "Didn't they have copies of the journals that published those guys' article?"

"Sure, but we have our own agents as well as those of ally governments everywhere. It wasn't that difficult to destroy almost all records. And, sure, there may have been stray copies in an individual's office or library here and there, but we removed Horowitz and Nishioki from access for any follow up by other scientists. In addition, we had them publish a subsequent article retracting their hypotheses and findings."

Rickover seemed to shudder. "How exactly did you 'remove' them?" he said.

Franconia looked at Christie and both men smiled at Rickover's naivety.

"We did it in a very positive fashion," Franconia said. "They were hired by the Agency at three times the sums they could have made anywhere else, given very generous allowances for a fully equipped laboratory and anything else they needed. All their work was classified as top secret from that point forward."

Antonelli stopped rubbing his knuckles for a moment and said, "So what did you do with these guys, the genetic freaks?"

"First," Franconia said, "we put together a very special team to train them. All top Agency operatives and military people. It was a small group, maybe six people, not including the two scientists."

"Anybody left from the team?" Antonelli said and began rubbing his knuckles again.

"Two. Marine Corps Major General Roscoe C. McCoy and a retired Agency operative named Clifford Levell. There was a third, but he died this morning...Harold Case."

With the mention of Case's name, everyone around the table except Christie sat a little straighter and turned toward Franconia. Christie had heard this story earlier.

Rickover looked at Christie and said, "So, is the theory that Case's investigation into this old Agency project is what got him killed?"

Christie was sitting back in his chair, legs stretched out under the table with his elbows resting on the arms of the chair. His hands were folded under his chin. "At this point, we assume there's a connection," he said.

"What about the general and the agency person," Antonelli said. "Is anyone talking to them?"

Christie nodded. "They're at the top of my list to be interviewed, along with the surviving geneticist, Nishioki." He paused and looked at his hands for a moment then said, "Levell is retired and wheelchair-bound because of injuries suffered in an automobile accident. I doubt he could have killed Harold Case and the other three."

What about the other guy, the Marine?" Antonelli said.

"We've checked. He was at MARSOC headquarters at Camp Lejeune when this thing went down this morning."

"Back to the black ops unit, what was its purpose?" Antonelli said.

"They were utilized for very special wet work that remains too highly classified to discuss here," Franconia said. "They were operative for less than two years, then the project was terminated. That was almost twenty years ago."

"Why?" Rickover said.

"You don't need to know that."

Rickover looked at Christie, as if for support.

"Even I don't have that level of access," Christie said. "Jim, what else can you tell us about this project?"

Franconia had been finishing his notes on the flip chart. He turned back to the others and said, "Because of the nature of the work they did – essentially on call for the most sensitive operations, they were dormant a lot of the time. As a result, they were given the name Sleeping Dogs."

58

Rickover squinted and shook his head. "Sleeping Dogs? I still don't get it."

"It was the code name given to them," Franconia said. "For purposes of comparison, they were much more like wolves than dogs. But 'sleeping dogs' is a known term of art. Their purpose was to remain dormant until a specific situation arose which required their activation, after which they responded with the fury of Hellhounds."

"Yeah, Aaron, didn't your parents teach you to never wake a sleeping dog?" Antonelli said.

Rickover shrugged and turned his hands palms up.

"Dogs don't like to be startled," Christie said. "When you wake a sleeping dog, the sonofabitch just might bite you."

"These Dogs would more than bite you," Franconia said. "They would freakin' kill you."

"And what about these so-called Dogs?" Antonelli said. "What happened to them when the project was scrapped?"

"Some died on missions," Franconia said and turned back to the flip chart. He drew a death's head then drew a large X through it. Turning back to the others, he said, "The order was given to terminate every one of the remaining members with extreme prejudice."

The FBI personnel looked at each other, then back at Franconia.

"Is that what happened?" Antonelli said.

Franconia thought about his answer for a moment then said, "Yes and no. It seems that someone involved with the unit was having an affair with the wife of a deputy director at the Agency. The DD foolishly let it slip in a conversation with her. She told her lover, and the Dogs all vanished." He paused.

"That's it?" said Antonelli. "They just vanished and no one knows what happened to them? Did anyone ever look for them?"

Franconia shrugged. "Sure," he said. "But we didn't have to look for very long. Two weeks later they showed up in Puerto Rico and stole a C-130 Hercules from Coast Guard Air Station Borinquen, the old Ramey Air Force Base." He paused for effect and watched all of the people seated around the table lean forward. Christie remained as before; slouched in his chair, chin resting on his folded hands.

"So where did the plane land?" said Antonelli.

"Didn't. It crashed right after takeoff. Into the ocean off Puerto Rico."

"Did anyone check for survivors or proof that all were dead?" said Antonelli.

"Where they crashed is the Puerto Rican Trench. It's the deepest part of the Atlantic Ocean, more than five miles deep. There was no wreckage to examine and no survivors to worry about."

15 POTOMAC, MARYLAND

The city of Potomac, Maryland is located about fifteen miles northwest of Washington, D.C. along the marshlands that border its namesake river. It has a population of about fifty thousand people and is home to some of the region's most affluent neighborhoods nestled among the rolling hills. Many highly successful and wealthy business executives, professional athletes, and political operatives reside in the area.

On a good day, it's about a thirty-minute drive from the nation's capital depending on the route that's taken. In traffic, it easily can be forty minutes or more. Today, traffic on the Beltway and its arterials was heavy. Howard Morris, sitting in a heated rear seat of the Bentley Mulsanne limousine, began to fidget. In contrast, Shepard Jenkins, seated next to him, was the picture of calmness.

Jenkins looked over at Morris and said, "You're uneasy. Why?"

Morris didn't answer right away. He stared out the window at the passing scene as his fingers nervously twisted the edge of his overcoat. He paid no attention to a brown delivery truck passing in the other direction toward town. In large yellow letters on its side was the company's name, Custom Appliances of McLean. A short time later a black Cadillac Escalade driven by an oriental man also passed in the other direction. After a while he said, "I'm not uneasy. I just don't understand why Laski wants to see us. Right now, I mean. What could be so damned important?"

He turned from the window and glanced at the back of the head of the limo driver. He didn't know how much conversation the man listened to, and wanted to be cautious about what he and his political strategist, Jenkins, discussed in the man's presence. Surely, Morris thought, he reports everything back to Laski.

The man was large, well over six feet tall and north of two hundred and fifty pounds. He looked to Morris like a very rough customer. One ear was cauliflowered, his nose was flattened, and he had a number of facial scars. One particularly gruesome scar ran from the left side of his forehead through his left eyebrow, across what there was of his nose, and down his right cheek almost to the jawbone. He was typical of the people Chaim Laski surrounded himself with, at least the ones Morris had seen. These people frightened Morris. He assumed they had the same effect on everyone. That was part of their purpose in Laski's employ. Morris didn't want to think of the other duties they might perform for Laski.

Jenkins smiled to himself as he ran his hand over the semi-aniline finish of the full grain leather covering the seats. He felt the warmth coming through from the seat heaters and knew that in warm weather the seats were cooled. The heat felt very good on this cold, wintry day. He didn't know how much Laski had paid for this custom commissioned Bentley, but he knew these incredible machines could easily cost more than three hundred fifty thousand dollars. It weighed more than six thousand pounds and was powered by a twin-turbo pushrod V8 engine generating more than five hundred horsepower. It boasted an eight-speed transmission and was one of the few cars in the world that was built entirely by hand. He admired the man's taste. It certainly was impressive and fitting for a man worth many billions of dollars.

The driver had chosen to exit Washington via Constitution Avenue and crossed the Potomac into Virginia on the Theodore Roosevelt Memorial Bridge. From there he had taken the George Washington Memorial parkway west along the south bank of the river, then north into Maryland on the Capital Beltway. He exited onto River Road and drove west into the town of Potomac.

Laski lived in a very large French country-style mansion on several acres of land off River Road just west of the town.

As they neared their destination, Jenkins reached over and tapped Morris on the leg to get his attention. "Buck up, Howard. His wanting to see us can only be a positive."

Morris glanced again at the back of the driver's head. "I don't know, Shep. With all the shit that happened with Case this morning, why does Chaim need to see us now? What couldn't wait until tonight, maybe dinner together?" He looked in the rearview mirror and was further unnerved to see the driver looking at him. He unconsciously pressed himself back in his seat as if to put distance between himself and the man with the frightening countenance.

"I think it's perfectly plausible why he'd want to see us," Jenkins said. "Case being killed is unfortunate, but he managed to deliver the information we needed before his death. Now, we're poised to blow the lid off a great story, one that will only enhance your standing with Laski and his organization. For Christ sake, man, look at the positives. You're practically a shoe-in for the party's nomination for president."

The tires on the Bentley's twenty-one inch wheels crunched on the gravel as the car passed through the electronic gate set between high, sturdy looking walls. Both passengers couldn't help but notice the surveillance cameras mounted on the walls. Armed guards were patrolling the grounds with the largest, ugliest dogs either man had ever seen. The limo wound down a long, twisting driveway that led to Laski's palatial home. It was only one of several he owned in the United States and other parts of the world. When the car rolled to a stop in the motor court, another Laski employee, also large and menacing-looking and with an earpiece, opened the door for Morris. The driver did the same for Jenkins on the other side of the car.

"You vill please to follow me," the second man said in heavily accented words and began walking toward the steps that led to the front entrance of the sprawling structure. Morris had been here before and, although it was palatial in every sense of the term, he didn't particularly like it. It was *too* big – thirteen bedrooms and sixteen bathrooms. All told, it housed more than twenty thousand square feet under air conditioning. This did not include the separate caretaker's bungalow or the additional guest quarters located on the other side of a small lake.

As they reached the top step, an older man in a butler's livery opened the door. In a distinctly British accent, he said, "Welcome, gentlemen. Please follow me." He led Morris and Jenkins through the entryway and down a wide hall that was all glass on one side overlooking an enclosed garden area. The other side of the hall was lined with a series of double doors all of which were closed, except for the last one. It housed a well-stocked library. At the end of the hall was a glassed-in sunroom. The butler stopped at the entrance to the room and motioned for the two men to enter, then turned around and retraced his steps down the hall.

Laski was sitting in a very comfortable looking chair and talking on a cell phone. He broke off the conversation when he saw Morris and Jenkins and laid the phone on the table beside his chair. He was short and somewhat stout. He looked to be somewhere in his mid- to late seventies. He had a roundish face and gray hair that twisted naturally in several directions, giving him the look of someone who had just gotten out of bed. Morris had heard that Laski slept about three hours a night, rising at four every morning to start his day with reports from the markets in Europe and Asia.

"Zenator und Zchep, iss goot to zee you boze. Please zid down," Laski said in his thick, guttural accent. His voice and speech pattern always reminded Morris of Henry Kissinger. In some ways it also reminded him of his own father's accent, and in some ways not so much.

The two men sat and Morris got right to the point. "Chaim, while it's always a pleasure to see you, I have to admit I'm puzzled why you called us here on such short notice."

Laski laughed. It was a cold and shallow laugh. "Is not to vorry, Zenator. I only vant to discuss important zituation vit you."

Morris and Jenkins looked at each other for a moment. "It must be pretty important for you to call this meeting," Morris said.

"Yes, wery important." He always seemed to Morris to reverse the pronunciation of his v's and w's. He knew Laski was a Polish immigrant, but somehow his accent seemed to defy placement in any particular Eastern European country.

Vhat I vant to know iz details ov Mr. Case's evorts."

"Well," Morris said, "I thought we were simply going to leak that information to our friends in the press or through an organization like WikiLeaks. I'm surprised you have such a strong interest in it."

"I am surprising man, Zenator," Laski said and laughed the mirthless laugh again. "Please to tell me vhat you know." He glanced at his watch as if to indicate that Morris should waste no time in delivering a summary of Case's findings. Morris knew the watch was a Patek Philippe World Time Platinum watch that retails for about forty thousand dollars. It had a hand-stitched blue alligator strap that matched the color of the watch's inner facing. It kept time in twenty-four separate zones, which was important to a man like Laski whose financial dealings were worldwide. Morris had heard, however, that Laski's World Time Platinum actually was the original one of a kind produced in 1939. Its last known price was more than four million dollars paid at an auction in 2002. That one kept time in forty-two cities around the world.

Morris sat back in his chair and looked at Jenkins again. "Shep, fill in anything I might leave out." Then he told Laski everything he had learned from the files Case had sent him. When he was through, he looked questioningly at his host.

Laski sat quietly for several moments, running the new information over in his mind. After a while he looked at Morris and Jenkins and smiled broadly. "Gentlemen, dis iss goot information. Iss vhat vee are zeeking," he said. "Tomorrow, Zenator, you vill call meeting of your committee viss press present. You personally vill release ziss information. Iss not for VikiLeaks and zuch. Zat does not have zame effect for benefit of your prezidential aspirations" He made a stabbing motion with his right hand. "Tomorrow vee drive anohzer big shtake in heart of American goody two shoe capitalist fantazy."

Jenkins moved uncomfortably in his chair. He had come a long way from his humble beginnings in the projects of Birmingham, Alabama. In some measure, he believed the American system had greatly contributed to his success. He wasn't sure how he would have fared in Laski's view of a single world order. He had heard enough over the past few years to know that it was a vision of global Marxism ruled by a small intellectual elite endowed with every privilege imaginable. The remaining global mass of humanity would subsist according to the directives of this intellectually superior order of beings. Dissidents would not be tolerated. By hitching his fate to Laski's organization, which included Morris, Jenkins hoped he would be included in the ruling elite.

16 FREDERICK, MARYLAND

Mitchel Christie had missed the last MARC train because of the lateness of the hour when he left Bureau headquarters. He caught a ride to his home in Frederick, Maryland with a coworker who lived a few miles farther north.

Christie lived in a comfortable home on a side street a few blocks from the town's historic district. Although it had been renovated many times since it was built in the early part of the twentieth century, it retained its original look. He and his wife had moved there before their son, Brett, the first of their two children, had been born. Although they could afford to upgrade based on his current salary, they never had developed a desire to move. It was home. His son and daughter, Samantha, went to nearby schools that had excellent ratings, and they all genuinely liked the neighborhood.

Frederick is about an hour and a half from downtown Washington, D.C. whether by car or the MARC light rail line. Generally, Christie caught the 6:05 train in the morning, arriving at Union Station about quarter to eight. It was a brisk seven or eight minute walk from there to his office. Because this day had started so early with the incident in Georgetown involving Harold Case, he had taken the earlier 5:38 train, but the last returning trip on the Brunswick line had left Union Station at 7:15 while he was still in conference with Franconia and the other special agents assigned to him on this matter.

Bone weary and cold, he checked his watch as he slipped into the dimly lit house. His wife, Deborah, had left the outside light on over the front door, as well as a small lamp in the living room. After all these years, she had grown accustomed to the unpredictable hours demanded by her husband's career.

It was almost one o'clock in the morning. Christie had been up for nearly twenty-four hours and he could feel it. He was not looking forward to the next day. He had an early meeting scheduled with the Bureau's Deputy Director and various functionaries of the Metropolitan Police Department. Later that morning he was scheduled to fly to Georgia to meet with special agents in the Bureau's Atlanta field office. The following day he planned to fly to the West Coast to interview the surviving geneticist, William Nishioki, whose name had surfaced in the CIA records that Harold Case had uncovered. But first, he thought, I have to find another bottle of Mylanta. Then I have to shower, pack, be out of here in time to catch the 5:38 train to D.C., and somehow grab a couple of hours sleep along the way.

Just inside the front door he slipped off the shoes he'd been wearing since four o'clock that morning. His feet immediately felt better. He quietly crossed the living room floor, sticking to the carpeted areas in preference to the underlying hardwood. Christie paused to look at a framed photo on the coffee table. It had been taken a few weeks earlier as the family celebrated Thanksgiving. Christie stared for a long time at each face: his wife's, his son's, and his daughter's. He felt a sense of anxiety in the middle of his chest. Time was passing rapidly, too rapidly. His kids were growing up too fast and he wasn't able to spend as much time with them as he believed he should. And he missed his wife. There just didn't seem to be enough quality time for their relationship. He knew he needed to do something, but he wasn't sure what it was.

Christie showered in the downstairs bathroom to avoid disturbing his family's sleep. His wife had left his pajamas and a blanket and pillow on the couch in the living room, knowing from experience that he would sleep there rather than take a chance on waking her.

Afterward, as he lay groggily on the couch waiting for sleep to take him, he thought about recent conversations he and his wife had had. What was it she had been urging him to consider? Wasn't it something about leaving the Bureau and taking a cushy job in management with a private security firm? It was beginning to hold some genuine appeal. He could lead a normal life like so many of the other husbands and fathers in his neighborhood. There would be time for his son's soccer matches and his daughter's swim meets. He actually could plan to take his wife out and know that nothing would come up abruptly to interfere with it. Maybe, he thought, after this current situation was resolved.

PART TWO

STRAY DOGS

17 TAMPA, FLORIDA

The Delta flight to Tampa took just over four hours with a change of planes at Hartsfield International Airport in Atlanta. Whelan had mingled unobtrusively with the thousands of other travelers in the Atlanta airport, moving just quickly enough to make his connecting flight, but not so swiftly as to call attention to himself. On the other hand, nothing escaped his notice. He had been trained too well to begin with, and the sense of self-preservation developed from living on the run for almost twenty years had only served to sharpen this awareness.

In Tampa, he moved easily with the flow of passengers through the Airside E Concourse that Delta shared with United and Air Canada to the tram station. The tram shuttled passengers to the Main or Landside Terminal. Once there, Whelan located the arcade that led to the Marriott Tampa Airport Hotel and turned into it. He had been awake and on the go for thirty-six hours and knew he needed to sleep if he was going to be fully operative for what lay ahead.

Along the arcade he paused at a clothing shop and purchased two pairs of clean socks and underwear, a dress shirt and a tie. A few doors down he entered a sundry shop and picked up a toothbrush and disposable razor as well as travel-size containers of shaving cream and toothpaste. He moved on to the hotel and, using the Murkowski ID and cash, he checked in for the night. After dropping his purchases off in his room, he went upstairs to the revolving restaurant at the top of the hotel and had poached salmon, steamed broccoli and two beers.

Later, he called a number Levell had given him. He arranged with the party on the other end to meet him the following morning in front of the Delta arrivals area outside the Main Terminal. After that, he showered, slid into bed and slept a deep and peaceful sleep.

The next morning Whelan wiped down anything in the room he might have touched, bagged up his dirty clothes and checked out of the hotel. He crossed back to the Main Terminal and descended to the Delta baggage claim area. Near the exit to the curbside pickup he spotted a man with a military bearing. He was wearing jeans, a white turtleneck sweater and brown leather jacket, and was holding a small, handmade sign with the name "Mr. Murkowski" on it.

Whelan approached him and said, "I'm Murkowski."

The man offered his hand and introduced himself. "Major Pederson. Tom Pederson."

Whelan shook hands and said, "You're one of General McCoy's people."

"Yes, I am."

"Then you're with USSOCOM at MacDill?" Whelan said in reference to the United States Special Operations Command. It is the unified combatant command charged with overseeing the various Special Operations Commands (SOC or SOCOM) of the Army, Air Force, Navy and Marine Corps of the United States Armed Forces. USSOCOM is part of the Department of Defense, and is headquartered at MacDill Air Force Base in Tampa, Florida. The Marine Corps component of USSOCOM was commanded by Major General Roscoe "Buster" McCoy.

Whelan gave Major Pederson the address of his destination on Orient Road. It was about a twenty-two minute trip via Dale Mabry Highway and Interstate 275. Pederson led him to a beige colored, late model Dodge Caravan in the short-term parking area. From the scattering of youth sporting gear that cluttered the interior of the van, Whelan knew it was the Major's personal vehicle and not military issue. He was pleased to note that McCoy and the other members of the Team, which presumably included Pederson, were following measures to keep their activities off the radar screen.

Whelan hadn't been in Tampa in almost two decades. The town was bigger, glossier, more heavily trafficked, but still dirty and industrial at its core. Orient Road was part of that core. Dusty and rutted, it was lined mostly with tired, ugly, squat buildings that had not aged well. The major exception was the Hillsboro County jail, a huge, rambling, multistoried mass of concrete. The asphalt parking lots were losing the battle with the weather in West Central Florida despite recent restriping. The landscaping was as ugly as the buildings, brownish grass and large bare areas where only the hard, dry, Florida soil showed. The trees, what there were of them, were spindly and stunted, struggling to find nutrition in the wretched dirt. This was a part of Florida that its Chambers of Commerce didn't want tourists to see.

Pederson stopped a short distance past the jail complex on the opposite side of Orient Road. The address Whelan had given him was a building long past its prime, if it had ever had one. The building was low and flat-roofed. The parking lot had more potholes than pavement. The door, and the two windows that flanked it, appeared not to have been washed in years. They all were reinforced on the inside with steel bars like buildings in a high crime neighborhood. Whelan noted the irony of a jail surrounded by such an environment.

The words "Bail Bonds" had been painted on one window. There was a phone number painted on the other. Both were badly faded. Pederson asked Whelan if he wanted him to wait. He shook his head and said, "Give me a number where I can reach you if I need something locally." Pederson gave him his personal cell phone number and Whelan entered it in code in his own cell phone directory. He waved Pederson off, turned and walked across the shabby parking lot, pulling his thin leather gloves on as he walked.

Whelan opened the door. As he did, a buzzer sounded somewhere in the back. Whelan estimated the room to be about thirty-five feet deep by twenty-five feet wide. There were two rows of battered metal desks running along the walls from near the front door back about twenty-five feet to a scarred and battered partition. A doorway in the partition indicated more space beyond. The place looked like it hadn't been cleaned in awhile, and hadn't been painted in a really long while.

A very beefy man with a shaved head was sitting at the last desk on Whelan's right. He was wearing a tee shirt that said Gold's Gym and appeared to be working a crossword puzzle in a newspaper. After several moments, and without looking up, he said, "So whaddya want?"

Whelan didn't answer right away. Instead, he walked toward the man at the desk.

The man looked up, pushed the paper away, and leaned back in his chair, crossing his thick arms in front of him. The skin below the sleeves of his tee shirt was covered with tattoos. He cocked his head back and examined his visitor through narrowed eyes. He sized Whelan up – the moustache, the glasses, the suit, and the briefcase. Another pussy lawyer, he thought. "I asked you a question, bud," he said.

"I'm looking for someone." Whelan said.

"Yeah? Whaddo I look like, a fuckin' information service?" A sneer seemed to be his default expression. As Whelan reached his desk, the beefy man stood.

He was about five feet nine, but well over two hundred pounds and powerfully built. Built like a typical bail bondsman, Whelan thought. It was rough work on occasion. "I'm looking for an employee of yours, Arne Olaffsen," Whelan said, giving the alias Larsen currently was using, according to Levell.

"Whaddya want with Arne?"

"He's an old army buddy."

"Yeah? He never told me nothin' 'bout no army. Besides he ain't here and I ain't got time to fuck around jawing with nonpaying customers. Now get out." He jerked his head toward the front door.

"Somebody needs a lesson in good manners," Whelan said.

"Somebody's gonna give you a lesson in ass-kickin', you ain't out of here in ten seconds."

Whelan was sure the bondsman knew where Larsen was. He saw two options. Try to wait around until Larsen showed up or beat the information out of the bondsman. It wasn't even close. He chose the second option. He knew that the other man, despite his bulk, would be very quick as well as strong. He would try to use his low center of gravity to bulldoze an opponent. Whelan knew better than to grapple with the man.

"I'll just wait here until Olaffsen comes back."

The bondsman cocked his shaved head to one side, squinted at Whelan, and peeled his lips back into an even bigger sneer. "You'll wait your ass outside," he said and reached suddenly for Whelan's suit lapel with his left hand while drawing back his right fist.

Whelan responded with lightening speed. In a single, smooth motion, Whelan dropped the briefcase and drove his right arm up, bent ninety degrees at the elbow and his wrist rotating inward. With his two hundred twenty-five pounds behind it, his forearm slammed into the bondsman's left wrist sending his arm flying to the side. He then snapped the same forearm, wrist rotating back to the outside, into the bondsman's right arm as he tried to deliver the punch to Whelan's head. The man grunted in pain as each blow was struck.

As part of the same technique, and without pause, Whelan snapped a back-fist strike to the man's nose, crushing it. The bondsman staggered back a half step, but Whelan moved with him, driving a knee into the man's groin that caused his knees to buckle. Whelan kicked his legs out from under him with a sweeping technique.

The man fell heavily to the floor and tried to get back to his feet. Whelan kicked him flush in the face. The force of the blow split open the skin over the bony area above his right eye. Blood began to flow freely down his face. He fell again to his hands and knees. Whelan stepped behind him and kicked him hard in the groin again with the toe of his lace-up. The bondsman collapsed to the floor and vomited.

Whelan waited patiently for him to recover enough to try to regain his feet, then grabbed him under the right arm and hoisted him up. The man staggered and tried to throw a wobbly right-handed punch at Whelan. But he only had the use of one eye and his depth perception was off. Because of his injuries, so were his speed and timing. Whelan threw the man against a wall face-first and viciously twisted his arm up behind his back. He kept forcing it up until he was satisfied that he had heard the snapping sound of the arm dislocating from the shoulder.

The man screamed and collapsed again. As he slid semiconsciously down the wall, his injured eye left a smeared and bloody trail. Whelan picked up his briefcase and walked around behind the man's desk. He laid the briefcase on the desktop and opened it. He knew the bondsman was right-handed because of the way he fought. He opened the top drawer on the right-hand side. Not unexpectedly, it contained a snub-nosed Smith & Wesson Bodyguard 38. Whelan stuck a pencil through the trigger guard, lifted it out of the drawer and dropped it into his briefcase, and closed it.

He returned to the bondsman who was in the fetal position on the floor, his right arm twisted at an odd angle. The man was groaning loudly through clenched teeth. He probably never had been on the receiving end of so savage a beating and was thoroughly defeated for the first time in his memory. Whelan eased him to his feet. "Tell me where I can find Arne," he said.

"Lunch, he's at lunch," the man said without unclenching his jaw.

"Where does he go for lunch?"

"Earl's Place."

"Where is it?"

The man drew in a deep breath and let out a long slow groan. He was very pale and beginning to shake as shock set in. Whelan slapped him on the damaged shoulder to get him to focus. "Ow, Jesus, ow! It's down the street, two blocks," he motioned with his head indicating a right turn on exiting the building.

"Where's your car?" Whelan said.

"You're gonna steal my ride?" The man paused and said, "You gonna kill me? Please don't kill me. I gotta wife and kid."

"A family? I bet you're the kind of guy who slaps his wife around, and probably the child too."

"Only when they need it." There was a distinct whine in his voice. "Please don't kill me, please." He started to cry.

"Give me your car keys," Whelan said.

The man said, "They're hangin' on a hook by the back door."

Whelan turned him around toward the rear of the building and pushed him, not hard, but not gently. He left the briefcase on the desk and together the two of them walked to the back door of the building. Whelan grabbed the key ring off the hook by the back door. He nudged the man aside, carefully unlocked and opened the door, and looked around. There was an old Cadillac sedan parked outside the door, but no one in sight.

Whelan pushed the bondsman out the door and toward the rear of the Cadillac.

"Whaddya gonna do to me, Mister? Please don't kill me. I won't tell no one about this. I swear. I only got a little bit of cash inside, but you can have it."

"I'm not interested in your money. It's Olaffsen I'm looking for."

"Jesus, you're just like that rough-assed sonofabitch. Whaddya gonna do to him, kill him?"

"None of your fucking business," Whelan said as he unlocked and opened the Caddy's trunk. It was filthy. There were greasy rags and clothes, a nearly bald tire, and assorted tools. Whelan took one of the rags.

He looked quickly around to be certain no one was watching. He grabbed the bondsman's good shoulder and turned him around so the trunk was behind him and the backs of his legs were against the bumper. "Get in the trunk," he said. "And if I was you, I'd try to land on my left shoulder."

The bondsman turned and looked at the trunk with his one good eye. The right eye had swollen completely shut. He hitched his butt up on the edge of the trunk and toppled over to his left. It didn't go so well. He lost his balance and turned in midair, landing face first. His right shoulder hit the rim of the tire. He screamed.

"You want to live, do exactly as I tell you," Whelan said. "I'm going to be around for a while. If I hear any noise, anything at all, I'm going to open the trunk and kill you nice and slow." With that, he slammed the trunk lid closed.

Wearing the thin leather gloves had prevented leaving any fingerprints, so he walked back through the bonding office and out the front door. Outside he turned right and walked down the street toward Earl's Place.

18 TAMPA, FLORIDA

Although it was Florida and the sun was shining, it wasn't a Chamber of Commerce day. The early January weather was raw and windy. The sky was a cloudless, cobalt blue. The temperature was dropping and the air held a promise of a cold, damp, mean evening. Whelan put on his sunglasses as he left the bondsman's office and walked the two dusty, forlorn blocks to Earl's Place.

The parking lot looked like a replica of the Bondsman's. The only vehicles in the lot were an old Harley with a torn leather saddle, a dirty and battered pickup truck that had seen a lot more than forty miles of bad road in its day, and an ancient and badly rusted Chevy Nova, its trunk held down with two frayed bungee cords. A rusty and dented pole that looked as if it once may have been painted white was planted in the middle of the parking lot. The dents and scars near its base testified to the countless number of times drunks had backed into it. The pole supported a neon sign that identified the establishment as Earl's Place. The neon tubes were broken in several places and Whelan wondered what it really spelled out at night. Hanging beneath the neon sign on two short chains was a rectangular piece of flat rusted metal that said "Beer & Eats". The rusty chains screeched in complaint as the gusts of cold north wind bullied the sign back and forth.

The building was squarish with a flat roof. The walls were badly in need of paint. An ancient and bent TV antenna was attached to a sidewall and swayed slowly in the wind. There were no windows along the front of the building, just a large, heavy-looking door. Whelan took his sunglasses off and put them in the breast pocket of his suit coat. He eased the door open and stepped into the dark interior, moving quickly to his left along the wall while he waited for his vision to adjust to the change from bright sunlight. As it did, he scanned the interior. The U-shaped bar dominated the room. Its closed end was against the far wall. There was a row of booths along the wall to his right and several tables and chairs between them and the bar. There were three pool tables and a few more tables to the left of the bar. A jukebox hugged the rear wall to the left of the bar between the entrances to the men's and women's restrooms.

The walls were barren of any decorations and the floor was bare concrete, dirty and cracked. Two middle-aged men dressed in work clothes sat in one of the booths on the right. The logos on their shirts indicated they were county employees. Probably grounds keepers or custodial workers at the jail, Whelan thought. A younger man wearing a worn leather jacket and a bandana was shooting pool by himself. A young woman was working the bar.

Unless someone currently was using the restroom, the only other occupant that Whelan could see was a man with a shaved head sitting at the bar with his back to the door. Even though the bar was relatively warm compared to the raw outside temperatures, Whelan saw that the man was wearing thin leather gloves very much like the ones he had on. They were thick enough to prevent the leaving of fingerprints, but thin enough to allow unrestricted use of the hands, such as in hand-to-hand combat. Whelan connected the dots. Trouble was brewing.

The man was very powerfully built with trapezius and deltoid muscles so thick it appeared that his shoulders joined his head at the base of his ears. He was watching Whelan in the large mirror that ran across the front of the bar. It was Sven Larsen, The Man With No Neck.

A broad smile spread slowly across Whelan's face. He walked to the bar and stood next to Larsen. In a replay of an inside joke that dated back twenty years, he said quietly so that no one else could hear, "Didn't you used to be Sven Larsen?"

There was a faint, but familiar smile on Larsen's face. He had two smiles, a good smile and a bad smile. This was his good smile. "I used to be a lot of things," he said, as he climbed off his stool. The two men embraced.

"It's been a very long time," Larsen said. "You look like you've kept yourself in good shape."

"I try," Whelan said. "And you still don't have a neck." He smiled when he said it.

"Us good-looking ones never do." Again there was the faint smile. "I got a call from Levell saying to expect you."

"He tell you why?"

"No, he said you'd fill me in when you got here." Larsen sat down on his stool. He nodded at the one next to him. As Whelan sat, Larsen said, "Levell knew about the bonding office, but how did you find me here at Earl's?"

"The bail bondsman told where to find you."

Larsen arched one eyebrow questioningly. "Is he still alive?"

"He'll survive."

Larsen made a grunting sound. It was as close to a belly laugh as he ever got. "You've clearly not lost your skill sets. Ross..., the bondsman, is a tough sonofabitch, though not as tough as he'd like to think he is."

"So, you been bonding for the past twenty years?"

"Not exactly. I got the license, but I'm a specialist of sorts."

"I can't wait to hear this," Whelan said.

Larsen took a sip of beer from the bottle in front of him. He held it in that odd, almost dainty way that truly powerful men sometimes do. Whelan wondered if it was because they were concerned that a firmer grip might cause the bottle to shatter.

"As a rule, bondsmen are a tough bunch, but even they have their limits," Larsen said. "There are some people who scare even them. When one of those types skips bail, I get the call to bring them back." He paused and smiled his bad smile, the cold, mirthless, menacing one. "I always get the sonofabitch."

"Maybe you should have been a Mountie."

"Naw, too freaking cold in Canada and the money is no where near as good."

"Kill anybody in the process of dragging them back?"

"Not yet, but I keep hoping. It's interesting that you asked. One of the things I like about the job is the fact that when a person skips bail, the law says the bondsman must 'produce the body'," he emphasized the last three words. "Doesn't say there has to be any life in the body." Again, the faint mirthless smile flickered across his face.

"Sounds like you've found your life's work," Whelan said.

Larsen motioned to the bartender. Although it appeared she didn't have much to do, she took her time coming over. As she did, Whelan saw that her face was badly beaten. One eyelid was swollen and discolored. Her bottom lip was puffy, accentuating her natural pout. There were cuts on her nose and right cheek and bruises on several other parts of her face and neck. Her sleeveless top revealed more ugly black, blue, and yellow bruises on her arms. There was no sign of life in her eyes, just a certain look of resignation. It seemed to Whelan that, despite her young age, she had abandoned any sense of enjoyment of life, or, perhaps it had been beaten out of her.

"Yeah?" she said. Her voice sounded tired and cheerless.

Larsen motioned his head sideways at Whelan. "Susie, this is my best buddy. I think he needs a beer."

Susie didn't say anything; she just stood in front of Whelan looking down at the bar with a sullen expression on her face. Judging from the place, he knew it would be a waste of time to ask for an import or microbrew. He looked at the bottle in front of Larsen. It was a well-known American brand. "Still drinking that watered down bat piss, I see."

"How do you know what bat piss tastes like?"

"I'm Irish. I know a lot of things."

"Some things I don't want to know and that's one of them." Larsen smiled his good smile.

Whelan looked at the girl behind the bar, grimaced and said, "I'll have what he's drinking." She walked away slowly.

"You and Sharon still together?" Whelan said.

"Celebrated our twenty-first anniversary last month."

"Kids?"

"We have two boys. Rolf and Erik."

"Sounds like names for Viking warriors. Do they take after their old man?"

Larsen shrugged. "Of course," he said. "Now you know about me, where have you been?"

"Ireland. A town called Dingle. It's on a peninsula in the southwestern part of the island."

Larsen nodded. "That's right, you were born there. Still speak the language?"

"Sure and begorrah," Whelan said.

"How do you make your living?"

"We..., Caitlin and I, run a B and B, a bed and breakfast."

"So, Caitlin is it?" Larsen said in an attempt at a brogue. "And would she be red haired with green eyes and freckles?"

Whelan shook his head and smiled. "Contrary to popular belief, not all the Irish are redheads or freckled. Caitlin has raven black hair and ice blue eyes. She's a stunner."

Susie walked up and placed a bottle of beer in front of Whelan. He nodded his appreciation, and she moved away to another part of the bar. He had no intention of drinking it and just left it sitting on the bar.

"How did you two meet?"

"She was in a pub with a couple of her girl friends and a guy was giving her a hard time. She looked like she could use some help. So I helped."

"Did the guy survive?"

"Mostly," Whelan said.

"And I guess she was very grateful and the rest is history."

"Not exactly. Her father was the local law at the time, the sergeant in charge of the sub-district. He threw me in the brig. Turns out the pub owner was a cousin of his and had had trouble with the guy before. He appreciated my work and spoke to Tom, Caitlin's father. Shortly after that I was sprung. Family goes a long way in Ireland."

"And how did things go with Caitlin?"

"Not so good at first, but I managed to wear her down with my inimitable charm and boyish good looks."

"Yeah. And now?"

"And now we have Sean and Declan."

Larsen looked at Whelan for a moment. "Interesting," he said. "And how are you getting along with her father now?"

"He figured it out pretty quickly. He's ex-SBS."

Larsen nodded. "The Brits' top special ops unit. How'd an Irishman get into the SBS?"

"He enlisted. Ol' Tom is one of the toughest s.o.b.s I've ever met. The Brits weren't about to turn down a prospect like him over a piddling matter like citizenship."

"Your boys have his bloodline as well as yours. That's a hell of a combination."

"Kinda' scary, isn't it?"

"Could be. He still a cop?"

"Yeah, he was promoted some years back. He's district superintendent now. My brother-in-law, Padraig, has Tom's old job as sergeant in charge of the sub-district. He's former SBS, too. He calls on me from time-to-time when there's a serious disturbance."

"How does that settle with Caitlin?"

Whelan smiled. "She's given her brother hell for it on a few occasions."

"The girl has a temper?"

"She's Irish."

"Sure and begorrah," Larsen said.

19 ATLANTA

The Hartsfield-Jackson International Airport in Atlanta, the busiest airport in the world, was it's usual beehive of activity. Mitch Christie's flight from Reagan National in Washington, D.C., had arrived on time at gate 18 in Terminal A. He was pleasantly surprised at the on-time arrival considering the weather. Now, he thought, if my luggage arrived on the same flight, it will be a good day regardless how the rest of it goes.

He decided against taking the People Mover tram, instead walking the Transportation Mall from Terminal A to the Baggage Claim Area located directly under the Main Terminal. He strode along quickly oblivious to the African-themed artwork and photographs lining the walkway between Terminals A and T. He still felt groggy from the combination of the pressure of the Harold Case situation and the minimal amount of sleep he had gotten the previous night. A brisk walk seemed like a good way to get some exercise. He hoped it would get his blood flowing faster and clear some of the cobwebs from his brain.

His suitcase was very nearly the last bag to come out of the baggage chute. Christie wondered why it was that a bag tagged "Priority", because of his business class ticket, wasn't one of the first ones to emerge. He pulled it off the carousel, extended the handle, attached his briefcase to a strap at the top, and rolled it to the exit from the baggage claim area. As he did, he saw a younger man he recognized as an agent in the Bureau's Atlanta office. He approached the man and extended his hand. "I'm Mitch Christie. Were you sent to pick me up?"

"Yes sir," the man replied, shaking Christie's hand. "I'm Ted Schiavo and I have a car waiting for you at the curb." He took Christie's wheeled suitcase and, motioning for him to follow, threaded his way through the crowded terminal area.

There was a late model gray Ford Taurus sedan idling at the curb outside the baggage area. A man in a dark gray suit was leaning against a front fender chatting with an airport security guard. Christie assumed the man was another agent from the Atlanta field office.

Schiavo opened the trunk of the Taurus and placed Christie's bag in it, slammed the trunk lid, and opened the right rear door for Christie to enter the car. He climbed into the front passenger seat and the other man slid behind the wheel. The other man turned his head and said, "Agent Christie, I'm Bill Tate with the Bureau's Atlanta office."

"Nice to meet you," Christie said. "Thanks for picking me up."

Tate exited the airport onto Interstate 85 and wound along it for the twenty miles it took to get to the field office on Century Parkway on the northeast side of town. After parking the car, the three men immediately went into one of the Bureau's conference rooms. It was small and furnished with what looked to be mishmash of castoff furniture from other offices and conference rooms. Christie set his briefcase down on a battered faux wood credenza and took a chair at the small round table. Two other people already were in the room. Both of them were women. One was a specialist in medical matters, the other in computer technology. Schiavo introduced them.

Christie shook hands with each of them and said, "I appreciate your being able to meet with me on short notice." Three of the five nodded. The other two just stared at him. He knew they all were busy in their own areas and probably didn't have the time to spare for this meeting. It was the kind of situation that can cause resentment, and he didn't blame them.

"Look, I'll try to make this as brief as possible," he said. "Bring me up to date on Walter Bailey."

The others looked at Schiavo, indicating he had seniority in this matter. He looked at the medical specialist and said, "Earlene, you've been following up this part of it, what do you have for us?"

Earlene was African-American, fortyish with thick glasses, slightly overweight, and wore her hair pulled back in a tight bun. She adjusted her glasses on her nose and glanced at some papers she was holding. She said, "Mr. Walter Alfred Bailey, Caucasian, was born in Marietta, Georgia on August ninth, nineteen seventy to Alfred Carlyle Bailey and Marie Celeste Bailey née Hopkins. He weighed seven pounds, four ounces at birth." She shuffled the papers and continued. "He graduated from Marietta High School in 1988 and attended the University of Georgia in Athens for two years. He had average grades with no discernible major and dropped out after two years."

"Any military record, Earlene?" Christie said.

"No."

"Wife, kids?"

She shuffled her papers again and said, "Yes, he married Charlotte Lynne Evans two months after leaving UGA. They had one child, a daughter, Amber Lynn, born in nineteen ninety-two."

"What kind of work did he do?" Christie said.

Earlene glanced at her papers again. "He was the manager of a paint store in Smyrna, Georgia. Apparently, he worked there from the time he dropped out of college until his death in nineteen ninety-eight."

"He have any hobbies or interests?"

"Fishing and NASCAR."

"That figures. Was he religious?"

"It doesn't appear so."

Christie said, "Any criminal record?"

"He was busted in high school with some of his classmates for under-aged possession of alcohol. He was cited twice for speeding as a teenager. That's it."

"Did he belong to any clubs, organizations, political groups, anything like that?" Christie said.

"Kiwanis."

Christie said. "He sounds to me like an everyday, plain vanilla kind of guy." He thought for a moment, then said, "What about his medical records and death certificate? Anything of interest there?"

"He was overweight, diabetic, smoked heavily, and had a family history of atherosclerosis." She looked up, adjusted her glasses again, and said, "That's the build up of plaque in the coronary arteries." She glanced down at her papers again and continued, "By age twenty-eight he was experiencing eighty-five to ninety percent blockage in several coronary arteries and suffering from severe angina. He was scheduled for triple coronary artery bypass surgery – the left anterior descending coronary artery, the right coronary artery, and the left circumflex artery. He didn't survive the surgery."

"A hellova note," Tate said. "Poor guy goes into the hospital to save his life and ends up losing it."

Everyone turned their head and looked at him for a moment with blank expressions.

"It's not so unusual under the circumstances," Earlene said. "He was in very poor health by the time he chose to have the surgery."

"Do we know anything at all about this man that might indicate how his identification showed up in use more than a decade after his death?" Christie said.

Everyone looked at Earlene. She shrugged.

"Stealing someone's identification is not so difficult," Schiavo said, "particularly if they're dead. First, you find a dead guy who was born about

81

the same time you were. Then you get a copy of his birth certificate from the office of vital statistics. Then...."

Christie held up his hand, stopping Schiavo. "I know the drill," he said.

The speakerphone in the middle of the small conference table buzzed. Schiavo leaned over and punched a button. "Yes?"

A voice at the other end of the line said, "There's a call for Special Agent Christie on line four. It's a Mr. John Deutch. He says he's in Forensics at Bureau headquarters."

"I'd like to take this call in private," Christie said.

"Sure," Schiavo said. He motioned to the others to clear the room.

When the door closed behind them, Christie picked up the receiver and punched the flashing red button for line four. "This is Christie," he said.

Deutch's nasal voice came from the other end of the line. "Supervisory Special Agent Christie, this is John Deutch in Forensics."

"Yes, John. You're a little late getting back to me. I expected to hear from you yesterday afternoon. What do you have for me?" Christie was irritated that Deutch hadn't gotten back to him earlier, as expected. The irritation showed in his voice.

"Well, I have some, ah, good news and...not so good news." Deutch's voice had a slight quaver in it.

"What is it?" Christie said. There was a tightening in his jaw, but he was struggling to be patient.

"Er..., you'll recall that there were blood samples from the Georgetown crime scene that were badly degraded and unusable for DNA purposes?"

"Yes."

"And there was another sample taken from the jacket sleeve of one of the victims?"

"Yes."

"Well, that one was in much better condition, and we were able to decode it. It definitely does not belong to any of the victims."

"Excellent, John. Do we have a suspect?"

"Well, I'm afraid that's where the bad news comes in, Special Agent Christie." The quaver in Deutch's voice was more pronounced.

"How so, John?"

"We checked the DNA results twice against our computer banks and could not come up with a match. I'm sorry." Deutch sounded like he might start to cry.

Christie's briefcase was on the credenza on the other side of the room, beyond his reach. There was a bottle of Mylanta in it. He eyed the briefcase longingly. "Goddammit, John, there's got to be a match." He thought for a few moments, and then said, "Look, here's what I want you to do, John. Get a hold of Franconia, the Agency liaison with the Bureau. Charlotte has his number. Have him check with Langley to see if there's any record of DNA or blood work for anyone involved in the Sleeping Dogs unit. If so, check it against the blood found on that victim's jacket. Got it?"

"Yes, I think so," Deutch said with a slight stammer. "Charlotte, Franconia, Sleeping Dogs…I'll do my best."

Christie gritted his teeth then said, "Yes, John, I'm sure you will. Thank you." He punched the release button and the line went dead. He went immediately to his briefcase, took out the bottle of Mylanta, shook it, and took a big gulp.

He took a deep breath and let it out slowly. Christ, he thought, I've endured an early meeting that didn't go so well with the Bureau's Deputy Director and a team from the D.C. Metropolitan Police Department, I've got more work to do here in Atlanta followed by a flight to San Francisco first thing in the morning. Thank God it's nonstop. Maybe I can sleep on the plane.

20 TAMPA, FLORIDA

With a gust of wintry air, the door to Earl's Place swung open behind Whelan and Larsen. Both men glanced in the mirror behind the bar. A tall, lanky man in his late twenties strode into the room. Four other men, all about his age, piled in after him. From the other end of the bar, Susie whined, "Bobby, I done tole you not to come down here no more when I'm workin'."

The man stopped about five feet inside the bar. His companions stood behind him trying to look tough. All five of the men wore jeans. Two wore sneakers and the other three wore engineer boots. One wore a ball cap, another wore a bandana on his head, and two of them wore Stetsons. The fifth had on a watch cap. Some were wearing plaid flannel shirts over white tee shirts and others wore sweatshirts. Bobby was wearing a tattered baseball jacket. There was a faint smile on Larsen's face. It was his bad smile. Whelan knew trouble had arrived.

"Shut up, bitch," Bobby said with a snarl. He spoke with a hillbilly drawl that Whelan thought seemed disingenuous as if he thought it made him seem tougher. "Ain't no woman gonna tell me where I can go and cain't go. That's a good way to get yore ass kicked. Again." He turned to his companions and grinned.

The two county workers sitting at a booth in the back stared at Bobby. The biker stopped shooting pool and stared also. "What the fuck you assholes looking at?" Bobby shouted. "You want some of me?" He jammed his finger into his chest for emphasis.

The two men in the back looked down at the tabletop and seemed to slither down in their seats. The biker shrugged, turned back around and resumed shooting pool.

Larsen literally flowed off his stool as smooth as rainwater on a windowpane. As he did, he placed a hand on Whelan's shoulder with enough pressure to indicate that he should remain seated. He stepped in front of Bobby and said, "I don't know about Susie, but I'm in a mood to get my ass kicked. Only, I hit back. Think you're up to it, Bobby-boy?" His bad smile was on full display.

While Bobby had three inches in height on Larsen, he spotted him about fifty pounds in body weight, and he had nowhere near the musculature of Larsen. Very few people did. But, with his four friends to back him up, he felt a strong sense of confidence. He turned and looked at them and grinned. "This motherfucker has a death wish. Shall we help him out, boys?"

They all nodded in agreement and tried to muster their most menacing looks. One of them pointed to Whelan and said, "What about him?"

"I'm doing you girls a favor by keeping him away from you," Larsen said. "If you don't piss me off, I plan to just rough you up. But him," he motioned toward Whelan with his head, "he's always in a bad mood, and he never leaves survivors behind."

Taking the cue, Whelan looked at the county workers, Susie, and the biker. "Anyone who looks like they might be using their cell phone, even to text, isn't going to leave here alive." Something about the way he said it caused the others to keep their hands where he could see them.

Bobby made a scoffing sound in his best macho man imitation and threw a right-handed punch at Larsen. Like most brawlers and wannabe brawlers, he telegraphed it badly. Larsen stepped inside and blocked it with his thick left forearm. He followed it with a pile driver of a right hand to Bobby's midsection. The wind exploded from Bobby's lungs with a savage grunt and he shot backwards, knocking two of his companions down and causing a third to stagger backward in order to maintain his balance.

"I'm disappointed," Whelan said, as he looked at the three men on the floor and the two still standing. "That's only a spare. I've seen you bowl better than that."

Larsen was moving to his left now, on his toes, smooth and quick like a lightweight. He began to softly whistle *Sweet Georgia Brown*.

The two men who had gone down with Bobby scrambled to their feet. One moved warily to his left, the other to his right. Bobby, having trouble breathing, was struggling to get to his hands and knees. A fourth man was trying to assist him. The one man who had not yet been affected sidled along the wall to the right of the front door. Someone had left a pool stick resting against the wall. He picked it up, reversed it, and, gripping it with both hands, began inching toward Larsen from the rear.

In a single, quick motion, Whelan snatched the bar stool Larsen had vacated and flung it with force at the man. It knocked him sideways into the wall. He shook his head to clear it and a second bar stool hit him with greater force. The seat struck his head and bounced it off the wall. His knees buckled and he slid semiconsciously to the floor.

Larsen snapped a glance at Whelan and said with a snarl, "This is my fight. You want a fight, go get your own."

Whelan smiled. Same old Larsen, he thought. Good to know some things never change.

The two men circling Larsen glanced at each other. One nodded and they both charged. They intended to grab Larsen around the head and upper body and grapple him to the floor where he could be kicked and pummeled into submission. It was a silly ploy. Larsen simply grabbed each man by the neck, lifted them off the ground and smashed their skulls together with extreme force. It concussed both men, sent them into unconsciousness, and split open their scalps. Larsen released their throats and both men collapsed to the hard concrete floor in unison. Blood began pooling around their heads.

Whelan was enjoying watching the Man With No Neck at work again after all these years. Three down, two to go, he said to himself.

The fourth man had helped Bobby get to his feet. He moved slowly on a direct line toward Larsen, paused and made some movements that looked vaguely like martial arts routines or what he may have thought were martial arts routines. Throwing is head back he screamed, "Kee-yaaah!" and charged. He attempted a poorly executed and well telegraphed head high roundhouse kick.

Larsen brought his left fist up to the side of his head and stepped into the kick, catching the force of it on the meat of his thick shoulder and arm. Immediately as the kick landed, Larsen grabbed the pant leg of the man's kicking leg with his left hand. Holding the leg in place, he delivered a massive blow from his right hand into the man's thigh fracturing the femur bone. Seemingly without pause, Larsen sent the same right hand in a back-fist strike to the side of the man's face. The force was such that it nearly dislocated the second cervical vertebra from the first.

He held on to the pant leg for a moment and grabbed the front of the man's sweatshirt. Looking over his shoulder he saw Bobby trying to tug a pearl handled automatic from the pocket of his baseball jacket. Larsen didn't hesitate. He flung the unconscious man at Bobby, knocking him the ground again. Bobby kept struggling to get the weapon free from his jacket pocket.

Moving fast and fluidly, Larsen closed the gap to Bobby in an instant and stamped down hard on his wrist and forearm pinning the arm against the hard floor. Bobby squealed in pain, "Ow, you motherfucker, that hurts."

Larsen stopped whistling *Sweet Georgia Brown*. "How do you think Susie felt when you were slapping her around," he said.

Still struggling for breath, Bobby said, "I'm...gonna kill...you, man. One day...I'm fuckin'...gonna...kill you."

"You're a real badass, Bobby-boy," Larsen said as he bent down and ripped the pistol from Bobby's jacket pocket. With his foot still on Bobby's arm, he removed the clip and ejected the round from the chamber, snatching it in midair with a motion almost too quick to see. He dropped the clip in his own jacket pocket along with the extra round, disassembled the gun and threw the pieces toward the back of the room.

He walked over to the semiconscious man that Whelan had knocked down with the bar stool, picked up the two stools and placed them back at the bar. Have to give him credit, Whelan thought with amusement. The man does clean up after himself.

Larsen picked up the pool cue and easily snapped it in two about six inches back from the tip. It left a sharp and jagged end like a spear. He raised it in his right hand and drove it down, piercing the man's chest in the meat between the clavicle and the scapula. The man screamed in pain. "You like using a pool cue," Larsen said. "Try that one."

Still down on the floor, Bobby screamed, "Susie, you fuckin' little slut, I'm gonna make you fuckin' pay for this. You'll see!"

Larsen walked back over to him, grabbing a bar stool on the way. He stood over Bobby and said, "Bobby-boy, you're a danger to society. It's time to reform you." With that, he grabbed the seat of the bar stool with both hands, raised it in front of him, and slammed it down so that one leg crashed into Bobby's mouth. It smashed out several teeth and rolled his tongue back, ripping it partially free and stuffing it down his throat along with the leg of the stool.

Bobby, wide-eyed and panicked, tugged desperately at the object lodged in his throat. Just before he choked to death, Larsen yanked the stool leg free. Bobby rolled over on his stomach and began vomiting blood and pieces of teeth. He was gagging, screeching in agony, and sobbing all at the same time.

"It'd be good if you stay the hell away from Susie," Larsen said calmly. "If not, I'll be back. And, if there *is* a next time, you won't get off this easy."

While Larsen collected the cell phones and motor vehicle keys from Bobby and his comatose friends, Whelan did the same with the county workers, Susie and the biker. They put it all in Whelan's briefcase. He also went behind the bar where there was a landline and yanked it out of the wall. "We're going to wait outside for a while. If any of you sticks his or her head out that door, you're going to lose it," he said. None of them looked like they wanted that to happen.

Susie said, "Is Bobby gonna be alright?"

"He'll likely survive," Larsen said. "But he's not going to have much to say for a while." Susie had come out from behind the bar. Larsen walked over to where she was standing and said, "Just a suggestion, Susie, but you should stop settling for second best when it comes to men."

"I know. I always end up with losers, but I don't know why anyone else would have me. Look at me, I'm a fuckin' mess." She started to cry.

Larsen put an arm around her shoulders. "Listen, Susie, you're a pretty girl when you aren't all battered and bruised by a current boyfriend. Get out of bartending. Go to night school and learn new skills. Get an office job. Join various groups and meet a better class of men; guys who are going someplace in their lives. Guys who know how to treat a lady."

She nodded her head up and down slowly, but didn't' say anything. Larsen and Whelan glanced at each other. They both knew how her story was likely to turn out. They also knew that each individual was responsible for his or her own life. If it didn't turn out well, there was no one else to blame.

The two men left the bar. "Where's your car?" Whelan asked.

"Behind the bonding office, next to Ross's."

Whelan thought for a moment. "Leave it there. Won't take long for the police to be on to us for that little scuffle at Earl's Place. We'll take Ross's Caddy." He smiled and said, "I'm sure he'd want it that way."

Larsen grinned his, good grin.

21 HART SENATE OFFICE BUILDING

Senator Howard Morris was feeling an adrenal rush. In just a few moments, he would call to order the most important press conference of his nascent campaign for the office of President of the United States of America. This was to be the launch pad and he was the rocket. His position on the Senate Select Committee on Intelligence had provided him with the opportunity to chair its Subcommittee on Central Intelligence Agency Activities.

Thanks to Shepard Jenkins he had found Harold Case, and Case had provided him with the material he needed to expose the Agency's illegal covert activities. While he didn't have the type of direct evidence needed for proof of guilt in a court of law, he did have a smoking gun. With a liberal media that distrusted and disliked the Agency, that was all Morris needed to accomplish his goal. There would be outrage on the left. As their hero who exposed these crimes, he would be in a prime position to ride that surge of outrage to the party's nomination.

He leaned over the balcony rail on the seventh floor, where his office was located, and watched people scurrying through the atrium area. He recognized some of them as members of the print and broadcast media. They were all gathering for his big announcement. He was elated, but not nervous, thinking about how important a player he was becoming on the national scene. What would his late father, the immigrant tailor, have thought of that?

He held his hands out in front of him and admired his well-manicured nails and deep artificial tan. He was wearing his newest and most expensive suit, a two button navy blue Armani in wool crepe that he had purchased at the Neiman-Marcus store on Mazza Gallery. His personal stylist had made a visit to Morris's office and had trimmed and coiffed his hair. What an incredible specimen I am, he thought. Ladies, form a line. Lost in his reverie, he jumped slightly as Shepard Jenkins tapped him on one shoulder.

JOHN WAYNE FALBEY

"'Bout time we headed down to the conference room, don't you think, Senator?" Jenkins said. He was dressed in a dark blue, well-tailored Brooks Brothers suit, and smiling broadly. This was to be a big day for him also, the day his dog got into the hunt.

The Hart Senate Office Building has two sets of elevators referred to as the North elevators and the South elevators. The two men walked toward the North elevator area with its six identical elevators, three elevators on the west wall of the elevator area and three on the east wall. They entered one of the elevators and Jenkins punched the button for the second floor.

Although there is a large meeting room, 902, on the ninth floor of the building that is used for conference purposes, Morris purposely chose to hold the event in the large central hearing facility on the second floor of the Hart Building. It was designed for high-interest events that attracted crowds that couldn't be accommodated in other facilities in the building. The facility offered more seating, better acoustics, and movable side panes where television cameras could operate without distracting the participants or audience members.

Morris entered the central hearing facility through a side door and strolled confidently to the dais where other members of the subcommittee were sitting. He nodded at them and paused for a moment to gaze at the Senate seal affixed to a white and gray marble wall. It contrasted nicely with the wood-paneled sidewalls. There were several members of the press corps sitting in the audience whom he knew. He waved to each of them individually and called out their names as he did so. A young female member of the press was sitting near the back because of her lack of seniority. Morris not only waved at her, but also blew her a kiss.

Standing to the side of the dais, Shepard Jenkins watched as Morris preened and pranced for what he believed to be his adoring audience. Jenkins had a lot of his career ambitions invested in this man and needed him to succeed in his political quest for the White House. To be sure, there had been other successful politicians like Jack Kennedy who couldn't leave the ladies alone. But they at least had been discrete in these activities. Morris made little effort to conceal his extramarital affairs. And these were different times. In the transparent 24/7 world of the Internet, it was more difficult than ever to cover one's tracks even if you exercised a great deal of discretion. Jenkins had spoken to Morris about these concerns and the conversation hadn't gone well.

After awhile, the media crew supervisor looked at Morris and gave a thumbs up signal. Everything was in place and working properly. Time to begin the show. Morris tugged on the hem of his jacket, straightened his silk tie and strode purposefully to the podium. The room became still as everyone's attention focused on him.

Morris cleared his throat and said, "My dear friends of the print and

90

broadcast media, I deeply appreciate your presence here today. I guarantee you will find what I am about to disclose to you to be of great significance." He paused for effect and looked around the room. "I have worked diligently to uncover this information." There were sounds of papers being shuffled, throats being cleared, and people moving about in their seats behind him. He glanced at the other members of the subcommittee and quickly said, "Of course, I have been ably assisted in these efforts by my distinguished colleagues on this Select Subcommittee who are seated at the dais behind me." Morris emphasized the word "Select".

He turned back to the audience. "What I am about to disclose to you is of critical importance, and I shall be brief. As you know, this Select Subcommittee is charged with the responsibility of monitoring the covert activities of this country's Central Intelligence Agency. Throughout the past several decades, the CIA has, on occasion, been guilty of heinous criminal acts all in the name of national security. As a result, Congress has found it necessary from time to time to enact laws designed to control this sort of behavior."

Morris again paused and lowered his head, wagging it slowly back and forth, as if in disappointment and sorrow. He raised it slowly and said, "Today, ladies and gentlemen, it is my sad duty to report to you that I...we" he corrected himself, "have uncovered indisputable evidence of the CIA's treachery and blatantly criminal behavior."

Morris felt powerful, in command. He was on a roll. He couldn't help himself and began to depart from anything that could be supported by facts. "Thanks to this Select Subcommittee's hard work and exhaustive investigatory skills, we have discovered the existence of an illegal covert operation set up years ago by the CIA. Its purpose was to create and train a special group of super human beings to assassinate world leaders, disrupt foreign governments – allies and those not particularly friendly to this country alike – and perform other hideous acts of warmongering. I ask you, is it any wonder that the United States has so few friends on this planet?"

He paused to savor the reaction of the audience, as its members turned to one another and exchanged whispers. "While we are not at liberty at this time to reveal documentation on this matter, we are prepared, within certain constraints, to answer a few questions at this time. More information will be revealed in the next few days."

Several hands shot up. "Yes, Marc," he said and pointed at a man from ABC News who had long been instrumental to the success of Morris's career.

"Senator, how long has this operation been going on?"

"Yes, we have evidence that it began prior to the First Gulf War."

"And can you tell us the names of the persons at the CIA who are responsible for the operation?" Marc said.

Morris shook his head. "Not at this time, Marc, but all that will be disclosed in due time." He pointed to the young woman sitting at the rear of the audience whose hand had not been raised and with a big smile said, "Yes, Janie, I believe you had a question."

She reddened visibly and made a nervous gesture with her hands.

"I believe you were going to inquire whether there was a name for this unit, were you not?" She nodded her head vigorously. "It appears that the unit was known as the Sleeping Dogs, although I'm not exactly sure why."

A man from the New York Times, sitting in the front row, said, "What did you mean when you called them 'super human beings'?"

Morris leaned forward across the podium, and with a lowered voice that he hoped sounded like he was revealing confidential information for the benefit of his audience, said, "It appears they may have been genetically engineered to be superior to us real people." He straightened up and returned to his usual speaking tone. "I'm sorry, but I am not at liberty to discuss that issue further at this time."

The man from the Times persisted. "Have those individuals been brought to justice, Senator?"

"Yes, divine justice. They all were killed in a plane crash several years ago while trying to elude capture."

"Can you tell us what their purpose was, Senator?" It was Marc again.

"Yes, from what we've uncovered so far, they were the most clandestine unit in the government; part military, part intelligence. Highly trained in the use of deadly force, and completely without morals or conscience, they were turned loose upon any person or government that had the misfortune to be deemed a threat to America's goal of world domination."

He pointed to a woman from another media outlet.

"Senator," the woman began, "has there been any reaction from the CIA?"

"Absolutely, Marge, and it has been frightening and barbarous. It appears they have murdered in cold blood a former employee of the CIA who, working for this Select Subcommittee, was instrumental in assisting us in locating the evidence of these activities." There was an audible and collective gasp from the audience and everyone's hand shot into the air accompanied by yells of "Senator, Senator" in an effort to get Morris's attention.

"My friends," he said, "I realize there are many questions, and we don't have the answers to all of them yet. But we will. And as we learn them, we will share them with you. You have my word on that."

He beamed at the audience, pausing in particular to smile at the young woman seated near the rear of the group. "In closing this session, I want to share this comment with you. Our great nation has been disgraced once again by its trusted servants. We have stooped to a new low in the eyes of the rest of the world. We have allowed a cancerous organization to be fostered within our own government. This no doubt is the result of poor leadership in the Executive branch of government."

Morris paused for effect then pounded his right fist onto the podium. "But I pledge to you today that I will not rest until this wrong has been righted. I will ferret out the guilty parties and see that they are punished to the full extent of the law. I will see that the Central Intelligence Agency and all similar agencies are brought into full compliance with our laws and remain there. I will provide the missing leadership that has allowed us to be dragged down this ruinous and disgraceful path. You have my word on it."

After a brief pause, Morris said, "Thank so very much ladies and gentlemen for your kind attention and for sharing your valuable time with us." He motioned toward the other Subcommittee members sitting behind him. He walked over to them to thank them and to measure their response to his presentation, but the two members of the minority party already were walking toward the side door behind the podium. Morris refused to see that as a reflection on him, preferring to chalk it up to partisan politics. He shook hands with the remaining members and thanked them for their participation, although he didn't believe they lent anything of value to his efforts.

Morris left the dais and exited through the side door where Shepard Jenkins intercepted him. With a look of smug satisfaction, Morris rubbed his hands together and said, "Well, Shep, what did you think?"

"I believe we achieved exactly what we wanted to at this point, Senator. Or should I get used to calling you Mr. President?" Jenkins said with a smile.

"It does have a lovely ring to it, doesn't it?" Morris slapped the other man on the arm and began to walk down the hallway in the opposite direction from the elevators that would take him back to the floor his office was located.

"Where are you going? I thought we were going back to your office to discuss our strategy for moving forward on this CIA issue."

"Not now, Shep," Morris said over his shoulder as he walked away. "I have a meeting with little Janie Gottlieb. I told her I had some exclusive information for her." She was the young woman who had been sitting near the rear of the audience in the press conference.

"Shit," Jenkins said under his breath and shook his head in disgust. "Be discrete, Howard, for God's sake be discrete." It's no wonder, he thought, that many Beltway insiders had nicknamed the man "Senator More-Ass". Or that members of the opposition party referred to him as "Senator Morass".

22 POTOMAC, MARYLAND

Dimitri Nikitin shifted uneasily in the large overstuffed chair. Although it was covered in the finest top grain leather and surrounded his tired body like a cloud, the direction of the conversation was making him very uncomfortable. He tried to distract himself by gazing around Chaim Laski's den. It was as opulent as the rest of the sprawling mansion in Potomac, Maryland. From the towering vaulted ceiling to the smallest accessories, the entire home was a shrine to the excesses of Western decadence and capitalism. God, how I envy Laski's lifestyle, Nikitin thought, comfortable in the knowledge that his Russian bosses had not yet developed a means for reading his mind.

He lit another cigarette from the embers of the last, took a long, deep drag and exhaled a cloud of smoke toward the ceiling high above. The three men had been in this meeting for more than two hours and Nikitin was getting bored and restless. He held the important office of Counselor and reported directly to the Minister-Counselor for Trade at the Russian Embassy in Washington. He was only two steps removed from the Ambassador himself. But at this meeting, he was simply window dressing, a diversion for the prying eyes, and more, of the American intelligence community. The real muscle here, in addition to Laski, was Kirill Federov, a mere attaché at the Embassy and ostensibly Nikitin's underling.

It galled Nikitin to be ordered around by Federov, but he knew that Federov reported directly to the Chief Deputy Director of the Sluzhba Vneshney Razvedki or SVR, Russia's primary external intelligence agency. That person in turn reported directly to the SVR Director, who reported directly to the president of the Russian Federation.

The conversation, conducted in Russian, was becoming somewhat heated between the other two men. Federov was leaning forward in his chair toward Laski. He was angry and his voice had become louder. He pounded on the arm of the chair to emphasize his point. "Comrade Laski, need I remind you that your *success*", he said the word as if it had a bad taste, "is due to the efforts, planning and expenditures of the Sluzhba Vneshney Razvedki, not your self-indulged belief in your own prescience and acumen. Without us, you would still be pimping whores in Gdansk!"

Laski's face was deep red, indicating his own level of anger. Somehow, he managed a conciliatory smile and turned his hands palms-outward in an effort to disarm the angry Russian. "My dear Colonel Federov, Kirill, I am well aware of the assistance so generously provided to me by the SVR."

"Assistance!" Federov spat the word out. "To the world you are a billionaire wizard of international finance and investment. In reality, we provided you with the funds for your activities. We made and destroyed markets internationally to provide you with the appearance of having earned all that nice clean money. Do you forget so easily?"

"No, Kirill, I may be getting older, but I am not yet senile."

"Are you not also aware that it was through our international network and many more billions of dollars that we created and advanced global unrest? Over the years, we have fostered and linked a vast array of organizations abroad and here in America for the purpose of destroying this country from within and without. It is we who have organized and funded the jihadist movement globally. And it is we who control it."

"Have you ever thought you could be playing with fire, Colonel?"

The Russian scoffed. "What? With these Muslims? Don't be ridiculous. They are imbeciles. They believe they are running the show. They are fools and are under our control. And, when the appropriate time comes, we will easily dispose of them."

With a sly smile, Laski said, "And do you also control the Chechens who slaughtered the students in one of your schools and many others in the opera house?"

The comment so enraged Federov that he was speechless for several long moments. Finally, between clenched teeth he said, "That is a different matter. It is personal between them and us. You are not capable of understanding. He paused for a moment before continuing. "What you must understand is that we are very close, Comrade Laski, very close to succeeding here in America."

"Yes, of course," Laski said. "I am well aware of that. And have I not wisely kept up appearances with my business activities while also funneling moneys to the appropriate unions, political causes, and various dissident groups both here and abroad? Have I not earned my reputation as the chief financier of the far left political movement in America?"

"And you have spared no expense indulging your every fantasy. Private jets, a fleet of the world's most expensive automobiles, homes in a dozen locations."

Laski interrupted him. "No! Only seven. And as a recognized billionaire investor am I not to live up to that reputation?"

Federov shook his head. "Once a pimp always a pimp. In Poland you ran sexual whores. Here you run political ones. But even pimps get lucky. This new scandal involving the CIA is good political theater for us. It brings further disgrace on America, weakens its relationships with its allies and generates even greater hatred for it across the globe. Nurture it, Comrade Laski. Use it to help win the nomination for that preening, weak-kneed puppet of yours, Howard Morris."

"I shall, Kirill. You need have no concerns over this matter." With that, the meeting ended.

23 TAMPA, FLORIDA

Sven Larsen, who had been living in Tampa for the past several years, was driving the bail bondsman's older model Cadillac with Whelan riding shotgun. They had bound and gagged Ross, the bondsman, and stuffed him in a closet in his office. He was tied so restrictively that any movement on his part was impossible.

Larsen was driving north on Orient Road toward Interstate 4. "What's the plan?" he said.

"The people back at Earl's Place will be singing like birds any minute now. If they didn't know who you were, the cops will figure it out pretty quickly. I'm sure they know you from your bail bonding activities."

"True," Larsen said.

"Plus in a rare moment of sentimentality, you opted not to kill Ross. Once the cops have you in mind, they'll go to the bond office and find Ross. Then they'll be looking for this car."

"So what's our next move?"

"We need to get you out of town in a hurry."

"What about Sharon and the boys?"

"They go too. It's been a long time, but Levell told us always to have a safe haven available in case something like this should occur. I assume you have one."

"Sure," Larsen said. "One of my uncle's was a bachelor. Had a cabin in the Green Swamp. It's the part that isn't in the state's wildlife management area. I was his favorite nephew. When he died, he left it to me. That was a long time ago; pretty much everyone has forgotten about it."

"You check on it lately?"

"Every six months or so. It'll do for now."

"How fast can you get Sharon and the kids in gear?"

"Are you kidding? We're talking about Sharon, you know. When has she ever done anything in a hurry?"

"Sharon and the boys need to leave now. Call them."

Whelan pulled the special cell phone Levell had provided from an inside pocket of his suit coat and handed it to then other man.

Larsen looked at him and said, "I got my own phone."

"Yours is easily traceable. This one isn't."

The Man With No Neck took the phone and dialed a number. After a moment or two he said, "Hey. Remember the line of work I was in when we met and got married? And remember how that ended, but we knew that someday it might come back to be a problem for us?" He paused then said, "Today's the day. You and the boys need to get the hell out of the house right now. Do not stop to pack anything or waste a minute of time."

He paused as if listening to his wife's response. His jaw tightened visibly and his eyes narrowed in anger. "Goddammit, Sharon, don't argue with me on this! Do you remember why we've been living under assumed identities for damn near twenty years? Once the government knows I'm alive, they'll come after me to complete the death warrant, and they'll start with you and the boys. Now get your asses out of there!"

Larsen turned and looked at Whelan. "She wants to know where she should go."

"Tampa International, long-term parking, southwest quadrant, level three near the elevators."

Larsen relayed the information to his wife, then terminated the call. "Women," he said, as he handed the phone back to Whelan

Whelan studied an image he had punched up on Google Maps for a few moments, then dialed up the number given him by Major Tom Pederson. After three rings, Pederson answered. "Major, it's your friend from the airport," Whelan said.

"Yes, sir. How can I help you?"

"I need you to drive a friend of our mutual friend and his family somewhere. Do you have a personal vehicle that can be used?"

"Yes, sir. We have the proverbial soccer van you rode in from the airport. That should work."

"Good. Are you able to drive them…take about two hours round trip?"

Pederson said, "Yes, sir. I'm not on duty today. Where do you want me to meet you and when?"

Whelan gave him the same directions they had given Sharon Larsen, then punched the disconnect key.

Larsen already had turned west on Interstate 275 heading toward the airport. "How long do we stay holed up in the swamp?"

"I'll let Levell know your situation. He'll see that the Team provides you with the necessary identities, location, and funds. He'll let you know when and where the Dogs will reunite. In the meantime, here's some cash to tide you over." Whelan handed Larsen a thousand dollars from the money he had received from Rhee. Then he opened his briefcase and took out the revolver he had acquired at the bail bond office. He slipped it under the front seat. "It's Ross's weapon. Just in case you need it."

"What about you? What's your agenda?"

"After my adventures here, I should cover my tracks. I'll catch a direct nonstop flight to Charlotte on US Airways. The Team will have a car waiting for me with more cash. I'll drive down to Atlanta and catch a plane from there."

"What's your destination?"

Whelan smiled. "Hawaii," he said.

"Hawaii? Damn. You do have the luck of the Irish. Which one of us is in Hawaii?"

"Stensen."

"Stensen? I'm surprised he's still alive. You suppose he's still crazy?"

"Always was, always will be."

Larsen shook his head. It seemed to swivel on the neckless shoulders. "Watch yourself around him," he said.

24 IN FLIGHT

Mitch Christie had worked late at the Bureau's Atlanta field office then spent a restless night at the Hyatt Place Atlanta Airport South. Although the room had been comfortable enough, Christie couldn't get his mind off the case he was working. There were so many pieces, but what did they mean? How many pieces were still missing? He sensed that timing was essential, but things just weren't moving fast enough to suit him.

He was groggy the next morning when he checked out of the hotel and cabbed to the terminal. The two cups of coffee he drank while waiting to board his 8:20 a.m. flight to San Francisco only soured his stomach. That started him on his daily ritual with Mylanta. It was a direct, nonstop flight and he hoped to get some sleep on the five and one half hour flight. He would need to be sharp for his interview with the geneticist, William Nishioki. He suspected that regardless the quality and amount of sleep he might get on the plane, he would have a difficult time understanding the science of genetics under any circumstances.

Christie was flying Business Class and was among the first to board the big Boeing 767. He stuffed his briefcase in the overhead bin and settled into his window seat, 3G, hoping the aisle seat next to him would not be occupied. He was not in a mood to engage in conversation. He soon was disappointed. A tall, good-looking man with an athletic build and an air of quiet confidence about him slipped his carryon suitcase into the overhead bin above Christie. He slid into the aisle seat in what seemed to Christie to be a single fluid motion, and stowed a small briefcase under the seat in front of him.

Christie, his cop instincts always in play, sized up his traveling companion. He judged the man to be a few years younger than himself with smooth, even features, light brown hair that was well groomed, neither long nor short and a trimmed moustache. His blue eyes were the color of Alpine glacial ice, striking but cold. There was a physical presence, a sense of power about the man that Christie couldn't identify. He looked like he could have been a professional athlete or Hollywood action hero. Unhappy with his own physical appearance due to the rigors of his job – insufficient sleep, eating on the run, and little time for physical exercise, Christie felt some pangs of envy. The man was well dressed, and Christie appreciated that. He, too, was wearing a dark suit, the Bureau's standard dress code. It seemed to him that airline passengers today, even in First and Business Classes, competed to see who could dress most like a slob.

* * * * *

Whelan had caught a flight directly from Tampa to Charlotte, North Carolina. Before leaving Tampa, he had spoken by phone with Levell following the instructions given him by Rhee, and brought him up to date on Larsen's situation. In turn, Levell had arranged to have a car available for Whelan at the airport in Charlotte along with additional cash. He had driven the two hundred and fifty miles from Charlotte to the airport in Atlanta and spent the night at the Atlanta Airport Marriott Gateway.

The next morning, Whelan wiped down the hotel room, checked out and cabbed to the terminal to catch his flight to San Francisco, the first leg of the journey to Hawaii. He found a men's clothing store and acquired a few pairs of underwear and socks, a pale blue dress shirt, a blue and gold Jerry Garcia tie, a pair of jeans, and two Tommy Bahama polo shirts. At a runner's shop a few doors down, he bought a comfortable pair of Brooks running shoes. He bought a small carryon suitcase at a luggage shop and packed it with his purchases. After a single cup of coffee with cream and a blueberry scone, he bought a Wall Street Journal and walked to his boarding gate, arriving as the First and Business Class passengers were boarding.

As he moved through the mob of fellow travelers crowded around the entryway, he calmly looked around, taking in the scene with the experienced eyes of a well-trained operative, as well as those of a man who had lived the past twenty years looking over his shoulder for possible pursuers. As he did, he pondered a couple of questions. First, he wondered why passengers whose tickets clearly had them boarding in later stages, insisted on crowding tightly around the boarding passage and all but blocking the way for those who had earlier boarding privileges. He also wondered what had happened to Americans in the past two decades that caused them to dress so shabbily for air travel.

Boarding the plane, he assisted an older woman in stowing her luggage in the overhead bin. It gave him a chance to check out the plane and passengers already seated in First Class. It seemed a fairly nondescript group, but there was something about the tall, lean man sitting in the seat next to 3F, the one assigned to Whelan. It was as if he wore a sign proclaiming him to be a government employee. From his rumpled dark blue suit with mismatched green tie and brown shoes to his slumped posture, he looked the part of a career bureaucrat. There also was something about his expression, a sort of glum look as if he didn't feel well. Was it his stomach? Although Whelan thought him to be about his same age, maybe a few years older, the man's once dark hair was graying and thinning, and his face was lined more than it should have been at that stage of life.

Whelan sat down and nodded at the other man who he noticed had been studying him as well. "Morning," Whelan said.

"Morning," the other man said, but it came out as more of a grunt than a statement.

A flight attendant appeared next to them. He was a chubby young man with decidedly feminine traits. Placing a hand on Whelan's shoulder he leaned in and said "Oooh, don't you two gentlemen look handsome in your suits. I so wish more people saw fit to dress up for their air travel." He smiled at Whelan who didn't return the gesture. "May I get you gentlemen something to drink before we depart?"

Whelan nodded at the other man, indicating he should go first.

"Some club soda would be fine," he said. "No ice."

"Very good," the attendant said and turned to Whelan. "What may I get for you?" He gushed when he said it and squeezed Whelan's shoulder.

Whelan thought about snapping the offending arm off at the elbow. He never had liked being touched by anyone who didn't have his express invitation to do so. That was a very short list populated solely by the members of his immediate family. "Water," he said.

"Seems a little light in his loafers, doesn't he," said the man next to him.

"At least he's cheerful for this hour of the morning."

The other man stuck his hand out. "I'm Mitch Christie," he said.

"Nice to meet you, Mitch." Whelan shook his hand and said, "Mike Murkowski."

"You don't look like a particularly talkative kind of guy, Mike, but I thought I'd tell you that I have some sleeping to catch up on and plan to do that on the flight. Hope you're not offended."

"Nope. I plan to bury myself in the Journal." He held up the folded newspaper.

"Good reading," Christie said. Passengers still were boarding, so he hadn't yet turned off his cell phone. He felt it vibrate and pulled it out of the inside pocket of his suit coat. He looked at the number of the incoming call, then pressed the receive button. "Yeah, this is Christie. Shoot."

Whelan pulled the first section of the Wall Street Journal away from the remaining three and placed them in the seat pocket in front of him. He opened the first section and began to read the op-eds while eavesdropping on

Christie's phone conversation. There was something about the man that said, "cop".

Christie's call was from John Deutch in the Bureau's Forensic Analysis Branch of the FBI Crime Laboratory at the Quantico Marine Corps Base in Virginia.

"I have some good news for you, Special Agent Christie," Deutch said. There was a certain eager-to-please quality to his tone.

"It's about time, John. I need some good news for a change."

"Well," Deutch said, "it turns out that there was some information in the Agency's files on that special unit, what was it called?"

"The Sleeping Dogs," Christie said.

It was all Whelan could do to stifle a reaction.

"Yeah, that's it. The Sleeping Dogs," Deutch said. He paused, as if expecting a few kind words for his news.

"Dammit, Deutch, get to the point. Did you get any matches?"

"Um, yes sir, right away sir." There was a gulping sound from Deutch's end of the line, as if he had swallowed hard. "There was a match, ...I mean is a match. One of the members of the unit...a Brendan Whelan, sir."

Christie suddenly leaned forward in his seat. "Are you certain about that, Deutch? He's supposed to have died in a plane crash with the other members of his unit nearly twenty years ago. If he's still alive, maybe more of them are, too. Maybe the damn crash was staged."

Suddenly, the ambient temperature wasn't as cool and comfortable as Whelan would have liked it to be. He reached up and opened the air conditioning valve above his seat. While he couldn't hear Deutch's end of the conversation, he had heard enough from Christie to know what was happening. So much for the theory that there are no such things as coincidences, he thought. *Of all the seats on all the planes going to San Francisco today, I end up sitting next to the Fed who's heading up the investigation involving Harold Case.*

"Alright, good work, John," Christie said into the phone. "What other information do we have on this Whelan guy? Photos? Next of kin? Background materials?"

"I was told that there are photos of all of the men in the unit in the Agency's files and some background info, but I've been focusing on the DNA end of it."

"Christie was silent for a moment, then said, "Okay, see if you can switch me over to Antonelli at HQ."

After a few moments, he heard Antonelli's gruff, Brooklyn-accented voice on the other end. "Yeah, Mitch, what's up?"

"You know we got a match on the DNA?"

"Yeah, I heard. A guy named Whelan."

"Right. What else do we have on him?"

"Not much. A twenty-year-old photo of a young guy in combat gear, face covered in camo paint. Some bio info. Born in Ireland, raised in the U.S., parents are dead. Not much to go on. A lot of the files with personal information on these guys appear to have been destroyed over the years."

Look, Lou, get me a copy of the photo. I'm on my way to San Francisco. Wire the photo to the field office there and have someone bring it to me at the airport when I get in around ten-thirty their time."

"It's on its way," Antonelli said.

Christie hung up just as the flight attendant returned with the beverages. He unscrewed the cap from the small bottle of club soda and took a swig. He tried to politely disguise the resulting belch. "You ever have stomach problems, Mike?" he said to Whelan.

"I might be about to get some," Whelan said.

25 SAN FRANCISCO

Mitch Christie slept fitfully on the flight to San Francisco, waking frequently and struggling to find a comfortable position. By the time the plane landed, his suit, rumpled when he got on the plane, looked as if he had fought trench warfare in it.

Seated next to him, Whelan had coolly reviewed his situation. He was sitting next to the FBI agent who now knew he was alive, and that he had killed Case and his bodyguards. Worse, he soon would have a photograph of Whelan from the CIA's files. An old photograph to be sure, but it added to the risk factors. He could kill Christie and prop him up in his seat to look as if he were in a deep sleep. But the deed likely would be discovered before he could safely exit the airport. He could tail Christie in the airport and hope to find an opportunity to terminate him, but he knew the man was to be met at the arrival gate by personnel from the Bureau's San Francisco field office. That left little likelihood that such an opportunity would arise. Escaping after killing two or three agents in a crowded airport terminal didn't seem feasible.

Whelan realized this unscheduled turn of events required a change of plans. He was to have caught an afternoon flight from San Francisco to Honolulu. The ticket would be waiting for him at the Delta Airlines counter. Instead, he would have to call Levell and arrange alternate travel plans. Levell also would have to arrange to change the Delta flight to another destination and get someone to fly using the Murkowski name. It had to appear as if Murkowski actually had flown to the new destination.

As the plane taxied toward the arrival gate, Christie sat up from his slumped position and attempted to straighten his jacket. He fished his cell phone from his pocket, checked the directory for the number of the Bureau's San Francisco field office, and punched it. When the receptionist answered, he identified himself, asked for the special agent in charge and was transferred to his phone. "Newell?" he said. "This is Mitch Christie. Has Lou Antonelli from headquarters been in communication with you?"

"Yes. We got the photo. I sent an agent, Dave O'Connor, to meet you at your arrival gate. You need a car or anything from us?"

"No thanks. I have a rental lined up. Just need that photo. I'll be looking for someone at the arrival gate." He disconnected, checked his email for anything that might be deemed urgent, decided there wasn't any and put the phone away.

When the plane docked at the arrival gate, both men stood in the aisle and retrieved their respective bags. "It's been nice traveling with you, Mike," Christie said. "I hope my tossing and turning didn't disturb you."

"Not at all, Mitch. It reminded me how hard it is to get any decent sleep these days."

The First and Business Class passengers deplaned first. The two men walked up the gangway in silence. At the top, Christie spotted a man holding a small sign that said "Mr. Christie" and went over to him.

Whelan kept walking, even picking up the pace briskly. He wanted to call Levell, but knew he needed to get clear of the terminal without delay. He took the escalator to the ground transportation level, walked past the baggage claim areas and exited the building. He was in luck. There was a very short line at the cabstand. In moments he was on his way to the Red Roof Inn south of the airport on Anza and Airport Boulevards.

He had the driver let him off in front of the hotel. He entered the lobby and was relieved to see that the desk clerk was preoccupied with checking a guest into the hotel. Striding confidently and purposefully as if headed to a specific room or location, he went across the lobby and exited the building on the other side. He went across Anza Boulevard and entered the Crown Plaza. Once inside, he located a pay phone and, using the thin leather gloves, picked up the receiver and called the number he had memorized. He let it ring three times and hung up. Less than a minute later his Smartphone rang. It was Levell.

"Are you on your way to Hawaii?" Levell said.

"Yes, but we're going to need a change of plans."

"What happened?" Levell sounded genuinely concerned.

"My seat mate on the flight this morning appears to be the FBI agent in charge of the Case matter."

"What! You've got to be kidding."

"No joke, sir. I overheard his phone conversations. The Bureau knows about the Dogs, and worse yet, knows I wasn't killed in the plane crash."

"Shit! We expected the Bureau would get its hands on the Agency's records as a part of the investigation into the circumstances of Case's death. But how the hell did they get on to you?"

"Did the Agency keep records of our DNA?"

"The original records kept track of everything; preferred hair color in your women friends, favorite flavor of chewing gum, how many pieces of toilet paper you used to wipe your asses. Everything. Hell yes, DNA too."

"Then I'm guessing that nick on my finger must have deposited a bit of blood at the scene of Case's death, maybe on one of his goons. That and some good guess work ID'ed me."

Levell was silent for a few moments, then said, "Where are you now?"

"Are you sure no one can tap or trace this call?"

"Yes. It's scrambled better than a well-cooked egg and encrypted with algorithms that all the world's supercomputers together couldn't crack if they had eternity to do so. And we're using chained proxy servers located in countries unfriendly to America. The Agency's and NSA's top tech people are with us. They make sure we stay ahead of the curve".

"Good," Whelan said. "I'm in the lobby of the Crown Plaza Hotel near the San Francisco Airport."

"Sit tight. I'll have someone pick you up in fifteen minutes or less. He'll be holding a white handkerchief as if he's got a runny nose or something. Get in the car. He'll take you to a safe house. We'll put together a new plan in the interim," Levell said.

"Better get the original Delta flight changed to a new destination. And have someone who resembles me use it." Whelan said and hung up.

Several minutes later a late model navy blue Ford Focus pulled up on the far side of the wide porte-cochére that sheltered the entrance to the hotel. The driver appeared to be blowing his nose into a white handkerchief. Whelan walked quickly to the car, tossed his briefcase and carryon bag onto the backseat and slid in next to the driver.

Forty-five minutes later they were in a private home in San Jose near the University. A few hours later Whelan had wavy reddish-blonde hair and full beard, thicker eyebrows, a larger nose, and brown eyes thanks to the makeup artistry of one of Levell's people. He also appeared to have gained thirty pounds thanks to padding and clothes. The Whelan who left the place looked nothing like the one who had entered. He was handed a used and somewhat battered suitcase filled with additional clothing and toiletries. He was now David C. Taggard, an attorney from Kansas City.

When he left, he slid into the passenger seat of a new GMC Acadia and passed the next six hours being driven down the 5 to LAX. He spent some of the time familiarizing himself with Kansas City on his Smartphone using Google and Wikipedia. He also studied Google aerial photographs of the Hawaiian island of Maui then slept most of the rest of the way. At LAX he caught a late afternoon Alaska Airlines flight and arrived in Kahului on Maui a little less than six hours later.

* * * * *

When Christie approached the FBI agent sent to meet him at the San Francisco Airport, he nodded perfunctorily and said, "Are you Agent O'Connor?"

"Yes, Sir."

"Do you have the photograph?"

"Yes, Sir," the man said and handed Christie an eight-by-ten manila envelop.

Christie took it and said, "Walk with me. I've got to make a stop."

"Yes, Sir. The men's room is right across the aisle." The agent pointed at it.

"Not that kind of stop." As he walked, Christie slipped a thumb under the flap of the envelope and ripped it open. Inside was a grainy photograph of a muscular young man, maybe twenty years old. He appeared to be standing in a jungle area, as there were vine covered trees and a lush assortment of tropical plants in the background. The man was wearing full combat gear and his face was covered with camo paint.

"Do you recognize the man, sir?"

"Besides the fact that it's an old and not very well preserved photo, the gear, helmet and camo paint pretty well disguise whoever it is." Christie looked up and saw that they were approaching a sundries shop along the concourse. He motioned to the other man to wait for him outside, and went into the shop. He found the largest bottle of Mylanta they had and bought two of them, which he slipped into his briefcase.

When he left the shop, the other agent said, "Where to now, sir?"

"I'm going to pick up a rental car and drive down the coast. I'm meeting with someone who had an involvement in this matter many years ago."

"Do you want me to drive you to the rental car garage? It's pretty far from here."

"No, I've been here before. I'll take the tram. Thanks anyway." He started toward the escalator that led to the tram level, then stopped and turned around. "On second thought, O'Connor, there is something you can do for me."

"Yes, sir."

"Have one of our sketch artists do an update from the photo…what this guy might look like today."

"Yes, sir. I'll get right on it."

"Good. I can't put my finger on it yet, but there's something vaguely familiar about this guy.

26 SANTA CRUZ, CALIFORNIA

Christie picked up a silver colored Hyundai Accent at the airport rental car garage in San Francisco. He drove south on the 101 then skirted San Jose on the 85. Eventually he turned onto California State Highway 17 and wound along spectacular views through the coastal mountains. He loved the rugged, almost pristine, countryside of this area of California. He gazed wistfully at it and thought about relocating here with his family when he retired from the Bureau. For a change, his stomach seemed settled by the vista instead of the ubiquitous antacid. Eventually he came to the town of Santa Cruz. The drive took him an hour and a half. He spent another twenty minutes locating William Nishioki's home. It was a modest bungalow on a shady street in a new retirement community south of town, just off Cabrillo Highway.

He parked at the curb in the shade of a large eucalyptus tree. He was about thirty minutes early for his previously schedule meeting. As he rang the doorbell, he hoped Nishioki would accommodate him. The sooner they started, the sooner Christie would be able to drive back to the airport at San Francisco and find a hotel, hopefully for a long restful sleep. He had a scheduled six a.m. departure the following morning for Reagan National Airport in Washington.

The door was answered by a man of medium build with thick hair that was cut somewhat short. While gray on the sides, it was still dark above. He was dressed in a lightweight black *gi*, the uniform of martial artists. It was cinched loosely low on his waist by a tattered black sash, or *obi*. Christie noted the man's smooth, almost wrinkle free, skin. This surprised him, as he knew Nishioki was in his early seventies. His features clearly were Japanese, and Christie knew he had been interned with other Nisei as a child.

"Dr. Nishioki?"

"Yes. You must be Mr. Christie." Nishioki smiled and extended his hand. "You are early."

Christie noted the firmness of the man's grip. "Yes," he said. "I apologize. I made better time than expected. I hope I'm not inconveniencing you."

"Not at all, but would you mind showing me your official identification?" It was said with a disarming smile.

Nishioki studied it closely and nodded in satisfaction. He handed it back to Christie and stepped aside, motioning for him to enter. As the Bureau agent did, he saw that the room was airy and bright with hardwood flooring, expensive-looking rugs, and furnishings that appeared quite comfortable. He looked around. "Do you live alone, Doctor?"

Nishioki hesitated then said, "Yes, why do you ask?"

"The nature of our conversation is extremely confidential. I'm sure you understand."

The other man nodded. He pointed to an urn on a mantelpiece and said. "My wife is very good at keeping secrets."

"Your wife?" Christie said as he realized that the urn contained Mrs. Nishioki's ashes.

"Yes. When it is my time, our ashes are to be spread as one over the sea." There was no hint of sadness in the statement, just calm conviction.

Struggling to cover his embarrassment, Christie said, "Well, you don't look like you're going anytime soon. You look amazingly fit, Doctor."

"I have studied and practiced *aikido* since childhood. I was practicing *kata* when you rang the bell."

"You must hold a very high rank." Christie looked at the ragged *obi* circling the older man's waist. Clearly he had held black belt rank for a very long time.

"Rank has no meaning to the true practitioner," Nishioki said. "It is the knowledge and how one applies it." He motioned to a chair and said, "Please sit down, Mr. Christie. I was just about to have some tea. Will you join me?"

"That would be nice," Christie said. He wasn't particularly fond of hot tea, but doubted it would bother his stomach as much as the coffee in the airport had.

While Nishioki went to the small kitchen to get the tea, Christie dug out his cell phone and called his office. When Charlotte answered, he said, "Hey, it's Mitch. Do you know the status of the sketch I asked for this morning?"

"I understand the artist is working on it now. Do you want me to call you as soon as we have something?"

"Yeah, please." He disconnected as Nishioki returned with a small tray containing a teapot and two cups. He placed it on a small table between two comfortable stuffed chairs and poured the tea, handing the first cup to Christie.

After settling into his chair, the scientist said, "I believe you have some questions for me about a project I worked on many years ago. Is that so, Mr. Christie?"

"Yes it is, Doctor."

"Please," Nishioki interrupted him, "call me Bill."

"Alright, if you'll call me Mitch."

"Agreed," Nishioki said with a nod. "You may begin, Mitch."

Christie took a moment to gather his thoughts. He could feel the fatigue, mental and physical, from the schedule of the past few days. "This concerns a project you worked on with Dr. Horowitz for the Central Intelligence Agency."

"Yes?" There was a slight smile on the older man's face.

"I believe it had to do with an operation that apparently was code named Sleeping Dogs."

Nishioki simply said, "Ah", and continued to smile.

"What can you tell me about that operation, Bill?"

The other man was silent for a few moments, than said, "There is nothing I can tell you about the military or political aspects. I was not a part of that, and I took great care not to be a part of it. I am a scientist."

"A scientist. Well, let's talk about that part of it."

"As you know, my field is genetics. The Agency engaged my late colleague, Jacob Horowitz, and me to provide scientific research for this particular operation."

"For what purpose."

"To, ah, identify certain individuals who possessed the characteristics desired for this operation."

"Tell me about those individuals. What makes them unique genetically?"

"They have somewhat different muscle fiber. It's denser, giving them greater strength. Their nervous systems transmit signals faster in their brains and throughout their bodies. Their hearts and lungs are larger, giving them the ability to process oxygen faster. They are quite formidable."

"Why you and Horowitz? Why not other geneticists?"

Nishioki's smile changed. He seemed a bit self-conscious. "Because we had developed a theory that fit well within the parameters of the operation."

"Did this involve identifying individuals who were...," Christie hesitated, groping for the right words..."genetically superior to...ordinary men?"

"I believe the term you are searching for is 'more genetically evolved'. And the answer is yes."

Christie sat back in his chair and tried to sip his tea. To his surprise he had emptied the cup without realizing it. It was very good tea.

"May I pour you some more tea, Mitch?"

Christie bobbed his head up and down, and said, "Please." Nishioki sat forward and refilled Christie's cup as well as his own.

"Can you explain in layman's terms how these men came to be 'more genetically evolved'?"

Nishioki settled back in his chair and said, "I can't guarantee the part about 'layman's terms', but please bear with me."

Christie shrugged. "I'll do my best."

"Genetics, as you undoubtedly know, is the science or study of the molecular structure and function of genes. This includes, among other things, patterns of inheritance from parent to offspring, gene distribution, variation and change in populations."

"I'm with you so far," Christie said. "But science never was my strong suit. Please explain what exactly a gene is or does."

"A gene holds information to build and maintain an organism's cells and pass genetic traits to offspring. They correspond to regions within DNA, which is a nucleic acid that contains the genetic instructions used in the development and functioning of most known living organisms."

Christie nodded his head. "So far, so good," he said.

"The main role of DNA molecules is the long-term storage of information. DNA is like a set of plans or a code, as it contains the instructions needed to construct other components of cells. The human genome is the entirety of this hereditary information and is encoded in our DNA.

"Over many generations, the genomes of organisms can change significantly, resulting in the phenomenon of evolution. Selection for beneficial mutations can cause a species to evolve into forms better able to survive in their environment. This process takes place, however, over many generations and is called adaptation."

"Let's pause for a second, Bill," Christie said as he held up a hand. "It's my understanding that these Sleeping Dogs people are not simply a generation better than the average Joe, but several generations."

Nishioki smiled a patient smile and said, "I'm getting to that, Mitch. The inherited instructions an organism carries within its genetic code is known as a genotype. Appearance and behavior, however, are subject to modification by environmental and developmental conditions.

"Thus, in contrast to a genotype, a phenotype is any observable characteristic or trait of an organism including development and behavior generated by environmental conditions. It is a fundamental prerequisite for evolution by natural selection."

"Natural selection? Isn't that Darwinism? Survival of the fittest? Law of the jungle?"

"Well, yes, in a manner of speaking."

"Then I don't understand. There are no sabre-toothed tigers around anymore. What would prompt this sudden spurt of evolution?"

Nishioki continued to smile as if he were a wise and patient *sensei* teaching a young disciple the finer points of a complex but necessary *aikido kata* or technique.

"Evolutionary change results from interactions between processes that introduce variation into a population. It's a form of stochastic process."

Christie gave the other man a puzzled look. "What kind of process?"

"It means random. In a stochastic or random process there is some indeterminacy in its future evolution. Genetic variation provides the raw material for natural selection. The main source of variation is mutation, which involves changes in a genomic sequence. Mutations are thought to be caused by radiation, viruses, and transposons, which are sequences of DNA that can move or transpose themselves to new positions within the genome of a single cell, as well as errors that occur during meiosis – a certain type of cell division - or DNA replication. These changes can be inherited by offspring. Another source of variation is genetic recombination, which shuffles the genes into new combinations."

Christie could feel a migraine headache coming on. And he wished he hadn't left his Mylanta in the car.

"Two main processes cause variants: natural selection and genetic drift" Nishioki said. "Natural selection is the process by which, over many generations, traits become more or less common in a population due to consistent effects upon the survival or reproduction of their bearers. Natural selection remains the primary explanation for adaptive evolution. Genetic variation provides the "raw material" for natural selection."

Christie raised his hand again. "You just said that natural selection occurs over many generations. These particular men, genetically speaking, are supposed to have jumped several generations into the future."

Nodding his head, Nishioki said, "I was coming to that. Another cause of evolution, which is not adaptive, but leads to random changes in common traits in a population is genetic drift, or the change in the frequency of a gene variant or allele in a population. It is an important evolutionary process, but contrasts with natural selection. Changes due to genetic drift are not driven by environmental or adaptive pressures, and may be beneficial, neutral, or detrimental to reproductive success."

Christie slumped lower in his chair. His head was beginning to throb. He hoped Nishioki was nearing the end of his explanation of genetics and the Sleeping Dogs operation.

"Genetic drift provides the basis for the neutral theory of molecular evolution advanced by a late colleague, Motoo Kimura. It asserts that the vast majority of evolutionary change at the molecular level is caused by random drift of selectively neutral mutants, and that most evolutionary change is the result of genetic drift acting on neutral alleles creating a new allele. These new alleles may become more common in the population over time.

"Although both natural selection and genetic drift drive evolution, genetic drift operates randomly without regard to fitness pressures imposed by the environment, while natural selection functions non-randomly on the ecological interaction of a population."

Nishioki had paused, so Christie said, "So, your theory is that these men aren't the product of natural selection, but of genetic drift instead?"

Nishioki shook his head. "It's not that simple," he said. "There is more than one theory involved."

Christie stifled a groan and reached up to rub the back of his neck. The pain in his head seemed to start there and pound its way upward through his head.

"One theory is that, while the urgency to produce stronger, faster, smarter humans in response to a hostile environment no longer is as great, some humans still carry the elements of that genetic code. It's more dominant in them. If a male carrier mates with a female carrier, there is a strong potential for one or more of their offspring to be more advanced genetically than other members of that generation.

"This is called Heterosis. It literally is the occurrence of a genetically superior offspring from mixing the genes of its parents. This ordinarily would be a result of the process of natural selection"

"You said that was one theory, Bill. Are there others?"

"Yes, there are. While Horowitz and I were never able to prove it, we proposed a variation on the theory of genetic drift. It just made sense to us that, because this genetic evolution was clearly more than generationally incremental, something akin to genetic drift is responsible."

Nishioki shifted slightly in his chair. "As you probably are aware, in human evolution there are…were a number of members of the genus Homo, the branch of hominids that includes our species, Homo sapiens. All other species are believed to have become extinct."

"Actually," Christie said with some pride, "I do know that."

"Well, Jake Horowitz and I wanted to do research on the possibility that there may have been another branch of the Homo genus that closely resembled us in many ways. Through interbreeding, which is known to have occurred among at least some of the species, their genetic material could have survived. It could manifest itself today in the right combination of genetic pairings."

Christie nodded and the motion sent new waves of pain shooting through his head. At this point, he literally was digging the tips of his fingers into the back of his neck.

114

"Basically, our hypothesis, although we were unable to prove it, is that a certain few individuals do carry some mutant form of gene. In the rare event that two of these carriers mate, there is something on the order of a one in four probability that the mutant genes can produce an offspring that is several generations more evolved than ordinarily is the case."

"So, if I'm following you," Christie said, struggling for the right words, "the...uh...probability that someone having this genetic superiority could be...uh...produced is extremely slim."

"That is correct. If our theory is correct, there are only a few such individuals in any generation."

"Why were you not able to prove your theory, Bill?"

Nishioki smiled a patronizing smile. "Genetics research is not like police work, Mitch. You don't simply catch the butler holding the proverbial smoking gun."

Christie nodded. He knew he was being chided and decided not to pursue the question. Most of what he knew about genetics research had just been told to him by his host. "Are we, the USA, the only nation who has produced such individuals?"

"No. Genetics generally does not recognize nationalities, and certainly not borders."

"So, the Russians or Chinese or anyone could have such individuals also?"

"Yes."

"Do you think they are aware of that?"

"Probably not yet, but in time they will figure it out."

"Speaking of figuring things out, I assume these Sleeping Dogs knew they were...ah...different."

"Of course. As I said they were very bright. They referred to themselves as 'gifted'."

"What did they call the rest of us who are not so gifted?"

Nishioki allowed an amused smile. "'Norms'," he said. "For normal."

"Besides their strength, quickness, and intelligence, were there any other distinguishing characteristics about these men?"

"Yes, two things. One was their eyes."

"What about them?"

"They each had very pale blue eyes ranging from Whalen's, which were the color of the Irish Sea, very cold. Stensen's were the palest, a whitish blue, then Larsen, Almeida, Kirkland and Thomas."

"Thomas?" Christie said. But wasn't he an African American?"

"Yes, but he was one of them, with the same genetic mutations. His eyes really were quite a striking feature."

"I bet they were."

"Incidentally, Mitch," Nishioki said, "For the record, Thomas didn't like the term African American. He referred to himself as a black man."

"Why? What was his problem with African American?"

"He believed it was a term of divisiveness, noting that Whelan didn't refer to himself as Irish American, nor Larsen as Norwegian American."

"Bill, you indicated there were two characteristics." Christie said. "Their eye color was one. What was the other?"

"They all had temperaments…short fuses and were capable of great physical violence. Whelan probably was the worst."

"So you're saying it wasn't a good idea to piss them off."

"Exactly," said Nishioki, who glanced at his watch.

Catching the hint, Christie said, "One last thing. You are aware that all of these genetically evolved individuals, the Sleeping Dogs, died in a plane crash almost twenty years ago?"

Nishioki nodded. "I was aware of that. Tragic."

"What would you say if I told you that one of them, Brendan Whelan, seems to be alive?"

The impassive expression on the geneticist's face never changed. He was silent for a moment, then said, "I would say good for him."

"Did you know him?"

"I knew all of them."

"How would you describe Whelan?"

Nishioki's lips curled into a faint smile. "Ruthless."

"Ruthless? You mean cruel, sadistic?"

"No, not at all. I mean ruthless in the same sense as a businessman who doesn't tolerate schedule delays, budget overruns, or taking focus off the big picture." Nishioki's smile broadened a bit. "You might say he's the six sigma advocate of the black operations business."

Christie stared at him for a moment. "Six Sigma? Isn't that the philosophy of zero defects or mistakes?"

"Yes."

"Would you say the world is less safe with him in it?"

"For people who misbehave. But for most of us, I would say it is a safer place."

Nishioki stood, indicating that the meeting was over.

Christie rose to his feet also, shook his host's hand and thanked him for his time. "I assume you'll be available, at least by phone, if I need to follow up with you on something."

"Certainly."

Christie started out the door, then stopped and said, "By the way, thank you for the tea. It was excellent."

"You are most welcome, Mitch. However, I don't believe it did anything for your headache."

Christie stared at him for a moment. "How could you possible know I have a headache?"

"We Orientals are not only inscrutable, but quite perceptive," Nishioki said with a faint smile as he closed the door behind Christie.

27 MAUI, HAWAII

It was a little after eight p.m. Hawaii-Aleutian Standard Time when Whelan's flight arrived at the airport in Kahului on the Hawaiian island of Maui. He had slept most of the way on the long, nonstop flight. Added to the catnap he got on the drive from San Jose to LAX, he felt rested, but not refreshed. It had only been three days since he left Ireland, but with the schedule he was on and the ten time zone difference between Ireland and Hawaii it felt like a week or more. He missed his routine, helping Caitlin get the boys off to school while preparing and serving breakfast to their B and B clientele. He missed his exercise routine and time spent with his sons. He missed the fellowship with the townspeople in the local pubs.

Most of all he missed Caitlin, her warmth and genuineness. Her gentle, loving touch. Her soft, raven black hair and cobalt blue eyes that flashed when she was angry. The scent of her. The way she fit perfectly in his arms. The fullness of her lips and her lush, lithe body. Her intuition, the way she just seemed always to know what his thoughts were. He had never considered himself a ladies' man, but neither had he spent much of his life without a woman in it. And then there was Caitlin. They had met casually, almost by accident. But very shortly they had become inseparable. Each just seemed to know, to intuit that they had met The One.

He appreciated the genetic break fate had given him. He was aware that not all of the Dogs felt the same. Whelan was very conscientious in maintaining his physical prowess. He trained relentlessly. Weights, martial arts, running, swimming, and cycling, especially cycling. Despite his size – he was considered to be too big to become a top cyclist, he was good enough that he occasionally trained with the Irish National Cycling Team when they were in Southwestern Ireland. He competed in local road races as an amateur and could easily whip the field, but he didn't. He always finished in the top

118

twenty, but purposely chose not to stand out. A man living a life underground was wise not to call attention to himself.

Whelan missed his regular workout routine. He felt stale. He and Larsen often had remarked about this. Both men became restless and uncomfortable when their training schedules were off. Right now he needed a good hard workout more than anything. He checked his Smartphone and found a fitness facility located about two and a half miles from the airport. It advertised that it was open twenty-four hours seven days a week. He picked up his rental car and stopped at a small tourist shop near the airport to buy shorts and a tee shirt. Now that he was in Hawaii, he would be happy to shed his newest disguise. The Bureau would be turning California on its ear trying to find him. Even with all the security cameras at LAX, they would never recognize him as a passenger on the Alaska Airlines flight to Hawaii.

The fitness facility offered one-day memberships. Whelan signed in as David C. Taggard, the Kansas City attorney. When he registered, a young man with a bad case of acne came out of an enclosed office area to sign him in and collect his workout fee. Afterwards, the man, who appeared to Whelan to be Filipino, disappeared back into the office from which Whelan could hear the sounds of a TV playing. It sounded like the young man was watching a NASCAR race.

Whelan warmed up for thirty minutes on a treadmill gradually adjusting it to the steepest incline. From there he moved to the floor mat for twenty minutes of stretching exercises. He followed that with thirty minutes of core strengthening routines. Finally, he moved on to the free weights. There were only a few people in the facility at that hour, another man lifting weights nearby and two women in very tight leotards cycling through the Nautilus equipment in a far corner.

Whelan was careful not to use weight totals that he thought might draw unwanted attention to himself, and, correspondingly, his unusual strength. But he was used to working out with friends and family in a small gym in Dingle, where his strength was legendary. He overestimated the strength of a Norm weightlifter, even the very powerful ones. Loading three hundred and fifty pound on the bench-press bar, he slid under it and began slowly and easily to crank out twenty full reps.

The man working out nearby ran over to stand behind him. "Shoulda' asked for a spot, man," he said.

"Thanks, don't need it. Yet." When Whelan finished the last repetition and replaced the bar in the rack, he sat up.

The man, who had short blonde hair and a decent build, stuck his hand out. "I'm Josh," he said.

Whelan shook the hand. "Dave," he said.

"Damn, Dave, you were pushing what…three fifty?"

"Something like that." Whelan realized he had misjudged the amount of weight he should have been using under the circumstances. His mind raced as he searched for a way to remedy the situation. It was at that moment that one of the women who had been circuit training on the Nautilus equipment walked up to him. She was petite with bleached blonde hair and green eyes, and wore a skin tight, bright green leotard without sleeves or leggings. She filled it admirably with very large breasts, tiny waist, flat stomach, slim hips, well-shaped buttocks and muscular, athletic looking legs. In his single days, Whelan would have found her interesting for a night, perhaps even a weekend. He judged her to be in her mid- to late thirties.

She smiled seductively at Whelan and seemed oblivious to Josh. "I haven't seen you around here before," she said to Whelan.

"Haven't been around here before."

She stood facing him with her feet spread about shoulder width apart and hands on hips and eyed him up and down. Whelan had a glimmer of understanding of what an attractive woman must feel when men are ogling her as a sex object. He had been there before.

She slowly licked her lips suggestively. Finally, she said, "I'm Renée."

"Dave," Whelan said.

She continued to appraise him, and, liking what she saw, said, "Dave, what are you doing after your workout?"

"Getting some rest. It's been a long day."

"Getting some rest, huh? How'd you like to join me after the workouts? We could go for a drink, then see what happens after that."

"Sounds like fun, but I've got other plans."

Her eyes narrowed and her lips tightened. Clearly, this was not the response she had been looking for. Rejection was rare and it made her angry. "Other plans?" She looked at Josh, then back to Whelan. "Are you gay?"

Josh reddened. Throwing up his hands he said. "Don't look at me. I'm not gay." He walked away.

"Neither am I," Whelan said to Renée. "I'm married."

"So when has that ever stopped anybody? I cheated on my husband like crazy when I was married."

"Moments to be proud of, no doubt," Whelan said with intentional sarcasm. "If you'll excuse me, Renée is it, I need to finish my workout and get on with some business activities."

She glared at him for a moment then said, "Shove it up your ass." She spun around and stormed back to the Nautilus area, where she continued to flash angry looks at him.

An hour of nonstop iron pumping later Whelan had achieved both an aerobic and a strength workout. It was not long enough to completely satisfy him, but it was better than no workout at all. Just as he was finishing, a man came into the facility. He was about Whelan's size, perhaps slightly taller and had a bodybuilder's physique. Earlene squealed and jumped into his arms, wrapping her legs around his waist and her arms around his neck. He spun her around for a moment then placed her on her feet.

Renée reached up and grabbed the tank top he was wearing and pulled his head down to her level. She was saying something to him and pointing at Whelan. The man scowled at Whelan, then straightened up and walked over to where the Irishman was stacking the weights following his last set of the night.

The man stopped in front of Whelan with his hands balled into fists and resting on his hips, blocking the way to the locker room. "Hey," he said belligerently. "My girlfriend says you propositioned her."

"Renée?"

"Yeah, Renée. And she says when she refused, you threatened to beat the shit out of her."

Whelan stared at the man for a moment then said, "I don't think so, Slick, now get your ass out of my way."

The man telegraphed his intentions by suddenly rotating his left hip and shoulder forward and his right hip and shoulder backward. It's what some fighters call "loading up"; in other words, coiling the body preparatory to throwing a punch.

Whelan didn't load up. That had been trained out of him decades earlier. He drove the palm of his right hand straight forward with blinding speed, smashing it into the center of the man's chest and driving the air from his lungs with an explosive grunt. The man flew backwards through the air for ten to twelve feet and landed semiconscious on his back in the middle of the gym. Whelan walked over, grabbed him under the chin and casually dragged him over to Renée and her female friend. "When he comes around," he said to her, "he's going to have lung contusions and a couple of broken ribs. He might want to have that looked into." He turned and walked away.

"You're an asshole, you know that? A huge fucking asshole," she shouted at Whelan's back.

After clearing his gear out of the locker that had been assigned to him, Whelan drove the short distance to the Maui Beach Hotel and checked in using the reservation someone on the Team had made for him. It was too late for most restaurants to be open, so he ate two Kashi GoLean bars he had picked up at LAX, washing them down with a bottle of Fiji water he bought at a Whole Foods store on the short drive from the 24 Hour Fitness.

He arose at five the next morning and, knowing it was three in the afternoon in Dingle, called Caitlin. She picked up on the third ring and answered in Gaelic. He spoke to her in Gaelic as well. It was the original language of the Celtic peoples of Ireland, but as a result of having been banned during the centuries of English occupation many in Ireland no longer spoke it. But Ireland was a difficult land to rule effectively before the twentieth century. Most of the English influence was in Northern Ireland and around Dublin, the capital. The southwest part of the country, where the Dingle peninsula is located, was as far removed from those areas as anywhere on the island. Whelan's parents had taught him the language as a child. Though it had gone underground during the long English occupation, the language was still spoken by the natives in addition to English. It was a safe language to use in the very remote possibility that Levell was mistaken and the call could be being monitored.

"I knew it was you," she said.

Whelan shook his head and smiled. "Now, how could you know it was me, Kate?"

"I just did, Bren," she said, calling him by her nickname for him. "We have a connection, the two of us, and it can't be explained. Doesn't need to be."

"Are you and the boys alright?"

"We're fine. We have Paddy" – her brother – "and my Da along with the whole village lookin' out for the boys and me. God help anyone foolish enough to give us any grief."

Whelan had to chuckle. He knew she absolutely was right. Her immediate family and the other residents of the Dingle area were really one very large, extended family. He couldn't help but worry about his loved ones while he was so far away from home with no real idea when he would return. But he knew that Caitlin, Sean and Declan were in as safe a place as there was.

"Things going smoothly in my absence?"

"The B and B, yes. The boys, not so much," she said

"Why? What's happening with the boys?"

"Well, *your* son, Sean…"

"Oh, it's *my* son now, is it?" he said with a chuckle. He knew there was no more devoted a mother on the planet than his Caitlin. "What has he done?"

"Yesterday, at school, a big bully of a boy two grades older than Sean and more than thirty pounds heavier picked a fight with him, shoved him down. And what do you think Sean did about that?" she said.

"Kicked his butt, I'm sure."

"Oh, it was a bit more than that, Bren. He sent the poor lad to the hospital with some serious fractures and other injuries."

"That's my boy," he said and smiled with fatherly pride.

"Yes, he most assuredly is your boy. But it's the younger one, Declan, who's most like you. No one's been foolish enough to pick a fight with him in two years or more."

"That's my boy, too," he said with basking in fatherly pride.

"It must just be somethin' in their genes," she said with a laugh, teasing him about his own genetic constitution.

He could image her here with him now. He could almost smell the sweet scent of her hair, and feel the warmth of her body. Suddenly he felt very homesick. He had never had occasion to be away from her and the boys for more than a night and now he missed them. He felt a sharp pang of longing deep within his chest as if his heart truly was suffering.

"You don't need to be worryin' about this, Bren," she said. "Their Uncle Paddy came over to the house when he heard about the fight and had a talk with Sean and Declan. He tried to sound very stern, but I caught him winkin' at them when he was finished. Honestly, he's as bad as you are when comes to settin' an example of peaceful restraint and turnin' the other cheek."

"Is that what you'd want me to do, turn the other cheek?" He was smiling when he said it.

"No, Bren, you know I truly love that strength about you. I enjoy seeing some troublesome fool get the bejesus knocked out of him. Remember who I grew up around."

"They don't get any tougher than Tom and Paddy," he said.

They chatted for several more minutes. At the end of the conversation, she said, "When are you comin' home, Bren. We miss you terribly."

"Not soon enough, Kate. Not soon enough."

28 HANA, HAWAII

The road from Kahului to Hana is world famous. It twists and winds along the seacoast and cliffs through six hundred hairpin turns and switchbacks in a little more than fifty miles. There are more than fifty bridges in the stretch, many of them only one lane wide. Countless creeks and streams tumbled toward the sea in a struggle to drain the lush, tropical rain forest growing on the wet easterly side of Mount Haleakala. Between the constant curves and switchbacks and the bumper-to-bumper tourists, it took him more than three hours to cover the fifty or so miles to Hana. Whelan didn't mind. He was motoring through a genuinely exotic paradise; one of the most beautiful and captivating drives on the planet - flowers, tropical foliage, streams, waterfalls, bamboo thickets, and lush, impenetrable rain forest. Giant tropical trees that sprouted prehistoric-sized leaves. There were copses of rare rainbow eucalyptus trees with multicolored bark. He wished he were driving a convertible. More than that, he wished Caitlin could be there for him to share it with her. He vowed he would find a way to make that happen someday soon.

Along the way he stopped to buy some fresh fruit, fresh made banana bread and a bottle of water at a small stand by the side of the road. He took some extra minutes and followed a trail uphill to a scenic lookout. The majesty of the view was humbling. The flank of Haleakala fell away beneath him, a mass of green all the way to the azure pacific. What, he wondered, had the first Euro-American explorers thought when they discovered these islands. It was no wonder that doctors, lawyers, accountants, business executives and others left well-paying jobs on the Mainland to move to Hawaii and become guides, cabbies, or others employed in the tourist trade just to be able to go native in this paradise. Whelan understood what motivated them. The temperature was a balmy eighty-two degrees and the clean air was scented with soft, tropical fragrances. Back in the States, including Florida, people were enduring a bone chilling cold snap.

When he reached the small town of Hana with its population of little more than a thousand residents, he was tempted to stop for lunch at the Travaasa Hana, the former Hotel Hāna-Maui, a world famous resort and spa in the heart of the village. But he wasn't really in the mood for a sit-down dining experience. He drove on through Hana, past the historic Wananalua Congregational Church built in 1838, the several generation old Hasegawa General Store, and a bank that was open for business only ninety minutes each day. A short distance later he spotted a small food vendor's stand by the side of the road. It didn't seem to have a name, just a hand painted sign that said "Go Native. Eat Here." He pulled over and got out of the car.

As he walked over to the stand, the aroma of the food hit him. Whelan realized he was ravenous. A solid looking man who Whelan judged to be about five ten and two hundred fifty pounds was cooking ribs on a portable gas grill. He looked authentically Polynesian to Whelan, and he wondered if guests staying at the bed and breakfast in Dingle thought that he looked authentically Irish.

"Ho Brah," the man said. "You lookin' hungry to me. Want some food?"

"Whatever you got, and a lot of it," he said.

"You got it, Brah." The man heaped a paper plate with a mound of the ribs and handed it to Whelan. "Don't need no more sauce, Brah, but that's for you to say." He motioned toward a couple of unlabeled bottles containing a reddish brown sauce.

"I'll take your word for it," Whelan said and spent the next several minutes in silence as he savored the best ribs he had ever eaten.

When he finished, the man said, "You still look hungry, Brah. You want some more?"

Whelan shook his head. "No, that was just the right amount." He wiped his hands and face with some moist towelettes that were in a small basket on the rough wooden plank that served as a countertop. "I'm looking for someone, an old friend. Maybe you can help me."

The man had turned away to dispose of the plate and bones in a garbage can next to the grill. "Maybe. What's his name?"

"I believe he goes by the name of Brett Lange."

The man spun around and looked at Whelan and said "I never heard of him."

Given the man's otherwise laid back demeanor, it seemed to Whelan that he had moved and spoken too quickly. There was a raw nerve there somewhere.

"I understand he lives past the end of Pink Lokelani Lane off Highway 330 about two miles south of here."

"Don't nobody live there, Brah and don't nobody go there either."

"Well, if nobody lives there and nobody goes there, what's the harm if I go up there and have a look around?"

The man shook his head vigorously. "No, Brah. That's a bad place. You go there, past the end of the dirt road, you don't be comin' back."

"Why? What's to keep me from coming back…monsters?" Whelan had to stifle a grin. This was getting interesting.

"Maybe monsters, maybe demons. Don't matter, Brah. You don't be comin' back."

The ribs had been incredibly good and Whelan laid a generous amount of money on the makeshift counter top, then walked back to his car. He allowed himself a smile now. Monsters, demons – the man seemed sincere enough. But, as far as Whelan was concerned, the Irish had a lock on the supernatural – banshees, wizards, witches, leprechauns, and more.

He drove in a southerly direction along the Hana Highway. Not far past the point where the Haneoo Road looped back into the highway he saw a small sign identifying Pink Lokelani Lane. It was a narrow unpaved road that wound upward for about a mile and a half. He passed a variety of houses along the way, some clearly the luxurious vacation homes of the very well to do and some quite humble. Eventually he came to a point where the road ended and what appeared to be a little used trail snaked on up from there. At the trailhead there was a hand painted sign on an old post that said, "Stay out. Trespassers will be shot."

Whelan locked his car and started hiking.

29 J. EDGAR HOOVER BUILDING

When he had finished the interview with Dr. Nishioki, Christie drove back to the airport in San Francisco and returned his rental car. On the drive up he had used his cell phone to arrange to meet Dave O'Connor from the Bureau's San Francisco field office at the terminal.

He nodded as he approached O'Connor near the United counter in Terminal Three. "You got that sketch for me?"

"Yes, sir," O'Connor said and handed him a manila envelop.

Christie tore it open and removed the sketch. He studied it for several moments. It looked like the sketch artist had done a pretty good job of creating the current likeness from a twenty-year old photograph that hadn't provided much to work with anyway. Suddenly, he broke into a cold sweat. "Wait a minute…no…Jesus fucking Christ!"

Startled, O'Connor said, "What is it, sir? Do you know this guy?"

"Jesus fucking Christ!" Christie said again. "I'm not positive, but this looks like the guy I sat next to on the flight out here. It's a close enough resemblance that we need to get on this right now." He paused, staring at the drawing. "What the hell was he doing? Taunting me? The sonofabitch."

"What do you want me to do, sir?"

He looked at O'Connor. "Get this sketch to all agencies, federal, state and local. Turn this country inside out until we find this guy." He paused for a moment or two, then said, "I think his name…the name he's using is Murkowski. Mike Murkowski. Get on that right away. The usual sources — transportation, lodging, charge cards."

After O'Connor left, Christie spoke to his office and checked his email. Then he found a bar near his departure gate and had a double bourbon with a Mylanta chaser. He caught a United red eye flight and slept all the way to Chicago where he connected to a flight to Reagan National in Washington. He was at his desk before ten o'clock the next morning.

He gathered members of his team and briefed them, then they spent the next several hours on the phones talking with members of various law enforcement agencies and studying films from security cameras at West Coast air, bus and rail terminals. A video from LAX that included shots of a chubby man with a big nose, bushy eyebrows, and curly, reddish blonde hair didn't draw anyone's attention.

Eventually, someone in the Bureau's San Francisco field office, who had been checking with hotels in the airport area, came up with a lead. It was a video from the security cameras at the Airport Crown Plaza Hotel. It showed a man who matched Christie's description of Murkowski making a phone call in the hotel lobby. He never faced the cameras while on the phone, so the Bureau couldn't get a lip reader to assist. Another camera in the porte-cochére caught the man getting into a late model navy blue Ford Focus. The Bureau was able to zoom in on the license plate and enhance the resolution enough to read it. Christie ordered an all points bulletin. The car was found shortly thereafter abandoned in a mall parking lot in Sacramento. It eventually was determined that it had been stolen from long-term parking at the airport. It had been wiped clean of any prints, as well as hair, body fluids or other potential DNA evidence.

Christie was meeting with the members of his team in a small conference room at Bureau headquarters when he learned this last bit of information. He slammed his fist on the table and said, "Goddammit! Who is this guy?" He stared at the ceiling for several moments as he slowly regained control of his temper. Except for the soft hissing of the HVAC system, the room was quiet. No one said a word.

He could feel himself starting to lose it. There had been more than enough on his plate before the Harold Case matter was thrust at him. The pressure on him from Bureau brass, the Metropolitan police, the media, and others, combined with lack of rest, the travel, his stomach issues, and guilt about neglecting his family was taking a deeper and deeper toll on him. He desperately wanted another swig or two of Mylanta, but felt it would be a sign of weakness to do it in front of his team.

At last he leaned forward, resting his elbows on the table and said, "Look, this guy is too slick. He's no crazed killer. He's not like any professional hit man I've ever encountered. He moves too quickly. Changes directions on a dime. Has more identities that Lon Chaney. He's almost better at this than we are. There's got to be somebody helping him."

Antonelli, the veteran, said, "Got any idea who he might be working with?"

"Maybe," young Rickover said, "it's one of us."

All heads swiveled to look at him. "What are you saying?" Christie demanded. "That someone in this room or in the Bureau is working with a killer?"

"Well, I...no...what I mean is..." Rickover stammered, trying desperately to crawl out from under his last statement. "It could be someone in government, not the Bureau. No, I never meant the Bureau."

Christie continued to stare at Rickover. The young agent's eyes were wide open and his Adam's Apple bobbed up and down vigorously as he swallowed repeatedly. He had pushed himself as far back in his chair he possibly could.

"Someone in government," Christie said. "That's interesting. Hadn't thought of that, but it could explain the access to resources; how he seems to always be a step ahead of us." He thought some more, shook his head and said, "What the hell am I doing? Twenty-plus years with the Bureau and now I'm going to start spinning conspiracy theories?"

30 HANA, HAWAII

Whelan enjoyed the exercise he was getting, as he hiked up the trail on the south flank of Haleakala. It was steep and rough, but the sun was shining through the heavy foliage of the rain forest. The temperature was cool and the air was amazingly fresh. He was glad he had dressed in shorts, a tee shirt and running shoes that morning.

After about ten minutes, he came upon a second hand-painted sign that said, "This is your final warning. Turn back or die." He smiled and continued hiking. Has to be Nick Stensen, he thought. A few minutes later he came upon a third sign. It said, "You stupid son of a bitch. It's too late. Now I'm going to kill you." This time there was the skull of some kind of animal on top of the signpost. He continued climbing, but he could sense the presence of someone else.

Eventually he emerged into a clearing amidst a grove of tall, mature tropical trees. There was a small cottage in the clearing that looked as if it had been built by hand. Who ever did it had to have hauled the materials up here without any mechanical help. The trail was too steep and narrow for heavy equipment to pass. The cottage sat at the far end of the clearing on a steep slope. Whelan turned and looked behind him. The trees at the front edge of the clearing had been trimmed so that anyone in the cottage could see the Pacific. Whelan also saw that the trailhead was in view and so was his car.

He turned back around and was startled to see a huge black Rottweiler sitting on its haunches ten feet from him. Its baleful black eyes were fixed unwaveringly on him. The jaws in its huge mastiff-like head were dripping with saliva. A steady growl rumbled from its thick throat. Whelan gathered from the fact that it hadn't yet attacked him that it was waiting for a command from someone unseen.

He knew from instinct as well as the extensive training he had received as a Sleeping Dog that he had two options. He had always had some mysterious bond with dogs. It was something he had inherited from his father. The man could have the most vicious cur licking his hand in a very short time. Whelan, likewise, could attempt to calm the dog, try to win it over as a friend. Or, he could anticipate the attack; in which case he knew he would have one chance – and a slim one at that – to apply a technique that might cripple the animal. He decided to go with both, but he would try the peaceful one first.

He slowly sank to his knees never taking his eyes off the Rottweiler. He knew that he had to get down to the dog's eye level to communicate effectively. He spread his hands out in front of him, palms out and began talking softly to the dog. It just sat there with the growl rumbling from its chest.

"Nice try. And when it doesn't work and he attacks you, you're gonna throw yourself to the right, try to grab his right front foreleg and snap it out of joint with enough force to keep him from twisting his head around and biting you. Then, if you're lucky enough to do that, you start running, looking for a blunt object to hit him with or a tree to climb, all the while hoping you can outrun a three-legged dog." The voice came from behind him. It was Nick Stensen.

"Nice to see you too, Nick."

"What? You fucking Irishmen can't read English?"

"Would have been easier in Gaelic."

"Doesn't matter. I'm sure your sorry ass would have come up here anyway."

"Mind if I stand up?"

"That's between you and the dog."

"Fuck the dog," Whelan said and stood up.

The dog never moved. It was very well trained and sat waiting for a signal from Stensen. After a moment, Stensen made a sideways motion with his head and the dog stood and trotted off into the rain forest.

"In spite of the cute dog tricks, I know you were expecting me. Levell spoke to you," Whelan said. He looked into the other man's pale blue eyes and saw the familiar red dots deep in the center of each. They were not much more than pinpricks, meaning that Stensen's madness was almost dormant for the moment.

"Yeah? Doesn't mean I want to see your sorry ass."

"Call me sorry ass one more time, and I'll feed your sorry ass to your own dog."

"Goddam, Brendan, that's what I always loved about you, man. You really are a hard-assed sonofabitch."

131

"Goes with the territory. We Irish have had a hard time for centuries. Tends to give you an attitude."

"I don't know from Irish, but I can truthfully say I like being crazy."

"If you're crazy enough to claim you're crazy, you're not crazy."

Stensen looked at him. "Was that Gaelic? It didn't make any sense." Then he stepped forward and embraced Whelan in a tight squeeze. He stepped back and said, "I hate to admit this, but it's good to see you. Gets lonely on this mountain with just a dog."

"Might have more company if you took the signs down and lost the dog."

"Nah, when I want company, I go to town...well if you can call Hana a town. Hey, you want a beer?"

Whelan followed Stensen into the cottage. It was surprisingly comfortable for a veritable hermitage. It obviously was wired with electric current as evidenced by the small refrigerator and lamps. Stensen got two Fire Rock ales, a beer brewed in New Hampshire for a brewery headquartered in Kona on the Big Island. Even the suds industry has gone global, Whelan thought.

They went back outside and sat on a low bench, really nothing more than a two by twelve plank stretched between two tree stumps, gazed at the pacific and drank their beers. Stensen's cell phone rang. He looked at the number and said, "This will just take a minute."

He hit the connect button and said, "Yeah?" He listened for a minute then said, "Nah everything's fine. Just an old friend stopping by for a visit." There was brief pause, then he said, "Hell yes I have old friends...some, a few. Look, I appreciate your concern." He disconnected and put the phone back in his pocket.

"Neighbors worried about you?" Whelan said.

"No. Worried about you."

"Your neighbors seem to be on a friendly basis with you, Nick. What's up with that?"

Stensen smiled. "I have a good life here. I keep the peace. And the locals look out for me."

"Yeah? I passed the cop shop on the way into Hana. So what do you do, that they don't?"

Stensen reached his arm out and pointed into the distance. "You see all those big, expensive homes on the way in? The owners can go Mainland for months at a time and leave the places unlocked if they want to. Nobody will mess with them. I have unlimited access to their pantries, freezers, cars."

"How's that work?"

Stensen stretched and took a drink of his beer. "When I first got here, there was some crime...B and E's, vandalism, you know the litany. I made it a point to ambush the bastards in the act. They disappeared. Anyone who complained also disappeared. The guy that just called, he lives in one of those big ol' houses near the trailhead."

"The local cops don't have a problem with you exterminating the citizenry?"

"Why should they? I take out the trash. The only things they have to worry about these days are traffic violations. I handle everything else. Which, honestly, is the occasionally belligerent drunk tourist trying to pick a fight with a local or coming on too strong to one of the girls in town."

"So, if I have this right," Whelan said with a grin, "shit happens and the police shine a big spotlight in the sky with the stylized outline of a bat, then you come running?"

"Something like that."

"And the dog's name is Robin."

"How'd you know that?" Stensen said with a grin of his own.

"I asked about you in Hana'" Whelan said. "The locals seem to be terrified of you."

"Should be. But they like having me around. Bring shit to me, food and such. Leave it at the trailhead. Nobody comes up here." He took another swig from his bottle. "Hell, you're the first human who's been up here in years."

Whelan smiled. "Lady friends?"

"Plenty of that in town. I'm something of a legend among the ladies. I am, in fact, nothing less than the master of all I survey." Stensen swept his outstretched arms across the horizon.

Whelan said, "Kinda' tall for a Napoleon complex, aren't you?"

Stensen turned and stared at Whelan for a moment. Whelan knew he had touched a raw nerve. The ever-present tiny red dots of madness deep in the center of Stensen's pupils seemed slightly larger than they had been only moments ago.

"What do you say we go into town and get a drink or two?" Stensen said.

They hiked down the mountain to Whelan's rental car and drove back into Hana. Stensen directed them to a small, rundown bar on an unpaved side street in the small village. It was little more than a Quonset hut with a couple of window shaker air conditioning units stuck in the front panel of the building. It was rusty and dented, and badly in need of some maintenance efforts. There were no windows that Whelan could discern.

Entrance was through a battered wooden door that sagged on its hinges. The inside smelled of cigarette smoke and stale beer. It was dimly lit by a couple of bare light bulbs suspended from the ceiling on thin wires. The inside resembled the exterior: old, beat up, but serviceable. There was a scattering of mismatched tables and chairs, and an old jukebox in the front corner to the left of the entrance. A wooden bar extended along the wall to the right from a rear partition to a point halfway to the front of the place. The bar stools, like the tables and chairs, were an eclectic mix. Some were shorter than others. Some had backs, some didn't. Some had bare wooden seats, some had padding that had been taped and retaped many times with gray or blue duct tape.

It was mid-afternoon on a Friday and the bar was already crowded. Most of the patrons were Polynesian with a few Haoles scattered about. Two very bulky native Hawaiians were behind the bar. It got quieter for a moment when Stensen entered. Everyone looked up and either nodded, smiled, or waved. A few applauded. One *haole* man yelled, "Welcome O' Protector of the Innocent!" That drew several laughs.

"Hey, guys," Stensen said and put a hand on one of Whelan's thick shoulders. "This is an old friend of mine. He says he's come all the way to Hana just to beat the shit out of all of you. Says that, other than me, there's nothing but fairies in Hawaii." Stensen paused, looked at Whelan, grinned and said, "You gonna let him get away with that?" The red dots were much larger now.

Several men slowly stood up, all native Hawaiians. Their facial expressions were impassive, but their eyes smoldered with anger. They each were built like a Hawaiian Polynesian – thick and powerful. Whelan instantly counted twelve of them. His mind processed and weighed all options at the speed of light. Suddenly, his right fist flashed out toward Stensen's head. A man lacking Stensen's genetic gifts would have caught the blow square in the side of his head, possibly a deathblow. At the very least, he would have suffered a concussion and possibly a snapped neck.

Stensen, however, was almost as quick as Whelan. He was moving down and away when the blow struck. It caught him high on the side of the head and sent him flying into the jukebox. He sagged slowly to the floor, tried to get up then sat back down shaking his head to clear the stars that spun through it.

It was one of those proverbial "you could hear a pin drop" moments. The people in the bar, as did all the locals, regarded Stensen as almost god-like. It was unthinkable that any mere mortal, regardless of size or other qualities could drop him as easily as this stranger with the odd reddish blonde curls had.

Whelan looked at the crowd and said, "He's right. We do go way back. But I never made those comments. And he's never been able to kick my ass. Guess he forgot."

Most of the men sat back down, but one, the biggest man in the bar, remained standing. "What you want with us, Brah?"

"Just a cold beer and a few kind words will do," Whelan said with a disarming smile.

"You got it, Brah. What kind you want?"

134

"Fire Rock?"

"Sure, this is Hawai'i, Brah" the big man said and motioned to one of the bartenders.

Moments later an ice-cold ale was placed in Whelan's hand. "And my buddy needs one, too." He nodded at Stensen who was just getting up off the floor, but still wobbly.

"There's one other thing I need," Whelan said.

"Just say it, Brah."

"I need to get across the channel to the Big Island."

The big man smiled. "I got a boat. I take you there. When you wanna go?"

"Soon as I finish this beer."

A short time later the man, whose name was Akamu, the Hawaiian form of Adam, meaning, "Earth", took Whelan across Alenuihāhā channel separating Maui from Hawaii, the Big Island. The trip was rough, as the trade winds were blowing out of the northeast at ten to fifteen knots. This produced a strong following sea all the way from Hana to Kukulhaele on the Big Island. Once there, Akamu had a cousin drive Whelan to the airport in Hilo. There is another airport on the other side of the Big Island at Kona, but Whelan purposely chose not to use it. Kona is on the side of the island favored by tourists, and he wanted to avoid those kinds of places. Using his identification as David C. Taggard, the attorney from Kansas City, Whelan bought a ticket to San Diego on a flight leaving at nine that evening.

31 J. EDGAR HOOVER BUILDING

Christie sat at his desk staring out his skinny window at another snowy day in Washington. He was going over in his mind everything he knew about the Harold Case matter, Operation Sleeping Dogs and Brendan Whelan. He went back over his conversation with Bill Nishioki. His gut told him there was something big, maybe huge, involved in all this, but he couldn't connect the pieces yet. There was too much still missing.

There was a knock at his door and he turned his chair toward its source. Jim Franconia stood in the doorway. "Got a minute?" he said.

"Yeah, sure." Christie beckoned him in and pointed to one of his desk chairs. "What's on your mind, Jim?"

"I just wanted to tell you that the Agency hasn't come up with anything new on that black ops thing, the Sleeping Dogs. Your guys been able to make any progress?"

Christie brought him up to date, including the talk with Nishioki. Franconia seemed amused by the part about Whelan being seated next to Christie on the flight from Atlanta to San Francisco.

"You think the bastard was taunting me?" Christie said.

"Not likely. He's supposed to be an exceptionally smart guy and a stunt like that would be pretty dangerous. I'd chalk it up to a very weird coincidence."

"There's something very imposing about this whole case. Others are involved, too. Someone picked Whelan up in San Francisco. We had footage of the car with Freeway cameras, but lost it when it turned into a residential section. Whelan must have switched cars there, because he doesn't appear to be in it when the cameras picked it up again on the way to Sacramento."

"What about the parking garage at the mall in Sacramento?" Franconia said. "Did the security cameras pick anything up?"

"Yeah, a fat, frumpy woman got out and disappeared into the mall."

"Disappeared? How?"

"Clearly she...if it was a she, could have been a man for all we know, was wearing a disguise. Whoever it was must have changed out of it in the mall where cameras couldn't pick it up."

Franconia shook his head and whistled. "Too fuckin' weird, man. This is no lone wolf on a solo cross country tour."

"No shit. You see what I mean. This thing just keeps getting bigger. You got any ideas?"

Franconia tilted his head back in thought for a moment and stared at the ceiling. When he looked back at Christie he said, "What about the two older guys, Levell and McCoy? Got anything new on them?"

"Let's remember who these guys are. We're not talking about a couple of senior citizens playing shuffleboard."

"Right. One was the Agency's Deputy Director for Direct Actions, reporting directly to the DCI." – Director of Central Intelligence – "The other is the current Commander of MARSOC." - United States Marine Corps Forces Special Operations Command.

"We had people watching them, but they haven't given us anything that would raise suspicions. Then, out of the blue a directive came down from on high," Christie said with obvious disgust and frustration. "We were told to stand down on the surveillance. I know those guys are involved in some fashion, but I can't do a damn thing about it."

"So, what did you do?"

"What the hell do you think I did? I terminated the surveillance activities."

"Bummer," Franconia said. "You got anything going at all, like bugging their phones?"

"No."

"What about other forms of communication...Internet and all?"

"Yeah, yeah, yeah," Christie said impatiently. "We know the drill as well as you Agency spooks do."

"Probably because we taught you," Franconia said with a smile.

"Horseshit!"

Franconia's smile broadened and he laughed, then said, "Did you ever think that maybe we taught you everything you know, but not everything we know?"

"Double horseshit. We had everything in place that we needed to catch this guy Whelan and anyone else who's working with him. Except now it's no longer in place."

"My, aren't we the sensitive one."

Christie reached into the upper right-hand drawer of his desk and got out a bottle of Mylanta. He shook it several times, took a big gulp and put the bottle back in the drawer. "There *are* parts of me that are too damn sensitive," he said and patted his stomach. "Shit like having to shut down the surveillance damn sure doesn't help. What the fuck is going on in the rarified atmosphere of upper levels of government that they would order me, the SSA, to shut down what might have been one of our best avenues for developing solid leads?"

"Dunno," Franconia said. "Not ours to reason why. But moving right along, other than holding your hand on the flight to California then disappearing, is there any other news that might tie into this case?"

Christie rubbed his jaw. "Funny you should ask. There was a dust up in Tampa the other day. Somebody that kind of sounds like Whelan beat the shit out of a formidable thug operating as a bail bondsman. Then he seems to have sat in on a bar fight in which the guy he was with all but killed five pieces of trailer trash with his bare hands."

Franconia's lanky frame was sprawled out in the desk chair, one long leg hanging over an arm of the chair. He raised both eyebrows in a questioning look. "And your theory is?"

"Based on the bondsman's statements and those of the witnesses in the bar, one of them could have been Whelan."

"And the other one?"

"Sounds like he's as bad or worse. If that's the case, then there may have been others who survived the plane crash...if there was a plane crash." Christie leaned back in his chair and put his feet on his desk.

"Oh, there definitely was a crash. I saw the Agency's files. Photos and statements from the attempted rescue operation. But remember, no bodies were found."

"So someone arranged the crash to look like they all perished, then set them up with new identities and homes? And they've been living among us ever since? Hiding in plain sight?"

"Well," Franconia said, "let's not make it sound like these guys are space aliens or something."

Christie's head was tilted back and he was staring at the ceiling, thinking. "If they did survive, and if we can figure out where one or more of them may have gone to ground, we might be able to apprehend at least one of them."

"Sounds like the old needle in the haystack thing to me."

Christie shook his head. "Not necessarily. We know Whelan was born in Ireland. He knows the people, the culture, the lay of the land. Might even have had relatives there. And Ireland's a hell of lot smaller than the U.S."

Franconia sat up in his chair. "Look, that sounds like a waste of time to me. I wouldn't expend resources on it."

Christie leaned forward and picked up his phone with one hand and buzzed Lou Antonelli's office with the index finger of his other hand. When the other man picked up, he said, "Lou, it's Mitch. I got an idea."

"Yeah? Fill me in."

"I want you to gather all the info you can get on Whelan's Irish roots and work through the office of the AD IOD." - Assistant Director for the FBI's International Operations Division – "to get a team from the legat" – legal attaché – "in London to follow up. Have them circulate the sketch. Maybe we can pick up this guy's trail." He hung up.

32 SAN DIEGO

Wearing his fat costume and facial prosthetics again, Whelan flew from Kona-Kailua on the Big Island back to Los Angeles, then connected with a flight to San Diego. He slept much of the first leg from Hawaii to L.A. In San Diego, he picked up a rental car at the airport that had been prearranged for him by someone on the Team. He drove south on the 5 toward Chula Vista to an automotive dealership just off the Interstate. He asked someone in the service department where the detailing of cars was being done and was directed to an area behind the dealership.

As he approached the area, he saw two young people busily detailing a Chevrolet Suburban. One was a black male wearing a dark blue visor with a white bill. The word "CHARGERS" in white and a gold lightening bolt were stitched above the bill. The other person was a disturbingly thin white female with red hair and freckles on her very pale face. She was wearing a sleeveless blouse and her bony arms were covered with tattoos. Both people were dripping with sweat.

A short, stocky white man with bushy gray hair and a face full of gray whiskers was sitting in a ragged canvas chair in the shade of a small umbrella watching their progress. He was sipping a can of diet cola and smoking a cigarette. Despite Almeida's appearance after twenty years, Whelan recognized him.

"I'm looking for Colonel Sanders. Can you help me?" Whelan said with a smile as he walked up to the man in the chair.

The man took a long, deep pull on his cigarette and slowly blew it out before casually turning to look at Whelan. His eyes were a washed-out shade of blue, as pale as Whelan's, but not as pale as Larsen's or Stensen's. He appeared to be much older than his chronological age would indicate. His skin was wrinkled like that of man in his late sixties. His coarse, wavy hair was almost solid gray. He wore it long and in no particular style. It looked as if it hadn't been washed in awhile. After studying Whelan for a few moments he said, "Well, look what the cat dragged in. You look fat and gay with those stupid curls."

"And you look like a homeless old fart," Whelan said.

Raphael Almeida snubbed out the cigarette on the top of the soda can, set it on the ground beside the chair and stood up. He was several inches shorter than Whelan and had developed a noticeable paunch since Whelan had last seen him. He actually was slightly younger than Whelan, but he looked several years older. Whelan knew Almeida had a tendency toward substance abuse, and wondered if that explained his premature aging or if it was something else, something programmed by gene expression changes or a medical condition such as progeria.

Almeida squinted at Whelan for a couple of seconds, then said, "I heard you were coming."

"Levell?"

"Yeah. Whaddya' want with me?"

The two young people had stopped working and were watching Whelan and Almeida. "What the hell are you staring at? I don't pay you to stand around. Get your asses back to work," Almeida yelled.

"It's hot out here, boss," the young black man said. He took his visor off and wiped his brow with a forearm.

"Yeah," the girl said. "It's time for a break." She pointed to her wrist, as if indicating a watch.

Almeida stared at them. His lips were pressed tightly together as he struggled to withhold an angry response. He jerked his thumb toward a large metal building that housed the dealership's service department. "Alright goddammit take fifteen, but not a fuckin' second more or it'll come out of your pay."

The two workers tossed the cleaning rags they'd been using onto the hood of the truck and strolled off toward the metal building. The girl had her flame colored hair pulled back in a frizzy ponytail. She lit a cigarette as she walked away.

"Damn kids," Almeida said. "Can't find any good help these days and the turnover is awful."

"Maybe it has something to do with your bedside manner."

"Yeah, yeah, yeah, you smartass college types have all the answers." Almeida paused to light another cigarette. "So why are you dressed like a fat fairy with a big nose and shaggy eyebrows? Halloween's a long way off."

"It seems we've been outed. The Feds are on to us...on to me anyway."

"That why Levell wants us back together?"

"That's part of it."

"There's more?"

"Yeah. There's a mission."

Almeida tugged at his whiskers for a few moments, then looked at Whelan. "So, Levell and General Ball-buster expect us to just drop everything when they snap their wrinkled old fingers and come running after all these years."

"Something like that."

"Well, they can shove it." Almeida waved his arms around. "Look at this. I got responsibilities. I'm a business owner. I can't just drop all I've worked years to acquire and run off on some half-ass mission."

Whelan fixed Almeida with a cold, hard stare. Otherwise, his face was impassive. "Looks to me like you're hanging on by the skin of your ass. You look like you've been living in a cardboard box. You smell like a billy goat. There's booze on your breath at ten o'clock in the morning, and you're probably still abusing every recreational drug you can get your nicotine-stained hands on, colonel."

"Why you sonofabitch. I oughta' kick the shit out of you!" Almeida brought his clenched fists up to chest height. "And stop calling me colonel. I hate that fuckin' name, and I don't eat fried chicken no more."

"Have drugs fucked up your memory, Rafe. Fighting me never worked out for you in the past; you never even landed a punch. It'll go even worse for you now. Look at you. Pot-bellied, boozy, old before your years. If I was Levell, I'd tell you to go fuck yourself."

Almeida's arms slowly dropped to his sides. His body sagged visibly and he stared at the ground in front of his feet. "Truth is things ain't gone so well for me in recent years."

"So it appears."

"I got married some years back, but my old lady run off with a guy used to be a friend of mine."

"You abuse her?"

"Only when she asked for it."

"You're still an asshole, Rafe."

"I got to drinking and doing shit more and more. Only work I know how to do is detail these damn cars. Anymore I don't feel good enough to do the detailing myself. Have to get these fuckin' druggy kids to do it, and if one lasts a week it's a fuckin' miracle."

"Abuse them, too?"

"Only when they need it."

"Like I said, Rafe, you're an asshole."

"I'm scared, Whelan. I feel like I'm running short on time. I need to score some money. Real money." Almeida's face brightened and he looked up. "Hey, what's Levell going to pay us for this work?"

"That's between you and Levell."

"Bastard better pay me same as he's paying you. I ain't settling for hind tit no more."

Whelan looked at Almeida with the same hard stare. "If he pays you what you're worth, you'll end up owing him money."

"Horseshit! I want whatever you have."

As he looked at Almeida, thoughts of Caitlin and their two sons flashed through Whelan's mind. "Rafe, you'll never have what I have."

Almeida stared at him. He didn't know what to say.

"My best advice to you is to be where Levell tells you to be, and when he tells you to be there."

"Yeah, and if I don't want to go?"

"Big mistake. Levell will send someone, maybe the Man With No Neck. He'll bring you back dead or alive." Whelan paused, then said, "Or maybe he'll send Stensen. In that case the alive option is off the table."

There was genuine fear in Almeida's eyes. "Stensen? That crazy bastard still alive?"

"Very. I was with him yesterday."

"He's nuts, a butcher, gets off killin' people."

Whelan nodded. "Yep. Make it a point to be where you're told to be…and on time."

Almeida shook his head. "I ain't got any money, man. How'm I supposed to go anywhere?"

"Levell's people, the Team, will be in touch. They'll provide whatever you need."

33 FAIRVIEW BEACH, VIRGINIA

Almost due south of Washington, D.C. and less than two hours by motor vehicle is a small town on the banks of the Potomac River in the Tidewater country of King George County. It's known as Fairview Beach. The townspeople are predominantly young, working-class, Southern Baptist and Republican. The town is somewhat isolated and small. Only a few hundred people live within the town limits. The countryside around the town is heavily wooded in many areas and sparsely settled. A few narrow, paved two-lane roads connect the town to Highway 218, also known as Caledon Road.

There are a few dirt lanes that lead back into the woods from the few collector roads. At the end of one of them, sitting in the middle of a eighty-acre tract and isolated by dense woods from its few neighbors in the area, is a nine thousand square foot, two-story building with the appearance of a hunting lodge. It's exterior is made of large logs with a brick chimney at either end of the lodge. It's clearly posted as private property and would-be trespassers are cautioned not to enter in five different languages. An ultra sophisticated electronic and video system provides twenty-four hour surveillance of the entire tract. Nothing moves in the eighty acres that isn't instantly detected. A staff of very professional, highly trained security people responds immediately.

While the exterior of the lodge was designed and built to convey a rustic, masculine simplicity, the interior is something else entirely. Immediately behind the exterior façade, all walls, ceilings, and floors are lined with a material that resists all efforts to penetrate with infrared, ultrasound, and all other surveillance devices. Communications facilities are designed, installed and maintained by the best minds in the CIA, NSA, and private sector. They are designed to remain superior to anything available to the planet's top security agencies.

144

The interior is comfortably decorated and furnished in homage to the style of a luxurious western ranch. The lodge has eleven separate bedrooms and bathrooms, a large dinning hall, ultra modern kitchen, library, gymnasium, and boardroom. A separate facility houses staff, shelters motor vehicles, and provides a few spare bedrooms and bathrooms for occasions when the main lodge is fully occupied. The two facilities are connected by a tunnel.

The library has stone floors overlain with throw rugs that reflect Southwestern style and colors. The light switch on the wall beside the door that gives entry to the library serves two purposes. It does turn on the lights recessed in the lower part of the tray ceiling, providing accent for the fireplace and bookcases. If flipped ten or more times in rapid succession the switch activates an electrical motor. The motor causes a three-foot by three-foot stone plate in the floor to recess and pull back under the adjoining flooring. This reveals a set of steps leading down into a chamber under the library. There is a long, well polished, mahogany table and several comfortable chairs in the room. Bottles of fine wine are stacked in specially crafted shelving that keeps each bottle in a prone position so its contents can work on the cork. The walls, floor, and ceiling of the chamber are lined with lead and other materials that defy any attempts to probe the activities that occur there.

The lodge is owned by a company that's owned by another company that's owned by yet another entity and so on through a mind-boggling chain of twists and convolutions that are impossible to decipher. The ultimate owners, if the chain could be unraveled, are three billionaire brothers of a decidedly hard-line libertarian bent. Alfred, Hermann, and Tomas Mueller are part of the Team, which also includes certain top military brass and senior members of the security agencies that helped design the facility and keep it on the cutting edge technologically.

While Whelan was in San Diego recruiting Almeida, Clifford Levell rode from his home in the Georgetown suburb of Washington, D.C. to the lodge in Fairview Beach. Along the way, he had his personal attendant and driver, Rhee Kang-Dae, stop near Quantico to pick up General McCoy. The men were aware that government satellite surveillance could, and undoubtedly would, track their movements. But, once they entered the lodge, all such efforts would be futile.

There were no legitimate grounds on which government agents could arrest them. They were members of the private club that operated the lodge. In the unlikely event government agents picked them up for questioning, Levell, McCoy and the other members of the Team knew that the Mueller brothers would have the best civil liberties attorneys on the matter in minutes. In the minds of most members of the Team, such lawyers were liberals, socialists and part of what was wrong in America to be sure, but they were the best money could buy if you needed them.

After cocktails and a magnificent dinner of roasted elk loin in an elderberry sauce with pureed sweet potatoes, Levell, McCoy and others descended into the chamber beneath the library. Two husky staffers assisted McCoy down the steps and to his seat. Although he was the titular head of the Team, Levell made it a point to sit at a chair in the middle of the table rather than at either end. He knew that the positions of greatest power were at the ends of the table. The seats next to them were next in line in the power game. The weakest seats were the ones in the middle.

Such was Levell's confidence and the power of his personality that he purposely chose the weakest position. Not surprisingly, McCoy always sat at one end of the table. Harriman Floyd of the NSA and Chester Sturges of the CIA always tried to get the seat at the other end of the table. To stifle their squabbling, whichever one of the Mueller brothers was in attendance took that seat. Tonight it was Tomas, the youngest at seventy-eight. Most of those in attendance tonight were men. The lone female this evening was the chief executive of one of the largest technology company's on the planet. The others were the secretary of one of the nation's military departments, and a senior senator from a western state who was ranking minority party member of the senate's select committee on intelligence.

Levell looked calmly around the room, making eye contact with each of those present. The room became quiet and he called the meeting to order. "Friends and fellow patriots, it's been some weeks since our last gathering and a lot has happened."

"And there's a hell of a lot of work to be done," the NSA's Floyd said in an effort to seem more important and powerful than he actually was.

Levell nodded and silently held Floyd's gaze until the other man looked away. It was a message from Levell that interruptions wouldn't be tolerated. "I believe all of you are aware of the incident that occurred in a Georgetown residential neighborhood a few mornings ago. A former Agency employee named Harold Case was shot and killed at an intersection. He had three associates with him, all formidable bodyguards. Two of them were likewise killed. The third man had his brains permanently scrambled. He will be in a nursing facility for his remaining days."

The others around the table nodded. They had heard the news. McCoy smiled, as he knew where Levell was going.

"They were all victims of a single individual, who probably didn't break a sweat doing it." Levell said, smiling at the thought of Brendan Whelan destroying the three large Ukrainian thugs.

"How do you know this?" the Senator said. "Do you know the individual's identity?"

"Know him? Hell, Buster and I trained him." He motioned toward McCoy at the end of the table.

The CEO from the private sector, Maureen Delaney, had a puzzled look. It was shared by the others at the table. "I don't understand," she said.

Levell nodded his head up and down. "There's no reason why any of you would know anything about him. He was part of the most elite special ops unit this world has ever seen. Buster…General McCoy and I assembled the group based on their extraordinary genetic make up. In a way, they're freaks. Smart, fast, strong, deadly freaks."

"But, God, you gotta love 'em," McCoy said.

"What happened to them? Where are they today?" Tomas Mueller said.

"Some were casualties of missions. The survivors were deemed to be potentially an embarrassment by some pantywaist in the White House. That's all part of this inexorable march to the left that's afflicted our country for the past several decades." Levell shook his head in disgust. "A secret order was issued calling for their termination with extreme prejudice. They were able to escape, but appeared to have been killed when their plane crashed in the Caribbean."

"Appeared to have been killed?" said Maureen Delaney.

"The crash was staged. The General and I arranged it. We set the boys up with new identities, new lives. They've been gone to ground for almost twenty years."

"How does that concern us, our plans?" Floyd said. He seemed exasperated that Levell was wasting the group's time with what he deemed to be superfluous information.

Levell gazed at the NSA man for a moment, then said, "You've no idea what assets these boys are. Due to circumstances beyond our control, it appears they've been outed. The FBI is seeking one of them and sooner or later will figure out that the others also are alive."

McCoy said, "What Cliff is suggesting is that these men…the unit was known as the Sleeping Dogs, are the final and most important piece of the pie. They are the scalpel for excising the Marxist tumor that is destroying the traditional American way of life. It's what we've been missing."

"Are we talking about…ah… domestic political assassinations here?" the Senator said.

Without hesitation, Levell said, "This is nothing new, Senator. It's been on the table since the beginning. Frankly, it's always been understood, tacitly anyway, that America's enemies have gained too strong a grip on the country to break it at the ballot box or through more reasonable means. Our counterattack must be swift, certain, and permanent."

All eyes were on the Senator, who tugged nervously at his collar. "Well, yes," he said, "I know this was always an option, but it seems so extreme." He looked around the room. "If we take out theirs, they might take out ours."

"You mean take you out." McCoy said.

"Yes…I am a public figure, a United States Senator, and a recognized spokesperson for conservative ideals."

"If you truly are committed to those ideals, Senator, you would value them above your own well-being," the CIA's Sturgis said. "Every member of the Team, those of us here tonight, and the many hundreds of others who are not, are risking everything we have in this endeavor. If we are discovered, in all likelihood we will be executed for treasonous activities. As it is, it's a challenge each and every day to keep our activities and identities off the radar screen. And we are able to do that only because the positions we hold provide us with the ability to operate in the most sensitive areas and filter and amend, as appropriate, information that otherwise might register on someone's radar screen."

"Treason?" said Floyd. "How can you suggest that our actions might constitute treason? We're not trying to overthrow the government of the United States. We're trying to restore it."

Sturgis fixed his NSA counterpart with a hard stare and said, "Remember *who* the government is. Our actions would be considered treasonous to *them*."

Levell looked steadily at the Senator. "Is there anyone at this table who has reservations about our mission, about restoring the capitalism-based democratic republic that provided to everyone the opportunities for achieving the American Dream? Opportunities, that is, for those willing to work for them. If anyone here has such reservations, now is the time to speak up."

The room was silent for several moments as the people in the room looked at each other as if waiting for someone else to speak first. After awhile, Maureen Delaney spoke up. "I don't have any reservations whatsoever. I am living the American Dream that Cliff mentioned."

Levell blushed slightly. Although he had never said anything to her, he was smitten by Maureen's basic attractiveness and levelheaded business manner.

"I don't know whether any of you knows this, but when I was little, we lived in a trailer. Not a mobile home, an honest-to-God trailer. We were very poor. I applied myself in school and with a scholarship and part time jobs I became the first in my family to earn a college degree. I also earned a Master's degree.

"After college, I worked harder than anyone else…partly because of the constraints of the glass ceiling and partly because of a fear of returning to poverty. Today, as you do know, I'm President and CEO of one of the largest and most financially successful electronics and technology companies in the world.

"I've worked hard, but I've also been fortunate; fortunate to have been born in this great nation at a time when hard work, risk-taking, and a little luck could take you beyond your wildest dreams. I want succeeding generations of Americans, native born and immigrants, to have those same opportunities. It's part of what makes this nation the greatest on earth."

She smiled at Levell as she finished. He reddened a few shades darker.

Tomas Mueller spoke. "Very inspirational, Maureen. Your story is a classic example of how an individual can change their social and economic status in America. It truly is a Land of Opportunity...or was. Today, I'm afraid the concept of individual opportunity is becoming a thing of the past. Instead of a government by the people, for the people, it has been replaced with statist ideology. The governing elite believes, or wants us to believe, that the individual is too weak and too stupid to make good decisions; thus, the state must make them for us. And in this Orwellian society who prospers? That same governing elite, just as is true in every socialist society that's ever existed."

He paused and took a sip of tea from a small cup in front of him. "My grandfather immigrated to this country as a young man more than a century ago. He arrived alone, penniless, and spoke no English. By the time he passed away, he was a very wealthy man who had vertically expanded his original farming operations into packaging, distribution and wholesaling. My father grew the business further by expanding horizontally to acquire competing interests and their markets at every step in the process.

"My brothers and I have moved onto the global stage and now have significant interests in mining, manufacturing, shipping, and a host of other areas. In the process of doing this, we have generated enormous wealth, yes. But we also have created many thousands of jobs, resuscitated failing companies to preserve more jobs, and generated substantial revenues for the coffers of local state and federal governments."

"And," Levell said, "You have generously given many hundreds of millions of dollars to charitable, educational, civic and social organizations that have helped thousands upon thousands of people."

"You're very kind, Cliff," Mueller said. "My point, of course, is that this country has provided generations of people with opportunities that exist nowhere else in the world. If you are ambitious, industrious, determined, if you persevere and aren't a quitter, there is no limit to what an individual can achieve on America. All that's required is ambition and a level playing field.

"At least that's how it was. Now, I fear, there is a left wing, socialist, perhaps even Marxist authority emerging in this country that intends to destroy the concept of the individual and reduce us to a mindless, faceless mass who will be dictated to by an elite ruling class that will make all decisions for us. Maureen, and gentlemen, if this happens in American, we may be on the verge of entering the second coming of the Dark Ages, a thousand years of human misery and suffering." He paused, and looking at Levell, said, "I pray these Sleeping Dogs of yours can help us."

34 NEW ORLEANS, LOUISIANA

Whelan took a late afternoon flight from San Diego to New Orleans connecting through Dallas. Although the flight was little more than five hours in duration, because of time zones it was after eleven o'clock in the evening when he arrived at Louis Armstrong New Orleans International Airport. By the time he picked up his rental car and checked into the Doubletree Hotel near the airport, it was past midnight.

Even with the six-hour difference in time zones, it was still too early to call Caitlin. But it wasn't too late to call Levell. The man had always seemed to survive without sleep. Whelan had dialed the appropriate number from a pay phone in front of a convenience store between the airport and the hotel, let it ring three times and hung up. He was bothered by the thought that if the Bureau or another government agency was tapping the phone, it wouldn't take a lot of brain cells to figure out the incoming call had been placed near the airport.

The agency would alert local authorities and, if they thought he was involved, they would circulate his likeness all over the area. Fortunately, he didn't have to check in with the car rental office. The vehicle was waiting for him, unlocked with key in the ignition. But the desk clerk at the hotel was a different story. Still, with his fat clothes, facial prosthetics and funky hairstyle, he didn't at all resemble the person Mitch Christie had sat next to on the Atlanta to San Francisco flight.

His cell phone rang as he was sliding back behind the wheel of his rented navy blue Chevrolet Impala in front of the convenience store. He asked Levell to call him back in thirty minutes. That gave him a chance to check into the hotel and settle into the privacy of his room. The former Marine that he was, Levell called exactly thirty minutes later.

"What's your situation?" the older man said.

"Tired, hungry, need a good workout."

"Stensen in the fold?"

"Yeah, I think so."

Levell detected something in Whelan's voice. "Was there a problem?"

"Sort of."

"I know he's unbalanced. What was it this time?"

"He tried to set up a brawl between me and a dozen or so very stout Hawaiian men."

"So what did you do?"

"I knocked him on his ass. That seemed to defuse things."

Levell chuckled at the image. "How did you leave it with him?"

"Says he'll be there."

"You think he will?"

Whelan paused. "Like you said, he's crazy. Hard to say what he'll do, but I think he wants some new action. Paradise is beginning to bore him."

Levell changed the subject. "I understand you flew out of Hilo and not back out of Maui."

"Yeah, I was in involved in a small dust-up at a fitness center in Kahului. Figured it was a good idea not to go back there."

"Was there a woman involved?"

"Sure. Wars are fought for economic reasons. Fights are always about women."

"No shit," Levell said. "How'd you get to the Big Island?"

"When I dropped Nick on his ass, I gained a bunch of new admirers. One of them took me over in his boat."

"What about the Colonel in San Diego?"

"Says he doesn't like being called Colonel anymore and no longer eats fried chicken either."

Levell whistled. "Well there's a news bulletin," he said. "Is he on board?"

"I'm not sure. He's become an obnoxious little bastard."

"More so than before?"

"Yeah. And he looks like hell. Booze, drugs, the whole nine yards. He's fat and appears to have aged rather badly."

"Did you have a problem with him?"

"A couple of times I thought seriously about dropping him on his ass."

This time Levell actually laughed. "What is with the Irish? You seem to like fighting better than drinking or screwing."

"Not entirely true," Whelan said dryly. "We like to sing and dance too."

"Tomorrow you're going to speak with Kirkland?"

"Yeah."

"After your reunions with Stensen and Almeida, I think you'll enjoy your visit with Marc."

Something in the way Levell said that roused Whelan's curiosity. "Why's that?"

"You'll see." Levell changed the subject again. "After that your last stop is in Nashville."

"Yeah, Thomas is the last one."

"Did I tell you he has a Ph.D. in philosophy?"

"No, but it doesn't surprise me. He always was a very deep thinker."

"He's a tenured professor."

This time it was Whelan who chuckled. "Glad I don't have any daughters going to school there." This made him think briefly about Caitlin and the two boys at home in Ireland. The tight feeling in his chest returned.

Levell seemed to read his mind, a scary talent that he had always had. "Speaking of family, there's something you should know."

There was a sudden icy spot in the middle of Whelan's chest. "What is it?"

"It's nothing for you to be concerned about, but one of our people in the Bureau advised us that they're using assets from the Bureau's legat in London to look for leads in Ireland."

"And why am I not to be concerned?" Whelan said. There was an edge to his voice. "They have a sketch of sorts of me and, from records that weren't destroyed as they should have been, some knowledge of my origins in Ireland."

"We know that, and we've got people closely following the situation. I personally guarantee your family's safety, Brendan."

"Yeah, Cliff, and you personally guaranteed that the Agency's records would be destroyed."

"Dammit! I thought they had been destroyed until Case started nosing around."

"If there's any hint that my family's in danger, I'm gone, Cliff. Do you understand that?"

"Yes," Levell said.

Whelan hung up and paced around his small room. It was very late and he was weary and jet-lagged, but he also was energized by the anger in knowing that his family might now be involved. He reflected on the irony of his situation. For almost twenty years he had been able to lead a somewhat normal life despite having to cast one eye over his shoulder from time to time. Then, an incompetent Agency minion, an egotistical self-promoting senator, and a greedy ex-Agency operative had started events in motion that tore the cover off his comfortable existence. Now, he felt a strong temptation to withdraw from this mission that had been thrust on him without invitation and return immediately to Ireland. On some level, however, he wondered if that was what the Bureau expected him to do. Wouldn't they be watching the airports in Dublin, Shannon, and even Belfast?

Whelan knew that no one could protect his loved ones quite like he could, although he knew that Caitlin's brother, Paddy, and her father were the next best thing. He also knew there was nothing he could do at the moment, and that he needed to sleep in order to be at his physical and mental best. He showered and sat quietly using a meditative technique for twenty minutes. When he was finished, he was calm and relaxed. In a few more minutes he was asleep, but troubled by dreams that he was being pursued by parties unseen through a dense and very dark forest. The trees seemed to be animated, reaching out at him, clawing and clubbing him with their branches, slowing him down as the pursuers drew ever closer.

35 NEW ORLEANS, LOUISIANA

When he awoke the next morning, Whelan felt stale and listless. He knew the cure was a hard workout. The fitness facility in the hotel was far too inferior for what he needed. He drove a few miles down Veteran's Parkway to a sprawling modern facility that occupied two floors and offered the equipment he sought. It even had an outdoor track that circled the roof above the second floor. He spent two hours on the weights and machines; being very careful not to draw attention to himself by the amount of weights he hefted. He topped the workout off with another thirty minutes on the track doing sprint work. In spite of the cool January temperature, sweat was running off of him in small, steady rivulets when he was finished.

He showered and dressed, then stopped for a late breakfast at a pancake house on Veteran's Boulevard near the fitness center. Afterwards, he checked out of the hotel, but used a payphone in the lobby to call Levell again. He was walking across the parking lot to his car when the callback came.

"What's your current status?" Levell said.

"Just checked out. I think it would be wise to change IDs again and pick up a new ride."

"Jesus Christ. You go through IDs like a dose of salts."

"What?"

"Never mind, it's an old metaphor."

"I guess I'm not that old."

"Fuck you, smart ass. Look, you have to go through Houma. I have a contact there. An ex-Marine who Buster and I trust. He runs a martial arts studio. His wife is a beautician. I'll arrange for her to alter your appearance." Levell gave Whelan the address and directions.

"The car?" Whelan said.

"It'll be waiting for you when you get there. Call me after you speak with Kirkland." Levell hung up.

He navigated the rental car along Route 61 and then onto the on ramp for I-310. Checking his watch, he was mildly surprised it was almost one o'clock in the afternoon. That meant that it was going on seven p.m. in Ireland. He picked up his cell phone and dialed Caitlin's number.

His older son picked it up on the third ring. "Hello, the Fianna Bed and Breakfast. Sean speaking." He spoke with a distinctive Gaelic accent, which Whelan knew his boys affected whenever they spoke to guests at the B and B or around Caitlin's family. Other times, the boys spoke American accented English like their father

Caitlin had chosen the name, the Fianna House. In Celtic mythology, the Fianna were a caste of elite warriors who protected the high king of Ireland. They were thought to be almost godlike in their martial prowess. Knowing of her husband's genetic gifts and special operations background, Caitlin thought the name was the most appropriate one. In her mind, her husband was a contemporary version of Fianna warrior. It was something of an insider's joke with her and Whelan. Tourists generally thought Fianna was a lady's name and frequently asked if she was about. The boys, Sean and Declan, had grown tired of trying to explain its meaning and, when asked, would simply say, "She's on holiday".

A warm glow spread through Whelan's chest when he heard Sean's voice. "Hi, son. It's good to hear your voice."

"Dad! Where are you? Are you coming home?" There was genuine excitement in his tone.

Whelan felt a mixture of homesickness and guilt when he answered. "No, Sean, not yet. There still are some business details that need to be wrapped up."

"Oh." There was a clear air of disappointment in Sean's voice. "Then when *will* you be coming home?"

"As soon as I can, son. But I'm not sure just when that will be." He shifted the subject. "How are you and your brother doing in school?"

"Well, I guess you heard about the fight."

"Yeah."

"Seamus O'Donnell picked a fight with me and I finished it."

"I've always asked you and Declan not to start fights, but if someone else does, it's good to be the one who finishes it."

"Seamus won't be picking another one with me."

Whelan smiled at the thought of Sean taking down the much larger O'Donnell boy. He knew the O'Donnell family, and knew that Seamus was something of a bully. His father, Aidan O'Donnell, was a mean drunk who sometimes started problems in the local pubs, especially with tourists. Now that the main industry of the town of Dingle had changed from commercial fishing to tourism, Aiden O'Donnell's behavior was viewed as something of a threat to the economy.

Whelan's brother-in-law, Padraig, Sergeant in charge of the sub-district, kept a tight lid on O'Donnell's antics. When Padraig was not available, Whelan took responsibility for O'Donnell and any other altercations in the town. O'Donnell in particular was such a belligerent pain in the ass, that Whelan and Padraig each enjoyed the opportunity to rough him up.

No matter how often it happened, Aiden O'Donnell never seemed to understand that he was never going to best either man. He even came at Whelan with a cricket bat on one occasion. The thirty-eight inch bats typically are made out of solid willow and weigh about three pounds. Used as a cudgel, it can be lethal. Whelan was so enraged by the attack that he beat O'Donnell badly enough that he spent two weeks in the hospital in Tralee, the nearest town of any size. To send a message to any other would-be assailants, and with the pub-goers looking on, Whelan snapped the bat over his knee, a feat thought to be humanly impossible.

"I'm sure the lad has learned a valuable lesson and won't be a problem in the future," Whelan said to Sean. "But keep your eyes open. You don't want him creeping up behind you and splitting your handsome skull."

"Don't worry, Dad. Declan and I can handle ourselves."

"I know you can. That's one of the reasons I can be out of town and not worry too much about the safety of you boys and your mother." He heard Caitlin in the background asking Sean who was on the phone.

Sean handed the phone over to her. "Bren, are you all right?" she said. There was concern in her voice.

"I'm fine, Kate," he said. "I'm just homesick for you and the boys." They spoke for several minutes. Whelan told her the Bureau was sending people through Ireland armed with a sketch of him. He didn't want her or the boys to be shocked if they heard it from someone who had been approached. With a population of about four and a half million people in Ireland, the Bureau would simplify the task by limiting the inquiry to law enforcement agencies. He asked Caitlin to let Padraig and her father, the Superintendent of the District Police Force, know about the Bureau's actions.

"It's probably going to be several more weeks before I can come home, but if I can do anything to get there sooner, you know I will."

"Just promise me you'll do nothing foolish, Bren."

"You know you can count on that, Kate. And, in a short while, I'll be in the company of a group of old friends."

"Old friends?" she said. "Then they're people I've never met."

"True, but not to worry. In some ways, they're very much like me."

She laughed and said, "God help us all."

36 NEW YORK CITY

Dimitri Nikitin and Kirill Federov rode in silence in the private elevator that was whisking them soundlessly to the top of the tallest residential structure in Manhattan. Nikitin, First Deputy Counselor to the Minister-Counselor for Trade at the Russian Embassy in Washington had never ridden in such an elevator. Undoubtedly, he thought, the elevator cost more than his humble dwelling in Moscow. He was uncomfortable in the silence, but had grown used to it. His companion in the elevator, Kirill Federov, rarely spoke to him. Federov considered Nikitin unworthy of conversation. Perhaps he was correct, Nikitin mused. After all, while he was merely a career bureaucrat, Federov was a mere three steps away from the Russian Federation's president.

Nikitin's role tonight, as was usually the case, was to provide cover for Federov's meeting with Laski. It was designed to appear as though he, Nikitin, and Laski were meeting to discuss some international trade situation, and that Federov was merely accompanying him as his aide. In reality, the discussion would take place between Federov and Laski and had nothing to do with commerce.

Without ever having seemed to move, the elevator had swiftly ascended almost nine hundred vertical feet above Fifth Avenue in New York's Upper East Side. The door opened and the two men stepped out into an extraordinarily large foyer, Federov first, as always. They were met by a liveried servant who welcomed them to Chaim Laski's primary residence in the city. Nikitin had been here previously and knew something about the opulent Neo-Georgian penthouse that occupied the top three floors of the glass-skinned building. It contained almost fourteen hundred square meters, or more than fifteen thousand square feet, of living space, and included ten bedrooms, a large library, indoor/outdoor pool, sauna, two bars, private roof

159

garden, movie theater, and a full gym. Nikitin knew the gym got a lot of use. Not by Laski, of course; he was in his late seventies. But he employed a number of husky, younger men for security purposes.

As they followed the servant across the vast entry foyer highlighted by a huge chandelier with thousands of cut glass droplets, Nikitin marveled at the simple, yet elegant, Neo-Georgian motif of the place. The furniture was of dark woods. Some of the fancier pieces displayed ivory marquetry. The Toile de Jouy style of design was repeated in the upholstery of several winged armchairs and sofas. It all seemed somewhat dainty and refined in style; many of the pieces had ball and claw feet. Nikitin was sure that the furniture was originally designed by Chippendale, Sheraton, and Hepplewhite. He could easily appreciate the strong influence on the style of classical Greek and Roman, Rococo, Gothic Revival, and French Aristocratic motifs.

They were led down a wide hallway. The high walls of the hallway and other rooms that opened off of it were divided into three sections: a paneled or decorated lower part or dado defined by a horizontal stained oak molding; a middle section that was wallpapered in some parts, hung with fabric panels in others, or painted rich but muted golds, yellows, reds, or deep blues; and an upper area with picture rails hung with expensive looking artwork and elaborately carved friezes beneath the cornice molding with its egg and dart pattern. Even the ceilings were painted in these colors. At various points along the hallway there also were classical style busts, statues and silhouette pictures. Although it was not to his personal and somewhat proletarian tastes, Nikitin conceded that a fortune had been invested in the design and furnishing of the place.

Like a good Marxist, Dimitri Nikitin had been dutifully raised to despise Western capitalism as the scourge of civilization. Yet, as he looked around, he could not avoid feelings of envy and a wistful desire to experience even a fraction of the wealth and opulence by which he was surrounded at the moment. How is it, he wondered, that it was Chaim Laski who was chosen for this role and not him. Instead, Laski enjoyed the life of a multibillionaire, while he was relegated to the ignominy of a mid-level bureaucrat whose career consisted of little more than shuffling papers and following orders.

The servant led the two Russians across the entry foyer and down a hallway. Along the way, Nikitin marveled at the flawlessly waxed natural wood flooring and the impossibly expensive rugs in neo-classical or Turkish designs. He glanced into other rooms as they passed by. Each seemed to have fine, large mirrors with elaborate gilded frames and its own fireplace of what appeared to be white marble. The rooms along the exterior walls of the building were floor to ceiling glass and draped with light colored fabrics printed with scenic designs in the Toile de Jouy fashion.

Eventually the hallway opened into another large area. In the middle, a marble and wrought iron staircase spiraled up three stories in a glass-topped atrium. Nikitin couldn't resist the urge to gaze up through the glass at the night sky above. He regretted the action almost instantly and could feel Federov's contempt for him for behaving like a tourist. While he despised Federov, the man also frightened him. Federov was a tall man, almost two meters in height – Americans would say he was about six feet three inches tall. He had broad shoulders and the trim physique of a good athlete. Nikitin knew that Federov, like Putin, was an expert *judo-ka*, and that he also was an outstanding runner and tennis player, as well as a former Olympic marksman. He also had heard the rumors circulating in the embassy that Federov was a former member of the *Spetsnaz GRU*, Russia's top Special Forces group. Nikitin knew it was the best-trained unit in the Armed Forces of the Russian Federation. If the rumors were true, and he believed they were, Federov indeed was a man to be feared.

They were led across the room and around the staircase to another elevator on the far side of the room. This second elevator serviced the three floors of the penthouse as well as the garden and pool area on the roof. The servant pressed a button and the door slid open, then he stepped aside. Federov didn't hesitate to brush past Nikitin in entering the cabin. When the other Russian had dutifully followed Federov in, the servant pressed the top button on the panel. "Mr. Laski is awaiting you by the pool, gentlemen," he said in a clipped British accent.

The two Russians rode in silence. Nikitin actually was grateful not to have to try to make small talk with the brooding Federov. Although he knew why they were meeting with Laski, he could think of nothing to say to the SVR operative. He was relieved when the door opened and they exited the elevator onto the rooftop garden area. A very large man, larger than Federov, was waiting for them. He wasn't wearing servant's livery, but instead wore an ill-fitting wool suit of a badly dated style still common in Eastern European countries. The large man raised an arm and pointed down a walkway that wove through a lush green area. It was glass enclosed and the verdant plant life seemed to thrive in the warm, humid atmosphere. "He is waiting there," the man said.

The two men followed the path and came upon the pool area. Beyond it Central Park spread out below. The pool was both indoors and outdoors with a glass wall separating the two sections. The outdoors area was enclosed in a glass dome. There also were bar areas on both sides of the glass partition that separated the two pool areas. While the outdoor pool area was open, the bar was partially sheltered by a trellis affair covered with leafy vines. A powerful looking man was sitting on a stool in the outdoor bar area sipping a drink of some kind. He wore light gray slacks with double pleats, a dark blue polo shirt with thin red horizontal stripes, and well-shined cordovan tassel loafers. The man's neck and shoulders were thickly muscled and his arms bulged against the fabric of his shirtsleeves. He regarded the two Russians for a brief moment, then turned away almost contemptuously. Federov bristled at the seeming affrontery, but Nikitin simply shrugged. What do I care, he thought; this man is just another member of Laski's hired muscle.

Near the pool was a custom-built granite hot tub. Laski, naked, sat on the edge. A naked young woman was on her knees with her head between his wrinkled, saggy legs performing oral sex on the elderly man. Laski saw the two Russians and waved them over. He tapped the young woman on top of her head and she looked up. He motioned for her to leave. Seemingly relieved at the opportunity, she wasted no time in doing so. She dove into the pool, swam under the glass partition and disappeared into the interior part of the house.

Federov appeared to be oblivious, but Nikitin was horrified at the scene. It is an outrage, he thought, that this flabby, wrinkled old man engages in such an act with a very attractive and very young woman. He looked at Laski, who had just stood up. His penis is all shriveled up, he thought. Why, then, does the man do these things? Because he likes to humiliate the woman? Because he can afford to do it? Because he's a sick old bastard? All of the above? It was a mighty struggle on Nikitin's part not to show anger or revulsion. He never had cared for Laski. Now, he added loathing to dislike.

Laski had wrapped himself in a thick Turkish towel. He walked over to a table near the bar and sat, motioning to the two Russians to do likewise. When they all were seated, Laski pointed to the man who was sitting at the bar, and in Russian said, "That is Maksym. He is in charge of my security matters." He smiled darkly and added, "He is a most unusual man."

"How so?" Federov said.

Still smiling, Laski said, "Let us pray you never have to find out, my dear comrade."

Federov shrugged and lit a cigarette, the first of many, but Nikitin turned to look at Maksym. The man was sitting motionless on the bar stool staring at the two Russians. It was a look of unmistakable arrogance. Nikitin shivered in the warm night air. There was something deeply malignant and frightening about the man. He hurriedly lit a cigarette of his own.

"So," Federov said, "we are having this meeting so you can report on the progress you are making in achieving our next set of goals. What do you have?"

Laski picked up a pair of glasses off the tabletop and put them on. He looked at Federov intently. "We are progressing as planned, everything is on schedule."

"Tell me again about this grand scheme of yours," Federov said.

"Of course." Laski smiled a benign smile that effectively hid his frustration at having to go over the plan with Federov one more time. "Our adversaries on the *Team*, as zhey call it," he scoffed at the word, "especially Mr. Levell, have done us an extraordinary favor. By reactivating these so-called Sleeping Dogs for the purpose of achieving political machinations, they provide us with the perfect cover for our own activities. Senator Morris already has revealed the existence of the unit. Now, we will make it appear that they are crazed right-wing anarchists and terrorists on a massive killing spree at the direction of the military and intelligence communities. Moderate and independent voters will swarm to our candidates seeking protective action. With the White House and a super majority in both houses of Congress, we will complete the dismantling of traditional American society."

He paused, then said, "There is, however, a small, unanticipated problem."

Federov snorted derisively. "Another unanticipated problem? You seem to have a talent for attracting such things. First, the killing of Harold Case with his information ending up in the hands of Levell and the other running dogs of capitalism. Next, the FBI is almost able to put together the dots..."

"I believe you mean connect the dots, Kirill," Laski said with a patronizing smile. "And I was able to derail the FBI's efforts, was I not?"

"Fuck the dots! And do not address me as Kirill. I am Colonel Federov." He glared at the older man. "Following that, you engaged in some foolishness in the UK that resulted in two of our operatives, who were posing as agents of the FBI, disappearing. Now what is it? "

Laski made a small dismissive motion with his right hand. "It is a small matter, and I already have plans underway to remedy it. By now, I would hope you would be well enough aware of my acumen in business and elsewhere that you would have confidence in my ability to deal with problems."

Federov snorted in contempt. "Your acumen! Do not make me sick, you old fool. You give yourself undeserved credit. Your wealth was created for you by Mother Russia, and it was done for one purpose. World socialism under Russian leadership. It is not for use in having sex with young women," he said in reference to the earlier scene in the hot tub.

Laski sat back in his chair, his face reddened slightly. "Ah, that. Surely you would forgive an old man a vice or two."

"You should be careful, comrade, how you spend the funds that are provided to you. You may appear to the world to be an investment genius, a titan of international finance. But, in reality, you are nothing more than a money distributor. We provide you with the means and the opportunities to acquire wealth, and we direct you where to send it."

He pointed his finger at Laski and said, "It has taken us decades to co-opt critical American institutions such as labor unions, education, news media and others. We are close, very close to achieving our goal of the destruction of American capitalism that has poisoned so much of the world.

It is not your job to indulge your vices and," he opened his arms wide and looked around, "live like the fucking Czars."

Federov paused for a moment then said, "What is this new problem you have 'unexpectedly' encountered?" He pronounced the word with derision.

"As I said previously, my dear Colonel, it is a minor thing and I already have put into motion the means for the solution. We shall be joined shortly by our good friend and colleague Senator Howard Morris and his strategist, Mr. Jenkins. It is Mr. Jenkins who is the actual pawn in my scheme, so we must take care to set him up properly."

"What is so special about this man Jenkins? He is a black man, is he not?" Dimitri Nikitin said. Federov and Laski ignored him, as was their usual habit. He slid lower into his chair and lit another cigarette.

"Minor or not," Federov said impatiently, "what is the nature of this problem?"

Laski smiled benignly and said, "There are two aspects. Our adversaries, Mr. Levell in particular, are somewhat more astute than we originally credited them. Left unchecked, it is possible they could interfere significantly with the success of the major event we have so carefully planned."

"And the second aspect?" Federov said.

"The FBI's Supervisory Special Agent of the Harold Case matter, a man named Christie, continues to be an annoyance."

"How do we know this?"

"We know this, dear Colonel, because we have our own source within the Federal Bureau of Investigation." Laski's smile conveyed a certain smugness.

"I distinctly remember you telling me that you had arranged to have this man Christie put on a short leash. Is that not so?" said Federov.

Nodding, Laski said, "Yes, the orders came directly from the President through the Department of Justice. This man, Christie, however, is like a bulldog. He has quieted his investigative efforts, but he will not give it up."

"I do not understand, comrade Laski. Is the president not one of our people, who we arranged to have elected? And is the attorney general not also one of our people who we directed the President to appoint?"

Laski turned his hands palms up and shrugged. "Yes, this is so. But you are well aware that the man we arranged to have elected as president is a buffoon. He is so pitiful as a leader that he has alienated the great majority of the American electorate. We have had to take steps to ensure that he will not run for reelection. You are aware of those steps."

Federov and Nikitin nodded in unison.

"We now will champion Senator Morris, once the current president has been removed from the picture."

"And the attorney general? He runs the Department of Justice, of which the FBI is a part. Is he not able to muzzle this FBI agent?"

Laski sighed and said, "He is like a clone of the president. Infatuated with the sound of his own voice. He is ineffective and incompetent. He will be replaced immediately following the next election…assuming we are able to co-opt another election. That remains to be seen, given that we have lost much of the Jewish vote over the incumbent's handling of the Israeli situation. His incompetence regarding jobs and the economy has rebuffed the youth and the independents."

Federov waived his hand in dismissal. "Morris is a Jew. That will keep their votes in our pocket. Also, we still have our allies in labor, the media, education and the Negroes. And let us not forget the sympathy vote that will follow the misfortune that will befall the current president. That is, if you are able to stop this man Levell and his colleagues from interfering. The election may be close, but we will win."

"I'm sure we will, dear comrade," Laski said.

"What about this rogue FBI agent. Should we have him terminated?"

"Killing an FBI agent would be foolish. Think of the furor it would occasion."

Federov's eyes narrowed. "We will make it appear to be an accident."

Shaking his head, Laski said, "No, his death would only focus unwanted attention on the matters he is working on, specifically the Harold Case affair."

"Then what do you propose?" Federov said impatiently. And lit a new cigarette off of the butt of the pervious one.

A sly smile spread slowly across Laski's wrinkled face. "He can be made to do whatever we require of him if he believes his family's well-being is in danger."

"So you have a plan to achieve this?"

"I do. It is being worked out even now."

"And the problem with this man, Levell?"

"Ah, that, my dear colonel, is part two. I will share that with you later. It is time now, however, to bring Senator Morris and, particularly, Mr. Jenkins into the picture."

Federov looked long and hard at Laski for a few moments. "How exactly is it that this Jenkins is to be involved?"

"Because of his position with Morris, we have delved deeply into Mr. Jenkins' background. It seems he has a certain weakness."

"Drugs, prostitutes, alcohol?" Dimitri Nikitin said. "Black people are famous for having these vices."

Laski and Federov both turned their heads and looked at Nikitin. "You are an idiot," Federov said. "Your role is to sit with your mouth permanently shut. I do not want to remind you of that again, Comrade Nikitin. Do you understand?" There was an unmistakable threat in Federov's tone of voice.

Nikitin bobbed his head up and down and fumbled for another cigarette. His face reddened as he felt Maksym's eyes drilling into the back of his head. No doubt the man held him in contempt for allowing Federov to speak to him in such a way.

"As I was saying," Laski said to Federov, "Mr. Jenkins has a weakness. It is gambling. He likes horse races and bets on them in a spectacularly unsuccessful fashion."

Federov snorted and said, "Americans are such fools."

"In any event, he has accumulated considerable debt. This presents him with certain issues involving the organized criminal element. As a result, Mr. Levell and his comrades have been able to turn him."

"So," Federov said, "he is now their mole in our midst."

"That is so, but it is a good thing, because we are able to feed him whatever information or misinformation we want Levell and the others to have. We now can manipulate them."

"And this somehow factors in to the troublesome situation involving the agent for the FBI?"

"Yes," Laski said.

Federov studied him for a moment before saying, "And this man Jenkins, he will be useful in solving this problem you say you are having with Levell?"

"Indeed, but at this time, it would be advisable for you and Mr. Nikitin to withdraw, as I do not believe it would be good if Morris and Jenkins knew that two of the finest members of the Russian Federation's diplomatic corps are involved in what I am about to disclose to them."

"Agreed," Federov said and stood. Nikitin joined him immediately. "I expect you to keep me informed of all developments in a timely manner, Comrade Laski," Federov said. He turned and strode back through the garden toward the elevator, purposely ignoring Maksym. Nikitin, however, couldn't resist stealing a glance at Laski's security man. He immediately regretted it and hurried after Federov like a frightened child racing to catch up with his parent.

Laski watched the two Russians until they had disappeared into the elevator, then, turning to Maksym, he said, "Bring the Senator and Mr. Jenkins to me."

37 BAYOU COUNTRY, LOUISANA

The chilly temperature had eased, but the sky remained gray and leaden. There was a sodden quality to the air that permeated everything, making it seem colder than it was. Whelan drove west on Interstate 310 through what looked like farm country gone to seed, large formerly cleared areas that now were being swallowed up by weeds. He crossed the Mississippi River between New Sarpy and Destrehan. As he drove over the bridge, he noticed there were several groups of what looked like old barges fastened together on the river, and pondered their purpose.

After a few more miles, farmlands and industrial uses gave way to the wetlands of Bayou Country, also known as Acadiana. It extends through the twenty-two parishes in South Louisiana that, beginning in the seventeen hundreds, were settled by the Acadians, political refugees from French Canada. Acadiana makes up about one-third of Louisiana. The region also is called "Cajun Country".

He exited I-310 onto U.S. 91 west, the main transportation corridor prior to the advent of the Interstate highway system, and began passing through enclaves of trailers and homes that clearly had not been well cared for. There were industrial and commercial operations scattered along the old highway. Most appeared to be struggling to survive.

He drove through the town of Paradis. It appeared to be surrounded by scrublands and more abandoned farmland. The area seemed dismal and barren of hope. In the majority of homes visible from the highway, the yards were overgrown and unkempt. It occurred to Whelan that real grass, the green kind, might not grow in such a depressive environment. Even the ubiquitous churches, Catholic and Southern Baptist, seemed forlorn, with treeless parking lots and weeds growing up through the cracks in the asphalt. It appeared to be a stereotypical dusty, dirty, poor Southern town. Then

167

abruptly he was through the town and back out in the open empty spaces occasionally interrupted by an intersection with a narrow country road.

He passed through a nameless little residential area and into the town of Des Allemands that was split by a small muddy, sluggish river that drained Lac des Allemands through Dufrene Ponds, Petit Lac des Allemands, and Bayou Gauche into Lake Salvador. From there it would wander through the lower reaches of Bayou Country and eventually into Barataria Bay and the Gulf of Mexico.

Traffic was sparse and what there was of it was mostly local, as travelers would be using Interstate 10 to the north of Highway 90. The traffic consisted of battered pick up trucks hauling small bayou scows or farm products, oil tankers, and freight haulers. Route 90 curved south outside of Des Allemands with the small river on one side and rusty weed covered railroad tracks on the other. The overall atmosphere in this part of the country seemed to be one of hopelessness and despair. Whelan wondered what the Cajuns had done for God to have exiled them to this sad, forlorn environment.

The road curved to the west again and he was back in farm country although there were no crops of any kind to be seen. He wondered if cotton, sugarcane and rice still were grown in the area. He recalled that forestry was Louisiana's chief industry, but doubted that it played much of a role in the economic fiber of the surrounding wetlands and scrublands.

Eventually, he exited Route 90 onto Highway 182, also known locally as New Orleans Boulevard. Very soon he was in Houma, named after an apocryphal tribe of Native Americans supposed to have inhabited the area before the Europeans arrived. To Whelan, it seemed to be a town of sagging electric distribution lines and very few sidewalks. The road was lined with rundown motels, dingy-looking gin mills, auto repair shops, empty storefronts of failed businesses and a plethora of gas stations, many boarded up, all evidence of the days before Interstate 10 siphoned off most of the traveling public. While Highway 182 was paved, the side streets were dirt-topped and dusty. As he neared the downtown area, curbs and sidewalks began to appear, although they were cracked and broken. Traffic picked up a bit as he neared the heart of town, but many of the motorists seemed to drive poorly. Or, Whelan thought, maybe they just didn't have a reason to give a damn.

West Main Street was narrow and metered for parallel parking and there were plenty of empty spaces available. The street was lined on both sides with one-story buildings, most of them in need of painting and maintenance. There were tattered awnings on some, patched up windows on other, and a lot of spaces that had gone dark.

The *dojo*, or martial arts studio, that Whelan was looking for was on West Main Street wedged between a sports bar and a printing shop. It stood out with a fresh coat of paint and a new sign that announced the Paul

Fontenot Academy of Martial Arts. There was oriental script painted on the front plate glass window. Whelan recognized it as Japanese. This was confirmed by the dojo's martial arts style also painted on the window in English: *Shotokan*. The system had been developed by an Okinowan, Gichin Funakoshi, who immigrated or was brought to Japan prior to the Second World War. Whelan was a student and practitioner of many different styles of martial arts, and considered *Shotokan* to be one of the best of the linear, or "hard" styles, in terms of practicality and effectiveness.

He parked the car in front of the *dojo* in one of the many available spaces and went inside. It was mid-afternoon on Sunday, but there were a few students stretching or working on *kata* – detailed choreographed patterns of movements designed to simulate unarmed combat. One student was pounding the *Makiwara*, a padded wooden post used to development striking power and toughen the hands. The students all wore white *gis* – the heavy cotton canvas uniform of the *karate-ka* or practitioner. There was one black belt working out with them. The others wore *obis*, or sashes, of other colors, indicating lesser rank.

The *dojo* had a hardwood floor and white walls on which there were a number of photographs, including the ubiquitous one of Master Funakoshi hung in a central place of honor. Three neon light fixtures that ran in a line front to back were hung from the exposed ceiling.

The black belt noticed the powerfully built stranger with the odd reddish blonde, curly hair respectfully removing his shoes by the entrance to the *dojo*. From the look of him, the black belt suspected he might be a guest *karate-ka* visiting from out-of-town. He walked over to Whelan and asked if he could help.

"I'd like to speak with *Sensei* Fontenot. He's expecting me," Whelan said.

The black belt nodded and walked over to a small office cubicle that had been partitioned off from the rest of the *dojo*. In a moment, a large man wearing a black *gi* and a worn and tattered black *obi* emerged and walked over to Whelan. His hair was cut short in a military buzz cut. Figures, Whelan thought; once a Marine, always a Marine. The man was an inch or two taller than Whelan and heavier, probably in the range of two hundred and fifty pounds. It always amused Whelan that a large and powerful man would master the martial arts when nature had already provided him with all the physicality he probably would need to protect himself in a fight. Then, he thought of himself and the other Dogs, and realized it was a rhetorical question that had no answer.

"You the fella Cliff said to expect?"

"Yes."

The man stuck his hand out and said, "I'm Paul Fontenot. Cliff's an old and very good friend. Tell me what you need and I'll see that you get it."

The students all had stopped their activities and were staring at the two men. "Thanks," Whelan said and shook the man's hand. "Is there a place we can speak in private?"

Fontenot motioned with his head for Whelan to follow him. He strode across the floor to the rear of the building and exited into an alley. He opened a door on the other side and entered what turned out to be the backroom of a beauty salon. The place was closed but there was a buxom, dark haired woman inside. Her long, black hair was pulled back behind her ears and held in place by two tortoise shell barrettes. She wore a lot of make-up and a lot of cheap jewelry. The deep red polish of her long fingernails matched the color of her lipstick. She had on a mauve blouse that displayed an admirable amount of cleavage. The tight black skirt stopped well above her knees.

"This is my wife Leonie," Fontenot said.

Whelan nodded. "A pleasure." She graced him with a sultry smile.

"Cliff said you need a new look, new ID, and a car," Fontenot said.

"I do."

The shades over the front window had been drawn. Fontenot motioned toward the rearmost chair in the salon and said, "Have a seat. Leonie will get started on creatin' the new you. The car's out front. I'll bring it around to the alley when you're ready. Meantime, I'll check on the status of your new ID."

Leonie had just spread a sheet over Whelan below his neck to protect his clothes when she squeezed his left bicep. "My," she said in a provocative drawl, "are you this hard everywhere?"

Whelan was suddenly uncomfortable. Leonie was an attractive, sexy woman and the message seemed clear, but he had always been faithful to Caitlin and didn't want to change that status now. "I train a lot," he said.

"I'll bet you do, darlin', and I'll bet you're really good at it, too." She winked at him. Leonie made a production out of dropping her comb and bending over to pick it up, giving Whelan a view of her impressive cleavage. She smiled

"Like what you see, darlin'?"

A few minutes later, she reached over him as if to get something from the shelf and pushed her breasts into the side of his face. She stepped back, hands on hips, and said, "Why aren't you the little dickens. Ah'm jest gonna' have to keep mah eyes on you." Another provocative smile spread slowly across her face.

Paul Fontenot couldn't return quickly enough to suit Whelan. Despite her flirtations, Leonie did a competent job. Whelan's hair now was jet black and combed straight back in the fashion favored by male movie actors in the 'thirties. She also had raised the level of his sideburns to a point almost level with the top of his ears and used a small amount of gray dye to create a salt and pepper effect on the sides. He had had a three-day growth of beard. She trimmed it down to a pencil-thin moustache and soul patch. Stepping back to admire her work, she said, "Darlin', you look like you been born and raised in N'Awlins." She turned to get something from a cabinet behind her.

She bent at the waist, which had the effect of hiking up her short skirt. It exposed a lot of leg, and Whelan had to admit it all looked good. She stood and handed him a tube of lubricating jelly. "Keep your hair slicked back with this stuff," she said. "And KY Jelly is good for somthin' else, don't you know, darlin'." She gave him a lascivious wink.

She was just finishing blowing his hair dry when her husband returned. He had a new driver's license, credit cards and other indicia of identity for Whelan. He took a small camera off a shelf in the back room of the salon, lined Whelan up against a dark green curtain and took his picture. He removed the card from the camera, stuck into a slot on the front of a small photo printer and made a four by six print. He cut it down to the appropriate size, glued it on the license and covered it with clear plastic. Whelan offered to pay them for their services, but they refused, saying that Levell had already taken care of it.

Fontenot had brought an aging red Dodge Charger around to the alley between the salon and the *dojo*. As Whelan was getting into the driver's seat, Fontenot said, "Cliff told me some things 'bout you. Says you're 'bout the best fighter he's ever seen."

Whelan shrugged noncommittally.

"It's a shame you can't spend a little time here. Would'a been good to work out with you. Don't get many guest martial artists around here; 'least any with real skills. Would'a been good for the students too."

Whelan said, "If I'm ever in these parts again, consider it a done deal." He started to get in the car, but paused and said, "Do you put a lot of hours in the *dojo*, Paul?"

The other man looked at him. "Yeah, seven days a week. Nights too. Why?"

Whelan studied Fontenot for a moment considering how to phrase what he wanted to say. "I think you need to find a way to spend more time with Leonie." He was prepared for the other man to react angrily or aggressively.

Fontenot didn't respond immediately. He stared at Whelan for awhile, then said, "Cliff told me you were smart. Pick up on things quickly."

The two men looked at each in silence for a few moments, then Fontenot offered his hand and said, "That's good advice. I'll do my best."

Whelan drove off to continue his mission to find Marc Kirkland, retracing his path down West Main Street for a few blocks then turning west on Lafayette Street for several more blocks until he reached Honduras Street. It became Tunnel Boulevard and took him east under the river to the intersection with Highway 52, also known as Grand Caillou Road. It was a tired commercial strip featuring the three Ps: power lines, parking lots, and pylon signs. 52 would take him to his destination, Dulac, Louisiana.

The local traffic was moving slowly along the two-lane asphalt road. He wondered if it was any better on weekdays. The route took him past an industrial park, farmlands where there were signs of actual crops, and trailer parks. In his mind, these humble places didn't rise to the fancier level of mobile home subdivisions.

The road was running south now, and, as he got deeper into Bayou Country, the farm fields gave way to wetlands and an increasing number of drainage canals. Traffic began to thin out and the scenery turned decidedly junkier. Trailers were scattered singly along the road, their yards filled with pieces of cars and other machinery. A canal paralleled the road to the west. Driveways and unpaved side streets ran off to the east. In some places, brackish water came almost to the edge of the road. The newer looking houses were built on pilings. He wondered how often the road flooded, and what people did when it was closed.

Whelan was aware that Louisiana contains forty-one percent of wetlands in the United States. Now, land was beginning to give way to backwaters filed with rotting debris - tires, buckets, tarps, pieces of Styrofoam coolers, cans, bottles, fragments of wood, partially sunken derelict boats and more. He passed a small two-story elementary school that was next to a cemetery. All of the graves were aboveground crypts because of the extremely high water table. The graveyard was positioned in front of a Catholic Church. Spanish moss drooped limply from the scraggly branches of trees scattered in clumps along the road.

Eventually he came to an area that was more densely populated and suspected he was arriving in Dulac. There were some newer homes scattered incongruously among tin-roofed shanties and commercial operations, most of them connected to the fishing or shrimping industries. There were a number of shrimp boats tied up along the canal to his right. He passed a restaurant called Schmoopy's. He would later learn that it was Dulac's top dining spot. A few moments later he saw a large water tower announcing that he had arrived in Dulac.

It was a low-lying bayou town in the Houma–Bayou Cane–Thibodaux Metropolitan Statistical Area, a census-designated place (CDP) in Terrebonne Parish. The population in the Dulac area is less than three thousand people. Oil and commercial shrimping are the area's largest employers. Whelan was amused by a faded, seemingly antithetical billboard he passed touting the annual Shrimp and Petroleum Festival in Morgan City. The Gulf oil spill meets the seafood industry, coming to a theater near you, he thought.

Much of Dulac appeared to be an industrial zone, stained with oil and petroleum products and reeking of exhaust fumes. It helped to explain why it was burdened by poor air quality standards compared to the national average. There are an inordinate number of superfund sites in the area. The rate of high school grads was little more than half that of the nation as a whole. More than forty percent of households in Dulac earn less than twenty-five thousand dollars per year. Given the poverty evident in the area, Whelan had been surprised to learn that sixty-nine percent of the electorate was registered as Republican.

The road and adjacent canal seemed lined with boat and construction yards, pipelines and processing plants. Trash littered its streets and waterways. Stray dogs and cats wandered aimlessly or lay listlessly in the middle of the side streets.

Whelan drove through Dulac, such as it was, and around a couple of bends in the road. He turned off on 4-Point Road, also known as Parish Road 67. Five miles later the road ended in a small fishing village. It terminated at the front door of a run-down, tin-roofed shanty listing slightly to the right on pilings that raised it a few feet off the ground. Fittingly, the building housed a bar. The name of the bar, painted in badly faded letters over the front door, was simply The Bitter End.

He parked the Charger across the street in a vacant lot that was more water than dry land and walked over to the bar. The lot and the road were topped with crushed rock or marl, a white, claylike substance that quickly turns viscous in wet areas. It stuck to Whelan's shoes like mud.

There were three wooden steps leading up to a narrow porch or veranda that was sheltered by an overhang of the tin roof. Two battered and rickety cane-backed chairs flanked the heavily patched screen door that was the entrance to the bar. A well built but slender man in a nicely fitted three-piece white linen suit sat in the chair to the left of the door. He looked very out-of-place amidst the surrounding brownfields and industrial blight. Even more incongruous than the rest of his outfit, were his black *kung fu* slippers. As he sat, he casually twirled what appeared to be a highly polished walking stick. His dark hair was slicked back in a short ponytail. He wore a well-trimmed goatee and sunglasses that were so dark they seemed to be opaque. Although Whelan couldn't see the man's eyes, he was certain they were fixed on him. It took him a moment or two to recognize Marc Kirkland.

38 NEAR DULAC, LOUISANA

"I've been expecting you," Kirkland said.

"Everyone seems to," Whelan said.

Kirkland waved toward the other chair. "Have a seat."

As Whelan settled into the chair, Kirkland said, "Would you like a drink?"

Whelan looked at his watch. Five after five. He thought of his late Irish father. The man always said that it was improper to drink alcohol prior to five o'clock, but once that magic hour was reached, the drinking lamp was lit. "Sure," he said. "I'll have a beer."

Kirkland called out "Remy."

After several moments a heavyset, unshaven man with long, curly, dirty blonde hair shuffled to the screen door. He walked with a noticeable limp. "What you wan', mon ami?" he said.

"My friend would like a beer. Very cold, as I recall." He looked at Whelan.

"What kind you wan'?" Remy said.

"Something local with a lot of hops," Whelan said.

The man disappeared back into the bar and returned a few minutes later with a bottle of Abita Jockamo IPA. He handed it to Whelan. "You don' look like a man what need de glass," he said with a thick accent that hinted of French.

After he left, Whelan said to Kirkland, "You not drinking these days?"

"In awhile. I have some business to take care of first."

"What kind of business?"

"The troublesome kind. A gang of bikers has taken to frequenting the place. They beat up Remy's regulars, take their money, get kinky with their women. Pretty much destroyed his business. He got hurt pretty bad shrimping awhile back and can't do that kind of work anymore. His wife ran off and left him with five kids to raise. This bar's all he's got to support his family."

"You want some help?"

"No thanks. There are only fifteen or twenty of them," Kirkland said in a matter-of-fact tone.

This should be interesting, Whelan thought as he took a long pull of the well chilled, nicely hopped beer. He looked at Kirkland's walking stick. "That heavy?" he said.

"You tell me," Kirkland said and casually tossed the stick to the other man.

It was about four feet in length and slightly less than an inch in diameter. It was made of wood that had a mottled black and white consistency, but was surprisingly heavy as if made of lead. Whelan hefted it and studied the grain. He noticed that the stick narrowed at each end to slightly less than a half inch in diameter. Each end was tipped with a hard substance that looked like carbon fiber. "Lignum vitae," he said as he handed it back to Kirkland.

"Yep. Sometimes known as ironwood."

They sat quietly for several minutes discussing Levell, the Team, and the pending reunion of the Sleeping Dogs. After awhile, Whelan heard a low rumble that began to build to the north. It grew louder as the moments passed. In a short while, a group of eighteen motorcyclists appeared in the distance. They came to a stop in front of the bar but continued to gun their engines for several moments. The resulting roar shattered the previously quiet atmosphere. Eventually they shut down their bikes and began to climb off the saddles.

Kirkland rose from his chair in a swift, fluid movement and moved to the top of the steps. He paused with his hands resting on the top of his walking stick. Knowing that Kirkland had been a highly dedicated and avid student of the martial arts, Whelan knew that the "walking stick" actually was a formidable oriental weapon commonly known as a j☐ stick. In the hands of an expert j☐ jutso-ka, it could be quite deadly.

The martial applications of the j☐ are believed to have been developed by Mus☐ Gonnosuke Katsuyoshi in seventeenth century Japan. The techniques supposedly came to him in a dream following his loss in a sword duel with the immortal Japanese sword saint, Miyamoto Musashi. Musashi, who was a master of the two-sword technique, is reported to have fought and won more than sixty duels. He is said to have lost only his final one. That one was a rematch with Gonnosuke in which Gonnosuke used his j☐ stick techniques to overcome Musashi's masterful two-sword technique.

Whelan was amused by the bikers' fashion sense. Some of them had shaved heads; others wore long, oily ponytails. A few had faded bandanas wrapped around their heads. None of them wore helmets. Many of them were wearing sunglasses. Some wore shirts with the sleeves ripped off. A couple of others were wearing tee shirts that touted heavy metal bands from the 'seventies. One was shirtless with what appeared to be empty bandoliers crisscrossing his chest. All were wearing scuffed engineer boots and grime stained dungarees. They came in all sizes from a short, thin man to a six foot seven inch giant. None of them had shaved in awhile. All of them were heavily tattooed

The leader of the pack was a powerfully built man who stood more than six feet tall with huge arms and thick shoulders that stretched the fabric of his sleeveless shirt. A forest of tattoos covered all of his exposed skin except his face and the palms of his hands. His head was shaven and his face was covered by a mass of dirty, matted whiskers. An ugly white scar started about an inch above his right eye and plunged through the eyebrow skipping the eye itself, but continuing for another couple of inches down his right cheek. There was a chain of some kind dangling from the right side of his belt.

After he climbed off his bike, he took his sunglasses off and perched them on the top of his shiny, bald head. He began to climb the stairs to the porch fronting the bar. Kirkland blocked his way. "Who the fuck're you, Colonel Sanders?" His voice was deep and raspy.

"I'm the new bouncer."

"Yeah? Who the fuck you plannin' to bounce?"

"Anyone who's not back on his bike and gone in the next twenty seconds."

The biker was standing one step below the porch, but was almost eye level with Kirkland. He eyed the man in the white suit with a malevolent stare. If only looks could kill, Whelan thought, as he watched the drama unfolding in front of the bar. Kirkland was about five feet ten inches tall and weighed in the range of one eighty five. Whelan knew he had the same genetic gifts that he also enjoyed. Kirkland was lightning quick and enormously powerful. It didn't hurt that he also was a gifted practitioner of the martial arts including the $\int$.

Someone standing behind the gang leader said, "Kick the little pansy's ass out of the way, Deke. I need me some beer."

Whelan heard a noise behind him and turned to see Remy, the barkeep, standing behind the screen door with an ancient short barreled ten-gauge shotgun in his hands. Whelan stood, walked over and opened the door. He took the weapon from Remy. Cradling it in the crook of his left arm, he walked over to the wooden two-by-four railing that ran around the porch. He sat on it facing the gang of bikers and said, "This man" he nodded at Kirkland "is about to beat the pure shit out of each and every one of you. In fact, I'd be surprised if all of you are still breathing at the end. But..." He held up the shotgun for all to see "to keep it fair, I'll cut anyone in half with this if I see a weapon being pulled."

Just then, Deke made his move. He was surprisingly fast for a man of his bulk, but not fast enough. Only a small handful of people on the planet, including Whelan, Sven Larsen and Nick Stensen were. Deke attempted a roundhouse punch with his right hand, expecting to catch Kirkland on his left temple. The jō stick flashed and spun. Deke's right arm became dislocated at the shoulder and he started to cry out in pain, but the whirling jō stick lunged and crushed his larynx, or voice box. If he survived, it was unlikely that he would ever speak again.

He staggered backward, falling into some of his gang members. For an instant, no one moved, then, as if on cue, the bikers tried to swarm up the steps at Kirkland fueled by rage and the belief in their self-created reputations as unholy terrors. Kirkland was a blur of white. The jō stick whirled, flashed, lunged in nonstop motion. Kirkland's feet moved just as fast as he effortlessly shifted from one technique to another. Occasionally, one or the other of his feet would snap up or out, crushing testicles or destroying a knee. The perpetual motion of the jō stick cracked skulls, gouged out eyes, and destroyed joints. In less than one minute it was over.

Three bikers were standing at the bottom of the steps, backing slowly toward their bikes. Their eyes were wide with fear. One of them said, "We ain't got no beef with you, Mister. We jes' wanna ride outta' here."

Kirkland nimbly leaped from the porch to the ground in front of the men. In seconds they lay motionless beside their bikes.

Whelan did a quick appraisal. Some of the bikers clearly were dead and a few others were in the process of joining them. The few remaining ones were either unconscious or crying out in pain.

Kirkland turned to Whelan and made an exaggerated bow, as a stage actor might following a performance. "How'd I do?"

Whelan set the shotgun down and held up ten fingers, rating Kirkland's performance. "Nice," he said. "You do have some blood on your suit, but it's not yours."

"No problem. I was getting tired of the damn suit anyway. Time for a new look."

"Tell me about it," Whelan said.

"Yeah," Kirkland said. "The Johnny Depp thing just isn't you."

Whelan picked the gun up again and opened the screen door for Kirkland. Inside, Remy had placed two cold beers on the bar, another Jockamo and a Restoration Ale, also by Abita.

Kirkland drained the Restoration in a single pull. He nodded to the bartender for another one and said, "Remy, *mon ami*, you won't be having any more problems with bikers."

The man nodded, opened another bottle and placed it in front of

Kirkland, then opened one for himself. *"Merci beaucoup,"* he said.

In a few minutes, Whelan heard the sound of several vehicles pulling up in front of the bar. There were sounds of men talking and grunting as if toiling at something. Then there were metallic sounds and a noise that sounded like a machine was being used for some purpose. He looked at Kirkland.

"Remy's clean up crew."

The bartender laughed. The sound came out like a snort. After several minutes, the door opened and a man walked in wearing the uniform of a parish sheriff. He strode directly to the bar, took off his hat and laid it on the top of the bar. Whelan looked at Kirkland. Kirkland looked at Remy.

"Boys," Remy said, "meet Sheriff Arsenault. We're first cousins." With that, he placed four shot glasses on the bar in front of each of the men. He reached deep into a cooler behind him and brought out a bottle of Don Eduardo añejo tequila. Remy filled each shot glass to the brim and placed a shaker of salt and bowl of lime wedges on the bar in front of them.

The Sheriff picked up a lime wedge between the thumb and index finger of his left hand, raised the hand to his mouth and licked the crotch between his thumb and forefinger. He sprinkled some salt on the wet spot, then picked up a shot glass with his right hand. "Boys," he said, "they gonna be some fat, happy 'gators in the Bayou tonight. I personally guarantee it." He tossed back the shot and bit deeply into the lime wedge.

Remy raised his glass and, with a distinct drawl, said, *"Laisser les bons temps rouler"* - Let the good times roll.

39 J. EDGAR HOOVER BUILDING

The weather in Washington was a little better for a change, although the air remained crisp. The snow was starting to melt off, but still covered the ground. It wasn't fresh anymore and had begun to turn brown and even black in places where the detritus of urban activities had left its mark. The sun had begun to burn away patches of the sooty gray cloud cover, allowing the brilliant blue sky to peek through with the promise of better days ahead.

Special Agent Mitch Christie was in one of the kitchen areas in the massive Bureau headquarters building. He had poured his fifth cup of coffee of the morning and laced it with six shots of cream to make it easier for its passage through his digestive system. The excess cream had cooled the coffee to something less than lukewarm, so he nuked it in the microwave oven for sixty seconds. As he waited for the oven to complete its task, he unconsciously rubbed his stomach, as if to warn it that the coffee was on its way. His thoughts turned to the nearly empty bottle of Mylanta in one of the drawers in his desk.

As he was taking his first, tentative sip, Lou Antonelli walked in and said, "Thought I might find you here. Something came up that might be relevant."

Christie nodded toward the door. "Let's go to my office." As they walked along the corridor toward his office, Christie said, "So give."

"We got word from officials in Hawaii about a situation that's developing there."

"In Honolulu?"

"No, a couple of places on Maui. One of them was in a little town called Hana."

"Hana?" Christie said with surprise in his voice.

"Yeah, you know the place?"

179

"Vacationed on Maui with the family a few years back. We visited Hana. It's very quiet and scenic. Charles Lindbergh's remains are buried nearby."

Antonelli looked at him for a moment. "Thanks for sharing," he said dryly.

"So what's going on in Hana?"

They began walking again. "It seems," Antonelli said, "that there were a couple of dust ups a few of days ago. The first one was in a place called Kahului." He pronounced it 'Ka-hoo-loo-eye'.

"Kah-hoo-looie," Christie corrected him. "That's where the airport is. What happened?"

"Some guy who paid for a single day pass was working out at a fitness facility and a local babe put the moves on him."

"The moves."

"Yeah. He apparently rejected her. So, when her boyfriend shows up a little later, she must have told him the new guy offended her somehow. The boyfriend was a big stud and something of the resident bully."

"Yeah?"

"Well, the boyfriend goes over and takes a swing at the new guy. The new guy swats him like he was a tennis ball. Then he picks the big sonofabitch up with one hand and drags his ass over to the babe. Knocked the s.o.b. out cold."

"Then what?"

"Then the new guy says to the babe something like "Lucky for you, your boyfriend's probably too stupid to figure out you're the one that got his ass kicked'."

"So?" Christie said, "That shit happens everywhere, including inside the beltway. Boys will be boys."

"Yeah, but the new guy was hefting weights in amounts and repetitions that a guy his size…hell, maybe any size, shouldn't have been able to handle. And he was lightning quick, too."

"So what size was he?"

"About six two, maybe two twenty, two thirty."

Christie stopped again and turned toward Antonelli. "So, what are you saying, Lou?"

"I'm saying this guy might be our boy, Whelan. Right size. Freakishly strong. Freakishly quick."

After a moment of reflection, Christie said, "But how the hell could he have gotten to Hawaii from San Francisco? We had all the bases covered."

"Dunno, but wait 'til you hear the next part." They began walking again and Antonelli said, "The next day, in that Hana place, there's another similar event."

They had reached Christie's office and went inside. Christie shut the door and waved Antonelli to a chair. "Go on," he said and settled into his desk chair.

"A local guy known as Brett Lange goes into a local bar with a stranger. Lange isn't a native, but he's lived in the area for a long time. He's supposed to be some kind of physical freak. Stronger, faster than anyone had ever seen. Locals liked him, but with a healthy respect...maybe more like fear. He lived in a cabin on the side of the mountain above town."

"Haleakala," Christie said.

"Whatever. The thing about Lange is that ever since he showed up in the area, crime just about dried up." Antonelli paused for a moment, then said, "And hard core criminal types simply disappeared."

"And what did the local cops think about this coincidence?"

"They didn't seem to mind. They got to issue parking tickets and Lange got to deal with the bad guys."

"So, what's this got to do with the Whelan case?"

"Seems this Lange guy, just for sport, tries to promote a brawl between the stranger he brought with him and the rest of men in the bar."

"And."

"And, the stranger puts a quick end to it by swatting Lange across the room. Fast as Lange is supposed to be, he couldn't quite evade the blow."

"This stranger, what did he look like?" Christie said.

Antonelli grinned. "That's the interesting part. He sounds like the same guy from the fitness center in Kahului."

"The possible Whelan?"

"Yeah."

Christie stood suddenly and turned to gaze out his narrow window. "Shit! We need to lock down that whole island and sift through it until we find this guy."

"Don't waste your time," Antonelli said. "I've been following up. One of the locals took this guy by boat over to the next island."

"Hawaii, the Big Island?"

"Yeah. There's two airports there. One on each side of the island. I have people on the ground tracking his steps there. But there's another element to this too. An eerie one."

Christie shrugged. There was a sour expression in his face as if he had been sucking on a persimmon. He unconsciously opened the top right hand drawer of his desk and rummaged around until he found the Mylanta. "As if having to deal with genetic mutant super beings wasn't enough. What is it now?" He took a swig of the Mylanta and put the bottle back in the drawer.

"The locals were concerned about Lange, so a couple of cops went up to his place. Had to tase a big-ass dog to get on his property. It was clean. The guy had left."

"So?"

"So, while they're up there, the cops poke around in the area behind the house and find a freakin' bone yard."

Christie spun around and stared at Antonelli. "A bone yard? You mean a cemetery, a burial ground?"

"Yeah. Looks like Lange is a serial killer. Kind of explains what happened to the criminal element that disappeared from the area."

Christie sat down again in his desk chair and leaned forward with is elbows on the desk and his chin resting on his hands. He stared at the wall behind Antonelli. "I'm starting to see more here than just Whelan."

"Like what?"

"First, there was that incident in Tampa where a guy that might have been Whelan was involved. His partner was a thickly muscled Incredible Hulk lookalike without the green skin. He takes on a gang of toughs and slaps them around like ping pong balls. From what I've read of the files on the Sleeping Dogs, that guy could have been the one they called Larsen, the Man With No Neck."

"You mean there are two of these guys still alive?" Antonelli said.

"Worse. This guy in Hawaii, the suspected serial killer, he could be the one known as Stensen. According to the files, he was a bloodthirsty nut case."

"So you're thinking there may be as many as three of these guys instead of just Whelan."

"I'm thinking maybe there are even more. Maybe they're all still alive. Maybe none of them died in that plane crash twenty years ago. Maybe it was all a ruse."

"Jesus," Antonelli said.

"Yeah, Jesus. If this is true, then Whelan is going around to each one of the Sleeping Dogs. Collecting the strays, as it were. But why? Is he recruiting them? And for what?" He looked at Antonelli and said, "This thing just got a hell of a lot more complicated and more dangerous." He picked up the receiver of the phone on his desk and pushed a button. After a moment, he said, "Charlotte, see if you can get that geneticist, Nishioki, on the line for me."

40 NASHVILLE, TENNESSEE

Whelan spent the night at Kirkland's modest cottage on Bayou Dularge Road near the small village of Theriot. They nursed a few beers and talked about the reuniting of the Dogs and what Levell might have in mind for them. Later, Whelan asked whether Kirkland ever worked out at Paul Fontenot's dojo in Houma.

"Very, very infrequently," he said. "I have to hold back and try to act as ungifted as the rest of them. It's like fighting with one arm and one leg tied behind my back."

"Ever meet Paul's wife?"

"Leonie?"

"Yeah. She ever come on to you?"

"Sure. Leonie comes on to everything that's got a cock."

"Paul know this?"

"Probably not. Otherwise, some people would have been badly fucked-up by now. He spends too much time focusing on his *dojo* and the martial arts, and she's not the kind of woman who will tolerate being neglected."

"That's too bad," Whelan said. "He seems like a decent guy. But I've got a gut feeling that things aren't going to go so well."

"Yeah, the drill usually goes something like this - some night an anonymous someone is gonna drop a dime on him at the *dojo*. Ask if he knows where his wife is and who she's with. That's when the fecal matter will hit the rotor blades."

"Like the line from the Bob Seger song," Whelan said, " 'above all the lights, it's the passion that kills'."

Despite the lumpy sofa at Kirkland's, Whelan slept very soundly. In a way he was surprised, because alcohol usually interfered with his sleep, and he had had a lot of beer and tequila over the course of the evening. It was his first decent night's sleep since leaving Ireland more than a week earlier. It was also the first night he was not the sole and only guardian of his corner of the universe.

The next morning he left before sunrise on the next leg of his travels. He drove up Bayou Dularge Road to the southern outskirts of Houma, then skirted the town and retraced his path back to Kenner on the outskirts of New Orleans where he picked up Interstate 10. A short time later he veered onto Interstate 55, threading his way between Lakes Pontchartrain and Maurepas. 55 took him north through Mississippi to the outskirts of Memphis, Tennessee where he switched to Interstate 40 for the journey into Nashville.

He took his time, and, with stops, it was a twelve-hour trip. He pulled up to his hotel near the campus of Vanderbilt University at exactly five o'clock. There were other routes he could have taken that might have been faster, but he liked sticking with the Interstate system and blending in with the heavier traffic. His initial plan had been to fly from New Orleans to Nashville, but his gut instinct told him to avoid the airports. He knew that the government employed facial recognition technology in airports and other places. Although primarily used by TSA for anti-terrorism purposes, he knew the Bureau could co-opt it for their purposes too. The facial prosthetics had been designed to evade FRT, but he wasn't so sure the new look given him by Leonie Fontenot would achieve the same purpose. He glanced at his reflection in the car's rearview mirror. He thought his new appearance, with the slicked back dark hair, pencil moustache and soul patch, made him look somewhat like Johnny Depp. If I had my druthers, he thought, I'd rather look like a young Clint Eastwood.

He checked into the hotel. It was almost across the campus from the university. Later he found the fitness facility and worked up a drenching sweat. It felt good after the long hours in the car. After showering, he called Caitlin and the boys. Things were in good order at home. Her father and brother hadn't heard of anyone looking for Whelan on behalf of the Bureau. He made another call, this time to Levell, to report on his meeting with Kirkland and to get details on his next and final recruit, Quentin Thomas.

The next morning, following a restless sleep filled with dreams in which he was a desperate prey stalked by an unknown force, Whelan went over to the Vanderbilt campus. It was a short but brisk walk through the chilly January air of Middle Tennessee. He thought the campus was beautiful, even in the cold, gray winter gloom. It had been designated a National Arboretum and featured over 300 different species of trees and shrubs. The university was founded in 1873 and the oldest part of the campus is in the northeast corner almost across the street from Whelan's hotel.

He quickly found Furman Hall. Tucked behind the law school on Twenty-First Street South, it is one of the oldest buildings on campus. It is the headquarters for the school's College of Arts and Science, where Professor Thomas had his office. Thomas wasn't in, so Whelan asked a young office worker in the Philosophy Department when the professor might be expected. She seemed hesitant to volunteer any information.

"I'm an old friend and only in town for a short time. I'd hoped to be able to visit with him briefly while I'm here," he said, hoping this might encourage her.

"Well, he usually comes in around ten..., but if you don't have an appointment...." She trailed off.

"Perhaps I can meet up with him before then. Where would he be now?"

The girl scrunched her face up in indecision. Whelan smiled pleasantly and waited. Finally she said, "He usually works out in the mornings before he comes to the office. You might find him at the gym. Memorial Gym."

Whelan thanked her, got directions to the facility, and walked over to it. The gym was located across campus from Furman Hall and gave him a chance to view modern college life in a splendid Southern cultural environment. Although the trees and ground were bare and few people lingered outside in the crisp air, the scene was almost idyllic. The old, but finely crafted buildings, and the solitude recreated the ambiance of an era that had long passed in America. A certain feeling of wistfulness briefly engulfed Whelan.

He found the school's gym without difficulty and quickly located the weight room. As he expected, Thomas was lifting. Like all the Dogs, he possessed enormous strength. He was not the strongest. That was Larsen, but he did have the quickest reflexes of any of them. He was finishing his tenth set of bench presses, smoothly raising and lifting the bar with three hundred fifty pounds of weight, ten repetitions, each seemingly as effortless as the first. There were a few other students in the weight room. They were very large young men, football players from the look of them. They all watched Thomas enviously out of the corners of their eyes.

"Need a spot?" Whelan said in jest as he approached Thomas, referring to the precaution of having another person available in case the lifter needed assistance. He knew Thomas wouldn't need a spot unless he attempted considerably more than the three fifty.

"No," he said, setting the bar back on the stanchions, "but thanks for offering." He sat up, perspiration running off his head and body like rain off black granite that had been chiseled by a master sculptor. He glanced up at Whelan with pale blue eyes that were a striking contrast to his dark skin.

When he saw who it was, he said "You! Cliff told me to expect you. How the hell are you, man?" He rose and clasped Whelan's hand in a vise-like grip.

"Been a long time, Quent," Whelan said. "But you don't look like you've missed a day of conditioning."

"You either, brother, you either. What's it been? Goin' on twenty years?"

"Yeah."

They looked at each other for a few moments, then Thomas grinned and said, "What's with the Johnny Depp look?"

"Long story. I've been outed by the FBI, but, so far, I think the rest of you are safe."

"Shit, I can't believe it. Brendan Whelan, the Prince of Wolves. Man, we got some catchin' up to do. Let me get showered and dressed, then we'll go grab some breakfast."

Twenty minutes later they were sitting in a small café on West End Avenue across from the campus. The few coeds in the place were stealing peeks at Professor Thomas and his friend who they thought looked a bit like a very large Johnny Depp. They giggled as they toyed with their Skinny Caramel Macchiatos.

"Don't you have office hours at ten?" Whelan said.

"Oh, that's just academic masturbation. Kid's today are totally digital. They want to confer with me, they text. If it's lengthy or involves attachments, they use email."

"What about classes this morning?"

Thomas laughed and made a dismissive motion with his hand. "I don't have classes on Tuesdays. If I did, I'd have a grad student teach it for me, so I could spend this time getting' caught up with you."

Whelan shook his head. "You, a college professor. I always thought you would have been an all-pro running back if it hadn't been for the Sleeping Dogs."

Thomas was suddenly serious. "No, man. I always wanted to study and teach philosophy. It's a great life. I'm a tenured fulltime faculty member."

"What exactly does that mean?"

"Tenured?"

"No. Fulltime."

Thomas leaned in closer and lowered his voice conspiratorially. "The Dean would have my ass if he heard me say this, but fulltime in academia is far different than in the private sector. With teaching, including preparation and test grading, research and publication, and service on various faculty committees, I work about a twenty-five hour week. Some of the others use grad students to teach and research. They probably don't work fifteen hours a week.

186

"I get paid very well, have lots of free time including regular sabbaticals, and access to the athletic facilities. It's a sweet life, brother." He sat back in the booth and smiled.

Whelan looked casually around the coffee shop. "There are a lot of raging hot young women on any campus. I've heard the stories about how some male faculty members use their positions to cut a wide swath through the coed population. Is that a perk, too?" There was a teasing note his voice.

"You heard right. Some faculty members do take advantage of their positions in that regard. They're hot alright, but after dealing with kids all week, I want a mature woman as my off-work companion."

Whelan nodded. "Got a main squeeze?"

"Not really," Thomas said shaking his head. "I was married for awhile, a fellow doctoral candidate, but it didn't work out after we graduated and started teaching. We'd be in school all day, then come home and discuss our respective experiences. It was like there just wasn't anything else. These days I'm happy playing the field, as they say."

"Of all of us, you were always the deep thinker. It doesn't surprise me that you chose philosophy as your discipline."

"Like they say, the mind is a terrible thing to waste. What you don't use, you lose."

"Is that Plato?" Whelan said with a sly grin curling up one corner of his mouth.

"No. It's Quentin Thomas."

At that moment, two of the coeds who had been eying the muscular professor and his equally powerfully built friend, came up to the table. One of them, a blonde girl wearing designer clothes, said, "Hi, Professor Thomas. Remember us from your Asian Philosophy class, Kailee and Lindsay."

Thomas looked up and said "Of course, ladies. Nice to see you."

While Kailee flirted with Thomas, her friend focused on Whelan. "I haven't seen you before, and I'd remember you if I did. Do you teach at the University, too?"

Whelan, somewhat irritated by the interruption nevertheless smiled and said "No. I'm an old friend of the professor's just passing through town."

Lindsay, wearing a tight sweater, crossed her arms beneath her full breasts and raised them slightly. It was an impressive sight. "Do you need someone to show you around town?" she said and smiled provocatively.

Whelan was mildly flattered. "Thanks, but I'm not going to be in town long enough to see any of it."

"Oh," she said with a little pout and tossed her long, thick brown hair in feigned petulance.

"Look, ladies," Thomas said, "my friend and I have some important business to discuss. I'll see you in class, okay."

The girls flounced back to their table and sat. The motion hiked up their very short wool skirts. There was a lot of firm, bare thigh showing above the tops of their knee-high, faux fur-trimmed, leather boots. Thomas sighed. "In another life, perhaps."

They got refills – coffee for Whelan and green tea for Thomas – and began to discuss Levell, the Team, and the days ahead. As they finished, Whalen said, "To recap, Levell has an as yet unspecified mission for us, after which we go back underground; hopefully for good this time."

"Do you know anything about this mission?"

"No, but it will happen soon. Levell will get in touch with each of us and tell us when and where to rendezvous. After that the game is afoot."

"Thanks, Sherlock," Thomas said, "but, as Sam Goldwyn famously said, 'include me out'. " He put his cup down, stood up, and pulled his coat on. "I've worked hard to build just the life I want. Unlike your situation, my cover's not been blown. I wish you luck, brother, but this time it's not my fight." With that, he walked away.

PART THREE

OLD DOGS, NEW TRICKS

41 DINGLE, IRELAND

Dingle is a hilly town with winding, narrow, ancient streets and brightly painted homes and shops. It is the only town on the entire Dingle Peninsula, a mountainous finger of land that stretches some forty miles south from Tralee in County Kerry in the Southwest of Ireland. The area evidences signs of human habitation dating back some six thousand years. Until the modern era, it was on the far edge of the known world. Accordingly, it was the ugly stepchild through centuries of wars, invasions, famines and miseries.

With the mountains that form the spine of the peninsula at its back and a protected cove at its feet, the town of Dingle developed over time into a large and important port on the west coast of Ireland, second only to Galway. Even so, it's a small town with a population of approximately two thousand residents. The town also boasts fifty-two pubs, one for each week of the year.

Nearby is Mount Brandon. At more than three thousand two hundred feet, it is the second highest mountain in Ireland. Mythology holds that it was the site of an ancient pilgrimage during the Iron Age as part of the worship of the Celtic god *Lughnasa* during the harvest festival. The mountain is named for St. Brendan the Navigator. Legend has it that he scaled the mountain around AD 530 and had a vision of the North American continent. His fame endures as the first European allegedly to sail to the Western Hemisphere and back. The story of his voyage was translated into every European language by the twelfth century.

Today it is the scene of a pilgrimage by Irish Catholics in honor of St. Brendan. The route is called *Cosán na Naomh* or Saints Road. It begins near the southern end of the peninsula and ends at *Sáipéilín Bréanainn* or Brendan's Oratory at the summit. Brendan's Oratory is the remains of a small stone building that legend says was used by Saint Brendan.

Brendan Whelan, himself named for the saint, sat at the top of the mountain a few feet from the ruins of the oratory with his sons, Sean and Declan. They were gazing west toward the setting sun across the gray, cloud-mottled Atlantic.

"Da," Declan, age thirteen, said.

"Yes."

The younger boy hesitated a moment. "Do you believe St. Brendan really sailed all the way to America? I mean, it was only the sixth century. Way before Columbus or even Leif Erikson."

"I believe it's possible," Whelan said. "A Brit named Tim Severin replicated the voyage in nineteen-seventy using a *curach* or *naomhóg* similar to the one St. Brendan's crew would have used."

Sean, age fifteen, had been sitting quietly with a handful of pebbles, slowly tossing them one-by-one down the hillside. "What's a *curach*?" he said without looking up.

"It was a boat made of dried ox hides that were cured with oak bark and stretched over a wooden frame."

"Wouldn't that leak pretty badly?" Sean said.

"They used tar to seal the joints, but I suspect there still was leakage."

Declan thought about that for a moment. "Did they have to row all the way across the Atlantic and back?"

"I'm sure they did a lot of rowing at times, but they usually rigged a sail on a mast in the middle of the boat."

Sean shook his head slowly back and forth.

"Don't tell me you're a nonbeliever, Sean, and with you being Irish at that." Whelan said.

"It's not that I don't believe. I want to believe, but it's just that the boats were so small and primitive and the Atlantic is so big. And there are ferocious storms and all."

Whelan smiled. He was pleased that his boys were bright and bold enough to express some skepticism. "Is there a storm that's more ferocious than a determined Celt?"

Both boys laughed and shook their heads.

"Good point," Sean said.

Although it was August, a chill was beginning to settle into the wake of the setting sun. The three of them got up and made their way back down the hill to their car.

The Fianna House Bed and Breakfast sits on high ground just south of the town of Dingle overlooking the harbor. The original part of the structure was built as a small farm bungalow in the late eighteenth century. That was expanded into a two-story manor house early in the twentieth century. Brendan and Caitlin Whelan bought the property and modified the structure into a ten-bedroom, ten-bathroom inn with kitchen, dining room,

191

library/sitting area, and a small office. It had taken a lot of work and money to renovate the antiquated and obsolete plumbing, electrical, and heating systems. But the two of them loved their lives as innkeepers in a town that enjoyed steadily increasing tourism. They employed a staff of four people to assist with the running of the inn.

As Whelan and the boys drove through the gate into the large motor court surrounded by hedgerows, Caitlin was waiting for them at the front door. Her face glowed with a warm and tender smile; her three boys were back from their latest venture. Her husband had returned from six months in the States a few weeks earlier. She knew he had unfinished business there that required him to return in less than a week. Although she felt as if she couldn't get enough time with him herself, she encouraged him to spend as much time with their boys as possible.

As both boys tried to rush past her in search of snacks, she reached out and grabbed them. "Now just a minute. Where's a mother's hug?" The boys each gave her a perfunctory embrace than dashed off. "get cleaned up," she called after them. "We're going to your grandparents' for dinner."

As Whelan approached her, a last ray of the setting sun found a hole in the cloud cover and bathed her in a lovely glow. The sight of her beauty – raven black hair, cobalt blue eyes, perfect body, striking features made Whelan's chest tighten.

She put both fists on her hips and gave him a mock stern look. "You had better show more affection than those lads just did," she said.

He put his arms around her and pulled her close. He felt the fullness of her breasts against him as he kissed her with a slow, deep, passionate kiss. He slid his hands down the small of her back past the narrow waist and tenderly squeezed her firm, shapely bottom, pulling her in even tighter.

As they separated, she gave him a come hither look and said, "I do believe I felt your interest rising."

"Indeed you did," Whelan said.

They both laughed, and arm in arm, they strolled into the inn.

Tom and Ciara Murphy, Caitlin's parents, lived in a comfortable, centuries-old farmhouse a few miles outside of Dingle. It was a two-story structure with dormer windows on the second floor and a chimney at either end of the house. The original thatched roof had long since been replaced with slate tiles. It sat along the coast road surrounded by the famous lush verdant fields of Ireland. It was warm and cozy and exuded a beguiling charm that seduced every visitor with an irresistible sense of homecoming. Tom and Ciara had moved into the house shortly after their wedding. It was the only home Caitlin and her brother, Padraig, had known until they married and moved into homes of their own.

Whelan enjoyed visiting the Murphy's. They had accepted him as if he were their own son, something that didn't seem to trouble Padraig at all. In fact, he and Padraig had grown close, almost as brothers. He knew there was nothing the Murphy's wouldn't do for him, and he felt the same about them.

The moment he and Caitlin and the boys entered the house Whelan felt a deep sense of peace. Maybe it was the history of the place. Maybe it was the homey touches Ciara had added. Maybe it was the bond between all of them. Whatever it was, Whelan knew years earlier that he had found his home in the beautiful green hillsides of County Kerry.

Ciara greeted them at the door with warm embraces. In her early sixties, she remained a striking woman. She was not as tall as her daughter, but it was clear where Caitlin had gotten her raven hair, cobalt blue eyes, alabaster skin, and statuesque figure.

In the United States, many people may have assumed the women had inherited their dark hair from the "Black Irish", a term essentially unknown in Ireland. The misguided theory is based on an assumption that survivors of the sunken Spanish Armada, destroyed off the shores of Dingle Peninsula in 1588, swam ashore and intermarried with the indigenous Celtic peoples of Southwest Ireland. In reality, the numbers of such survivors would not have been significant. Recent genetic research strongly suggests that the original Celtic peoples migrated to Ireland from Northern Spain twenty five hundred years ago.

Padraig, Caitlin's brother, and his family had arrived earlier. His wife, Megan and two boys were sitting in the large family area near the fireplace. Even in August, the nights often had a chill to them. When Sean and Declan spotted their cousins they fist-bumped them then all four boys ran outside to play football (soccer). The spirited play would keep all of them occupied until time for dinner.

Tom and Padraig were in the small but well organized and spotless kitchen. They looked up as Whelan entered. Each gave him a bear hug. Both men were about six feet tall with muscular builds, although they were not remotely as powerful as Whelan. Tom, in his mid-sixties, was ramrod straight. He had sandy brown hair flecked with gray, a square chin, and large powerful hands. Padraig was the image of his father, but without the gray flecks.

"So," Tom said, "my daughter tells me you'll soon be off to the States again."

"Regrettably," Whelan said. "There's unfinished business there."

Tom reached into a cabinet and brought out three tumblers, placing one in front of each of them. He pulled a bottle of Old Bushmills Black Bush Irish whiskey from a cabinet next to the sink and poured a generous amount in each tumbler. He held his glass up to the light and looked admiringly at its contents. "As beautiful an example of the fine art of Irish distilling as there is," he said.

All three men took a large sip and rolled it around on their tongues before swallowing.

"As good as life gets," Padraig said, and the three of them drained their glasses.

When Tom had poured another round, he said, "Brendan, as a father, I thought there would never be a man good enough for my Caitlin." He paused and took a sip of his whiskey. "She's a strong-willed woman, just like her mother."

"They *are* Irish," Whelan said with a smile.

"Aye, they are that." Tom took another sip. "When you first started courtin' her, I thought you were just some damned American ex-pat lookin' for a barroom brawl and a wench to bed.... I was wrong. Truth is, she couldn't have done better."

"That means a great deal to me, Tom, but I'm not sure any man is worthy of Caitlin," Whelan said. He was a little uneasy, not knowing where his father-in-law was taking the conversation.

Tom raised his hand as if to cut Whelan off. "What I have to say is not an easy thing for a man to say." He paused as though searching for the right words.

Padraig sensed his brother-in-law's discomfort and refilled the three tumblers.

"What I'm trying to say, Brendan, is that you are as much a part of this family as any of us. You're like a second son to Ciara and me, a brother to Padraig. You're the love of my daughter's life, the father of two of my grandsons. If you're in some kind of trouble, there is nothin' any of us wouldn't do to help you."

Whelan digested this last comment as he rolled a large sip of the Black Bush around on his tongue, savoring the unique taste. It was created by the significantly greater proportion of malt to grain whiskey and the flavor imparted by Spanish Oloroso sherry-seasoned oak casks that matured the malt. Later it was blended with delicate, sweet, single grain whiskey. After a few moments, he said, "Tom...Paddy, I'm an Irishman. I was born here and, God willin', my earthly remains will be interred here when I'm gone."

"But I'm also an American. The country was very generous to my family and me. Gave us wonderful opportunities that we might not have had anywhere else. Close friends of mine, people I care a great deal about, are struggling against a cancer that's destroying that great country from within and without. They've asked for my involvement and I feel an obligation to help them."

Tom looked into his tumbler and slowly sloshed the contents around. "Bren, a person doesn't have to be a citizen of that great land to appreciate all she's done and what she means to those of us who love liberty and free choice." He looked unwaveringly into Whelan's eyes and said, "I know Caitlin and the boys mean more to you than anythin', but I also know that a man's got to do what a man's got to do. Paddy and I will see to your family while you're away."

Whelan, still gazing steadily at his father-in-law, said, "They couldn't be safer. Thanks for understanding."

Tom said, "There's somethin' you should know, but it's not for Caitlin's ears."

Whelan put his empty tumbler on the countertop and placed his hand over it to signal to Padraig that he didn't want a refill.

"Awhile back," Tom said, "before you came home, the Yanks' Federal Bureau of Investigation sent a request for information to the *Garda Síochána* (the Irish National Police force). It was about you. Fortunately, Paddy saw it and notified me. I deleted it from the District records." Tom paused and took a sip of his drink, and continued. "Right after that, no more than a few days, we learned through security channels that the Yanks had called the whole thing off. Apparently that order came from very high up in the U.S. government."

"Interesting," Whelan said.

"More so than you may think, Bren," Tom said. "I have a friend who is the District Superintendent in one of the northern counties in Leinster. We were in the SBS together. I saved his life in that bit o' nastiness in the Falklands in 'eighty-two." He nodded at Paddy, indicating he should contribute to the conversation.

"Less than a week later," Paddy said, "Da and I learned from our friend in Leinster that two gents claiming to be FBI agents would be travelin' south from Belfast."

"For what purpose?" Whelan said.

"Claimed they were looking for a rogue Yank Special Ops person who had gone to ground in Ireland. That sound like anyone you might know?" Paddy grinned as he said it.

"What happened to them?"

"They were..., shall we say, intercepted just before they crossed the border."

"Intercepted?" Whelan said. "What happened to them after they were 'intercepted'?"

Tom and Paddy looked at each other for a moment. "They were kind enough to answer some questions before they went swimmin' in a deep lough, what the Yanks call a lake, not far from Castleblaney on the Brits' side o' the border. It was made to look like the deed was done by the Northerners," Tom said, referring to the citizens of Northern Ireland.

"A permanent swim," Whelan said.

"Yes."

"What was the nature of the questions?"

"We wanted to know if they had any information that would lead them to you here in Dingle. I'll not have my daughter's husband harmed or taken away from his family if it's in my power to prevent it."

"I appreciate that very much, Tom. Did these would-be agents know anything of interest?"

"Well now," Tom said with a slight shake of his head, "turns out they didn't know a bloody thing, just followin' orders it seems. Someone in the States sent them based on old records that showed your family immigrated to America from the area around Shannon in County Clare." He paused and looked directly into Whelan's eyes with a steady gaze. "Seems they knew you were in the States. It was Caitlin and the boys they were after."

An icy chill spread swiftly from the pit of Whelan's stomach throughout his body. It was replaced almost instantly by a mixture of concern for his family and rage against those who would attempt to harm them. "There may be more of them as time goes by. Under the circumstances, I can't go back to the States and leave my family."

Tom shook his head. "No, Brendan, you've got a job to finish there. But you can rest assured that someone is always watching your family."

"But there's only two of you," Whelan said.

"Look, everyone in this whole bloody area loves you and Caitlin and the boys. Many of them are relatives of ours or dear friends. There are men watchin' over the Fianna day and night, as well as wherever your family members go. No strangers will get near them, I can assure you of that. Not live ones anyway."

Paddy, who had remained silent in deference to his father, the family patriarch, said, "Clearly, you're a man with an interesting past, Brendan. It would appear that you're caught up in something that has to do with that past. Hell, we all know what's goin' on in the States. It happened in most of the countries in Europe after the war. Even Ireland has far too many freeloaders who are easily seduced by the siren song of socialism and worse. But what's happenin' in America seems more pernicious and evil. To stop it at this point is such an imposing task that I doubt it can be done. On the other hand," he paused and laughed then said, "That sounds like somethin' a bloody economist would say."

Whelan smiled and nodded.

"What I mean is," Paddy said, "that if ever there was a man created for such a task, it would be you. And if your associates are anythin' like you, the leftist bastards behind all this are in over their heads."

Tom said, "As you well know, Paddy and I are no slouches when it comes to dealin' with problems of a physical nature. But you, Bren, are not like anyone we've ever known or heard tell of. And if some of these friends of yours in the States are of the same stock as you, I expect there'll be a lot of folks departin' for the afterlife. All I ask is that you take care in all this wet work that's to come, that you aren't one of the dear departed."

"While there are no guarantees," Whelan said, "like you and Paddy in your SBS service, I've seen a lot of nastiness…people dying, sometimes at my hand, usually very ugly deaths at that. But I can promise you, as I did Caitlin, that my top priority is to come home to her and the boys alive and whole."

Tom put his empty tumbler down on the countertop and looked at Whelan. "Just about the time you went to the States back at the first of the year, some senator over there made a big deal of exposing an old CIA-military special operations unit. Somethin' that was deadlier and more effective than the Navy SEALs or Delta Force. Paddy and I," he shot a glance at his son, who nodded, "have been wonderin' if you were a part of that."

Whelan stood silently for a long time looking back and forth at each of the other men. Finally, he said, "Yes."

"And are these associates of yours also part of the same unit?"

Another long pause then Whelan said, "Yes."

A sense of relief seemed to come over Tom. "Christ," he said, "I feel better already. C'mon, lads, let's eat."

Later that evening, when Whelan and his family had returned home, he lay awake with a sleeping Caitlin wrapped in his arms. The boys were long in bed. He and Caitlin had made love. It was long, slow, patient, and passionate. They were so familiar with each other's bodies and the ways that pleasured each of them to the point of ecstasy and beyond. It was much more than lovemaking. It was a breathless, dizzying sojourn on Olympus.

Afterwards, an exhausted Caitlin quickly fell asleep in his arms. Whelan, though, lay there in the dark pondering all of the question marks that lay ahead in the immediate future. That future would start very soon with his pending return to the United States and a final reunion with the Sleeping Dogs.

42 THE APPALACHIANS

Less than a week later, Whelan lay awake in his bunk in the drafty old cottage that had been provided to the Dogs during their retraining. Determining who owned the cottage would require a lifetime of effort by a skilled title tracer. It was made of fieldstones mortared together many decades ago. The sagging trusses supported a roof of cedar shake shingles that were warped with age and darkened with the accumulation of mold. The interior was chilly and damp, and smelled faintly of mildew. It sat in a small clearing in the midst of a thick, old growth forest in the mountains of North Carolina adjacent to the Pisgah National Forest and not far from the town of Brevard.

It was beneath an umbrella created by the tall Fraser fir and red spruce trees that only grow above the four thousand foot mark in the Southern Appalachians. Their interlocking branches blocked much of the sunlight during daylight hours. A few small, grimy windows further dimmed the sparse light that managed to trickle through. It created an atmosphere that seemed perennially to border on gloom. Although officially it was referred to as "the Cabin", Whelan and most of the others had redubbed the place "the Cavern". Almeida referred to it as "Hotel California". He said the place reminded him of a line in an Eagles song: "You can check out anytime you like/but you can never leave". The overall encampment of which it was a part was known as "the Camp".

It was four-thirty in the morning and Whelan could hear the other Dogs stirring restlessly in their beds. The late geneticist, Jacob Horowitz, had suggested that their seeming inability to achieve deep slumber was a trait of their genetic construct. He proposed that, because they were disposed to be warrior-like in attitude and physicality, it was their natures to be alert and ready to respond to threats at all times, even when sleeping.

The long six months of conditioning and training exercises had had the desired effects on their bodies, knowledge bases and reflexes. But it also had become boring, the day after day repetitiveness of the exercises and assignments. Even the benefits of the brief ten-day respite allowing them to visit their families – those who had families, had quickly worn off. The men all were growing restless, including Whelan. They wanted to carry out the mission, whatever it would be, and get on with their lives.

Whelan reflected on memories of his recent trip to Ireland. When he thought of Caitlin and his sons the familiar ache welled up deep within his chest. Like the others, he had grown weary of the endless exercises. Some had been in better condition than others. Despite his expressed desires to the contrary, "Colonel" Rafe Almeida had been rounded up forcibly by Larsen and brought into the fold. After a few days, he had realized that it was the best thing he had going. The promised payoff at the conclusion of their mysterious mission was substantial. Just the same, Almeida rarely stopped grousing or whining.

Even the philosopher, Quentin Thomas, had undergone a change of heart and showed up in the second week, on a year's sabbatical from the university. When Whelan had asked him why he changed his mind, Thomas had said, "Guys like us need to live our lives on the surface of our bodies, not hiding deep in its interior like pussies. I felt myself withdrawing from the surface, growing stale. I need this challenge. I need to know that I'm still good enough." With the exception of Almeida, they all were in excellent physical condition. Even Almeida had improved noticeably in the six-months of training and conditioning. Part of that was due to the rigor of the program and part was due to the particulars of their genetics.

Finally, Whelan kicked off his blanket that warded off the mountain chill and stood up. Padding into a small bathroom, he brushed his teeth while staring at his unshaven countenance in the mirror. He affected a snarl and was reminded of an old movie. The Wolfman returns, he thought. He pulled on a pair of ragged cargo shorts, a tee shirt and battered running shoes, and went outside. Although it was still dark, he could see the small glows of gas grills in the mess tent a hundred yards away. The smell of coffee and breakfast foods wafted through the trees and he realized he was hungry. Breakfast was at five o'clock. Those who were on time ate. Others would have to wait until lunch.

As he approached the tent, he could hear the sounds of bacon sizzling in the frying pans and see the cook and her helper moving about. He was almost to the tent when he noticed someone sitting on an old tree stump holding a cup of coffee. The steam wafted up in a dancing pattern above the rim. The man held the cup with both hands as if to capture the warmth. It was Buster McCoy. "'Morning, Brendan," he said from behind the cup.

"General." Whelan nodded at him as he took a cup from the stack on one of the long wooden folding tables and drew some coffee from the urn that was next to the cups.

"Come and sit over here," McCoy said. "I'm glad to have a chance to talk with you one-on-one."

Whelan sat on the damp, cold ground near McCoy and leaned back against a red spruce tree that was at least eighty feet tall. The cook was several generations a southerner and had added chicory to the coffee. It brought a certain bitterness to the already dark, potent brew. He blew across the top of the cup to cool the surface then took a sip and savored the strong taste.

"How did things go in Ireland?" McCoy said. "Family doing well?"

"It was too long in coming and passed by too quickly," Whelan said. "Yeah, everyone's fine."

McCoy sipped some more coffee and said, "The flight go okay? No issues on entering Ireland or the U.S.?"

"Traveling to and from small airports in a private jet with very well crafted fake documents does have its advantages."

The General chuckled. "Yes, the cooperation of the Mueller brothers and their almost unfathomable wealth provides unlimited opportunities for us." Then he turned serious. "What's your assessment of our status, the preparedness of your colleagues? It's been, what, twenty years since your last combat operation?"

Whelan considered his response carefully. The General's career, reputation, and perhaps his life were on the line, as was true for Levell and the other far-flung members of the Team. "Some of us are more ready than others."

"You're being enigmatic. I presume you're referring to Almeida."

Both men sipped their coffees for a while. "Yeah, he's not in the kind of condition, physically and emotionally, he needs to be in for a mission," Whelan said. He paused and looked at McCoy.

"Who else?"

"Stensen is ready physically, but he's a loose cannon. He'll more than carry his share when the killing starts, but his pernicious bloodlust is a twenty-four seven affliction."

McCoy had been pondering the contents of his coffee cup. He raised his head and said, "Are you aware that he is a serial killer?"

"Yeah."

"It seems, however, that he only kills bad people."

Yeah, but it's in accord with his definition of 'bad'."

"Are you suggesting that those two should not be included in the mission?"

"No. That's going to depend on the nature of the mission. I'm just suggesting some of us might become casualties, and others of us might incur unnecessary collateral damage on occasion."

At that moment, Kirkland materialized in front of them, startling McCoy and causing him to spill some of his coffee.

"Jesus, Kirkland, where the hell did you come from?"

Kirkland was casually twirling the *jō* stick in his right hand. "Just out for my morning constitutional, General."

McCoy shook his head and rose slowly and stiffly from the tree stump. He walked over to the urn and poured himself another cup. "Either of you men want coffee?" he said.

Whelan moved his head back and forth a few times indicating he wasn't interested.

"I don't touch the stuff," Kirkland said. "Makes me jumpy. Interferes with my combat instincts."

Still angry about being startled, McCoy said, "Well, we certainly wouldn't want that to happen, would we." There was more than a note of sarcasm in his tone. He turned to walk back to his tree stump perch.

Kirkland reached into the pocket of his windbreaker and made a slight flicking motion with his hand, so fast as to be almost imperceptible.

The cup in McCoy's hand shattered, sending hot coffee splattering onto his pants. "Ow, goddammit", he said. "What are you doing, you crazy bastard."

Kirkland nodded at a tall Fraser fir behind and to McCoy's right. "I was practicing my *shuriken* technique on that tree over there," he said referring to the Japanese throwing star. "But I missed. Guess I need more practice." Kirkland grinned at Whelan, who just shook his head.

McCoy, still angry, grabbed a new cup and poured more coffee. He shook his head and said, "Sometimes I think all of you bastards are as crazy as Stensen."

"Possibly," Whelan said, "but no one does what we do as well as we do it."

Taking a sip of his coffee, McCoy said, "Very soon you're going to get an opportunity to prove that statement." He turned and walked away.

All of the Dogs, except one, were up in time to have breakfast. Rafe Almeida, as usual, missed it. Afterwards, as the day was breaking, they all went for a long training run on a narrow dirt road. It wound up the steep slope of the mountain and through the damp, earthy-smelling forest. Angry at missing breakfast, Almeida sprinted off the front. He very quickly ran out of steam and was swallowed up and passed by the others like an overzealous rider in the Tour de France. He cursed them as they pulled steadily away from him. Stensen gave him the finger.

The run, which circled the top of the mountain at an elevation of almost six thousand feet then returned to the base camp, occupied most of the morning. Following an hour for lunch and recovery, they engaged in martial arts and hand-to-hand combat training. Rhee Kang-Dae, Levell's personal assistant, and Paul Fontenot were among their instructors. Levell had brought Fontenot from Houma, Louisiana in an effort to get his mind off his pending divorce from Leonie. He finally had accepted the realization that she had been sleeping around throughout their marriage. It was a recent, and still very painful wound. Whelan and the other five men respected Rhee and Fontenot for their high degree of skills in the martial arts. They all were aware also of the emotional beating Leonie continued to administer to Fontenot. He had left her in an effort to salvage his emotional and psychological well being, but she continued to find ways to taunt him with her past indiscretions and current affairs.

These training sessions were long and physically demanding. Rafe Almeida provided the comic relief, unwillingly. Because of his personal habits and attitude, he was the least conditioned of the group. Each time he finished last in an exercise, he complained bitterly that there had been an element of unfairness or that the others had cheated. Nevertheless, he regularly bragged about his superior prowess as an athlete, lover, fighter, and substance abuser. For the most part, the others tolerated his alternate whining and crowing, but there were points where Almeida's behavior crossed the line. Today was one of them.

Kirkland was working with Almeida in a simulated combat situation. Almeida had a SOG SEAL Team knife with a powder coated seven-inch combo edged steel blade. In this case, the edges and point had been dulled to avoid serious injury, but it still was capable of inflicting damage. Kirkland was unarmed.

Almeida feinted a couple of times then attacked. He was very quick. Kirkland was quicker. Using a smooth flowing *Tang Soo Do* technique, he blocked Almeida's thrust, applied a wristlock and swept him to the ground, disarming him at the same time.

Almeida landed hard on his back. For a moment he seemed slightly stunned. He looked back at Kirkland and a snarl formed on his lips. Jumping to his feet, he said, "You got lucky; that's all." He lowered his head and charged Kirkland. His intended target used another sweeping technique and Almeida hit the ground even harder this time.

After a few moments, he sat up and shook his head as if to clear it. When he was able, he climbed slowly to his feet. He looked around and spotted an axe used to chop firewood. Someone had left it resting against the trunk of a tree. He snatched it up and charged Kirkland again. As he raised the axe over his head, Larsen swept in with the speed of a jungle cat and yanked it out of Almeida's grip. At the same moment, Thomas swung a heavily muscled forearm into Almeida's exposed throat, clothes-lining him.

All activity in the camp had stopped as everyone turned to watch the action. Almeida lay on the ground in pain and struggling to regain his breath following the blow. Thomas straddled him and leaned over to speak to him. Pale blue-gray eyes deeply set in an impassive black face transfixed Almeida. "Give it a rest, Rafe," he said. Almeida managed a nod as he massaged his throat. Thomas leaned down and grabbed the front of Almeida's shirt. Swiftly, and with no apparent effort, he pulled him to his feet.

In a croak, Almeida said, "Get your fuckin' hands off me." Thomas released him. He staggered backward for a step then turned and stumbled toward the cabin.

Whelan and Levell looked at each other for a moment and Levell motioned with his head toward Almeida's retreating back. Whelan gave a barely perceptible nod in return and followed Almeida into the cabin.

Inside, Almeida turned to him and said, "What the fuck do you want?" His voice was still raspy.

"It's not what I want, Rafe. It's what I have to do. We need to talk."

"Fuck off, I ain't got nothin' to say."

"Good, then listen. You're not in the same condition the rest of us are. And your attitude is worse."

"So what. I'm more than a match for any Norm."

"Maybe," Whelan said, "but not by much. You're putting the mission at risk. And you're putting each one of us at greater risk. You're the weak link, Rafe."

"Yeah? So what are you gonna do, fire me?"

"It's too late in the game for that."

Almeida digested this last statement. "You mean you're gonna snuff me. Jesus Christ! A guy is dealing with really shitty personal problems and his reward is to be killed. Fuck!"

He turned away from Whelan. As he did, Whelan thought he caught a glimpse of tears welling up in the other man's eyes. "Look, Rafe," he said, "I don't want to see that happen either. We've known each other a long time, even been friends at times. You've saved my ass and I've saved yours. But you've just about worn out your welcome here. The Team is putting together an exercise that will wrap up our training. I've asked them to give you one more shot at proving you belong. If you fuck this up, it's all over for you. Really over."

Almeida slowly turned around, his gaze locked on the floor. There were twin glistening tracks on his cheeks. "Thanks, Whelan," he said softly. "I'll give it my best, but sometimes it just seems like I can't help but fuck things up."

43 THE APPALACHIANS

It was seven o'clock in the evening and, despite the effect of Daylight Saving Time, it already was dusk in the valleys of North Carolina's Blue Ridge Mountains. There would be a full moon later in the evening, but the thick covering of branches would obscure most of its glory. The temperature, warmed during the day, was beginning to drop toward the high fifties. Dinner was over and the cooking crew had cleaned up and left for the day. Only six men remained at the Camp – Whelan, Larsen, Kirkland, Stensen, Thomas, and Almeida. They were sprawled around a small campfire, each grateful that the long training period was over at last. Tomorrow Levell and McCoy would roll out their final training operation. Following its successful completion, they would learn of the ultimate mission for which they had been training for so long.

Whelan sat on the ground with his back against a towering Fraser fir. He sipped slowly from a coffee mug that contained Black Bush, one of his favorite Irish whiskies. Larsen and Thomas were sharing a log as a sort of bench seat. Larsen was drinking his fourth Diet Coke of the evening, while Thomas nursed his fourth beer. Kirkland sat on a tree stump sharpening his favorite *wakizashi*, a Japanese short sword with a blade less than two feet in length. Stensen lay on his back with his eyes closed, though he was not sleeping. Almeida sat cross-legged on the ground, resting a bottle of cheap tequila in the diamond shaped area formed by his legs. It had been full when he began; now, it approached half-empty. He had a small towel laid over one of his knees. Several slices of lime were on it.

No one had spoken for a while. Eventually Almeida said, "I'm glad this fuckin' gig is almost over." He took a pull from the tequila bottle and chased it with a bite out of one of the lime slices.

"Is that so?" said Stensen without opening his eyes. "As if you have a life to go back to."

Angrily, Almeida said, "Fuck you, you fuckin' weirdo. I got plenty of life to go back to. Lotsa' chicks. Big money jobs. The whole nine yards."

"Really?" Stensen said mockingly. "If that's so, why are you here in the first place, Bigshot?"

Almeida tried to ignore him by taking another slug of tequila and biting another lime.

Stensen continued. "You're here for the money the Team's paying us, because you haven't got a pot to piss in."

"Oh yeah, Smartass? What are *you* doing here?" Almeida didn't wait for a response. "I'll fuckin' tell you why you're here. You're a fuckin' killer, plain and simple. Levell and the others offered you a chance to whet your bloodlust and you fuckin' couldn't say no."

"Wow," Stensen said. "Imagine a little redneck cretin knowing how to use words like 'whet' and 'bloodlust'. And in the same sentence, too. Perhaps there's hope for America's public school system after all."

"Alright," Whelan growled, "get off each other's asses and stay off."

Larsen smiled the faintest of smiles and said, "The Alpha Wolf has spoken. Everyone take heed accordingly."

Whelan chuckled and said, "You mocking me?"

"*Moi?* Perish the thought." Larsen raised his can of Diet Coke in salute.

Whelan raised his mug in return. What a bunch of oddballs, he thought and shook his head.

"You know," Thomas said, "Nick raised a good point. What the hell is each of us doing this for? I, for one, would like to know." He turned to Larsen seated next to him.

The Man With No Neck laughed, a very rare occurrence. "Heck, that's easy. I'm getting away from my wife."

Everyone laughed. To know Larsen was to know of the uneasy relationship he had always had with his wife, Sharon. He also thrived on danger, as did the others. Levell and McCoy were providing him with the perfect opportunity to do both of the things he liked best.

"At the risk of stepping on your overly sensitive ego, Rafe, I think Nick pretty much spelled out what brought you here," Thomas said. "But what about you, Nick? Why are you here?"

Stensen, still lying on the ground with his eyes closed and his hands underneath his head, stretched languidly and sighed. "It was time to move on. Civilization, with its twisted concept of justice, was closing in on me."

"Twisted concept of justice?" Kirkland said. "You mean society's ideas of fair trials, lengthy appeals and decades before actually executing perps, or maybe just letting them go because prisons are crowded or for some other inane reason?"

"Yep, that would be it," Stensen said.

Kirkland nodded thoughtfully. "I see your point."

"So, what brought you back, Marc?" Thomas said.

Kirkland looked thoughtfully up into the rapidly gathering darkness for a few moments before saying, "Do you guys remember watching reruns as a kid of an old TV western called 'Have Gun, Will Travel'?"

"Yeah, I do," Almeida said. The others nodded.

"It was about a gun for hire in the Old West. A guy named Paladin traveled around helping people who were being oppressed by the ugly side of human nature." Kirkland paused and sighted down the razor sharp edge of the wakizashi's blade, turning it slowly in his hands, first one way then the other. Satisfied with what he saw, he leaned down and laid it gently on a cloth next to his right foot. "The show must have made a real impression on me, because that's what I do for a living." He looked at Whelan. "Like that little job at Remy's bar down in Louisiana."

Whelan nodded in recognition and smiled. "So, this operation gives you three squares a day, decent cash flow, and a chance to continue righting wrongs."

"That pretty much covers it," Kirkland said. He turned toward Thomas. "Alright, Quentin, why's a guy with a cush job in academia risking his neck?"

"Yeah," Almeida said, "and with all that college pussy around to hit on, you must be out of your mind?" He began to croon the rock classic by Dire Straits: "That ain't workin', that's the way you do it. Get your money for nothin' and your chicks for free."

Thomas drained his bottle of beer and dropped it next to the preceding three. "Well, gents, it's really very simple. Yes, I'm in a very good situation, and it's better than I imagined it would be. But there's just one thing." He paused for effect and grinned. "I couldn't live with myself if I let you bozos go off and screw up a mission or get yourselves killed."

There was a very brief silence then the others laughed and hooted. "Shit," Almeida said, "if it wasn't for watchin' out for your black ass, this mission would be a lot easier."

Thomas laughed. It came out a deep rumble like distant thunder. "Spoken like a true cracker, Rafe," he said.

Slowly, one by one, all heads turned toward Whelan. "What about it, Bren. You have a family and a good life in Ireland. What brings you here?" Thomas said.

"Yeah," Almeida said, "you're not even an American. Why should your Irish ass give a shit about the US of A?"

"Actually, Rafe, I have dual citizenship."

"Yeah? Is that like being a switch hitter or something?" Almeida laughed at his own attempt at humor. No one else laughed with him. Whelan looked at him for a few moments. It was a cold, hard look. Almeida squirmed and took a long swallow from his bottle of Tequila.

"Ignore the little shit," Kirkland said. "Tell us what brought you back to the unit."

Whelan picked up a twig from the ground and began to doodle in the soft earth with it. "You each have expressed interesting reasons for your being here, some of them even may be admirable," he said with a slight smile. "But mine really is very simple, and I believe it's the same reason each of you is here. Throughout history there always have been evil people who wanted to destroy large numbers of humanity and subjugate the rest. By my assessment, that scenario may be at its worst today."

"Ah," Thomas said. "It's the age old battle between good and evil. The *yin* and the *yang*."

"That's not quite correct," said Kirkland. "*Yin yang* merely expresses the interdependence between seemingly polar opposites, not the irrevocable divide between good and evil."

Thomas stared at Kirkland for moment. "Thanks for sharing, Obi Wan," he said.

"Quentin does get my point," Whelan said. "This country, America, has defended democracy and freedom of choice throughout much of the world for decades. Now, it's crumbling from within. When the light goes out here, it will be extinguished around the world. I don't want my children and grandchildren to inherit that nightmare.

"Levell, McCoy, the Mueller brothers, and all the other members of the Team understand the situation. They're risking their lives and fortunes to halt this long, accelerating slide over the brink. It really is as simple as choosing between good and evil." He turned his head slowly and made eye contact with each of the others one by one.

No one was laughing now. "Damn, dude." Thomas said after a while. "Do you think the six of us can make a difference at this point?"

"Of course. Ordinary people make a difference everyday. And we're far from ordinary."

With three-quarters of the bottle of tequila in his system and three sheets to the wind, Almeida said with a distinct slur in his voice, "From what I hear, you got a hot wife, kids…, your own business,… and you don't even live in this fuckin' country. You sure you want to risk all that as well as your life for *this* shit?"

Whelan, face impassive, looked at Almeida and said, "I'm here, aren't I."

44 THE APPALACHIANS

This was to be their final exercise before the actual mission was rolled out for them. Levell, McCoy and TEAM adherents from the highest levels of the Department of Defense and the CIA had carefully planned the operation. To determine their level of competence in the field, Whelan and his colleagues were to successfully carry out a simulated ambush of an elite military unit. In this case, that target was a ten-man squad of the Second Platoon, Bravo Company, Third Battalion of the Army's Seventy-Fifth Ranger Regiment headquartered at Fort Benning, Georgia. The 75th Ranger Regiment is a special operations combat formation within the U.S. Army Special Operation Command.

The exercise was to be observed by unmanned surveillance drones. In addition, a major in the Marines' FORECON, or Force Reconnaissance, had been assigned to the Ranger unit as an observer for this exercise. His role was to observe and report as well as to halt the exercise if he believed serious injury or death of a participant was imminent. The major reported via an encrypted cell phone signal to Levell, McCoy and other controllers. They were in a cabin a few miles away near the town of Rosman, just above the North Carolina-Georgia line. The drones transmitted signals to the same location. In addition, the Ranger unit also carried technology enabling them to receive the drones' signals. In theory, it gave them a decided advantage over Whelan's unit.

The strike would occur in the heavily wooded, mountainous terrain of western North Carolina. The Rangers had been told that this was a training exercise, but to be vigilant at all times for an attack by another elite group. Being Rangers, the men welcomed the opportunity to excel in a combat situation.

The Rangers had been transported by van to a spot just off NC 215, which had been closed to traffic north of Rosman for the duration of this exercise.

They were in full combat gear and carried weapons that bore close resemblances to M16A2 and M-4 combat assault rifles, but had been modified to fire projectiles similar to paintballs for war games purposes. They also carried specially designed, nonlethal knives that were designed to leave simulated bloodstains when used in close quarters combat.

They forded Diamond Creek, a tributary of the French Broad River, and hiked up and over a steeply sloped ridge to the west. At the bottom of the far side, they turned north and hiked along a narrow valley between two ridgelines. The steep slopes on either side of the small creek were thickly forested with Fraser fir, red spruce, fire cherry, yellow birch, mountain ash, and mountain maple. Patches of wild blueberry, mountain raspberry, red elder, and bush honeysuckle produced a pleasant fragrance. At various points, wildflowers such as ox-eye daisy, white snakeroot, purple-fringed orchid, St. John's wort and pink turtlehead added color to the surroundings. The area was devoid of human habitation, and the drones were equipped with thermal imaging technology that confirmed the absence of anyone else in the area except the Rangers.

Just after the late-falling darkness of summer hours descended, the Rangers came upon a small glade in the forest and set up camp. The Rangers' first task was to place a number of protective surveillance devises along a perimeter one hundred fifty yards from the encampment. They used the LKMD motion detector, a small, modular, unattended, tactical, ground sensor designed to provide early detection of the presence of intruders. Upon such detection, the LKMD would activate its light modules. It also can be programmed to send an audible or silent alarm to a hand-held remote control module.

Two sentries were posted. One was across the creek and upslope from the encampment. The other was above the bivouac area about fifty yards up the opposite slope. Each sentry had a hand-held remote control module for the LKMD detectors as well as a laptop for monitoring the signals sent by the drones patrolling the sky above. The sentries would be relieved every two hours throughout the night.

As the first two Rangers took up their posts, the others ate their Meals, Ready to Eat, or MREs, and turned in. The Marine Corps major carefully surveyed the surrounding area. Satisfied that nothing seemed out of the ordinary, he walked thirty feet back down the creek to a spot where a fallen tree had formed a bench-like seat. He climbed over the trunk and inspected it closely for insects that might be clinging to it. Finding none, he scraped the fallen pine needles, leaves and other soft forest detritus beneath it with his boot to from a small depression then climbed back over the trunk. The major dropped his pants, sat back on the tree trunk with his butt hanging slightly off of it, and responded to a call from nature.

When he finished, he used a small amount of tissue that he carried in his backpack and pulled his trousers back up. He stepped over the trunk one more time and began scruffing the leaves and other materials over the feces. Almost immediately, something caught his eye. There was a large white X painted on the tree trunk that hadn't been there only moments ago. In war games, it can be the symbol for a planted explosive device. He was stunned that someone could sneak up that close to him undetected. If this was a real combat situation, instead of a simulation, he realized he would be dead now. He suddenly had a better understanding of an earlier comment McCoy had made about the their opponents' senses of humor. "Goddammit," he said under his breath.

As quietly as he thought he had said it, one of the sentries said, "Something wrong, Major?"

"No. Just keep your eyes open. Stay alert."

Immediately, McCoy shouted through the Major's ear bud, "Goddammit, Major, your role is that of an observer. A *silent* observer."

Shit, the Major thought as he walked back into the encampment. First I get my ass blown off taking a dump, and then I end up on Ball-buster McCoy's shit list. He was angry, but he was developing a very deep respect for the Sleeping Dogs. Maybe the myths and legends surrounding them were true after all. One thing, he thought as he lay down on the bed of leaves and pine needles he had piled up, it was going to get interesting very soon.

45 THE APPALACHIANS

The Dogs had hiked down the west side of Diamond Creek from Macedonia Church Road the previous day. Their own well-placed and camouflaged surveillance devices had picked up the Rangers moving steadily toward them. Judging from the pace the Rangers were maintaining, and knowing they wouldn't want to continue through the rugged country in darkness, Whelan accurately identified the spot where the unit would bivouac for the night.

The Dogs were aware of the surveillance drones and the LKMD perimeter devices the Rangers were using, and they had a few tricks of their own. Each of them was wearing a specially made ghillie suit, a camouflage outfit designed to resemble the surrounding flora. It allowed them to blend perfectly into the background. The suits, long a mainstay for snipers, had recently been improved in a number of ways, especially for the military. They now are much cooler than the older, heavier ones that not only impeded movement but also retained the wearer's body heat like a thick sweat suit. Even more important, these new suits utilized a material that reduces the wearer's body heat envelope, registering on thermal imaging devices as a small animal about the size of a raccoon.

Stensen lay on the forest floor in a thick copse of red spruce. The ghillie sniper suit he was wearing was lightweight, and he could feel the late evening chill of the mountain air. Even so, he was beginning to sweat. He felt a bead of perspiration meandering slowly from his hairline to his right eyebrow. He blinked rapidly a couple of times, hoping to redirect it. It may have altered course slightly, but it didn't stop, eventually rolling over his eyebrow and down into the corner of his eye. He held a British-made L115A3 Long Range Rifle or 'Long', as snipers liked to call it. In the right hands, it had the capability of taking out targets from as much as a mile away. Ordinarily, it weighed fifteen pounds and fired 8.59-millimeter rounds, but

211

Stensen's had undergone major modifications. It now fired a very potent tranquillizer dart, but at a much reduced muzzle velocity in order to avoid seriously injuring its human targets. As a result of the modifications, its distance and accuracy also had been reduced to an effective range of approximately one hundred fifty yards.

This particular weapon had been equipped with a suppressor and a night vision scope. The scope worked wonders with the ambient light, but it reduced vision to two dimensions. Among the Sleeping Dogs, Stensen was the finest marksman. His job on this exercise was to take out the sentries at the appropriate time. He had been motionless for several hours, waiting along with the others for the signal to strike.

At last, about one-thirty in the morning and approximately thirty minutes after the third shift of sentries had assumed their posts, Stensen heard the sound of a small click in his ear bud. After two seconds, it was repeated twice in rapid succession. Whelan had given the signal. He sighted through the infrared night vision scope. Taking in a deep breath, Stensen exhaled slowly as he gently increased his finger's pressure on the trigger.

The dart flew true and straight. The head of the sentry posted on the opposite side of the creek from the encampment snapped sharply to the right. He felt a stabbing pain in his neck where the left carotid artery carried cerebral blood flow to his brain. In an adult, CBF is typically seven hundred fifty milliliters, or more than one and a half pints, per minute. It is equivalent to fifteen percent of total cardiac output. Instinctively, the Ranger grabbed at the spot of the sudden stinging sensation. As his hand felt the shaft of the dart, his brain slipped into blackness. Part of the surrounding forest rose up to catch him as he pitched forward. It was Kirkland in a ghillie suit.

On the other side of the creek and upslope from the encampment, the other sentry sat with his back against a balsam tree. While he was unaware of it, he was just beyond the critical range of accuracy for Stensen's modified L115A3 Long Range Rifle. The Ranger was watching the screen of his laptop for signals from the drone overhead that showed any signs of living creatures that approximated human beings in size. Other than a few small animals, he saw nothing remarkable. He knew that this rugged, virtually uninhabited area was home to bobcats, gray and red foxes, coyotes, chipmunks, cottontail rabbits, feral pigs, opossums, muskrats, striped skunks and other species. Most of these animals foraged at night, so their presence was neither unexpected nor unusual.

Periodically, the sentry put his night vision field glasses to his eyes and carefully swept the area. He saw nothing. Only rarely did he glance behind him toward the encampment, believing that area to have been secured previously. Even if he had done so, he would not have noticed Larsen in his ghillie suit slowly edging almost imperceptibly up on him. After a while, the

Ranger stood and began to stretch, his body stiffening in the cool night air and the cramped sitting position.

Suddenly, something than seemed like the incarnation of Bigfoot swept the Ranger off his feet and held him a few inches off the ground in a one-armed clinch that felt like a steel hawser being tightened by a capstan on a naval ship. His assailant's other hand clamped over his mouth so firmly he thought his face might be torn off. The Ranger was young, strong and well trained. He tried wiggling free, but Larsen's grip was so tight he almost couldn't breathe. Next, he attempted to smash Larsen's face with a blow from the back of his head, but Larsen had tucked his face into the Ranger's back leaving nothing to strike but air.

The Ranger instinctively tried to smash his booted foot down on the arch of Larsen's foot, but he was being held too high off the ground to succeed. In desperation, he tried to swing his heel backward into Larsen's shin. Larsen simply threw his left leg around both of the Ranger's legs and locked his left foot behind his right knee effectively neutralizing all motion by the other man. Using the hand gripping the Ranger's face, Larsen pulled the man's head around to the right until it reached the point where vertebra would begin to separate. His victim began making guttural sounds out of pain and a fear of death.

Larsen said in a low whisper, "This is supposed to be a simulation, and I'm not supposed to really kill you."

The Ranger grunted.

"But," Larsen said, "if you don't play by the rules of this exercise, I will snap your neck in a nanosecond. You understand?"

As difficult as it was, given the position his head was in and the strain on his neck, the Ranger managed a nod.

Larsen said, "When I take my hand away, don't make a sound, not even a deep breath. Your questions will be answered soon enough. Understand?"

Again, the Ranger managed a slight nod.

"I want you on the ground, face down," Larsen said. "I'm gonna truss you up. This will all be over in a couple of minutes and I'll be back to release you." He lowered the man's feet to the ground and slowly loosened his grip on his face. Pointing to the ground in front of them, Larsen eased the grip he had around the Ranger's arms and body.

The man knelt then stretched out face down on the forest floor. Larsen quickly bound his wrists behind him with plastic ties then did the same with his ankles. He bound both sets of ties together with a third one. Finally, he produced a cloth from beneath his ghillie suit and stuffed it in the Ranger's mouth, ensuring it would stay there with a strip of duct tape that he wrapped around his head. Then, just as quickly as he had materialized, Larsen was gone.

The Marine FORECON major was cold and uncomfortable. He stirred restlessly and tried to find a warm spot under his blanket. The slight mound of leaves and other decaying forest debris that formed his bed was damp and uncomfortable. He rolled over onto his back and raised his head for a look around the encampment. Nothing seemed out of place, yet he knew the Sleeping Dogs were wide-awake and close, very close. He glanced at the Rangers. All seemed to be sleeping peacefully, but he knew they were trained to awaken and leap into action without hesitation. When were their opponents going to strike? And how?

He saw one of the Rangers get up and walk a sanitary distance into the darkness for a latrine break. The man carried his modified M16A2 with him. The major doubted he would have an opportunity to use the weapon, and also doubted he would be returning. He was right. As the Ranger relaxed and began to relieve himself, a hand suddenly clamped over his mouth. Simultaneously, a rubber knife modified for war games purposes slid across his throat in an instant, leaving a red stain to simulate the gaping wound a real blade would have left.

Startled and angry that he had urinated on himself, the Ranger started to struggle. With a hand still clamped over his mouth like a vise and his assailant's other arm wrapped around both of the Ranger's so tightly he almost couldn't breathe, his efforts were wasted. The FORECON major stepped in front of him shaking his head in a negative signal and pointed to a spot on the ground. Very quietly he said, "Sit down soldier. You're out of the game."

Quentin Thomas nodded at the major and quickly gagged and bound the Ranger in the same fashion Larsen had trussed the sentry. Then, he slipped away into the darkness.

A few minutes before 3:00 a.m., two Rangers arose, stretched, and, picking up their weapons, began walking upslope in opposite directions toward the sentry posts. Each inadvertently triggered a trip wire and compressed air devices splattered them with a white, paint-like substance. It simulated the lethal damage of an explosion that a real device would have caused. Larsen wrapped up one of the Rangers like a boa constrictor crushing its prey. "You've been blown up and are out of it. Understand?"

The Ranger grunted something that sounded like "Uh huh", and Larsen released him. A few moments later he was trussed up similarly to the others who previously had been removed from the exercise.

Things didn't go so smoothly on the other side of the creek. Kirkland had grabbed the other Ranger who had triggered the other simulated IED and instructed him much as Larsen had done with his colleague. When he released the Ranger, the man was so frustrated he shouted, "Goddammit!"

Instantly, the five remaining Rangers were awake and reaching for their weapons. Two and a fraction seconds later Whelan and Almeida had fired rounds that, had they been using real bullets and not dye pellets that simulated wounds, would have been instantly fatal. A couple of the Rangers seemed confused by the suddenness of the ambush and appeared ready to react to the assault. The FORECON major shouted, "Stand down. This exercise is over!" As a Marine, he secretly was pleased that an elite Army unit had been taken down in an exercise. He was certain a Marine unit would have fared better. Still, it bothered him greatly that the winners, these Sleeping Dogs, were so secret that no one knew whether they even were a military unit.

The trussed-up Rangers were released and Whelan explained to the stunned unit how he and his colleagues had managed to take them out.

One of the Rangers, a Staff Sergeant, said, "I heard rumors about a special black ops unit. My brother served in the Gulf War. He said these guys actually infiltrated Saddam's palace, killed a couple hundred of his elite guards and came very close to killing that sadistic sonofabitch himself."

Whelan looked at the soldier with a steady gaze. "That's all that is. A bunch of rumors."

"That's a hell of a note," Almeida said. He spat the words out like they were flavored with vinegar. "Served our country and that's all we are. Just fuckin' rumors."

All eyes quickly turned toward him. Whelan locked him in a withering gaze and said, "Rafe!" The word came in a low, rumbling growl, threatening like the sound a lion would make just before attacking a cornered eland.

"Then who the hell are you guys, to be able to take us out like you did?" the sergeant said. "I mean we have LKMD perimeter devices, surveillance drones with infrared sensors, thermal vision night goggles. Who can get through that?"

Whelan shrugged. "Let's just say we're testing new gear that's still in the experimental stages." He paused then said, "That's enough Q and A. Anything else you need to know will be provided at the discretion of the Department of the Army." He motioned to the rest of his men and, except for Almeida, they rose in unison to leave. Almeida climbed wearily to his feet, sighed and began to trudge after the others.

A moment later Whelan's ear bud crackled and he heard Levell's voice. "Congratulations, men, for a job well done. Training is over. We'll take a day off then begin preparing for the mission."

46 THE APPALACHIANS

Following their successful operation with the Army Rangers, Levell had given the six men brief time off. Practice was over. In twenty-four hours, they would begin preparing for their real mission. There wasn't sufficient time for Larsen or Whelan to visit their families, but the six men were ready for some relaxing, enjoyable moments even if it was only for an evening.

The tavern was on an empty stretch of Highway 64 about halfway between Brevard and Rosman. It was in a relatively flat area in the valley carved over the eons by the convolutions of the steadily flowing French Broad River. The bar wasn't much to look at. It was built log cabin style and, judging from the glaring lack of symmetry and appearance, it had been expanded more than once over the years. The few windows, dusty and long in need of washing, were filled with neon signs advertising various brands of beer. The dust on the windows came from the unpaved parking lot. By the time the six men arrived at a few minutes past eight in the evening, the lot was filled with pickup trucks, SUVs, a few battered sedans and three or four motorcycles.

They squeezed the borrowed Hummer into a narrow strip between the edge of the highway and the tree line and walked back up the road to the bar. All of them wore jeans. A few had on sweatshirts; the others wore lightweight jackets over t-shirts. Almeida, wearing only a t-shirt to ward off the evening chill, led the way, eager to start drinking. Larsen purposely was close behind him to keep him on a short leash. Kirkland walked beside Larsen. His lightweight bomber-style jacket concealed the two *nunchaku* stuffed into the waistband of his jeans. Thomas, Stensen and Whelan walked together a short distance behind the others. Each of them quietly studied the vehicles in the parking lot, their license plates, the structure of the bar and its surrounding area and the traffic passing by on the highway.

Larsen and Kirkland weren't missing much either, but they knew they could rely on Whelan and the others to fully apprise them of anything threatening in the situation. Almeida couldn't have cared less. He threw open the door to the tavern, stepped in and, in a loud voice, said, "Uncle Rafe is here ladies. Line forms on the right."

Several men turned to look at him; some of them may have been of a mind to kick this brash stranger's ass. Then they saw the Man With No Neck. And the other four dangerous looking men with him. Everyone turned back to their drinks and conversations, any interest in Rafe Almeida vanished from their minds.

Whelan paused just inside the door and appraised the environment. Country music coursed loudly through the sound system. A few couples were using a small dance floor that was squeezed into the center of the room. There were booths along the front wall and down the wall to the left of the entrance. An L-shaped bar ran along the wall to the right and along the back of the room. A kitchen of sorts was squeezed into the area behind the bar in the rear. There was a small hallway to the left. A sign that said "Restrooms" hung over it. Whelan's gaze swept over the room and he identified the four bouncers. There were several other men in the crowd that looked like they could be brawlers. He watched Almeida swagger across the room, and thought, this could be one of those nights.

There still were several empty tables, but only one vacant booth. It was against the wall to the left. The men took it. Almeida sat on the outside with Thomas next to him and Larsen directly across from him. Stensen sat next to him on the inside. Whelan and Kirkland pulled chairs up to the end of the table.

The bar was filling up when the six men arrived. More than one hundred patrons already were there. Forty percent of them were women of all shapes, sizes and ages. Almeida kept up a steady commentary, specifically describing the sexual practices and positions he'd like to enjoy with each of the women. After several moments, Thomas elbowed him. "Give it a rest, Rafe."

Larsen, more than the others, generally was amused by Almeida. A surprisingly benign smile spread across his otherwise sinister features and he slowly shook his head back and forth. "He can't give it a rest, Quentin. He's a horny little bastard."

"Yeah, well, somebody please throw a bucket of cold water on him."

After a few minutes, a waitress walked up to the booth. She was in her mid-forties and about thirty pounds overweight, most of it in her thighs, butt and waist. That didn't stop her from wearing very tight, very short denim cutoffs. She wore a bright pink sleeveless knit top that was cut low over her ample breasts. Letters on the front said "Tit For Tat". On the back of the top it said "What's Tat?"

"Hey, Beautiful, where you been all my life?" Almeida said as he eyed her breasts.

"Waitin' for you, Sugah." She had a western Carolina drawl. "What can I get for you big, strong men?"

Everyone ordered beer of one sort or another. Almeida also ordered a shot of tequila. As the waitress took their orders, he slowly slid his hand up the back of her thigh from her knee to the bottom of her cutoffs. She quickly stepped away from him. "Sugah, y'all want that arm tore off and shoved up yore ass, just keep it up," she said and glanced at one of the bouncers who was watching her.

"Hell, Baby, it's always up," Almeida said and flashed his best effort at a killer smile.

Whelan kicked him under the table. Hard. "Rafe," he said.

The message was in his tone, but it seemed to be lost on Almeida. "What? What did I do?" He held his hands out, palms up, and looked around the table. "Shit, if you pussies just wanna sit around and cry in your beer, that's your problem. But tonight, Rafe Almeida's gettin' laid."

Stensen said, "Does that mean you're gonna' go into the men's room and whack off?"

"You motherfucker! I'll kick your ass!"

Stensen smiled his cruel smile and said, "Whenever you're ready." The red glow deep in the center of his eyes suddenly brightened.

Whelan leaned across the corner of the table and grabbed Almeida's arm. "If any ass gets kicked tonight, it's going to be yours, Rafe. I'll drag you out of here and beat you half to death. How many fuckin' times do you have to be told to get your shit together and keep it that way."

Almeida tried to pull his arm away, but couldn't break Whelan's grip. "Fuck you," he said. "Who says you can kick my ass."

Larsen leaned forward, and with a pleasant smile, said, "I do, for one."

"So do I," said Thomas, his face impassive as usual.

"I think we should draw straws to see who gets to fuck him up," Stensen said. Whelan looked at him. "Enough, Nick. Don't add fuel to the fire. We're just going to have couple of cold ones and leave." He released Almeida's arm and said to him, "Any problems with the Norms could jeopardize everything. Stay cool."

The waitress arrived with a tray of drinks. Almeida grabbed the shot of tequila off her tray and tossed it back. "Gimme another one, you little hottie. In fact, bring me a couple of 'em. I'm thirsty tonight. And feelin' lucky, too." She left to wait on another group a few tables away.

A couple of older men, probably in their seventies and clearly overdressed for a country bar, had come in with two very young and attractive women. Barely more than teenagers, they wore almost identical strapless, tightly fitted sheaths of shimmery Dupioni silk that stopped a foot or so above the knee.

218

One wore red, the other cobalt blue. They took a table across the room from Whelan and the others. The situation gave every appearance of older men having bought and paid for an evening's fantasy.

When the music switched to country rock, the girls jumped up and all but dragged their companions onto the dance floor. The old guys were game, but it wasn't even close. The two women knew that every man in the place was staring and they were perpetual motion. They spun, shimmied, and gyrated all in perfect time to the music. The sensuality was so strong it almost dripped from them. As they shook and jumped, their firm young breasts all but broke loose from the restraint of their bras. Their short dresses hiked up higher and higher.

Almeida couldn't stand it. He jumped up and quickly threaded his way through the tables to the dance floor. Whelan and the others watched him carefully. His attempt to cut in on one of the couples failed, but in the process it seemed to irritate one of the older men. His date for the evening stepped between the two men and, placing both hands on Almeida's chest pushed him slowly off the dance floor. Whelan could almost read her lips; something along the lines of "We're not available tonight. You'll have to find someone else to dance with."

Almeida shrugged and walked over to the bar. In just moments, he had struck up an animated conversation with two unescorted women who had come in together a few minutes earlier. Whelan and the others, except for Stensen, kept their eyes on him. Stensen nursed his beer and studied the ever-growing crowd - the jungle beast surveying the Serengeti in search of his prey. Slowly, the red dots in the center of his eyes brightened and grew larger.

Next to Whalen, Larsen's back stiffened and he leaned back in his seat, turning his head slightly as if to listen to something coming from behind him. It wasn't lost on the others. Whalen leaned toward Larsen and strained to hear. As his brain filtered out the loud music and the din of the crowd, he could distinguish voices coming from the booth immediately behind Larsen and Stensen. Mostly, it was a man's voice, snarling threats at someone. "You stupid fuckin' bitch. How many times I gotta beat shit outta' yore sorry ass before you start to git it?"

Whelan heard the voice of a young girl responding. "I'm sorry, Ricky. I...didn't...mean...no harm by it. But...they're my family. I know you hate my daddy 'cause he doesn't think yore good for me...but I...miss 'em and needed to hear my momma's voice. Please...don't hurt me again." Her voice was filled with fear as she stumbled through the words. She sounded as if she would begin sobbing at any moment. In some ways, it reminded him of an incident in Ireland a long time ago, an incident that led him to meet the love of his life. For an instant, he felt that familiar tightening in his chest at the thought of Caitlin.

"Oh, I'll hurt you again, Lorene, you ever talk to that bunch of pig fuckers you call family," Ricky said. "I got a good mind to bounce yore stupid fuckin' head offa' that wall behind you."

The girl gasped as if in pain and started crying. "Please, Ricky, don't do that, it hurts so bad. I won't ever talk to my family again, I promise."

Larsen had heard enough and spun out of his seat as if he had been ejected from a cockpit. He stood in front of Ricky, who was still facing the girl seated beside him, his left hand clamped around her upper right arm. She was in pain. Her free hand was trying to loosen Ricky's grip. Her eyes were squeezed shut in agony and tears streamed down her face.

"Let go of her and try slapping my head against the wall," Larsen said. His voice was hard and measured.

Ricky was young, mid-twenties, and stocky like he spent time in the weight room. Larsen placed him at a little less than six feet tall and about two hundred pounds.

Ricky turned slowly toward Larsen. "Well looky here. Some dumb fucker wants to get his ass k...." He stopped short as he focused on the pure physicality of Larsen: massive chest, shoulders and arms, the frighteningly sinister face on a clean-shaven skull, a skull that rested directly on those powerful shoulders without wasting space for a neck.

"Wha...? Who the hell are you?" Ricky stammered.

The younger man did have a neck, and Larsen's left hand shot out and grabbed it in a vice-like grip. He yanked Ricky out of the booth and held him four inches off the ground with one arm. From the lack of exertion he exhibited, Larsen could have been holding a dishtowel. The bar suddenly was quiet.

Whelan said, "Bouncers," and the others slid smoothly and quickly out of their seats. Together with Whelan, they formed a semicircle with their backs to Larsen and Ricky. Kirkland reached behind his back and closed a hand on one of the *nunchaku*.

The four bouncers all were large men. They looked like they could have been former college linemen. Three were in their twenties, but the lead bouncer was at least ten years older and looked like he had been plying this trade for a long time. He wore a short-sleeve denim shirt that was unbuttoned to his waist. The name "Fred" was stitched over a breast pocket. As they quickly closed in on the scene, Fred said, "We don't tolerate no trouble in here, boys. You got issues, take 'em outside." He motioned toward the door with his head.

"We don't have issues," Whelan said as he stared down the bouncer. "You do. Little Ricky here was abusing this young lady. From a legal perspective, that could be a problem for the owners and operators of this bar, including you, if she was to suffer an injury."

Fred looked uncertain. He didn't like being told what to do by anyone who wasn't paying him for his services. He liked the looks of these five strangers even less, especially the one with no neck. He had been around strong men all his life, but he never had seen anyone hold nearly two hundred pounds straight out with one arm. Especially when the effort seemed no more taxing to Larsen than holding an ice cream cone. He also was aware there was a sixth man dancing with two women he had just picked up at the bar. Fred had been in the muscle business for many years and brawled countless times. He had beaten up more men than he could remember, and he had faith in the toughness of his three young colleagues. But something about these six men said "Not this time".

The other three bouncers shifted uneasily from foot to foot and glanced at each other then back to Fred. Finally, he said, "I see yore point. I don't like nobody beatin' on women in my bar." He turned to the other bouncers and said, "Throw this piece of trash outta here and make sure he don't come back. Take the shotgun with you. Watch 'em, if he tries to get outta his car with any kind of weapon, cut 'em in half."

Larsen released his grip on Ricky's neck and the young man collapsed into the booth gasping for air. He wasn't there long. Two of the bouncers swept him up and literally dragged him to the door. The third bouncer followed along carrying a Mossberg 500 Tactical Cruiser, a six shot, 12 gauge shotgun with a pistol grip and an eighteen and a half inch barrel. Despite a disapproving look from Larsen, Lorene bolted out of the booth and ran after Ricky. He shook his head in disappointment and said, "Isn't that what the shrinks used to call co-dependency twenty years ago?".

Fred looked at Whelan and Larsen and said, "We don't need no vigilante justice in here. From now on leave the housekeepin' to us. If there's any more trouble, I'll have to ask you boys to leave. If you don't, I won't hesitate to call the sheriff. Unnerstand?"

Whelan nodded. As Fred headed back toward the bar area, they all sat down, except Stensen. "I'm going to take a leak," he said and walked toward the sign that said "Restrooms".

"What now?" Whelan said.

"Maybe the man really does have to take a leak," Thomas said. "We *are* drinking beer. Speaking of which." He signaled to the waitress to bring another round.

"Where's Lover Boy now?" Larsen said.

Kirkland nodded toward the bar. Almeida and the two women had left the dance floor and were sitting at the bar again, laughing and drinking. In a few moments, one of them stood up and took Almeida's hand. Instead of returning to the dance floor, they threaded their way through the tables and went out the front door. Twenty minutes later they came back inside. The woman's hair was tousled and she was trying to smooth out her skirt. Almeida had a big, sleepy, satisfied grin on his face. He deposited the first woman back at the bar, took the other one's hand and led her outside.

"Jesus, the man's a fucking satyr," Thomas said.

"Good to know some things never change," said Kirkland.

When they returned, it was like a rerun of the first episode except Almeida's grin was a little wider and a little sleepier. This time, however, the scene had changed. Two men wearing jeans with big belt buckles and western style shirts had joined the first woman while Almeida was outside with the other one. From the way the first woman had greeted the men, one in particular, Whelan and the others knew these were their dates. When Almeida returned with the second woman and she saw the two men, she stopped laughing and seemed suddenly nervous.

The first woman introduced the men to Almeida, but no one offered a hand. Her friend seemed upset and kept touching her face. Her movements were stiff and she didn't seem to want to face the two men. One of them, obviously quite angry, grabbed her arm and seemed to be demanding something, an explanation perhaps. The woman looked down and to the right and seemed to be struggling to think of what to say.

Suddenly the man spun around and threw a punch at Almeida who partially blocked it with his shoulder. Before he could throw another one, Almeida picked the man up and threw him over the bar. The other man grabbed Almeida's shoulder and tried to spin him around, his fist drawn back. Almeida turned in the opposite direction and drove his right fist into the man's stomach, doubling him over then brought his left fist over the top of the man's shoulder and into the side of his head. He went down and stayed there.

The first bouncer on the scene grabbed Almeida from behind in a bear hug. Almeida snapped his head back smashing the man's nose then simply burst loose from the restraint, turned and kicked him in the knee. The bouncer went down, scattering a couple of bar stools on the way. Almeida charged the second bouncer and picked up the three hundred pound man with ease, smashing the small of his back into the top edge of the bar where it formed an L-shape.

At that point, Fred arrived. He swung a sap in a short, powerful arc into the back of Almeida's head. Stunned and wobbly-kneed, Almeida was still on his feet. Fred sapped him again. After a third blow, Almeida slid into unconsciousness and sagged to the floor. Whelan and the others had closed the gap from their booth just as Almeida hit the floor. The crowd noise had ceased, although the music continued to blare. Everyone just stood and eyed each other for a few moments. Fred slapped the sap against the palm of his left hand, slowly. The fourth bouncer stood a few feet away with the pistol grip Mossberg aimed at Larsen's chest. They always point the weapons at the man with no neck, Larsen said to himself.

"Look, I done tole you boys there better not be no more trouble. Now, I want you to get on outta here. If you don't, I expect the sheriff will be comin' by in a couple of minutes."

Whelan nodded. He looked at Larsen then at Almeida's inert form. Larsen understood. He scooped Almeida up with one hand and laid him over a shoulder. It didn't appear that he used any more effort than he would have with an infant. Whelan motioned toward the door with his head. The men filed out after him and headed for their car.

When they got there, Stensen was sitting on the hood. The red glow was almost absent from his eyes. He looked at Almeida slung over Larsen's shoulder and said, "Why am I not surprised."

"I thought you were taking a leak," Whelan said.

"I needed some fresh air."

"This have something to do with Ricky?"

"Ricky who?" Stensen said with mock innocence.

"Fuck Ricky," Thomas said. "I hope you didn't harm the girl, what's her name...Lorene?"

"Shame on you, brother. I never harm women," Stensen said. The red glow in his pupils had shrunk to pinpoints.

47 THE APPALACHIANS

Levell was sitting at the battered kitchen table in the bunkhouse the men called the Cavern. Mr. Rhee had helped him move from the wheelchair to a simple wooden chair and then left the room. There was a cup of coffee in front of him that had long grown cold. The expression on his face was just the opposite. He was in a furious mood. He had summoned Whelan and, when he appeared at the kitchen doorway, Levell pointed to a chair across the table and said, "Sit."

Whelan remained in the doorway, gazing at the older man with a quizzical expression. After a few moments, he sat. "You wanted to see me, sir?"

"See you?" Levell said in a growl. "I'd like to wring your damn neck!"

Whelan leaned forward toward the other man and put his elbows on the table. "I take it this has to do with last night's events at the bar."

"Jesus H. Christ! How could you let shit like that happen when we're this close to the mission? We've come too far, invested too much, taken too many risks to blow it all in some redneck shithole." He paused for a few moments, as the two men held each other's gaze. He continued, "You of all people...the brightest, the natural leader, the alpha wolf...you couldn't have prevented that kind of shit from happening?"

"Cliff, it's been a long, hard six months of endless training and challenges. The men deserved an opportunity to let off some steam."

"Let off some steam? Shit, they were brawling. Do you not understand how dangerous it is for you men, with your unique abilities, to get into fights with Norms? It's a dead giveaway that you're not like the rest of us."

Whelan shook his head. "It wasn't like that, Cliff. It wasn't anything that you wouldn't have seen in any blue-collar bar. Hell, fighting is as much a part of that culture as it is in professional hockey."

"Wrong on a couple of counts. A guy Rafe's size tossing a three hundred pound man over the bar? Him picking up another three hundred pounder and running him halfway across the room and slamming him into the bar rail? A tough guy bouncer having to sap Rafe three fucking times in order to subdue him? Larsen holding another man off the floor at arm's length like he was a friggin' daisy or a petunia?"

Whelan waiting quietly. He knew there was more to come.

"And that's not the worst of it. There's the woman-abusing bastard that Larsen disciplined." He paused.

"What about him?"

"It's complicated. We know people who know people. It seems young Ricky has been killed. We got word earlier that the sheriff's office here in Transylvania County reported a homicide."

Whelan immediately thought of Stensen. "And...?" he said.

"And they're looking for you men. Think about it. Six strangers walk into the bar, all with extraordinary physical power, and get into it with Ricky. Then Ricky shows up murdered a short time later, his body propped up against a tree just uphill from the bar's parking lot. And he didn't die a pleasant death. Whoever killed him took pleasure in what he was doing."

"Are you suggesting it was Nick?"

"That's who I'd place my money on. Did you have him in sight the whole evening?"

Whalen shook his head. "No. What actions do you suggest?"

Levell stared silently at the scarred and stained tabletop for a few moments then looked at Whelan and said, "There's an APB out for the six of you and the Hummer. It's being dismantled as we speak and will be airlifted out of here and disposed of. We'll also airlift you men out and relocate you to a safe house in Virginia." He paused and stared hard at Whelan. "For God's sake, Brendan, keep a short leash on these men from now on. I have no doubt that last night's episode will end up on the Bureau's radar screen. They've been looking for you for months and they're smart people. They'll connect the dots and realize the Sleeping Dogs are wide-awake."

Whelan's back stiffened. "Wait a minute," he said. "The Team hasn't been exactly forthcoming with us." Levell stared at him, but offered nothing. "We have busted our asses for the past six months, training for some mysterious mission. Based on the kinds of operations you and your people put us into twenty years ago, there's going to be a high mortality rate. Yet we haven't been told a damn thing about it. And you have the balls to bitch about six very tired and bored individuals slipping off the reservation for one evening of R and R? That's bullshit, Cliff. Tell us what we're training to do. What's our objective?"

Levell made a sound that was somewhere between a snort and a chuckle and said, "Yeah, Brendan, I'd be pissed off too if I were in your position. But you know the situation this country faces. The communists and socialists, now euphemistically known as 'progressives', have gained all but an unbreakable grip on the power structure. They've managed to capitalize on what Nietzsche identified as resentment of the existing social order. They've used it to generate serious class warfare, getting a huge portion of the population to believe that the 'haves', the mythical 'one percent', are treating them unfairly. That they can't get a fair shake. That the deck is stacked against them. They resent others because they have an education, or a better job or a nicer house."

"Sadly," Whelan said, "this is, or was, the one place where anyone who was willing to put out the effort could get a quality education, so they could find a better job, and buy that nicer house."

Levell nodded his head vigorously. "But the problem now is that people are too willing to settle for second best when it comes to making an effort. But they resent having to settle for second best as a result of that effort. They've been lead to believe – or more likely want to believe, that the State is their ombudsman. That it will control the successful members of our society and force them to share their largesse with those who deem themselves less fortunate."

"Less fortunate or less ambitious," Whelan said. "The path of least resistance is the most attractive for many people. But it's a path that only leads down."

"A major key to all of this has been the careful nurturing and development of the entitlement culture. Roughly half the population is on one or more forms of federal or state dole. Entitlement programs now consume sixty percent of the federal budget. It was twenty percent in 1979. Over that same period, defense spending has fallen from forty percent of the budget to less than twenty percent. We're becoming a nation that won't be able to defend itself against aggression, and populated by a citizenry that mistakenly believes it can have a life of ease that will be paid for by future generations. The reality of it is that it's being paid for by a government that debases the coin of the realm by creating enormous amounts of it out of whole cloth. And, in addition, creating an unrepayable servitude of debt to foreign entities that clearly do not have our best interests at heart."

Whelan nodded thoughtfully. "As someone who has been living in Europe for the past twenty years, it is crystal clear to me that the U.S. is on a fast track to becoming a European-style welfare state. Given what we've seen happening on that continent financially, that would be an irreparable disaster."

"And that must not be allowed to happen," Levell said. There was a very hard edge to his voice. "It's why we've reunited the Sleeping Dogs back together. This operation may well be the blackest in history."

"Are you going to fill me in?"

"It's strictly on a need to know basis, and, right now, you and the other men don't need to know. But I can tell you this much. It involves one or more assassinations under very difficult conditions."

Whelan continued to lock eyes with Levell for several seconds then said, "Is it your intention to have us assassinate the President of the United States?"

An enigmatic smile spread slowly over Levell's face. "Like I said, need to know."

48 VIRGINIA TIDEWATER COUNTRY

Less than an hour following his conversation with Levell in the cabin in North Carolina, Whelan and the other five men had been picked up by an AgustaWestland AW109S Grand helicopter owned by a subsidiary of a company controlled by the Mueller brothers. The 109S Grand accommodates up to seven passengers and two crew members and is powered by twin Pratt & Whitney PWC207C turbine engines. It cruises at speeds close to two hundred miles per hour. It transported them three hundred and fifty miles to the lodge near Fairview Beach, Virginia in just under two hours.

Whelan and Larsen were assigned a room to share in the main building. The others were provided with rooms in the accessory building. Kirkland volunteered to bunk with Almeida, when it became clear that Stensen and Thomas would not. They were given a room to share next to Kirkland and Almeida.

The six of them spent the next week battling boredom. Not permitted to leave the buildings except by the tunnel that connected the lodge and its accessory building, they struggled to keep active. The accessory building had a small gym, but it was equipped for men of ordinary physical skills. It lacked sufficient weights to challenge the limits to which they had become accustomed. Rhee Kang-Dae, Levell's personal assistant, and Paul Fontenot had been brought in from the former camp in North Carolina to work with them in the martial arts. More hours were spent on the far too familiar subjects of calisthenics, weaponry, stealth tactics, and technology. They were not allowed to make any outside calls, which was particularly difficult for the family men, Larsen and Whelan.

Alcoholic beverages, ordinarily freely available to the lodge's guests, had to be locked away to prevent Almeida's abuse of it. On three separate occasions, he had been apprehended trying to slip off the premises – twice at night and once in the middle of the day. After that episode, Whelan assigned rotating shifts where each of them kept an eye on Almeida at all times during the day. At night they relied on the high tech surveillance gear and the staff security people to keep track of him.

On the seventh day, Levell, McCoy, and certain other members of the Team arrived. Whelan and the other five men were called to attend a meeting in the chamber concealed under the library. It was the first time any of them had been in the room. As they descended the stone steps, they took in the scene – long mahogany conference table lined with comfortable looking executive chairs and racks along the walls stacked high with bottles of wine, most of them quite dusty. The sight brought a smile to Almeida's weathered face. He liked this place.

Thomas did not. He shuddered slightly as he descended into the chamber and muttered under his breath, "This place creeps me out, man. It's like a freakin' tomb."

Levell's and Whelan's eyes met and the older man nodded slightly, a barely perceptible smile playing across his lips. He pointed to empty chairs at the other end of the table. The seats near Levell were already filled by other members of the Team. One by one, Whelan and the other men took a seat and looked around the table. They knew Levell and McCoy and assumed they would recognize, as public figures, the two men who were wearing hoods in an effort to conceal their identities from Whelan and his companions. The remaining three people were unknown to any of the Sleeping Dogs except Whelan. He recognized two of them. The lone female was Maureen Delaney, CEO of a major high tech company. He and Caitlin held stock in her company. It didn't pay dividends from its substantial earnings, but its growth in value was steady and significant.

A second person was Alfred Mueller, the eldest of the three billionaire industrialist Mueller brothers. The third person was unknown to Whelan. He was a well-dressed black man, tall and lean. He appeared to be in his early forties. Whelan wondered if he purposely had chosen the chair next to Levell or had been assigned to it.

"Everyone here knows who I and General McCoy are. Otherwise, introductions, for the most part, are not in order, as you may have gathered from our colleagues who have chosen to conceal their identities from our guests at the end of the table." He motioned toward Whelan and the other five men. "What is important is the situation that has just come to light."

McCoy was chewing an unlit cigar. Without removing it from his mouth, he looked at the six men sitting at the other end of the table and said, "You men are in luck. This involves a special mission that requires your exceptional skills."

"I take it this isn't the mission we've been training for," Whelan said.

"No. Consider it an additional training exercise, only this time you're playing for real," Levell said. He turned slightly toward the black man seated on his left and said, "This gentleman now works for us. We were successful in turning him in recent months. He's now our mole and is deeply embedded in the apparatus of this nation's domestic enemies. He's just learned of an operation they intend to carry out. While it isn't one we ordinarily would counter, we've decided to do so this time."

"Why?" Whalen said. Their body English and the expressions on the faces of his five companions underscored that he spoke for each of them.

"That's a fair question, and I'll answer it," Levell said. "Their operation is designed to co-opt the effectiveness of someone who is useful to us. Their plan involves potentially harming his family members and making it appear that it was done by you." Levell looked pointed at Whelan and each of his companions. "Because of this person's position, such an action could call unwanted attention to his current areas of responsibility. This might result in additional assets being employed on those areas of responsibility. We don't want that to happen. We believe countering it will send a message designed to confuse and frighten those responsible for this planned operation."

McCoy yanked the unlit stogie from his mouth and said with a growl, "We want them pissing in their pants." He realized Maureen Delaney was staring at him, and said, "Oops. Sorry for the language, Maureen."

She made a dismissive motion with her hand. "Don't worry about it, General. I grew up in an Irish Catholic family with six older brothers, all of them Marines. I've heard far worse."

"Well, now that we've got the housekeeping issues out of the way," Levell said dryly, "let's get down to business." He turned to the man on his left and said, "Please describe the situation to our guests."

The man looked around the room, making it a point to make eye contact with each of the Sleeping Dogs, especially Quentin Thomas. Black man to black man in a decidedly white environment. After several moments, he said, "My name is Shepard Jenkins."

The name didn't register with any of the men, who all glanced at Whelan to judge his reaction. Whalen shrugged.

"Ostensibly, I work as the chief political strategist for Senator Howard Morris, the senior senator from the State of New York."

The name was familiar to all of the men except Almeida, who always had been completely apolitical.

"Isn't he planning to run for president?" Kirkland said.

Jenkins nodded. "He hasn't officially announced yet, because the incumbent hasn't officially agreed not to seek reelection. But that's the plan. He has very powerful people and a great deal of resources behind him. The nomination is his if he can keep his pants on." He looked at Maureen Delaney.

She smiled knowingly. "His reputation in that area is hardly a State secret," she said.

"My kind of guy," Almeida said.

Continuing, Jenkins said, "I was in a meeting the other day involving the planned campaign, and overheard something that disturbs me greatly."

"It disturbs all of us. That's why we're here," Levell said. "Go on."

"Where was this meeting? Who was there?" Whelan said.

"I'm getting to that," Jenkins said. "The meeting was held at the Potomac home of Chaim Laski."

The six men nodded their heads in recognition of Laski's name. Even Almeida knew who he was.

"Man," said Thomas, "this senator dude does have some major resources behind him."

"Yes, he does," said Jenkins. "The others at the meeting included the senator and myself, Laski's chief aide for political affairs, a man from a leftwing union umbrella group – who by the way is a close friend of the current president. The last person was a large and nasty looking man who spoke to Laski in what sounded like an Eastern European dialect. Very guttural. Frankly, he scared me." He paused and looked at Whelan and the others. "If you men are who I think you are, maybe you aren't intimidated by people like that, but he seemed very menacing to me."

"I don't know who you think we are?" Stensen said. "But we're just regular folks." He smiled in a way that sent shivers down several spines in the room. The red dots in the center of his eyes flared as if something suddenly had fueled their fire.

"Time's wasting. Get to the point, Shep," Levell said impatiently.

Jenkins rested his elbows on the arms of his chair and slid his lanky body back farther in the seat. "The senator complained that a certain FBI agent in charge of the Harold Case affair in Georgetown late last year was becoming a pain in the butt. Laski said if he was successful in finding...well, you people, it would destroy an important plan they had been working on for a long time."

"Destroying us would destroy their plan. Interesting," Whelan said. "What plan?"

"I'm not exactly sure. I haven't been privy to that information. I don't know that the senator has either. But is seems to have something to do with creating a situation that will do great damage to the opposition, thus delivering a majority of the votes in the general election to the Senator and his party."

"Let me and the others worry about that," Levell said. "I want Shep to tell you about this interim action involving the fellow from the Bureau." He nodded at Jenkins.

231

"This FBI agent, Christie, Mitchell Christie, is like a pit bull. He's working this case like a dog worrying on a bone. He's determined to find you, all of you," he motioned toward Whalen and the other five men.

Whelan glanced at Levell and smiled. "I believe agent Christie and I were traveling companions a while back."

"Indeed," said Levell with a slight nod.

"Senator Morris," Jenkins said, "has tried going through certain channels to have Christie replaced by a somewhat less dedicated agent, but that didn't come about. Now, it appears that Laski has become involved."

Jenkins paused and looked around the room. His eyes came to rest on Whelan and the other five men, one by one. "I don't how much you know about Chaim Laski, but he enjoys enormous wealth, and, as a result, he wields enormous power. And he is quite ruthless."

"Ruthless? We can tell you about ruthless," Stensen said.

"Bet your ass," Almeida said.

"So I've heard," Jenkins said as his eyes locked with Stensen's. He saw the bright red dots in their centers and felt a distinct tightening in his sphincter. His mouth suddenly was dry and he swallowed hard. His Adam's apple bobbed up and down. He licked his lips nervously and said, "He plans to gain control of Christie through his family."

"How?" Whelan said. It sounded like a demand.

"The wife and kids will be abducted and held as insurance that Christie will play ball."

"Why don't they just kill Christie? Seems quicker and easier," Larsen said.

Levell raised his hand to stop Jenkins from responding. "It's too messy, killing a federal agent in a high profile case like this. Even if they could make it look like you men did it, it could always backfire. Using the wife and kids to pressure him is cleaner and safer. Plus, once Christie has compromised himself, they'll always have leverage over him."

"And we care about Christie...because?" Whelan said.

"Because we don't want any more attention drawn to the Harold Case investigation. We're hoping it eventually will grow cold and fade away."

This didn't add up for Whelan. The unit was too valuable, too much had been invested in it by the Team to risk the ultimate mission on something like this. There were other ways to handle it. He looked at Levell with a quizzical expression on his face. Barely, almost imperceptibly, Levell's right eye seemed to wink. To any of the others, it would seem to be a slight facial tic. Whelan knew what it was – confirmation that more was at stake than it would appear. Whelan thought about this for a few moments then said, "And you want us to see that this abduction does not succeed."

"Correct," Levell said.

PART FOUR

BAD DOGS

49 WASHINGTON, D.C.

Whelan and the other Sleeping Dogs, with help from Levell and other members of the Team, quickly gathered intelligence about the planned abduction of Mitch Christie's family. What they had learned from Shepard Jenkins was that Laski employed a number of very large, thuggish men, all of them Ukrainians. They formed his security cadre. They were hired muscle and rumor had it that they performed whatever dirty deeds Laski required. It appeared that they worked in staggered shifts and each had one day off per week. Using information gathered principally by satellite surveillance - provided by a corporation owned indirectly by the Mueller brothers - Whelan and the others learned how most of Laski's men used their respective days off. They usually sought female companionship at a certain nightclub on the outskirts of Georgetown near the Maryland state line.

Laski's minions appeared to be creatures of habit. They generally left the estate about the same time. They usually parked in the same area, arriving at the club at about nine o'clock. On busy nights, it wasn't unusual for there to be a line of patrons waiting to be admitted. The club's staff always waved Laski's people in immediately, regardless how long the line was.

Whelan's plan called for an activity inside the club. It had precise time requirements. Waiting in line was not acceptable, so he, Larsen, Thomas, and Kirkland arrived early before business picked up. They entered individually in order to minimize drawing attention to themselves. As it was, a black man with bright blue eyes and another man with the same eyes and no neck always drew attention. One from the ladies, the other from bouncers. Thomas briefly considered wearing sunglasses, but realized that could impair his vision inside the dark club. That alone could draw unwanted attention.

At a few minutes past nine, two of Laski's men entered the club. They were very large men, well over six feet tall and each weighing more than two hundred fifty pounds. The club was busy now. As they strolled through the tables on their way to the bar, they would pause for brief conversations with women. It didn't seem to matter to them that many of the women were with other men. From the expressions on the faces of some of the women, their remarks were neither appreciated nor well received.

The bar was crowded. Among the patrons, there were two young couples. The women were sitting side by side with their escorts seated on either side of them. When Laski's men got to the bar, they wedged their bodies between the women and the men who were with them. One of those men objected. He tapped the closest Ukrainian on the shoulder and tried to explain that the women were with them. The thug ignored him and slid his hand up the young woman's thigh and under her short skirt. Clearly startled, she tried to push the offending hand away, but it wouldn't budge. The man who had been with her slid off his bar stool and grabbed the Ukrainian's beefy shoulder, attempting to spin him around. He was six inches shorter and seventy pounds lighter. The Ukrainian slapped the hand away as casually as if he were swatting a fly. The man grabbed the shoulder again and the Ukrainian slammed a huge right fist into his stomach. The smaller man stumbled backward, crashed into a table, and sagged to the floor where he didn't move.

Two bouncers appeared immediately along with a couple of busboys. The busboys quickly straightened the table and chairs and hauled away the broken glassware. A cocktail waitress brought a fresh round of drinks to the people who had been sitting at the table. A bouncer each grabbed an arm of the victim and dragged him out of the club. One of them looked at the Ukrainians and winked.

Watching this scenario, it was clear to Whelan that the men in Laski's employ enjoyed special treatment at the club. It was the destination of choice for most of them on their day off and they probably spent a lot of money there. There also was the possibility that Laski either owned all or a part of the club, or paid to ensure that his men let off steam without causing problems with the club's management.

Whelan glanced around the club at his three companions. Each was located in a different section. Kirkland shrugged, as if he were unimpressed. Thomas, ever the impassive one, showed no emotion at all. Larsen smiled his bad smile, the cold, mirthless, menacing one. Clearly, he wanted to go over and beat the two Ukrainians within a fraction of their lives, maybe closer than that. The same fate would await any other bouncers who got into the mix. Maybe, Whelan thought, Sven will get his wish. If not tonight, then soon.

One of the women said something to the other one and they tried to slide off their bar stools, but the Ukrainians stopped them. One of the women pointed to the ladies' room. The Ukrainian who had slugged the man who had been with her shook his head in a negative gesture. He held up one finger, indicating that they would have to go one at a time. The women looked at each other and spoke for a moment. One of them slid off her stool, gathered her small purse and headed off toward the ladies' room, which was well inside the club, a long way from any exits. That was when Whelan made his move.

As the young woman moved away from the bar area, Whelan fell in behind her. "I can help you, but don't look around," he said. Naturally, her first instinct was to stop and turn around.

"They're watching you. Keep walking," he said it in a low growl. "The ladies' room is around the corner up there. When we're out of their direct line of sight, we'll stop and talk."

When they had rounded the corner, the woman turned to face the tall, muscular man with light brown hair and bright blue eyes. She had seen eyes like that somewhere, but not in a human. There was something feral in the eyes, suggestive of a wild beast. A wolf, maybe? Suddenly the Ukrainians didn't seem so menacing after all. Perhaps they were the lesser of two evils. "What do you want with me?"

"I see your predicament and I can help."

"Yeah? You're pretty big, but those guys are huge."

"Isn't it women who say 'size isn't everything'?"

She looked at him and said, "Are you being a smart ass?"

"Wouldn't be the first time. Seriously, though, I can help you, but I need you to do something for me."

A smirk came across her face. "Does this involve the backseat of a car in the parking lot?"

"No."

She eyed him for a moment. There was something calm, perfectly at ease in his manner. It was the most genuine kind of confidence. "What is it you want me to do?"

Whelan reached into his right hand pants pocket and pulled out a small vial. "When neither of them is looking, pour this into one of their drinks. Do it fast and pour all of it in there."

Her eyes widened. "You want me to poison them?"

"No. It's not poison. It's a highly concentrated dose of Furosemide."

"Fur...Fur...what?"

"Think of it as a medicine that makes you need to pee. Really pee and really soon. Just don't let either of them see you pour it into the drink."

"What if they don't both look away at the same time?"

"I'll see to it that they do. Just be ready."

"How is all this going to help me and my friend Amber?"

"Whichever one of those guys who drinks it is going to want to hit the men's room shortly afterward. I'll deal with him in there."

She looked at him in puzzlement. "Why the men's room?"

"Because it's private."

"The men's' room is private? With guys running in and out all the time?"

"It will be when I get him in there."

She nodded as if she understood. "And what will you do to him in there?"

Whelan's eyes narrowed and his lips curled in a smile that frightened her. "Behavior modification."

She took the vial from his hand and pushed open the door to the ladies' room, but paused briefly and looked back at him. All she saw was the back of his broad shoulders as he moved easily through the crowd.

A few minutes after she had returned to her seat at the bar, Whelan walked up and said to the Ukrainians, "I can't tell you guys how much I enjoyed seeing you belt that dweeb a while ago. I know the guy; he's an asshole. How 'bout I buy you a drink. What'd you say?"

Both Ukrainians looked at him, slight sneers on their faces. The one who had slugged the man earlier said, "We don't need you buy drinks. How you say in dees country…go be lost."

While the two thugs were staring at Whelan, the young woman he had spoken with earlier quickly poured the contents of the vial into the drink of the man nearest her. He was the one who had hit her date.

"Okay," Whelan said with a disarming smile, "I go be lost."

He went directly to the men's room. Larsen and Thomas were dressed similarly to the club's bouncers – gray slacks, black muscle tees, and black sport jackets. They had clipped small, rectangular brass nametags to the breast pockets of their jackets. Larsen's said "Darren". Thomas's said "Karl". They hung a sign on the door that said "Out of Order. Use Second Floor." and took up positions in front of the door to the men's room. They stood shoulder to shoulder with arms crossed and icy expressions on their faces. From that moment on, any men needing access to the rest room were told that it was out of order and advised to use the one on the second level of the club. No one argued.

Inside, the men's room appeared to be unoccupied. There were three urinals, side by side along the wall to the left of the door, and three stalls against the wall opposite the door. Three sinks and a large mirror faced the stalls. Two of the stalls appeared to be empty, but the door to the third was closed. A small surveillance camera was attached high in a corner.

In a few minutes, one of the Ukrainians rose off his bar stool. "Vasyl go take the peess," he said, using the third person. "Vhen Vasyl coming back, vee leave. Go someplace and fuck." He leered at the two women and swaggered off toward the men's room. The women's faces were studies in fear and loathing.

As Vasyl approached the men's room, Thomas reached into a pants pocket and pressed the send button on his cell phone. He and Larsen moved easily to the side and appeared to be having a casual conversation. As soon as the Ukrainian had entered the men's room, the two men repositioned themselves in front of the door.

Whelan got Thomas's signal that the Ukrainian was coming and stepped to the middle urinal as if to relieve himself. The big Ukrainian entered the room, paused for a moment then opted for the urinal on Whelan's left. He looked and Whelan and sneered. "So, eez the go get lost guy. Thees vhere you get lost? In peess house?" He snorted derisively and turned his gaze back toward the wall behind the urinals and began to relieve himself.

The Ukrainian was using his left hand to guide his stream and his right hand rested on his hip. Whelan zipped up and turned as if to leave. As he turned, he smashed his right hand into the other man's solar plexus. Vasyl doubled over as the air was driven from his lungs. He staggered backwards, spraying urine on the wall, the urinal and himself.

Putting out his right arm for balance exposed the man's rib cage and Whelan drove a huge left hook into it, cracking several bones. Vasyl grunted and his knees started to buckle. Whelan quickly slipped behind him. Grabbing the back of his jacket and the seat of his pants, he lifted the bulky man off the floor and slammed him headfirst into the wall above the urinal. Barely conscious, the Ukrainian went limp and Whelan shoved his head into the urinal, holding it there for several seconds.

Vasyl quickly realized what was happening and began to struggle, trying to get his feet under him. Using his right foot, Whelan stomped down on the top of Vasyl's right calf just below the knee. The blow ripped apart the anterior and posterior cruciate ligaments and severely damaged Vasyl's fibular collateral ligament, rendering his knee joint useless. Vasyl tried to rise again, using his left leg. Whelan drove his knee into the back of the leg, damaging the semitendinosus and biceps femoris muscles. Vasyl's injured legs collapsed and his left knee slammed into the tile floor, further damaging the joint.

The Ukrainian had both of his large hands on the rim of the urinal and, with great effort, began to push himself away from it. Whelan threw a powerful elbow strike, or *empi* technique, into the back of Vasyl's neck. He collapsed with his face again submerged in the urinal. Whelan held him there until he was satisfied that the other man had had enough to drink then he slung him backwards with great force.

Vasyl slid across the tile floor, stopping near the stall with the closed door. As he lay there choking and gasping for breath and grimacing with pain, the door to the stall opened and Kirkland stepped out.

Vasyl rolled his eyes toward the newcomer, hoping it was someone who would help him. Instead, Kirkland dropped on the Ukrainian, driving a knee into the pit of Vasyl's stomach and quickly bouncing up and back.

SLEEPING DOGS: THE AWAKENING

Vasyl's head shot forward and he vomited urine, booze, and remnants of an earlier dinner. His head fell back onto the tile floor with a cracking sound and he lay there groaning. His eyes rolled around in his head and it slowly wagged back and forth as if he was trying to disbelieve his current situation.

Kirkland knelt beside him and pulled a small instrument from his jacket that looked like a trident with the center prong considerably longer than the ones on the outside. It was a *Tjabang*, the smaller Indonesian version of the Okinowan *sai*. Like many farm tools used in Asia, it had become a weapon commonly used in the martial arts. Typically a *Tjabang* is somewhat blunt, but Kirkland had sharpened the middle prong on this one to a very fine point.

Whelan had joined Kirkland on the other side of the felled Ukrainian. Vasyl rolled his eyes toward Whelan. "Vhy you are doing dees?" he gasped.

"It's simple. Unless you tell me what I want to know, we're going to kill you. It's a matter of seconds, understand?"

Vasyl shook his head. "Some vun coming through door zoon."

"Guess again. There are two men, each as powerful as I am, barring that door on the other side." Whelan paused for a moment. "Tell me everything you know about a plan to kidnap the family of an FBI agent."

Vasyl looked around the room and saw the surveillance camera. Emboldened by it, he shook his head again. "If I tell you, dey vill kill me."

"You're wasting your time worrying about 'they'. We're going to kill you here and now. And it will be more painful than anything you can imagine." He looked up at the camera and said, "If that thing was working, someone would have arrived by now. He nodded to Kirkland, who slid the point of the *sai* through the skin under Vasyl's chin and into the geniohyoid muscle behind it.

With Kirkland kneeling on his right arm and Whelan on his left, Vasyl could only clinch his fists against the pain. His eyes opened as wide and as round as they could and tears rolled out of their corners. His body was rigid and a strange high-pitched sound emanated from somewhere within his throat.

Whelan nodded again and Kirkland slid the point of the *sai* deeper, piercing the genioglossus muscle just below the tongue. "Talk to me quickly, while you still have a tongue."

Vasyl nodded his head gingerly to avoid driving the sai any deeper. "I vill tell you." He rolled his eyes toward Kirkland, using them to plead for relief.

Kirkland looked at Whelan, who nodded. The *sai* slid out, leaving a small round hole from which a steady stream of blood oozed.

"The FBI agent. What is the plan?"

Vasyl swallowed carefully and licked his lips. The room was cold, but he was beginning to sweat heavily. "I not knowing much about diss. I am not big shot yet."

"What do you know?"

"Is to happen tomorrow. In afternoon. Vhen kids home from school. That is all I am knowing."

Whelan looked at Kirkland. "Time to go," he said.

"I assume we want this guy dead."

"Now you want to be like Nick?" Whelan said with a deadpan expression.

"Not exactly. I usually kill in bunches, not individually."

"Like on the front porch of a country bar?"

"Something like that."

Whelan looked briefly at the Ukrainian. "He's a liability. Kill him."

"No!" Vasyl screamed. "I tell you all I know. You promise I live."

"I lied," Whelan said.

Kirkland placed the point of the *sai* on Vasyl's chest, a little left of center, and shoved down with force. The tip penetrated the Ukrainian's jacket and shirt, pierced his skin and muscle tissue, and slid between the third and fourth ribs into his heart. When Kirkland yanked it out, Vasyl's dying heart pumped gradually smaller geysers of blood through the hole and onto his chest.

Kirkland wiped the *sai* on Vasyl's jacket and slid it back into its place of concealment beneath his own coat. The two men exited the room. Outside, they and Larsen and Thomas each strolled off in different directions, leaving the club quickly, but individually. Thomas, the last to leave, thought he heard some kind of clamor coming from the direction of the first floor men's room.

They reassembled at their car, a gray Jeep Liberty, parked on a side street about a block from the club. Stensen was waiting for them. He handed Whelan a videodisk he had removed from the surveillance equipment in the club's office. "You guys do nice work," he said.

50 FREDERICK, MARYLAND

Mitch Christie and his family lived in a house on a well-landscaped side street not far from the historic district in Frederick, Maryland. It was a two-story, red brick house with a gabled slate roof. The windows were framed with dark wooden shutters. A flat, built-up roof extended over the small portico on the ground level, supported by six white, smooth, tapered pillars. Four low, wide, semi-circular steps led from the entrance path up to the portico. The yard was well kept, with an abundance of shrubbery and flowers. A black wrought iron fence stretched across the front of the property interrupted only by two posts made of red brick that framed the gate. The path from the gate to the front steps was laid with brick pavers in a herringbone pattern.

It was just after two o'clock on a hot, muggy afternoon in late August. School had started for the Christie children that week. A sapphire crystal metallic Chrysler Town & Country minivan was parked in the single car garage at the rear of the driveway. The garage doors were open, giving a view of the interior where gardening tools and lawn equipment were neatly stowed.

Although pedestrian and motor vehicle traffic on the street was almost nonexistent at that time of day, no one paid attention to a white service van that turned onto the street a block away. It rolled slowly up to the Christie residence and stopped at the curb. On the side of the van, in blue letters, it said "Washington Gas Company". Below, "Frederick Gas Division" was printed in smaller letters along with a phone number. There also was a stylized blue flame painted next to the letters.

The van pulled to the curb in front of the house and two men climbed out. They each were wearing dark blue pants and work shirts of a lighter blue that stretched tightly over their muscular frames. The back of the shirts carried the same company information as the sides of the van, including the blue flame logo. Each wore a blue ball cap with the flame logo above the bill. Both wore sunglasses and carried tool bags. One of the men was black. There was a name stitched in navy blue thread on the flap over the left breast pocket of his shirt. It said "Ike". He was carrying a clipboard. The other man was white. "Will" was stitched on the flap above his shirt pocket.

The men opened the gate, walked up the brick pathway and steps, and rang the doorbell. After a few moments, Deborah Christie opened the door a few inches. It was secured by a swing type door guard, the kind often used on hotel room doors. She looked at the two men for a moment. Quentin Thomas (Ike) pretended to look at his clipboard and said, "Mrs. Christie?"

"Yes?"

"We're with the gas company and…."

"And you expect me to let you in the house," she said before he could finish the sentence. "I'm afraid that isn't going to happen. You may be legitimate, but my husband, who is with the FBI" - she purposely said the three letters slowly and precisely - "told me that the gas leak ploy is the oldest one in the book."

Thomas shook his head. "I'm sure it is, ma'am, but we don't need to enter the house. We're just checking the gas lines in the neighborhood, and didn't want you to be alarmed when you saw two men poking around in your back yard."

"That's fine. Do what you have to do. I won't interfere."

Thomas smiled and held up the clipboard. "Thank you, Mrs. Christie. If you don't mind, we'd like you to sign this form acknowledging that we were here. It's part of the company's customer service policy." He handed the clipboard to her through the narrow space with his left hand. As she reached for it, Thomas made a move as if to hand her the ballpoint pen he was holding in his right hand.

She looked up to grasp the pen, and he pressed its cap. A thin stream of odorless, invisible gas shot from the tip and struck her in the face. Deborah Christie's eyes opened wide in shock, then rolled back in her head. She crumpled unconscious to the thick carpet behind the door.

"Wow, that stuff acts fast," said Larsen (Will). He leaned easily into the door and, despite being anchored by two #10 screws each two inches long, the base of the door guard easily ripped free from the jamb. The door swung open and the two men quickly entered and shut it behind them.

Larsen scooped Mrs. Christie up and carried her over to a sofa. He quickly bound her wrists behind her back with a plastic cable tie from his tool bag. He similarly bound her ankles and stretched a piece of duct tape over her mouth. Thomas pulled a Motorola Talkabout MR350R walkie-talkie from his pants pocket and activated the send signal. "One down, two to go," he said.

Outside, a third man, who had remained in the service van, drove away from the house to a small commercial area a few blocks away. He parked and waited for the next communication.

Larsen took up a post in the front of the house and watched the street. From a spot in the clean, modern kitchen, Thomas kept an eye on the back area of the property. It was completely private, enclosed by thick green bushes and several trees. At about twenty minutes past three, Larsen saw a young girl, about thirteen, come up the sidewalk, enter through the gate, and approach the house. He buzzed Thomas on a walkie-talkie, "The girl's home". In a very few seconds, Thomas was there, flattening himself against the wall next to the door.

The girl rang the doorbell and said, "Mom, I'm home." Larsen whipped open the door and yanked her inside, wrapping her up in a bear hug and clapping a hand over her mouth. Thomas, who had reloaded the gas cartridge in his pen, inserted the tip in one of her nostrils, which were flared widely in terror, and depressed the cap. A moment later she was unconscious. "One to go," he said.

Larsen carried the girl over to the sofa and trussed her up as he had her mother. A few minutes later, a car pulled up to the curb in front of the house. A young man, about fifteen, climbed out on the passenger's side and turned to speak to the driver. "Thanks for the ride, Coach. See you tomorrow."

The car pulled away and the young man, with an air of youthful confidence and athleticism, walked up the pathway to the house. When he rang the doorbell, a scene similar to the one involving his younger sister took place. Soon, he was trussed and lying on the floor next to the sofa that held his mother and sister. All three remained unconscious.

The two men took up their positions once again. The phone rang a couple of times but they ignored it. The Christies began slowly to awaken. First the mother opened her eyes and looked groggily around the room. The son was next, followed shortly by his sister. As each of them came to the realization of their situation, their eyes opened wide and they began thrashing about as they struggled against their bonds. Strange, muffled sounds came from their throats.

Thomas held a finger to his lips. "We're not here to hurt you. It's just the opposite. There are some men coming here soon who do intend to harm you. Our job is to see that they don't. We'll take you somewhere safe after that."

Mrs. Christy continued to make the strange sounds.

"I think she's asking about her husband," Larsen said.

Thomas nodded. "He's not our problem, ma'am."

Tears welled up in the corners of her eyes and spilled over, running slowly down her cheeks. She tried to turn her head away so her children wouldn't see her tears. Deborah Christie was an attractive woman in her mid-forties with short dark hair, and the trim body of someone who diligently followed a workout routine. She had hazel eyes and a cute, turned up nose. Both men felt somewhat remorseful that she and the children had to be in this situation.

At four forty-five in the afternoon, a delivery truck pulled to a stop in front of the house. The large, burly driver hopped down and began walking briskly to the front door. He wore brown shorts and cap, and a brown short sleeve shirt with some kind of logo on it. There was a package under one arm. As he walked up the pathway, another man emerged from the back of the truck and moved swiftly toward the back of the house.

The man at the front door rang the bell and waited. A few moments later, in one smooth technique, Larsen whipped the door open, grabbed the big man by his shirt, and yanked him into the house, head-butting him as he did so. The man's knees sagged, but he still was conscious enough to reach behind him for the Glock that was stuck in his waistband. Larsen crushed a huge right uppercut into the man's jaw and he collapsed. Stripping him of the weapon and patting him down for others, Larsen swiftly bound the man and slapped a piece of sturdy packing tape over his mouth.

At the back of the house, the other man, equally large and menacing looking, had crept up the rear steps to the kitchen door. He stood on the top step and pressed his ear against the door. It suddenly burst open inwardly and Thomas pistol-whipped the surprised man's head with his HK45. His scalp split and blood began to flow freely. Grabbing the barely conscious man with his free hand, Thomas yanked him inside and closed the door. He quickly disarmed him and bound him with plastic ties. He spread a piece of packing tape over the man's mouth. Grabbing the collar of his shirt, Thomas dragged the bleeding man into the living room where Larsen had deposited the other would-be kidnapper.

Thomas pulled out his walkie-talkie again and said, "The gang's all here." Thirty seconds later the white service van pulled up in front of the house. Larsen walked out the front door and opened the driveway gate. The driver of the van backed it down the driveway to the rear of the house. Thomas and Larsen exited through the kitchen door at the back of the house. One carried Mrs. Christie. The other had a teenager slung over each shoulder. They gently placed them in the van then went back in and dragged the two beefy hostages out, tossing them in the van the way a farmer might throw a bag of fertilizer onto the bed of a pickup truck.

Sitting behind the wheel of the van in a uniform that matched that of Thomas and Larsen, Stensen surveyed the scene. "Ukrainians?" he said, nodding at the two trussed up men.

"That would be my guess," Thomas said.

The red dots in the center of Stensen's eyes flared large and bright. "Now it's my turn."

Larsen looked at him as he and Thomas climbed into the van and closed the doors. "I'm sure you'll have them singing like canaries."

51 FREDERICKSBURG, VIRGINIA

Stensen drove the gas company service van, with the three Christies and the two would-be abductors, out of Frederick, Maryland on Route 15 and across the Potomac. He stopped at a commercial center outside Leesburg, Virginia, pulling around to the rear of the center, which backed up to a heavily wooded area. Waiting for them was a medium-sized brown truck that would have been familiar to Whelan. Its markings indicated that it was a delivery vehicle for a chain of appliance stores. The name on the side of the truck in yellow letters said Custom Appliances of McLean. There were two men in the cab of the truck.

Larsen, Thomas, and Stensen took turns climbing into the back of the truck while two of them watched over their cargo in the service van. In the truck, they quickly changed into brown work uniforms, jackets, and brown ball caps. There were logos on the jackets and ball caps that matched the logo on the truck. They swiftly and gently transferred the Christies to the truck. The two thugs were tossed in unceremoniously. When they were finished, the two men in the truck climbed down from the cab, got into the service van, and drove it away.

Larsen and Thomas got into the back of the truck and closed the lift gate. Stensen climbed into the truck's cab, drove around to the front of the commercial center and back on to Route 15 heading south. An hour later, outside Warrenton, Virginia, he turned onto the Highway 17 Bypass. A little more than an hour after that, outside Fredericksburg, Virginia, he turned into a long driveway that wound through a thick stand of trees and stopped in front of a large country manor.

He got out of the cab, went around to the back of the truck and banged on the liftgate twice in rapid succession, paused briefly then banged twice again. Almost immediately, the liftgate slid up. Thomas jumped down to join Stensen. Larsen picked up Deborah Christie and handed her down as

246

gently as possible to Thomas. He handed her daughter, Samantha, to Stensen, then climbed down with the son, Brett, slung carefully over one shoulder. He closed the liftgate and secured it from the outside.

As they approached the manor house, the double doors in the front opened and a man in butler's livery came out to greet them. He directed the men to a suite of rooms on the third floor where the Christies would be confined in luxurious, but escape-proof quarters.

Thomas and Larsen returned to the truck and hauled the two thugs into the house. The butler led them down a hallway to the rear of the building, through the kitchen area, and into a large pantry. He stopped in front of a rack of shelves that stretched from floor to ceiling and held various canned goods. From a trouser pocket, he produced a small object that resembled a keyless remote for an automobile. He pressed a button on it three times in rapid succession. The entire wall swung inward soundlessly, revealing a set of stone steps that led down to the basement of the house.

Dragging the two prisoners behind them, Larsen and Thomas descended the steps. The basement was a large area, about one hundred feet square. It was dry and very cold. The walls appeared to be solid metamorphic rock with shiny crystals of minerals glistening in ribbonlike layers. The space looked as if it had been carved from a solid rock formation. The floor was made up of large, rough-hewn fieldstones. The space was empty except for three men standing in the middle of the room – Brendan Whelan, Marc Kirkland, and Rafe Almeida. From the grim expressions on their faces, the three newcomers knew something unanticipated had come up.

The two thugs were shoved to the floor in a corner of the room. "What are the three of you doing here? I thought we were to drop the Christie family and these two guys here, then meet up with you three at HQ," Larsen said. He knew by the look on Whelan's face that whatever had happened, it wasn't good.

"What's up?" Thomas said.

Tight-jawed, Whelan said, "The Christie family wasn't the primary target; they were a diversion. Levell was the target."

Larsen, Thomas, and Stensen looked at each other. "Holy shit!" Larsen said; strong language for him.

"What the f...?" Thomas said simultaneously.

Stensen said nothing, but the red dots in the centers of his eyes flared large and the corners of his mouth curled in a faint but grim smile. The other men knew what that smile meant. Stensen was in a killing mood.

"I'm not following you, man. What happened?" Thomas said.

"I don't have all the details yet," Whelan said. "But what I do know was relayed to me by General McCoy."

"Is the General okay?" Larsen asked.

"Yeah, he wasn't with Levell at the time. As I understand it, Cliff was on his way from the Lodge near Fairview Beach to his home in Georgetown. Rhee was driving and Paul Fontenot was additional security. The hit happened at sixteen hundred hours on Route 218 about a mile east of the area known as Goby."

"Shit, that's not even five minutes from the Lodge," Thomas said. "How did they pull this off?"

"Do we know who was behind this?" Stensen said.

"What's the status of Rhee and Paul?" Larsen said.

Whelan gave each man a hard look, as if to say, 'Hold the questions, I'm telling you all I know at this point'. After a few moments he said, "Paul Fontenot was shot dead. Rhee caught a couple of rounds but managed to escape into the surrounding woods and hid in a small creek."

"What's his status?" Stensen said.

"He was in surgery when McCoy spoke with me."

"Do they know if he'll make it?" said Thomas.

"I don't know. McCoy said he was in pretty bad shape when they got to him. Lost a lot of blood."

"Those motherfuckers," Almeida said. "Rhee was a slope, but I liked the little bastard."

Whelan and Thomas looked at him and shook their heads in disgust.

"You told us what happened to Rhee and Fontenot," Larsen said. "What do we know about Cliff?"

"The car was all shot up, but there was no sign of Levell."

"Bloodstains in the back seat? Signs of a struggle?"

Whelan shook his head. "The Bureau has a forensics team onsite. McCoy has an operative inside the Bureau and is trying to get the skinny. But, right now, it looks like whoever did it wanted Cliff alive."

"The big question," Thomas said, "is what is the purpose of this?"

"Don't know that either," Whelan said. "But someone in this room does."

The other five looked at each other then slowly turned and stared at the two would-be abductors laying face down on the fieldstone floor in a corner of the basement.

Whelan pointed to the larger of them, and said, "Cut him free."

Producing a sharp pocketknife, Stensen quickly severed the plastic ties that had bound the man's ankles and wrists. The man rubbed the joints vigorously trying to restore feeling. Eventually, he reached up and gingerly removed the packing tape over his mouth using his right hand. Whelan made a mental note of that. "Vhat you are vanting from us?" the man said in a thick Eastern European accent. It reminded Whelan of the Ukrainian in the nightclub.

"Simple," Whelan said. "If you can beat me physically, you and your comrade are free to leave."

The man rose to his feet and looked at Whelan suspiciously. "Is some kind of trick, yes?"

"No tricks. And it's the only chance you have to get out of here alive." The man continued to stare at him, trying to figure out what was going on.

"You're wasting our time," Whelan said and nodded at Thomas, who pointed his HK45 at the middle of the man's chest. From less than ten feet away it would be an absolute kill shot.

"Please, I am not understanding," the man said, trying to buy time.

"I don't beat on helpless men. You're not helpless anymore. But I'm losing what little patience I have. You best show me what you've got in a hurry, or my friend is going to pop a hollow point cap in you."

The man looked back and forth between Whelan and Thomas. Finally, he said, "I beat you, I not have to fight others?"

"That's right," Whelan said.

The man seemed to understand at last and began to circle to Whelan's right while inching forward steadily to close the distance between them. He moved in a grappler's crouch with his arms in front of him, hands a little farther apart than shoulder width and the elbows bent. Whelan held his ground, turning easily to keep his shoulders squared to his opponent. When he had closed the gap between them to about four feet, the man made a feinting gesture with his left hand and lunged forward to grab Whelan with his right. Whelan was expecting it. He had noted that the man had used his right hand to remove the packing tape that had covered his mouth.

Whelan slid smoothly to his left and smashed a palm heel strike with his left hand to the outside of his opponent's right elbow. It knocked the man's arm away and spun him slightly to his left. Whelan dug a powerful right-handed blow to the man's exposed back just above the right kidney then slipped away.

A cry of pain exploded from the man's mouth. He arched his back and reached quickly behind himself to try and touch the injured area. He slowly and painfully turned to face Whelan again. He looked at the Irishman, who at six feet two was a good four inches shorter and at least fifty pounds lighter than the Ukrainian. In his native tongue, the Ukrainian thought, what kind of man is this? Never have I seen a man move as quickly. Never have I been struck so hard. He began to feel something very unfamiliar to him – fear.

The man thought back over his years as a fighter and remembered something a coach had told him long ago – "if your opponent is faster, you must be stronger; overcome speed with force". He knew what he would have to do. Lowering his head, he began to growl and suddenly launched himself at his opponent. Whelan glided to his left again. Using his right hand, he grabbed the wrist of the man's grasping right arm and twisted down, around, and up. The big Ukrainian flipped over, landing hard on the base of his spine. He howled with pain as he hit the stone floor.

As he slowly got up, he stared at Whelan with a look of sheer hatred mixed with fear. Driven by pain and panic, he lunged at Whelan again, wildly swinging a huge right haymaker. Whelan swiftly stepped in and neutralized it with a left forearm block and pounded the man's midsection eight times with left-right combinations. His hands moved with such speed that, to the untrained eye, the entire sequence was no more than a blur. It took no more than a second to accomplish. The big man sagged to the floor and pitched forward onto his hands and knees. Whelan stepped over him and squatted down, locking the man's chest between his thighs. He wrapped his right hand around the man's chin and placed his other hand on the side of his head just behind his right ear. Stensen watched, hands on hips and a faint smile playing across his face. Larsen, Kirkland and Almeida also watched Whelan; their faces were expressionless. Thomas purposely turned away. With a mighty wrench, Whelan twisted the man's thick neck sharply to the right and heard the snapping sound of a cervical fracture – a broken neck. The man's body went limp. Whelan let go of the head and it smacked the fieldstone floor with a thud.

Almost in unison, the six men turned and looked at the other Ukrainian huddled in a corner. For the first time in many years, the man was terrified. He had seen his comrade, Bohdan, killed by a man using only his bare hands. How was such a thing possible? Bohdan had been a champion wrestler years ago in the Ukraine. He had even been an alternate on the 1984 Soviet Olympic team as a Greco-Roman heavyweight wrestler. Unfortunately for him, the Soviets had chosen to boycott the games in retaliation for the United States boycotting the Moscow Games in 1980. Bohdan had been respected, and, even more than that, feared, as a man of great strength with a deep streak of cruelty. If this stranger could kill Bohdan so easily, what chance did he, Fedir, have? For the first time, he began to regret the path he had chosen in life.

The men casually walked over and stood in front of Fedir. Whelan reached down and yanked the packing tape away from his mouth. A substantial amount of skin went with it, and Fedir yelled in pain.

"Do you speak English?" Whelan said.

"Yes."

"Better than your late friend over there?" Whelan motioned toward Bohdan's corpse.

"Yes, better than Bohdan." Fedir bobbed his head up and down nervously, his eyes wide with fear.

"What's your name?"

"Fedir. Fedir Shevchenko."

"Would you like to end up like your friend over there, Fedir?"

"No. No, please, I am doing whatever you are asking."

52 J. EDGAR HOOVER BUILDING

Mitch Christie hung up the receiver of the phone in his office and reached for his current bottle of Mylanta. He had gotten the voicemail message on his home phone on all three calls he had made that afternoon. He wondered why no one had answered. By now the kids would be home from school. One of them or their mother should have answered. It was possible that they had gone to the store or on a similar errand, but he had been calling since three o'clock and it now was after six. Deborah should be home now, preparing dinner for the kids and herself, hoping he wouldn't be too late for a change. Ordinarily, if the three of them were going to go somewhere at this time of the day, she would have called him.

He sat with his hand on the receiver for several moments running scenarios through his mind. Something didn't feel right. He called each of his family member's cell phones. He reached voicemail on all of them and left the same message: call me as soon as you get this message. He had just finished the last call when Lou Antonelli knocked on the jamb of Christie's open office door. "Got a minute?" he said. He was chewing an unlit cigar.

"Yeah," Christie waved the other man to a chair in front of his desk. "So how's the new house in Chevy Chase? All moved in yet?"

"It's comin' along. It's great to have all that room."

"Didn't you say it was five bedrooms and four and a half baths?"

"Yeah about forty-five hundred square feet under air."

Christie looked at the other man for a moment. "That's a lot of house for a government employee. What does something like that run – million and a half, two million?"

"It could, but I got a great deal. It's all in how you negotiate the deal."

"Yeah? You must be the Donald Trump of residential deals."

Antonelli made a dismissive gesture. "Sometimes you just get lucky."

"Well, I'm wasting your time with chit-chat. Whatcha' got for me, Lou?"

"You remember that ex-CIA spook, Levell, the old geezer?"

Christie nodded. "Yes, he was part of that Sleeping Dogs operation. We've had him under surveillance for months."

"Right. Him and his buddy, that Marine general, McCoy."

"Yes, as I recall, they've been spending a lot of time at a place in Virginia."

"Yeah, but we don't have that place under direct surveillance. Orders from high up in the DOJ made it clear that was off-limits."

Christie leaned back in his chair and placed both hands behind his head. "Yeah, Lou, and that's really got me pissed off. I have no doubts that we could gather high value intel from that place, what with the cast of characters that comes and goes."

"Major industrialists, politicians, high ranking military and intelligence officers just to name a few," Antonelli said.

Christie leaned forward with his elbows on the desk. "So what about this Levell guy?"

"Well, it seems he was involved in a shooting and may have been abducted."

Christie fixed his eyes on Antonelli's. "Explain," he said.

"He and his driver and a guy we think was hired muscle were in a car that was forced off the road near that place we were just talking about in Virginia."

"Casualties?"

"The muscle caught a round in the head. He's dead. The Jap…"

"Korean," Christie said.

"Yeah, whatever. Those people all look alike to me. Anyway he got winged pretty badly. May not make it."

"Levell?"

"MIA."

"Do we know why?"

"Negative."

"Do we know who?"

"Nope."

"For Christ's sake, Lou, what do we know?" Christie was getting hot. He'd been in charge of this operation for more than half a year, and felt that he barely had made any progress. His frustration level was off the charts. To further complicate the matter, orders had come from higher up the bureaucratic chain of command – rumor had it that it could be as high as the White House – that severely limited the parameters of the investigation.

"From the damage to Levell's Escalade, Forensics says something big, like a truck, must have forced it off the road."

"Any leads on that vehicle?"

"It was stolen. They abandoned it a couple miles down the road."

"Anything else?"

"Nothing so far. There are no houses or business establishments nearby, and, as yet, no one has come forward who might have been driving in the area when it happened."

"Does Forensics have *anything* of value yet?"

"They think the perps may have been Russians or Eastern Europeans."

Christie's brow wrinkled in puzzlement. "Why?" he said.

Antonelli shrugged and said, "Coupla' things. Judging from the number of bullet casings, the perps were using fully automatic weapons. The bullet casings are bottlenecked seven point six-two by twenty-five millimeter. At first, Forensics thought they may have come from the old Mauser C96 or a knockoff like the PASAM used by the Brazilians or the Type 80 machine pistol the ChiComs like. But when they dug some slugs out of surrounding trees they determined them to be from Tokarev cartridges. They're a match for the ones the medics dug out of Levell's driver. The interesting thing is they're copper-coated. That type of ammo is banned by federal law 'cause it's capable of penetrating armor. Still used in the Eastern Bloc, though."

"So what are you saying, Lou?"

The other man shifted in his chair and crossed his legs. "Forensics thinks it's likely the weapon or weapons were Russian-made PP-Nineteen Bizons. With the end of the cold war and the breakup of the Soviet Union, a lot of those weapons found their way into the hands of the criminal element in the Ukraine. Many of those guys found work as enforcers for the Russian mob. Some of them are known to be in the States."

Christie leaned back in his chair and began slowly rubbing his stomach. It was a subconscious gesture. He'd lived with digestive miseries for so long he did it automatically. After a few moments of reflection on what Antonelli had just told him, he said, "So, what is the evidence telling us, that Levell got sideways with the Russian mob and they've kidnapped him?"

Antonelli shrugged again. "Doesn't add up to me. What would a guy like Levell, who's got a few bucks and a hellova government pension, be doing with the Ruskies?"

"Gambling debts, prostitution, drugs?" Christie said. "Maybe he got uptight for cash and borrowed from them then didn't pay it back in full or on time." He shook his head, hoping to stir up something that would connect the dots.

"Look," Antonelli said. "I gotta go. I'm taking the little woman to dinner at a fancy place tonight to celebrate closing the deal on the new house."

"That's nice. Have fun," Christie said as he watched Antonelli walk out the door. First a very expensive house and now a pricy dinner. Something about that bothered Christie and he wasn't sure why it did. Was it simple envy? Or was it something more? After a moment, he shook the thoughts from his head and opened the upper right-hand drawer of his desk. Reached in, he withdrew a fresh bottle of cherry flavored Mylanta Ultimate Strength liquid. He shook it vigorously for a few moments then uncapped it and took a large swallow. After replacing the bottle in the drawer, he called each family member's cell phone and the landline at home. Again, all he got were the opportunities to leave voicemail messages. He looked at his watch. It was almost seven o'clock. Something definitely wasn't right.

Just after he had replaced the receiver following the final call, his assistant, Charlotte, working late again as usual, buzzed him. "Agent Christie, there's a gentleman on the line who says he has information that will interest you."

"Did he give his name?"

"He said it was Smith."

"Sure," Christie said with sarcasm. "Why not. Did he say what it was concerning?"

"He said it was related to the Harold Case investigation."

"Okay Charlotte, thanks. And," he added, "go home. It's late." He recradled the receiver and sagged back in his chair, rubbing his reddening eyes. They stung from the strain of reading innumerable reports and bulletins, as well as from the hours of staring at the computer screen. His stomach ached from too high a level of stress. Lately, he'd developed a slight tremor in his hands. In addition to his role as SSA – Supervisory Special Agent – of the Case investigation, which seemed to be moving at a snail's pace, he also was involved in a number of other matters for the Bureau. He couldn't remember the last time he'd been able to maintain any sort of regular workout routine. He was only forty-five, but felt like he was falling apart physically. He feared he was at the beginning of something akin to an aircraft in a graveyard spiral; a long, quickening slide to an early and ignominious death.

And where the hell was his family? Christie took in a deep breath, held it for a few moments. He released it slowly, as if trying to clear his mind by exhaling his growing concerns for his wife and children. He reached over, picked up the receiver and punched the button that was flashing at the base of the phone. "Christie," he said.

"Agent Christie, you may remember me. We met awhile back," said the man on the other end of the phone call.

There was something vaguely familiar about the voice. Christie struggled to connect it to a face. Fishing for clues, he said, "Where was it we met?"

The voice on the other end said, "Back in January, we sat together on a flight from Atlanta to San Francisco."

Christie's eyes widened and he sat straight up in his seat. Now, he recognized the voice. "Whelan," he said. A second later, he leaned forward and punched a button on the base of his phone that began a recording of the call. It also sent a signal to Bureau staff members in a tech area two floors below to initiate a trace on the call.

"I realize you have, or shortly will have, a trace on this call," Whelan said, "so forgive me if I'm brief." He was leaning against a decorative railing with his back to the Potomac River, watching the comings and goings of the people around him.

"No," Christie lied, hoping to buy time for the trace to succeed. "I'm on my phone in my office. I can't put a trace on it from here."

"Bullshit," Whelan said.

"My assistant said you have information about the Harold Case investigation."

"Not exactly. It's about your family."

There was a sudden feeling of fear and emptiness in the pit of Christie's stomach that the Mylanta couldn't reach. When the moment of initial shock had passed, he said, "What the hell have you done with my family?"

"They're fine and they're going to stay fine. They are in very good hands."

"You son of a bitch. You miserable son of a bitch. Do you think you can use them as leverage on me." He was on his feet now and practically screaming into the mouthpiece.

"No, but someone else was planning to do just that. We stopped it. And we captured the two Ukrainian thugs who were sent to pull it off."

"Where are they?"

"Your family is in luxurious accommodations and being very well treated. After this, they may not want to return to their lives in suburbia. As for the two thugs, they're dead."

"You killed them?"

"One of them. It caused the other one to spill his guts like he was making his final confession to a priest."

"Did you kill him too?"

"No."

"Who did?"

"I don't know. He was alive the last I saw of him."

"But he's dead now?"

"That's my understanding."

Christie paused for a second. "Listen to me Whelan. If any harm comes to anyone in my family, I swear on all that's holy, I will find you and I will kill you."

In a matter-of-fact tone, Whelan said, "Anything's possible Agent Christie, but I wouldn't hold my breath on that if I was you." With that, he terminated the call by tossing the cell phone into the Potomac River.

Whelan walked a short distance and climbed into an unmarked, but official looking, black SUV parked at the nearby Thompson Boat Center. Larsen was behind the wheel. "Did you get through to him?" he said.

"Yeah, he got the message."

As they pulled out of the boat center on Thirty-First Street Northwest, Whelan took off the ball cap, sunglasses and jacket he was wearing and put them in a brown paper bag. A moment later, as they drove across the bridge spanning Rock Creek, Larsen slowed the vehicle and Whelan handed the bag out the window to a man dressed as if he were hiking the trails that paralleled the creek. The man walked to a car, placed the bag in the trunk, and drove away. In a few minutes Larsen and Whelan were on Interstate 95 on their way to the large country manor outside Fredericksburg, Virginia. After the ambush of Levell, General McCoy had advised them not to return to the lodge near Fairview Beach.

Within minutes after they left, local police, FBI agents and other law enforcement officials swarmed across the Washington Harbour development. After thirty minutes of searching the premises and questioning patrons, the senior Bureau agent on the scene called Christie. "No sign of the guy you described, Mitch," he said.

"Witnesses?"

"A couple of young women were headed into one of the bars here, the one where Gen Y meets to hook up. They said they thought they saw a guy who might have been the one we're looking for. He was using a cell phone."

"They give you a description of the guy?"

"Yeah, they thought he had a nice build and was good-looking."

"That's it?" Christie's voice had a ring of frustration to it.

The agent squirmed a little. "They said he was wearing a ball cap, sunglasses, and a light jacket. Mind telling me what this is about?"

"Shit!" Christie said as he slammed the receiver back into its cradle. He turned and stared out his sliver of a window. Where were his loved ones, he wondered, and how could he get them back?

53 RICHMOND, VIRGINIA

In Henrico County, just northwest of the jurisdictional limits of the City of Richmond, Virginia, there is a sprawling industrial area that lies between West Broad Street, which also serves as US Highways 33 and 250, and Interstate 64. The area consists of older warehouse space, Class C on a good day. The neighborhood has long since surrendered to grunge in the form of high vacancy rates, run-down structures with little to no maintenance, and streets filled with potholes and trash. The curbs and sidewalks are broken or nonexistent.

In the midst of this inhospitable and forlorn area, surrounded by vacant industrial space in all directions, sits a single-story building isolated in the center of a weed-grown lot. It's entirely enclosed within a ten-foot tall barbed wire fence rigged with sensors to disclose efforts to scale or cut through it. No effort has been made at landscaping the mostly dirt yard, and any grass long ago lost the war with the few, scraggly weeds. There is a sagging gate in the middle of the fence on the street side. The gate is mounted on small rubber wheels enabling it to be swung open in the event a vehicle should require access.

The exterior of the building is made up of faded red brick walls topped by a flat, built up roof. There are a few small, barred windows set high on the walls and a battered, rusting metal door centered in the front of the building. Two rutted tracks run across the hard dirt surface from the gate to a tall, metal overhead door set into the front wall on the right side of the building. The only incongruity is the presence of four video surveillance cameras, one on each corner of the building.

The inside of the building is even less attractive than its exterior. The cracked, and in some areas buckled, concrete floor is stained with rust and a myriad of industrial and automotive fluids representing years of accumulation. The space is mostly open and bare except for a number of crates stacked in one of the corners. There is a small, enclosed area that looked as if it may formerly have been used as an office. A single bathroom is situated next to the office. Rusting round poles that showed the dents and scars of the building's history support bare metal beams. Rows of neon lights, most of which no longer illuminate, are attached to the beams. Loose wires dangle from the beams in several places. The interior walls, originally painted white, are filthy and peeling. The whole place smells of stale air, cigarette smoke and automotive fluids. It was here that Cliff Levell now found himself.

Following the ambush that had taken the life of Paul Fontenot and left his personal assistant, Rhee Kang-Dae, in critical condition, the Ukrainians had brought Levell to this place. In his lifetime, he had seen worse. His abductors had used propofol to render him unconscious following the ambush. When he regained consciousness, he was lying on the filthy floor of the old warehouse. His wheelchair was nearby, and with great effort he was able to drag himself into it. Being the old warrior that he was, he began immediately to assess his situation.

The place was empty other than the area just outside the old office cubicle. It was furnished with a rickety old card table and two mismatched chairs that usually were occupied by his guards. The Ukrainians rotated this duty in pairs. They rarely got out of the chairs between shifts except to drag Levell from his wheelchair and slam him into one of the chairs during interrogations. There was a small refrigerator in which the guards kept food and beverages. The crowning accessory was a ten-year old calendar hanging on the wall just outside the door to the office cubicle. It featured an amazingly busty blonde baring her all for the month of October.

When Levell needed to relieve himself, his only means was to urinate in an old can and pour it down a pipe embedded in the floor near a corner of the building. He took it to be an old plumbing fixture of some kind. For the more serious bodily function, the guards would drag him out of the wheelchair and toss him onto the toilet in the filthy bathroom. The guards also used the same toilet and never flushed it. It appeared not to have been cleaned in at least a decade. It disgusted Levell to use it, but he was reminded of an old adage – any port in a storm. The guards gave him old newspapers in lieu of toilet paper. There was no soap or other cleansing agent available to wash his hands.

He was given one meal a day – a small can of tuna in oil - which the guards would open for him. No utensils were provided, so he ate with his unwashed fingers. Liquids consisted of water from the sink in the bathroom, which came out discolored by rust and reeking of sulfur. He was forced to sleep in his wheelchair. The guards occasionally would cuff him and curse him because they were bored and resented being used for this duty, which they considered to be beneath them. Levell never gave the guards the satisfaction of seeing him respond to the beatings. He liked to think of himself in the same terms as an old advertisement for Timex Watches – "takes a lickin' and keeps on tickin'".

Levell knew that propofol had less prolonged sedation and a faster recovery time than many other anesthetic agents. He assumed that he had been unconscious for a relatively short period of time following the abduction. Because of the windows, he could keep track of daytime and nighttime and estimated that he had been in captivity for approximately forty-eight hours. Because of the short-term properties of propofol, he believed his current location was not more than two hours from the site of the ambush. Even so, he knew that covered an enormous area that stretched, at a minimum, from south of Petersburg, Virginia to north of Baltimore, and as far west as the foothills of the Blue Ridge Mountains.

Given the nature of his activities, he knew a massive search by law enforcement officials would not be undertaken. It simply was too large an area for the Team to be able to comb with any success, even with the considerable skills of Whelan and the others. He began to rue not having had a tracing device implanted somewhere in his body. No doubt, he thought, it would have been discovered by his abductors and removed in a dangerous and painful way. Levell resigned himself to the fate he was sure awaited him. His only real regret was that he might not have driven the Team far enough, fast enough, to effectively counter the foreign and domestic apparatus that was destroying his beloved country.

Late in the afternoon of his second day in captivity he received a visitor. Levell had been expecting someone higher up the ladder than the thugs who guarded him. He was surprised, however, by who the visitor turned out to be. He recognized Kirill Federov instantly.

The Russian had the two guards on duty yank Levell out of his wheelchair, drag him across the hard concrete floor, and slam him into one of the two chairs at the card table. The guards took up positions behind Levell. Federov, dressed in a well-tailored dark gray suit and immaculately shined black wingtips, sat in the other chair and studied Levell silently for several moments. When he spoke, his English was nearly perfect. "Mr. Levell, you and I have never met, but we have known of each other for sometime, yes?"

Levell nodded, never breaking his gaze from the Russian's cold, blue eyes.

When the American didn't reply, Federov continued. "It is unfortunate, perhaps, that we shall no longer be able to continue our adversarial efforts." He smiled sardonically, as if savoring this moment of triumph.

"Don't cash checks that haven't been written, Federov."

"Meaning what?"

260

"Meaning that I'm not critical to our success against you and your comrades. I'm just one cog in a big machine that's going to roll right over you, and soon."

Federov looked at him with one eyebrow arched in skepticism. "I think you do yourself an injustice. You *are* the heart and soul of this Team, as you call yourselves. Without you, their leader, the others will stumble, unable to perform effectively. The weaker ones will disappear into the woodwork, trying to hide from their treasonous activities."

Levell shrugged. "You give me too much credit and underestimate the others. The operation is so far along that it is virtually failsafe."

Federov shook his head in disagreement. "I can permit an old man the pleasure of his fantasies," he said.

Ignoring him, Levell said, "I'm not a national political figure. I'm not surrounded by Secret Service agents. You could have had me taken out at any time, why now?"

Smiling with more than trace of smugness, Federov said, "Because now is the appropriate time."

"How so?"

"You have done us the very big favor of reassembling these Sleeping Dogs of yours. They are the perfect weapon to provide the appearance of the ultimate transgression by your foolish patriots in their slavish devotion to their political orthodoxy."

Levell's eyes narrowed. "What do you mean?"

With even greater smugness, Federov said, "There is some wet work that we must do to repair past misjudgments concerning certain individuals. However, we cannot be associated with it in any manner. How fortunate we are that you and your would-be patriot colleagues on the Team now can be made to appear responsible."

"How, exactly, does that work?" Levell said with a puzzled expression.

Federov laughed easily. "Given your situation, I see no harm in sharing this with you."

"You mean, given that I'm not going to leave here alive."

"That's putting it rather indelicately, but, yes."

"I'm all ears," Levell said

Federov leaned back in his chair and put one foot on the card table. "We seem to have developed issues with the current President of your country."

"What a shame," Levell said in mock sympathy. "After all the trouble and expense you went through to get him elected."

Federov shrugged. "No one is more surprised or disappointed than are we. Nevertheless, he has gone, as you would say, off the reservation."

"Still seems to be pursuing an all out socialist agenda to me."

"Yes, but it is his agenda. He has forgotten to whom he owes allegiance. We have instructed him to step down, but he refuses to do so. He insists he will stand for reelection."

"But, as unpopular as he has become with the American public," Levell said, "I thought you and your comrades, including Chaim Laski, were grooming Senator Howard Morris to run against him in the primary."

"That is true, but it would be very divisive; undoubtedly handing the White House to another warmongering capitalist imperialist like Reagan. That would set our plans and timetable back substantially."

Levell snorted in derision. "You call Reagan's *Pax Americana* and the peace and prosperity it created warmongering capitalist imperialism?"

"Actually, Reagan was a great leader and a visionary, but from our side of the politico-economic spectrum he was the devil incarnate. We had achieved so much by the time we were able to engineer Jimmy Carter's election, then Reagan set us back a full twenty years."

"So what are these plans of yours and how is it you envision the Team being instrumental in realizing them?" Levell said.

Federov tilted his head back and seemed to study the bare metal beams that supported the roof. After a few moments, he looked at Levell and smiled. "Your Sleeping Dogs are going to do our wet work for us." He paused for effect. "Through our comrades in the news media they and the other members of your organization will be portrayed as right wing fanatics who sought the violent overthrow of your constitutionally elected government. Given the background of these men as highly trained CIA assassins working in concert with your Team, a pseudo-patriotic right wing organization, it will not be a difficult sell. Brilliant, yes?"

Levell thought for a moment about what Federov had disclosed to him. "How do you propose to pull this off?"

"Very easy, my friend, and you are going to be instrumental in making it happen."

"Not in this lifetime," Levell said. He had endured a great deal of pain and suffering in hot and cold wars, first as a Marine and later as a field operative for the CIA. He was prepared to die, no matter how painfully, before he would cooperate in any fashion with Federov and his colleagues.

"Actually," Federov said, "the plan already is underway. We have contacted your good friend, General McCoy, to arrange to release you as soon as our instructions have been carried out."

"You're a bunch of fools," Levell said. "McCoy and the others won't hesitate to sacrifice me for the good of the overall operation. I wouldn't if it were any of them. They're smart enough to know that you have no intention of sparing my life under any set of circumstances."

Federov smiled in self-satisfaction and said, "We'll see about that."

"And furthermore, you're beyond foolish if you think the Sleeping Dogs will assassinate the president and other public officials. They wouldn't do it if I ordered them to."

Federov glanced at his Rolex Day-Date Platinum watch. Lifting his foot off the table and putting it back on the floor, he sat up in his chair and said, "It is time for me to go. It has been an enjoyable conversation and, in some ways, I will miss you, Levell."

"Are you familiar with the sport of baseball?" Levell said.

Federov made a dismissive gesture with his right hand and said, "It is something capitalists use to divert the attention of the proletariat from their miseries."

"Really? Have you expressed that opinion to you comrades in Cuba?"

"Why would I do that?"

"Because Cuba fields the top amateur baseball teams in the world."

"What is your point?" Federov said impatiently.

"A beloved icon of American baseball, Yogi Berra, once famously said 'it ain't over 'til it's over'".

Federov shook his head with a puzzled look on his face as if he didn't understand Levell. "What kind of foolishness is this?" he said. "More silly, confused capitalism?" He stood abruptly and spoke to the guards. "You will receive a signal as previously advised." He jerked his head toward Levell. "Kill him when you get that sign and dispose of the body as instructed. Understood?"

The two guards nodded. Federov turned and walked away. As he left the building, the heavy metal door slammed shut behind him with a loud noise that reverberated through the empty warehouse.

54 WASHINGTON, D.C.

Mitch Christie's mind was awhirl with thoughts and fears. He was a man whose many years of investigating the seamier side of life for the Bureau had annealed him to the plights and misfortunes of others. But this time it was very different. This time it was his own family members' whose well being was involved. Questions raced through his mind: What was their situation? Were they injured? Were they even alive? Was this his fault? Could he have done a better job of protecting them? Where were they now? How could he find them? How much time did he have before they were harmed? Why had they been abducted in the first place? Who was responsible?

Christie knew that in abductions time always was of the essence. He tried not to think about the Bureau's metric in these matters. Based on historical data, it demonstrated that over a relatively short period of time following a kidnapping the chances of recovering the victim alive decreased rapidly. Thoughts of vengeance against Whelan brought him little solace at this point. He needed to act quickly and effectively.

He grabbed the phone off his desk and punched in the numbers for the Bureau's equivalent of a motor pool. When a voice answered at the other end, he said, "This is Special Agent Christie. I need a vehicle and I need it now. I'll be down in sixty seconds."

He slammed the receiver back on its cradle and turned his attention to his computer. Using the mouse, he clicked on the desktop icon for Contacts. When the file opened, he clicked on Emergency Numbers under the heading Groups then scrolled rapidly to Frederick Police Department. He snatched up the receiver again and tapped in the number.

After a few rings, a female voice said, "Frederick Police Department".

"This is Special Agent Mitchel Christie with the Federal Bureau of Investigation. I want you to get hold of Chief Raitt wherever he is. Tell him my family appears to have been kidnapped. Have him get an SRT (Special Response Team) to my home immediately." He gave the woman the street address and said, "I also want a CSU (Crime Scene Unit) standing by when I get there. No one goes into or out of the house until I arrive. Understood?"

"Yes, sir," the operator said. Her voice sounded as if she wanted to ask further questions, but Christie hung up and ran out of his office and down the hall to the elevator banks.

Just as he reached the elevators, young Special Agent Rickover arrived also. "This working late sucks, doesn't it?" he said cheerfully.

Christie looked at him for a moment while continuously punching the down button. "Come with me, I may need you for something."

Rickover looked bewildered and disappointed. "But my wife expects me home for dinner. It's Wednesday. That's our date night...kind of." His face colored slightly.

"Goddammit, Rickover, call her on your cell phone and tell her you're on assignment."

The elevator doors opened and Christie grabbed the younger man by an arm and yanked him into the compartment.

"But...but what do I tell her? What kind of assignment is it? When will I be home for dinner?"

As the elevator descended, Christie stared at Rickover. A crimson flush of anger began to spread upward from his collar to his forehead. "You tell her anything you want to tell her," he said through clinched teeth. "And I hope for your sake you never talk to her about any of your work at the Bureau."

"No, no...never." Rickover had paled in contrast to Christie's reddening.

"And I hope you're not one of the Gen Y twits who thinks he or she is entitled to some lame ass job that allows them to come and go as they please as long as it doesn't involve more than twenty-five hours a week."

Rickover wagged his head vigorously back and forth. "No, sir. The Bureau has always been my dream. I'm all in, whatever it takes." He swallowed hard and his Adam's apple bobbed prominently.

A large, black Chevrolet Tahoe awaited them. Christie sprang behind the wheel, activated the lights and alarm, and they were on their way to Frederick, Maryland. It was a drive that normally took more than an hour. At speeds exceeding ninety miles per hour on the Beltway and I-270, Christie made the trip in thirty minutes. Throughout, Rickover sat wide-eyed and ramrod stiff, his white knuckled hands clutching the seat cushion as if it were a security blanket. There were several occasions when he thought he might toss any undigested vestiges of his lunch.

The Tahoe screeched to a halt in front of Christie's house blocking the street, which was lined with police cars on both sides. Christie leaped out and immediately took in the scene. A brown delivery truck was parked directly in front of the house. His wife's sapphire metallic Town and Country van was in the garage.

A heavyset man wearing a police uniform and chief's insignia walked over to him. "Special Agent Christie?" he said. "I'm Lamar Raitt, the Chief of Police."

"Yeah," Christie said and flashed his Bureau ID at the man. Motioning at his companion, he said, "This is Special Agent Rickover."

Raitt said, "What's this about your family and a kidnapping?"

Christie filled the chief in on what he knew about his family's abduction, but did not mention Whelan's name. Instead, he said he had received a call from a man claiming to be involved, but the Bureau had not been able to trace the call successfully.

When Rickover realized what was going on, he said, "Mitch, I think you ought to report this to our people at the Bureau."

Christie gave him an icy look and said, "I will, Rickover, but the local PD was able to get an SRT here and seal the area sooner." He turned to the chief and said, "I want your CSU to comb the house. Look for anything, prints, blood or any other possible source of DNA evidence." He paused and looked at the delivery truck. "And this vehicle too. Let's go." He turned and walked quickly into his dark and empty home.

Behind him, Chief Raitt said, "Wait a minute. Are you saying this isn't even official Bureau business?" He turned and looked at Rickover, who shrugged. "Hell," he said in disgust, "it's no wonder local police don't like working with you heavy-handed jerks."

Early the following morning after a sleepless night, Christie showered, dressed, and caught the 5:12 a.m. MARC train Union Station in downtown Washington, D.C. He had sent Rickover home in the Bureau's Tahoe and spent most of the night pestering and attempting to oversee the Frederick Police Department's Crime Scene Unit investigators. They gathered evidence, including blood samples and strands of hair for DNA purposes and impounded the brown delivery truck. When they left around three in the morning, the Chief had taken Christie aside and said, "We will do all we can, Special Agent, and we'll keep you in the loop on anything we turn up. But let's be clear on something. This is *our* investigation, and unless and until someone with proper authorization from the Bureau advises us otherwise, it's going to stay that way. Understand?"

Christie did understand, and his intention was to speak to his boss, the Assistant Director of the Bureau's Criminal Investigative Division, as soon as he arrived in the office that morning. Instead, he was called into the office of his boss's boss, the Executive Assistant Director of the Criminal,

Cyber, Response, and Services Branch. Over the years, he had met the man on occasion, but didn't really know him well. From the scowl on the man's face, Christie wished he did know him better.

The EAD was standing behind his desk hunched forward, fists resting on the top. He didn't indicate that he wanted Christie to sit in one of the comfortable looking side chairs.

"You want to see me, sir?"

The EAD straightened up, but the scowl stayed firmly planted on his face. "Special Agent, what the hell were you thinking when you scrambled the Frederick PD last night for a personal matter, but played it like it was Bureau business?"

"It concerns my family, sir. They were abduc...."

The EAD cut him off. "I don't give a crap about your family, Special Agent. You did not have authorization to commandeer the resources of a local police department for your own purposes."

Christie could feel his anger beginning to surge. He stared long and hard at the EAD before saying, "And if it had been your family, sir, I think you would have done the same thing."

"You *think*, Special Agent? No, that's the problem; you weren't thinking. If you had been thinking, you would have notified your superiors in the Bureau and let us coordinate the investigation."

"I understand what you're saying, but the Bureau could not have mobilized resources on the scene as quickly as the Frederick PD. You and I both know that in situations like this time is the most critical element."

The EAD stared at him, neither man being willing to be the first to break eye contact. "We have assumed jurisdiction and I have so advised Chief Raitt. I've appointed Lou Antonelli as the agent in charge of this investigation."

"Antonelli! Why Antonelli, sir? It's my family. I have personal knowledge regarding the victims and that can be immensely valuable. I should be in charge of the investigation."

"It's precisely because it *is* your family that I want you as far removed from the investigation as possible. If I hear that you've attempted to meddle in any way, directly or indirectly, I will suspend you without pay until I determine, if ever, that you should be reinstated. Am I getting through to you, Special Agent?"

Christie broke the eye contact as his gaze drifted down to the floor in front of the EAD's desk. His senses were overcome with feelings of despair and desperation. Antonelli was a decent investigator, he thought, but he doesn't have the same degree of motivation because it's not his family's well being that's at stake.

"I understand how you're feeling," the EAD said. "And we'll keep you advised of all developments in the matter. Now, go back to your office and find something to keep you occupied...other than the investigation into your family's disappearance. In fact, I'm putting you in charge of the investigation into that shootout and purported abduction yesterday in King George County, Virginia east of Fredericksburg."

Given his personal situation, Christie had a difficult time focusing on the apparent abduction of Levell and the shootings of the two men who had accompanied him. He toyed with the connection between Levell and Whelan for quite a while, but couldn't find any thing of relevance that wasn't already known. Finally, late in the afternoon, he gave up and walked down to Rickover's office, passing Antonelli's on the way. He was deeply disappointed when he saw that it was empty. He had hoped Antonelli would have something to share with him about the investigation into Christie's family's disappearance.

Rickover was sitting at his desk reading a file with a puzzled expression on his face. Christie leaned in the doorway and said, "Hey, Aaron, got a minute?"

The younger man looked up and stared at Christie for a moment. "Sure, but I have to tell you, my wife is really pissed at you about last night."

"Yeah, look, I'm sorry about that. I really wasn't thinking clearly. I hope you got home in time for your date night."

"Not exactly. She made me sleep on the couch."

"I guess she's pissed at you as well. Do you want me to call her and apologize?"

"No," Rickover said hastily. "That wouldn't be a very good idea right now."

"I understand. Look, has Antonelli said anything to you about the investigation involving my family?"

"No," Rickover said and paused, looking at the doorway to his office, "but he just walked by."

Christie spun around and caught up with Antonelli just as he was returning to his office. "Lou, is there anything new on my family?"

The other man looked at him for a moment before waving him to one of the chairs in his cramped office space. "It's a hellova thing, Mitch. What's this fuckin' world comin' to when lowlife trash kidnaps the family of an FBI agent." He shook his head as if in disgust.

He went around behind his desk and sat down, leaning back in his chair. "I was gonna call ya'. We got a coupla' things. First the good news. We looked at medical records and none of the blood samples matched up with anyone in your family."

"As a favor to me, would you have Forensics check them against the old records we have for that outfit, the Sleeping Dogs."

"I'm way ahead of you, pal," Antonelli said. "There's no match there either."

Christie had a momentary flashback to something Whelan had said the previous evening about someone wanting to harm his family and the Sleeping Dogs preventing it. "So what's the bad news?" he said.

"Well, that delivery truck apparently was hijacked. The driver's body was in the back covered up with boxes and such shit."

Christie's mind was racing. "It seems clear that another vehicle was used for the extraction. Have the neighbors been questioned? Did anyone see anything unusual?"

Antonelli reached into one of the drawers of his desk and pulled out a cigar. He removed the wrapper, bit off one end and stuck it in a corner of his mouth. "This little beauty is pure Cuban," he said.

"I thought those constituted illegal contraband in this country."

"Yeah, but every man's entitled to one vice."

"I understand they're expensive as hell, too," Christie said.

"Like I said, entitled." Antonelli took the cigar out of his mouth and admired it for a moment or two before replacing in the same corner.

"Back on topic, the neighbors?"

"Yeah, we had people interview everyone on your block and a block in either direction. An old guy lives a block north of you was waterin' his lawn. Says he remembers seeing a white van of some kind pullin' outta your driveway."

Christie's heart began to race. "Did he describe the van?"

"Only what I just told you." Antonelli paused again to admire his cigar. "But, he continued, "the gas company reported one of their vans stolen yesterday afternoon. Two of their guys went in to some joint for a late lunch. When they came out, the van was gone. It was recovered in the parking lot of one of those regional malls over in Tysons Corner."

Christie leaned forward in his chair. "Did Forensics check it over?"

"Yeah,"

"And?"

Antonelli shook his head. "It was clean. Not a stray hair. No blood or sweat. Not a smudged print. Nothin'. It was cleaner than a new one rollin' off the assembly line."

Christie trudged back to his office, head down, shoulders hunched, hands jammed in his pockets. He was angry and depressed. And he felt helpless. Who, he wondered, doesn't leave a single clue or piece of evidence behind? Just who in the hell were these people, Whelan and the other Sleeping Dogs? What was their game? Who was helping them? Just how many people were involved in whatever was being planned? More important, what could he do to help his family? There didn't seem to be a clear place to start.

As he entered his own office, it struck him. Levell! There had to be a connection. Levell had been one of the original Agency people who created the Sleeping Dogs. Without question, he had to be involved in their recent resurrection. But now it appeared that Levell had been abducted too. Was that a coincidence, Christie wondered, or was it staged by Levell to get himself off the radar screen? Unlike the Sleeping Dogs, Levell had tangible elements that could be associated with him. He had a home in Georgetown and paid frequent visits to a private club he belonged to, housed in a large hunting lodge in the Virginia Tidewater country. And he had associations. There was his driver, the Korean man, and Marine General McCoy, as well as all those members of government and industry who spent time at that lodge in Virginia. On the other hand, he had been instructed by his superiors in the Bureau not to pursue any of those leads. But now it was different. Now his wife and children were involved.

He thought about where to begin. One by one, he thought about possible actions. He could search the house in Georgetown for any evidence that would shed light on the Sleeping Dogs and their whereabouts. He could raid the lodge near Fairview Beach. He could grill the government and industry leaders that he knew associated with Levell. He could question Levell's driver in the hospital. He processed a lot of additional thoughts, but in the end, nearly suffocating with frustration, he realized that any of those actions would constitute a violation of the investigative restraints he'd been placed under. No doubt the EAD would have his ass. His badge too.

And then he had another thought. He glanced at his watch. Five-thirty. It would be three hours earlier in California. He punched up the contacts list on his computer then dialed a number. The phone rang a few times before a calm voice answered at the other end, "Hello".

"Dr. Nishioki? Bill?"

"Yes?"

"This is Special Agent Mitch Christie with the Federal Bureau of Investigation in Washington. I visited with you back in January. Do you remember me?"

"Ah, Mitch. Yes, of course I remember you. How are you?"

Christie didn't know how to answer that question. "I...I'm fine. Is this a good time to talk?"

"Well, unfortunately, I am expecting guests very shortly. Perhaps we can speak at a later point."

"No, wait, listen...I'll make this quick, but I need to ask you just a couple of questions."

There was a pause at the other end of the line then Nishioki said, "Very well, as long as it's only a couple of questions."

"The last time we spoke, I believe I told you that Brendan Whelan was alive."

"Yes, you did tell me that."

"Well, since then, it appears that several other members of the Sleeping Dogs unit also are alive. I believe they have reunited for a specific purpose."

"Indeed?"

"You knew those men, as well as the members of the team that created them, Levell, McCoy, and others. Do you have any idea what they might be up to today?"

The other man thought about the question for several moments then said, "No, I would have no way of knowing. But, if they are planning to engage in some sort of action, I suspect it will be out of their concern for this nation."

"Could it be some sort of terrorist action...assassinations, bombings, anything like that?"

Nishioki responded immediately. "No. These men are patriots. Over the years, each has sacrificed a great deal in the service of his country."

"Then, some sort of vigilante justice against persons or entities they believe threaten America?"

"Perhaps, but I really must go. My guests have just arrived. I have enjoyed our chat, Mitch. I wish you well." Nishioki hung up the phone.

Christie was replacing the receiver on the cradle, when his cell phone rang. He looked at the information on the screen regarding the incoming call, but it was an unfamiliar number. He pressed the Answer icon with his thumb and said, "Hello."

"Hello, Agent Christie," Whelan said. "I have someone here who'd like to speak with you."

Christie lunged for a small black box on his desk next to his landline phone. He pressed a button on top of the box and it began immediately to monitor the cell phone call via Bluetooth. It also began transmitting it to the tech lab two floors below where an attempt would be made to trace it.

"Whelan, you miserable son of a bitch," Christie said.

"Calm down, Mitchel, everyone is just fine," his wife said.

"Deb?" he said in shock, realizing Whelan must have handed the phone to his wife when he was punching up the tracer. "Where are you? What's going on?"

"I'm fine, Mitchel, everyone's just fine."

"Where are you? Do you have any idea?"

"Not really, but wherever it is, it's like a fantasy."

"Fantasy? I don't understand."

She laughed. "This must be how royalty lives. We're in the lap of luxury, pampered morning, noon, and night."

"You can't be serious! Have they administered drugs or sedatives to you? Threatened you if you don't tell me you're doing just fine?"

"No, Mitchel, nothing like that. Everyone is treating us beautifully. In fact, Brett's outside right now playing soccer with three of the men who helped us."

"Helped you? Dammit, Deb, they kidnapped you!"

"Yes, and it's lucky for the kids and me that they did what they did."

"What? You must be suffering from Stockholm Syndrome or something similar."

"Stockholm Syndrome? What are you talking about?"

"Sometimes captives become enamored of their captors. It's been documented in several instances."

There was a sound of exasperation in her voice. "Mitchel, we are not *enamored* with anyone. What you don't seem to understand is that these men who are helping us actually prevented another group of very nasty, armed men...Ukrainians I've been told...from harming us yesterday. They have assured me, and I have no reason to doubt them, that they will return us safely to our home when we're no longer in danger."

"And when will that be?" Christie said. There was an edge of doubt in his voice.

"As soon as they've...uh, dealt with the people who intended to harm us." She didn't want to think about what Whelan and his colleagues were going to do to those other men. She sensed from their quiet confidence, the manner in which they carried themselves, and most of all their imposing physical presence, that whatever they did to those other men it would be ugly and it would be permanent.

"Sorry to interrupt the conversation," Whelan said, "but it's time to go. Mrs. Christie and the children will be back in touch later." The phone line went dead.

Christie tore out of his office and raced down the stairwell two floors to the tech lab. He burst in and said, "Who's got the trace on my cell phone?"

A middle-aged woman wearing glasses with a tortoise shell frame looked up and said, "I do, agent Christie."

He strode quickly the table where she was monitoring a complex looking piece of electronic equipment and said, "Where did that call originate?"

The woman slowly removed her glasses, using both hands, and said, "Nairobi."

Christie stared at her for a long three seconds. "Nairobi? Nairobi, Kenya?" His voice was raised near shouting level. "Goddammit, that's impossible!"

The woman smiled thinly and said, "Personally, I don't believe it actually did originate there. Whoever made the call must have some very sophisticated communications equipment."

Christie looked at her with a mix of confusion and anger. "But, wait a minute, I thought *we* had the best equipment in the world."

"That's what we all thought. But it appears that someone may have one-upped us."

Christie instinctively placed his right hand on his abdomen and gently rubbed it. The pain was building fiercely in his stomach. "So what do we do now? They'll call back and I absolutely must be able to trace the call."

The woman put her glasses back on, looked at him and said, "We can put a live tracer on your cell phone number."

"What does that mean?"

"It will monitor your phone twenty-four hours a day and automatically begin tracing any calls made to it. If your mother calls to remind you to wear clean underwear, we'll know it." She smiled pleasantly.

"If that's your idea of humor, it's real funny. Do that thing with the cell phone and, just for the hell of it, keep a tracer on my desk phone too."

Christy walked slowly back to his office. This time he took the elevator. When he got there, he rummaged through the top right-hand drawer of his desk and found the bottle of Mylanta. He took a big swig and was just replacing the cap on the bottle when his desk phone rang. He tossed the bottle back in the drawer and picked up the receiver. "This is Christie."

A voice with traces of an Eastern European accent said, "Agent Christie, my name is Maksym. I am in possession of your family. If you want to see them again, you will do exactly what I am telling you. I call back later." The line went dead.

55 FREDERICKSBURG, VIRGINIA

Whelan stuffed the phone he had let Deborah Christie use to speak with her husband in a front pocket of his jeans. "Sorry to have to terminate the call, but its purpose was achieved."

"To let him know the children and I are safe and being well cared for?"

"Yes."

"That was thoughtful of you," she said without a trace of sarcasm.

Whelan nodded. "The purpose of this operation is to protect you and the children, not to leverage action out of your husband."

"I understand that now."

"Also, I apologize for having to listen in on the conversation."

"I know. It's a security thing, isn't it."

"Yes."

"Is Mitch in danger from the same thuggish people who tried to harm us?"

Whelan thought for moment before answering. "I don't think so, Ma'am."

"Call me Deborah," she said, "and why do you believe Mitch isn't in danger?"

"I believe their plan was to use you to coerce some action out of him. Now, that's no longer possible. Also, he's a federal agent. Harming one of them could loose the hounds of hell on the perpetrators. These guys are up to something that doesn't need the kind of scrutiny that would bring."

She had strolled over to a window and was looking out at an expansive lawn. Her son had teamed up with Quentin Thomas in a soccer match against Larsen and Kirkland. "You don't seem to be concerned that the call could be traced. Why is that?"

"We use satphones, satellite telephones, with a high degree of encryption." What he didn't tell her was that the system of communications satellites was owned and operated by a Brazilian company that, in turn, was owned through a series of other international entities ultimately controlled by the Mueller brothers. The satellites operated commercially, but also harbored highly encrypted communications accessible only for purposes sanctioned by the Muellers. That meant specifically designated members of the Team, including Levell, McCoy and a handful of others.

The system utilized 1024 bit asymmetric encryption that would require three hundred billion MIPS-years to crack. MIPS means one million instructions per second. Thus, a MIPS-year is thirty-one and a half trillion instructions. Multiplied by three hundred billion, cracking the code becomes virtually impossible. In addition, the system utilized a second layer of 256 bit symmetric encryption. The system converts voice to encrypted data using a constantly changing mathematical formula. Typically, the encrypted stream would be deciphered by the receiving unit, which converts it back to voice. In this scenario, all calls are routed directly to the receiving unit by way of a direct space link, thus avoiding use of a ground station.

In situations, like Christie's, where the receiving unit is not a part of the system and thus susceptible to interception, another strategy is employed. Here the call is directed to a special ground station where the encrypted data is converted to voice and directed to the non-systemic receiver through any transmission link on the planet. In addition, the special ground station is mobile and can be transported quickly to a new location by truck, ship or aircraft. In this case, the call from Christie's wife was routed through a ground station in Kenya, so that the Bureau's tracer indicated his wife's call was being transmitted from Nairobi.

"You seem like a very decent man," Deborah Christie said. "And most of your associates, too."

"Most?"

"Well, the one you call Stensen, who has such strange eyes, and the... ah...countrified one."

"Rafe."

"Yes."

"They each have their virtues, some are just harder to find."

"Some of you must be married. Are you?"

"Yes."

"Children?"

"Yes."

"It must be terribly difficult for them. Do you miss them?"

"Second by second."

She was quiet for a moment then said, "When this, uhmm, business is over, will you be able to return to a normal life with them?"

"I hope so, but that remains to be seen."

Whelan felt his phone vibrate from an incoming call. He fished the device out of his pants pocket and thumbed the receive button. "Whelan," he said.

"It's McCoy. We've had a communication regarding Cliff Levell."

"Give me a minute, I'm not in a secure area." He nodded at Deborah Christie and said, "Please excuse me, I've got to take this call in private."

As he walked quickly out the door into the hallway, he heard her say, "Please come back when you can. I like talking with you." There was something in her voice that made him, a fully committed married man, uncomfortable.

At the end of the hallway, there was a set of French doors that opened onto a small balcony. Whelan stepped out onto the balcony and closed the doors behind him. Larsen, Kirkland and Thomas were playing a spirited game of soccer in the fading light of day with fifteen-year-old Brett Christie. They were about one hundred yards away on the lush green lawn. It was far enough that they were out of earshot.

"Okay, General, what's the news on Cliff?" Whelan said into the phone.

"Here's one we didn't see coming," McCoy said on the other end of the line.

Whelan didn't like the sound of this. "What is it?"

"The bad guys called me a short while ago."

"Did you run a tracer on the call?"

"Hell yes, I ran a tracer." McCoy sounded angered that Whelan would even ask the question.

"And," Whelan persisted.

"Turns out it was a stolen cell phone. Belonged to some college kid at GWU. Had it stolen in a Starbucks."

"Yeah, but the Bureau can locate cell phones through GPS even when they're not in use."

"I know that, wiseguy. Our highly placed friends in the Agency and the Bureau tell me it went completely dead after the call was terminated. We assume it was destroyed."

"What did they want?" There was a pause at McCoy's end of the line. "Seems they want to swap Cliff in exchange for services."

"Services?"

"Yeah, they weren't specific about the nature of the services, but they were real clear about who was to perform them."

Whelan had a suspicion who that would be. "The Sleeping Dogs."

"Bingo."

"Must be wet work. And something that makes their side look good and ours look bad."

"You're a regular fucking psychic, aren't you."

"Not hard to figure out," Whelan said, ignoring McCoy's sarcasm. "How does the Team want to proceed?"

"It's a tough decision to make because we all love Cliff, but there really are no options. We can't send the six of you on an operation that enhances the enemy's power and destroys all that we've been working for. Not to mention getting you guys killed."

"So we're just going to throw Cliff to the wolves."

There was genuine sadness and remorse in McCoy's voice. "It's a hellova thing for a man to have to do, sacrifice his best friend of many year's standing, but Cliff knew...hell, we all know, the risks involved."

Both men were silent for a few moments. Whelan spoke first. "Truth is, we don't know whether Cliff is alive, or would be if we did perform to the 'services'."

"There is that," McCoy said.

56 J. EDGAR HOOVER BUILDING

Following the very abrupt and shocking phone call from Maksym, Christie sat in his desk chair struggling to put together the pieces of a baffling puzzle. What he did know was that it appeared his family was being well cared for. He knew also that Whelan and his men were protecting them, although he wasn't sure what they were being protected from. He knew there was some kind of Eastern European connection. Whelan and his wife both had mentioned Ukrainians, and the caller, Maksym, had spoken with what sounded like an Eastern European accent. Christie didn't know what the involvement of Ukrainians or other Eastern Europeans meant. And he had no idea who Maksym was or why he had lied about having Christie's family as hostages.

He rose from his chair and walked back down to the tech area a couple of floors below his office. The middle-aged woman with the glasses with the tortoise shell frame was still there. As he approached her, he said, "When I was down here earlier, I asked about putting a tracer on my office line."

The woman looked up. Her face was expressionless. "Yes, you did."

"Well, by any chance, did you activate that tracer yet?"

She continued to give him the blank look for a few moments. "You asked me to do that, and I did it."

"I received a call a few minutes ago. Can you check to see if it picked up any information." He was trying to be patient with her, knowing he had gotten off to a bad start earlier.

The woman turned away from him and began working at her computer, her hands moving rapidly over the keyboard as she watched the monitor's screen. About a minute later, she turned back to him and said, "There was a call to your number about nine and a half minutes ago."

Christie felt a sudden wave of excitement. "Did you get any useful information?"

"Some, but it was a very brief call." She slid the glasses part way down her nose and looked up at him over the top of the frame. "It was a cellular phone and moving rapidly, as if in a vehicle. At the time of the call, it was on Interstate Ninety-Five heading south near Dumfries, Virginia. We were not able to identify the phone number, unfortunately. There simply wasn't sufficient time."

His voice heavy with disappointment, Christie sighed and said, "So that's it. We don't have anything very useful."

Using both hands, the woman slid the glasses back up her nose and said, "That's not exactly correct, Special Agent. Every mobile phone is manufactured with its own unique identification code embedded in it. We were able to capture the code."

"So what does that mean in non-tech cop talk?"

The woman smiled thinly without genuine warmth. "It means that I have entered that identification code into the software we use for these purposes. The next time that particular phone is used, the trace will pick it up immediately and we will begin monitoring it."

It was Christie's turn to smile. It was a smile filled with hope and satisfaction.

57 OFF THE EAST COAST OF FLORIDA

At three hundred and sixty feet in length, or almost one hundred ten meters, the super yacht *Feral* was twenty percent longer than an American football field. It had been custom made by one of the top shipyards in Germany for a billionaire Russian oligarch. The Russian had sold it for a reputed price of two hundred million dollars to Chaim Laski. Among all his worldly possessions, without question this was his favorite. The *Feral* had an aluminum superstructure atop a steel hull and was powered by twin MTU 20V 1163TB engines capable of generating almost nine thousand horsepower.

For his own comfort as well as that of his guests, Laski had installed an alternative propulsion technology utilizing an azimuth thruster. It's a configuration of ship propellers contained in pods that can be rotated in any horizontal direction in lieu of a rudder. An electric motor inside a pod is connected directly to a propeller without the use of gears. The twin diesels produce the electricity. The benefits include better maneuverability than would be achieved with a propeller and rudder system, lower maintenance costs, more efficient use of space, and best of all, reduced noise and vibration. Together with the onboard wastewater management system, it produced much less pollution than most other super yachts. Not that Laski cared; but he did enjoy impressing the largely leftwing green movement.

For the additional comfort of himself and his guests, Laski had anchor stabilizers installed, which provided increased shipboard stability whether in port or at sea. He also had an iPad app custom-made. It allowed his guests to control everything from the entertainment and climate systems to blinds and lights in their cabins from their touch-screens. Each of the four VIP suites and six guest cabins was equipped with an iPad. Every unit featured onyx countertops, baths carved from limestone blocks, marble floors, and Swietenia mahogany grown on plantations in Fiji. In the master salon, Laski enjoyed a mahogany and delft tiled wood-burning fireplace. In addition to its guests, the *Feral* could accommodate a crew of forty.

The opulence didn't stop at the guest accommodations. Three glass elevators and an open glass spiraling staircase connected the several decks. Transparent flooring had been installed in a majority of the public areas of the ship. While there were a variety of pools, hot tubs, and sunbathing areas - many of them enclosed and air-conditioned, it was the infinity pool on the main deck with its waterfall cascading to the down-level decks that stole the show. Its high glass wall also served as a movie screen, enabling guests to watch a film while enjoying the pool.

The ship also featured an expansive wine cellar with a French limestone fireplace, a beauty salon and spa with massage room, and a full gym and full-size racquetball court. It also had an art collection exhibiting many of the priceless works Laski had collected. There was a glass-enclosed garden area filled with exotic plants from the far corners of the world. For tax purposes, Laski sometimes conducted business aboard the *Feral*. To accommodate these activities, there was a suite of fully equipped offices on board along with meeting and conference facilities.

For Laski's own peace of mind, a fully equipped hospital was maintained onboard. Certain specifications inherited from the Russian oligarch who formerly owned the ship were even more reassuring. These included bulletproof windows and armor plating. In addition, there were two helipads, each equipped with a brand new Sikorski S-76D chopper. But even more important, the Russian's insecurities had led him to equip the yacht with an escape submarine that had the capacity to sleep eight guests and spend up to two weeks underwater. There also was his omnipresent phalanx of Ukrainian bodyguards. Most important was the man he had placed in charge of the bodyguards, Maksym. Laski felt confident that regardless what dangers might come his way aboard this ship, he would survive quite nicely.

On this particular day in late August, Laski was cruising aboard the *Feral* off the coast of Southeast Florida near its homeport of Fort Lauderdale. His guests included several young blonde women currently scantily clad or nude in and around the infinity pool. Also aboard were the Chief Operating Officer and Chief Financial Officer of his parent holding company. They were there to provide a cover of legitimacy. His special guest was Colonel Kirill Federov. Laski had flown all of them except Federov to Fort Lauderdale in his recently purchased Gulfstream 650 business jet. Federov had flown commercial to the same city under the pretext of attending an international trade show.

While the COO and CEO were teleconferencing their underlings at various company offices around the globe, Laski and Federov were holding a private discussion in the ship's elegant boardroom. Behind the walls richly paneled in Honduran mahogany, was a lining of a material designed to thwart all efforts to penetrate with infrared, ultrasound, and all other surveillance devices. The same material underlay the deck beneath their feet. Even the white tray ceiling with brown border on molding, and featuring a brown ceiling medallion was lined.

At the moment, Federov was staring out the large clear panel at the distant beach. The panel, too, had been impregnated with the same anti-surveillance material. After several moments he swiveled slowly in his chair, rested his elbows on the Bubinga wood conference table, and looked across it at Laski.

"Well, my friend, what do you think of my little boat so far?"

"I am not you friend," Federov said. It came out almost as a snarl. "As for this floating whorehouse, I am as disgusted by it as much as I am by all of the other toys on which you piss away the money of the State."

If the remark stung Laski, he didn't show it. "My good Colonel, it is all part of the charade I must play in order to be in a position to optimize my services to the cause."

Federov shook his head slowly back and forth, but never broke his eye contact with Laski. "So, what is the meaning of this silly name *Feral?*"

A smile spread slowly over Laski's face as he considered whether to tell the Russian the truth. At last he decided it would do no harm. "It is a term in English."

"Meaning?"

"A feral animal is one that has escaped from a domestic or captive status and has returned to that of a wild animal."

"That is stupid. Why did you choose such a name?"

Laski continued to smile amicably at Federov, but he decided that he would not answer that question. It was too personal. He had been a child of nine when the Germans invaded and occupied Poland. Prior to that time, his father had been a wealthy banker. That ended with the invasion. Laski's family was Jewish. The Germans rounded up the other members of Laski's extended family and sent them to the Auschwitz death camp. None of them survived.

Laski had been more fortunate. Fearing what the future soon would bring, his parents had sent him to live with the family of one of their servants, a Polish girl who was Catholic. The family protected him throughout the war and hid him from the Nazis. After the war, Laski, now a gaunt and undersized fifteen year-old, had found himself alone and destitute in a ravaged land. But some of the things his father had told him around the dinner table stuck in his mind. One of them had been that the key to success was to provide a product that the market demanded. Another was to align yourself with those held in power.

He utilized the first bit of advice very quickly. Post-war Poland was occupied by the Soviets. Their soldiers were everywhere. Here was his market.

What did soldiers want? Women. In that devastated economic environment, Laski had little trouble finding women, even young girls, who would consort with the Soviets in a desperate effort to feed themselves and their children. The problem was that older, larger, stronger men were going into the same business and saw Laski as needless competition. His life was threatened. He hired off-duty soldiers, many of whom were Ukrainians, as bodyguards. They were gleefully proficient at their task, and soon Laski had little competition.

In response to the second bit of fatherly advice, Laski plied the Soviet administrators, almost all of whom were Russian, with his youngest, most attractive girls and fine Polish vodka. Through his whoremongering efforts, he eventually built valuable relationships with the highest-level Soviet administrators. They found him to be extremely intelligent, possessed of an intellect that could process complex data, including financial data, almost instantaneously. Although he was mostly self-educated, he spoke a number of languages, including Russian and English, and had a remarkable grasp of geopolitical affairs.

The attribute that most impressed his Soviet masters, however, was his vision of one-world government, and socialist at that. He shared their perspective that the mass of humanity consisted of little more than drones. Individuals were incapable of clear thinking and rational decisions. They needed to be confined tightly within a strict, all-encompassing regulatory framework. All decisions needed to be made for them by the intellectual elite. If necessary, and it always was, brute force in the form of the police power of the State was to be used to tell the masses what to do, and where, when and how to do it. In essence, they needed to be told what thoughts to form.

Some of Laski's Russian acquaintances rose through the hierarchy of the Soviet apparatus. They remembered the intellectually gifted whoremonger they had met in Poland. Eventually, they realized he was the missing key piece in their strategy to destroy the West, especially the United States. He was the perfect choice to manage the cash flow that supported the efforts to undermine that bastion of capitalism. And so, he had risen from a starving orphan in a bombed out Polish ghetto to become one of the wealthiest individuals on the planet. He was jarred from his remembrances by the sound of Federov's palm slapping sharply against the top of the Bubinga wood conference table.

"Are you listening to me, Comrade Laski?" Federov said with a distinct snarl in his voice.

"Yes, of course."

"I asked you why you chose this strange word, feral, for the name of this vessel. You did not answer. Instead, you seem to be daydreaming."

Laski smiled a phony smile intended to disarm Federov. "I assure you, my dear Colonel, I was merely thinking about the answer to your question."

"And?"

"Please indulge me. It is a personal conceit. I have gone from being someone who depended on the charity of others for my daily bread to a man who controls the fate and fortunes of so many others. I am like the animal that once was domesticated, but has returned to a place of prominence in the wild."

Federov stared at him for a few moments, contempt etched on his broad Slavic face. "You are an arrogant fool."

Laski felt his face redden, but nodded to Federov in deference. He purposely held his tongue.

"Stop wasting my time, Comrade Laski. We are here to finalize the details of our plan for the holiday the Americans call Labor Day."

Laski nodded again. "All has been arranged. Everyone knows what they are to do, and will do it perfectly."

"You had better be right this time, Comrade. Those Ukrainian fools you employ botched the kidnapping of the FBI agent's family."

More color seeped into Laski's face. "That was not handled well, I admit. But the agent has no way of knowing what happened to his family. Thus, we have made him believe they are in danger and he must comply with our instructions."

The Russian gazed at him for a moment. "So, what are you telling me?"

"We have been in communication with him and advised him that we do have his family. Believe me, he will do exactly as we ask."

"And you are confident that McCoy and the others will exchange these Sleeping Dogs of theirs for that old cripple, Levell?"

"Yes. In their conceit, they undoubtedly will believe that these assassins of theirs somehow will outsmart us and escape."

"And you are convinced they will not?"

"It is a condition that Levell will be released only when the assassins have completed certain tasks for us."

"But he is not to be released?"

"Of course not. He will be killed along with the others when our operation is completed."

Federov stared thoughtfully at Laski for a few moments, unconsciously rubbing his chin with the back of his thick right hand. "So you believe that these men, these so-called Sleeping Dogs, actually will participate in killing the president of the United States and the others?"

A smile of confidence spread across Laski's face. "Yes, the president, the senate majority leader, the publisher of the very liberal Gotham Times, the chairman of the Progressives for Fair Government, one of the chief fundraising and propaganda arms we've used over the years, and, particularly fitting on Labor Day, the president of the Service Industry Union. Dedicated Marxists, everyone of them."

Now it was Federov's turn to smile. "How nice of that bumbling fool we manipulated into the White House to bring them all together for another of his robotic, monotonic and empty speeches."

"And in such an accessible place, the steps of the Capitol Building."

"Yes," Federov said. "Those bumbling fools, the president and senator, have gone off the reservation and must be removed."

"The others, of course, are expendable, but lend such credence to this being the act of right-wing extremists."

"You have your people ready to do the actual killing?"

"Of course. The two Ukrainian marksmen have been rooming at the Hotel L'Orange for the past two weeks. As discussed, they are using the cover that they are on a month long business trip. The fact that Labor Day falls in the middle of it is seemingly inconsequential."

"Tell me again, why this Hotel L'Orange?"

"It's the closest to the Capitol and my men have a clear line of sight to the steps of the building."

Federov rubbed his chin some more and said, "The FBI and Secret Service will find the bodies of Levell and his Sleeping Dogs in the room. How do the Americans say it, a gift wrapping?"

Laski nodded his head up and down slowly. "Indeed they will, Colonel, indeed they will."

58 FREDERICKSBURG, VIRGINIA

Following the phone call from McCoy, Whelan gathered the other five men in his unit. They waited for the general in the library of the country manor home outside Fredericksburg. He pulled up in front of the large ornate portico thirty minutes later dressed in civilian clothes and driving an unmarked, late model Ford Taurus. Although they were not military, all of the men except Almeida rose to their feet when McCoy entered the room. He made a quick dismissive motion with his right hand, indicating they should sit down. He placed a slim Apple laptop on the table in front of his chair and sat down.

Whelan studied McCoy's weathered face, trying to read his emotions. It was, he thought, like sampling a fine wine and identifying the essences on the palate. There was a grim set to his curbstone jaw line. Determination showed in his clinched lips. His body language evinced his famous no-bull-shit attitude in all things. But it was his eyes that stole the show. There was fieriness there, the anger of a man too long frustrated and longing for revenge.

Almeida sat at one end of the long, stained oak library table, an insecure man seeking power by claiming one of the two power seats at the table. The others sat at chairs along the sides of the table. The chair at the other end had been left vacant for McCoy. But he didn't take it. Instead, he chose a chair in the exact middle of the table, the weakest position of all. It was what Levell would have done. So powerful was the force of his personality, that he consciously, purposely chose such a position. Whelan was on his right, Larsen on the left. Stensen, Thomas and Kirkland sat across from them.

"I shared with the men what you told me on the phone, General," Whelan said.

McCoy nodded his head a few times, almost imperceptibly. "Thank you."

"What do you want us to do, General?" Larsen said.

McCoy fanned out the fingers of both hands on the tabletop and leaned forward using them for support. "Since I made that call to Brendan, there have been some new developments."

The others around the table glanced at each other.

"How so?" Stensen said.

McCoy sat back in his overstuffed conference chair. With both elbows on the arms of the chair, he brought his large, ruddy hands up near his chin, left hand over right fist. There was a certain gleam in his eyes and a slight smile of satisfaction on his lips. "We know where Levell is," he said.

After a moment's silence, all of the others leaned forward involuntarily and stared at McCoy.

"How?" Thomas said.

"Where?" Whelan said.

McCoy's smile broadened. He relaxed his hands and placed them on his gut. "The one thing the Team does well that no one in the government seems capable of doing is assimilate information from a wide variety of government resources."

"You mean processing information gathered by entities like NSA, the Agency, and the Bureau, which they don't share with each other," Whelan said.

"Exactly. Top people in those agencies and others are a part of our efforts. They share with us. We compile it and interpret it."

Thomas said, "I thought all that infighting and turf war crap was supposed to have been prohibited after nine eleven."

McCoy shook his head, "It was a great idea, but old habits die very hard among the entrenched egos in a bureaucracy."

"Not to be abrupt, General," Whelan said, "but where is Cliff?"

"In an old warehouse in the middle of an industrial area northwest of Richmond."

"And we know this...how?" Stensen said.

"It should come as no surprise to you to learn that NSA maintains photographic surveillance of much of the planet via a system of satellites."

The other men nodded.

"As luck would have it, one of their satellites happened to videotape the tail end of Cliff's abduction. By coincidence it partially tracked the truck the bad guys used.

Kirkland interrupted. "Wasn't the truck used to kidnap Cliff abandoned a short distance away?"

"Yes, but the NSA tape showed them changing vehicles. Then VDOT cameras unintentionally picked up the other car farther along the way."

"What's VDOT?" Almeida said.

"Virginia Department of Transportation," Larsen said.

"I'm assuming the NSA videos were obtained from someone high up in the agency who is a member of the Team in hopes that a satellite might have picked something up," Whelan said. "Then, when they found the shots of the abduction scene, the Team finagled the VDOT tapes."

McCoy smiled and nodded.

"Sounds like there was some luck involved here, too," Larsen said.

"You haven't heard the half of it," McCoy said.

"We were hoping there was more," Whelan said.

"Indeed there is," said McCoy. "VDOT cameras eventually lost the car after it left the Interstate and entered the back streets of Richmond."

"Then how do you know he was taken to a specific location in the industrial area?" Thomas said.

"We got lucky. DEA has been using their satellite surveillance system to track vehicles they suspect of being involved in drug trafficking."

"So, how did you establish the connection between NSA, VDOT and DEA?" Thomas said.

"With a hellova lot of man hours on the part of the Team and its resources. We specifically tracked down any government agencies' surveillance materials looking for a match to the car. We hit pay dirt with DEA."

"What did their stuff show?" Whelan said.

"I'm getting to that if all of you will shit-can the interruptions," McCoy said with a growl.

The others nodded. A couple of them sat back in their chairs.

"The DEA has been following up on suspected involvement in drug trafficking by some Ukrainian gorillas. They provide muscle for some rich bastard who lives in a mansion in Potomac, Maryland."

McCoy paused and looked around the room. "And who do you think Daddy Warbucks turns out to be?"

A couple of the men shook their heads or shrugged.

McCoy's lips peeled back from his teeth in an expression of contempt. "That commie bastard, Chaim Laski."

Whelan smiled. To McCoy, anyone who wasn't to the right of Attila the Hun was a 'pinko' or a 'commie bastard'.

"I don't get it," said Thomas, the *über* rational philosopher and university professor. "Laski's a billionaire financier and investor. Why would he get involved in something as dangerous and stupid as drug trafficking?"

McCoy said, "He probably doesn't know about it. For security purposes, he surrounds himself with these goons, mostly Ukrainians with lengthy criminal records. They're probably picking up cash on the side by moonlighting in the drug trade."

"So," Whelan said, "the DEA tapes connected this car with the warehouse in Richmond."

"Yeah. It made several trips back and forth. DEA thinks it's probably where they store the drugs."

"It does sound like a good place to stash Levell," Thomas said. "But do you think Laski knows anything about Levell's abduction?"

McCoy scoffed. "Know about it? Hell, that commie rat bastard likely arranged the whole thing."

"Why?"

"Not sure yet. Something's surely brewing. Maybe Cliff knows and we can find out from him when we extract him. If not, we'll beat it out of the guards."

Whelan shook his head. "The guards probably don't know shit. They're just hired muscle."

"How do we even know Cliff's alive?" Larsen said.

McCoy smiled slyly. "Satellite thermography."

"What the fuck is that?" said Almeida.

"Animals, including humans, emit radiation in the infrared range of the electromagnetic spectrum," Kirkland said. "Thermal imaging cameras use a series of mathematical algorithms to build an image of the emitting life form."

For a moment, everyone, including McCoy, stared at Kirkland as if he were an alien life form.

Finally, McCoy said, "Uh, yeah, that's pretty much it. Using it, we've been able to establish what appear to be two human beings, probably the guards, and a third one in a sedentary situation. We believe it's probably Cliff in his wheelchair."

"When do we extract him?" Larsen said.

McCoy shook his head impatiently. "Wait, there's an additional wrinkle."

"Isn't there always," Larsen said.

Ignoring him, McCoy said, "It seems the Bureau also had some surveillance footage that raises a whole different issue." He paused.

"Well, what the hell is it this time?" Almeida said impatiently.

McCoy fixed him with a hard gaze for a few moments.

"It seems there's also a Russian involvement."

"As part of the drug dealing?" Whelan said.

"There doesn't seem to be a connection there. The Bureau keeps its eye on members of foreign diplomatic corps posted to this country, especially those from nations that are not especially friendly to ours."

"That certainly would include the Ruskies," Larsen said.

"Right. Well, in this instance a certain lower level attaché named Federov made a visit to the warehouse. The DEA and Bureau tapes both show it."

"So, why would a lower level Russian attaché be visiting a warehouse where drugs are being stored and a kidnap victim is being unlawfully detained?" Whelan said, more for rhetorical purposes than anything else.

"He's not your average commie bureaucrat," McCoy said. "This guy is a colonel in the Spetsnaz. The Bureau has recorded him making numerous trips to visit Laski, usually in the guise of a lackey accompanying a Russian trade counselor."

"Maybe he's not so lower level," Whelan said.

"Not according to the Agency. Their dossier on this guy indicates he's highly placed in the Sluzhba Vneshney Razvedki or SVR, Russia's primary external intelligence agency. He reports directly to the SVR Director, who, in turn, reports directly to Putin."

"Did the CIA share this information with the Bureau?" Thomas said.

McCoy looked at him with a pained expression on his face. "What the fuck do you think?"

Thomas shrugged.

"If it wasn't for the existence and efforts of the Team, none of the dots would ever get connected. America would just assume the position and the Marxists of the world would shove their red hot branding iron clear up our collective ass."

Whelan said, "I don't think any of us gives a shit who or what may be involved in this cluster fuck. Let's get back to Sven's question, when are we going to go after Cliff? His life is on the line and every second counts."

McCoy smiled a thin smile that stretched the corners of his mouth straight out rather than up. There was a gleam in his eyes. He opened the laptop in front of him and said, "I hope you boys don't have any plans for this afternoon, 'cause we got work to do. Startin' now."

59 WASHINGTON, D.C.

It was late. The massive FBI headquarters building at 935 Pennsylvania Avenue, NW was virtually empty. The clock on Mitch Christie's credenza ticked and tocked with metronomic regularity. The sound filled the silent office space with a mind-numbing ennui. If anything, the carpeted floor and acoustical ceiling tiles seemed to amplify it. It rebounded off the walls, the furnishings, and Christie's eardrums.

He hadn't been home, or slept, or showered or shaved in two days. His appearance showed it. He sat slumped in his desk chair in the darkened room, elbows on armrests, fingers interlaced, eyes closed, face resting on his knuckles. Troubling thoughts flashed over and over again through his mind. Why was his family targeted in the first place? Why would Whelan and his colleagues care enough to take the risk of the preemptive strike? Who were the Ukrainians, and more importantly, whom were they working for? His wife and children were victims of a kidnapping. Why did Deborah seem so calm, even at peace, with the situation? Why was she letting his son play soccer with members of the Sleeping Dogs unit? They were stone killers. Surely she was cognizant of that.

He dropped his folded hands to his stomach and leaned back in his chair, head against the backrest and eyes still closed. Still the questions raced and spun through his mind, almost playing tag with each other. Who was Maksym? Clearly, he did not have Christie's family. Whelan did. Why would Maksym claim to be holding them? What was it he expected Christie to do in the belief that compliance would get them back?

Christie was exhausted but he couldn't sleep. He was running on copious amounts of black coffee and Red Bull. And Mylanta. Try as he may, he couldn't get the pieces to fit. He knew with a cop's intuition that there were connections. The shootout resulting in the apparent abduction of

291

Clifford Levell was one. The comings and goings at the lodge in Tidewater Virginia was another. So was the involvement of Ukrainians. As was the presence of Whelan and the supposedly dead members of his ultra black ops unit. Then there was the incident in Georgetown back in January, when Harold Case and three bodyguards had been killed.

He reached for his cup, took a sip of long cold coffee and grimaced. There was the discovery of the bone field in Hawaii shortly after someone – who may have been Whelan, passed through. Later there was the supposed sighting in Bayou Country about the time a gang of motorcyclists went missing. There was the barroom brawl in North Carolina where witnesses described a group of men who resembled some of the members of the Sleeping Dogs unit. The body of a local troublemaker was found behind the establishment with his neck snapped. Recently, there had been the incident at the nightclub outside Georgetown, near the Maryland state line. A large and powerful Ukrainian bodyguard employed by Chaim Laski had been beaten to death in the men's room. In addition to the killer, at least three others had to have been involved. Two men had been observed directing patrons away from the restroom that night. Another had entered the second floor office, killed the night manager and stolen the videos recorded by surveillance cameras. Eyewitnesses again described men who could have been members of the Sleeping Dogs.

Shortly after that, Whelan's men abducted his wife and children. She and Whelan both told him it was done to prevent a kidnapping by Ukrainians. Whelan later admitted to him that the Ukrainians had been killed. And what was the Ukrainian connection running through this scenario? Who was Maksym? Was he another of the Ukrainians? Was there an involvement with Laski? But why would a socially prominent and politically powerful person be involved in murder and intrigue? It was true that he was politically active, pursuing his one-world government vision, but this seemed bizarre.

Christie believed he was close to fitting the pieces together, but somehow the end game continued to elude him. Unconsciously, he reached for the bottle of Mylanta on his desktop. At the same time, his cell phone rang. Thinking, hoping, it was his wife, he dropped the Mylanta and grabbed the phone off his desk. The small screen showed an incoming call from a number with a 301 area code. He didn't recognize the number, but he knew the area code. It was for a strip in Maryland that ran north and west of the District of Columbia. His home in Frederick was in that area.

He quickly pressed the green incoming symbol on his Blackberry. "Hello, this is Mitch Christie."

"Christie, it is Maksym. Do you remember me?"

Instantly, Christy recognized the somewhat raspy voice with its traces of an East European accent. "Yes."

"You are ready to have your family returned unharmed, yes?"

"Yes, I am."

"That is good. They are missing you very much. Do exactly as we tell you, and they will be released."

Christie's mind was racing. He knew Maksym didn't have his family. They were with Whelan. He could not see how there could be any connection between Whelan and Maksym. So, clearly, Maksym was bluffing, and Christie knew how to call his bluff.

"I need to know they're safe. Let me speak to them."

Maksym never hesitated. "That is not possible."

"Why? If you have them, and if they're safe, as you say, then let me speak to my wife."

Maksym suddenly turned angry. "You are not in position to make these demands. You will shut up and listen carefully. Otherwise, you are signing death warrant for your family. You are understanding, yes?"

For just a second or two, Christie toyed with the idea of telling Maksym to go fuck himself. He believed his wife when she had told him that she and the children were safe and in good hands. Yet he wanted to know what Maksym's ploy was. Obviously, there was some kind of involvement because he knew they had been kidnapped. Who was he working with? What did they expect to gain? Clearly, it was a situation that merited investigating.

"Yeah, I understand," Christie said. "What is it you want me to do?"

"Good. You are smart man, Agent Christie. Now, listen carefully. Here is what you must do."

"I'm listening," Christie said tersely.

"A bad thing is going to happen."

"When?"

"Soon."

"Who is going to do this 'bad thing'?"

There was exasperation in Maksym's voice. "That is what I am telling you. You must stop with the questions."

"Okay."

"The men who will do this thing are evil. They seek to destroy your country. I will tell you where and when you can find them. It will be your duty as agent of FBI to stop them."

Christie was quiet for a moment. "When are you going to give me this information?"

"At the appropriate time. Until then, you must not speak of this to anyone. If you do, your family will be killed. Their deaths will not be pretty. Understand?"

"I understand."

"Good." With that, Maksym terminated the call.

Christie sat and stared at his cell phone for a few moments. He tried to imagine a person to match Maksym's disembodied voice. His gruff tone conjured up a large, powerful man. The calm manner in which he promised to kill Christie's family members suggested ruthlessness. Whatever his physical appearance might be, Christie assumed he was a very dangerous man.

He stood up and walked out of his office and down the hall to the stairs where he descended two floors to the communications lab. He was almost surprised that the woman with the tortoise rim glasses wasn't there. Then, he remembered the hour and realized there had been a shift change. There was only one person in the room. He was a thin, smallish young man with short, dark hair that grew forward as if to cover a hairline that was beginning to recede. He wore round, wire rim glasses, a white shirt open at the collar, and khaki pants that looked as if they had been purchased off the rack at The Gap. Typical of his generation, he had what appeared to be a one-day's growth of beard. He also had a mild case of acne.

The young man looked up from a comic book he was reading and said, "Who are you?"

"I'm Special Agent Christie."

"I've been wondering," the young man said, "what's the difference between a special agent and a just plain agent?"

Christie was almost dumbfounded. After a moment, he said, "Look, there's a woman who works in here on an earlier shift. She set up a tracer for me on my cell phone. I just got a call and I want to follow up. Can you do that?"

"I can do just about anything. You got identification or something?"

Now, Christie was dumbfounded. And angry. "Listen you Gen Y twit. How the hell could I be inside this building if I wasn't an authorized Bureau employee? Now, get off your prepubescent ass and check the tracer."

The young man sighed and slowly got up. "Some day I'll be running the whole show and you'll just be another old fart FBI person wasting away in a nursing home."

Christie was tempted to slap the kid hard enough to separate his jaw from his teeth. He held his temper in check. Barely.

The tech walked slowly over to the equipment the woman with the tortoise rim glasses had used and said, "What's your number?"

Christie gave him his cell phone number and watched while the other man manipulated the equipment. After several moments he said, "The call came from a cell phone that was being operated from 7570 River Rill Drive in Potomac, Maryland. Anything else you want?" He sounded bored.

"As a matter of fact, Sherlock, there is. What is 7570 River Rill Drive?"

The man smiled somewhat insolently and said, "It's an address."

With great personal restraint, Christie managed to resist the temptation to strangle the little shit and said through clenched teeth, "That's very observant, kid. What's at that address?"

The man sighed again and turned back to his equipment. After a few more minutes he turned back to Christie and said, "It's a house. A big one apparently. High rent district."

"Who owns it?"

"Look," the young man said in exasperation, "I'm not your personal search engine. You're the hotshot FBI agent. You should be figuring this out."

Christie had had enough. He drew his sidearm, a Glock 23C, snapped the slide back, chambering a round. He stepped forward and placed the weapon's muzzle hard against the young man's forehead and said, "I'm tired of your effete impudence. Get me the information or I'll do the world a service and blow your entitlement delusions clean out the back of your paper thin skull."

All the color drained out of the young man's face and he gasped as his body began to tremble. Christie pressed the muzzle harder into the man's skin and he quickly turned and busied himself with the equipment.

"It's owned by someone named Laski, Chaim Laski."

Christie was stunned. Chaim Laski was a well-known billionaire. He was a personal friend of the rich and powerful, including the president of the United States. "Chaim Laski? Are you sure about that?"

The young man's head bobbed up and down. His prominent Adam's apple reciprocated.

Christie eased the hammer down and holstered his weapon. He spun around and walked back to his office. The young man sagged to the floor in front of his equipment and began quietly sobbing.

When Christie reached his office, he sat at his desk and began thinking about this shocking new element. Chaim Laski was a very powerful man politically. He was wired directly into the Oval Office. Christie couldn't simply order a raid on the man's home in Maryland. He needed to take this up the chain of command. He walked down the hall to a lounge area and stretched out on a sofa. After a long while, he fell into a fitful sleep.

The next morning, looking like a drunk coming off a long bender, he brushed his teeth and went upstairs to the office of the Executive Assistant Director of the Criminal, Cyber, Response, and Services Branch (EAD). This was the same man who, very recently, had dressed Christie down for the manner in which he had reacted to the abduction of his family. Christie didn't particularly want to speak to the EAD, but, given that Laski now was involved, didn't see any viable alternatives.

Red-eyed, wearing badly rumpled clothes, and with two days' growth of beard, Christie waited impatiently in the EAD's outer office until his assistant showed him into the man's private office.

The EAD was standing behind his desk, glancing through what appeared to be routine reports. He was short, thin and balding. He was an accountant by training and looked the part with a large, bony head and small body. His white dress shirt was crisply starched and accessorized by a conservative red and blue rep tie. He seemed to be an unhappy man. Smiles were rare and laughs were nonexistent. He had a reputation for being priggish and difficult to work for. In the chain of command, Christie worked for the person who reported directly to the EAD. But he had had enough experiences over the years to know that the man came by his reputation honestly.

After several moments, he looked up at Christie. "Are you having problems with your dry cleaner or razor, Special Agent Christie?"

"No sir, I haven't been out of the building in over forty-eight hours. Sorry."

"Sorry doesn't cut it, Special Agent. The Bureau has standards. We all are expected to conform to them regardless of our situations or workloads."

"Yes sir."

The EAD stared at him for a few more moments then said waspishly, "Well, get on with it, Christie. I'm a very busy man. I don't have all day to entertain someone parodying the homeless."

"Yes sir." Christie related to the EAD the calls from Maksym and his wife, and the apparent involvement of Chaim Laski in some fashion.

The EAD walked slowly over to a window and stared pensively out for several minutes. Eventually, he half-turned toward Christie with his left hand in a trouser pocket and the thumb and forefinger of his right hand pinching his chin. "You're asking me to authorize a raid on Chaim Laski's home in Maryland?"

Christie nodded. "Yes sir."

"Are you insane? Do you not understand the kind of political power that man wields?"

Christie nodded again. "Yes, I do."

The EAD fixed him with a look of disgust. "Really, Christie, you disappoint me. I am not going to authorize any such thing. We will continue to monitor phone calls made by this Maksym person. But for the time being that is the extent of it." He dismissed Christie with a wave of his hand.

As soon as Christie had left his office, the EAD picked up his phone's receiver and punched five numbers into the keypad. A moment later, the executive assistant for his boss, the Deputy Director, answered his call and patched him through. He nervously explained to the DD what he had just learned from Christie, and what his instructions to him had been.

"That is very interesting, Richard. I think your actions are appropriate for the moment. We'll get back to you later if we want to go in another direction." The Deputy Director hung up.

He got up and walked out of his office. As he passed his EA, he said, "Virginia, I'm going out for a few minutes. I need to pick something up at the pharmacy." He took the elevator to the lobby and exited the building. Two blocks down the street he entered a CVS pharmacy and walked to a pay phone near the rear of the store.

Less than a minute later he was speaking with a Marine major, the personal assistant to General Buster McCoy. He shared with him what he had just learned from the EAD via Mitch Christy. He knew the Team would want to know about Laski's involvement.

60 RICHMOND, VIRGINIA

With assistance from several influential members of the Team, both civilian and military, McCoy had quickly gathered a wealth of information on the warehouse where Levell was being held. Whelan and other members of the Sleeping Dogs unit pored over building plans for the targeted warehouse and surrounding structures, transportation maps, satellite imagery, and ground level photographs of the neighborhood generated by Google Earth. Word appeared to have been sent from a top government law enforcement agency to the Richmond Police Department to the effect that the agency would be conducting a training exercise in the area of the warehouse that was vital to national security. The Chief agreed the Richmond PD would avoid the area until notified that the operation had been terminated.

Approximately twenty-four hours earlier, the Team had placed the warehouse and its neighborhood under round-the-clock surveillance after piecing together evidence that Levell was being held there. Using satellite thermography provided by one of the entities controlled by the Mueller brothers, it was easy to determine how many people were in the building at any time and where they were positioned.

The few small, papered-over windows set high on the walls of the warehouse made it extremely unlikely that those inside could physically survey activities outside the building. The main problem for the unit in its assault on the warehouse would be approaching it without being detected electronically by the guards inside. There were three issues that had to be confronted. The first was the video camera surveillance system set up on the four corners of the building. It was a wireless system, which meant that it probably was being monitored within the warehouse itself.

The second problem was the need to prevent the guards from sending cell phone messages to their colleagues if they became alerted to the assault. The final challenge was determining how to avoid cutting or climbing the sensor-armed, tall barbed wire fence that surrounded the building site.

Whelan solved all problems with assistance from the Mueller brothers. One of their offshore companies, an electronics manufacturer in Bangladesh, produced a device that jammed wireless camera signals. It had a range of one hundred meters and jammed video transmissions in the three standard ranges: 900MHz, 1.2GHz, and 2.4GHz. It also was capable of producing one hundred watts of power for jamming cell phones at a distance exceeding one hundred meters.

The sensors on the fence were hardwired. This called for a nontechnical solution. Again, the Mueller brothers provided the necessary equipment, a mobile crane. It was being used by one of their construction enterprises for the renovation of a commercial property in Reston. One of their most trusted lieutenants, an executive of the construction company, drove it down to the warehouse site. All commercial markings and other potential means of identification had been removed or covered. It had a hydraulic truss or telescopic boom, mounted on a turntable, which could be extended up to fifty meters or one hundred sixty four feet. At Whelan's request, the driver parked the crane on the side of the warehouse opposite its front entrance. Whelan and the other five Sleeping Dogs were crammed into a gray Toyota Tundra Crew Max parked behind the crane. They were watching the front of the building by satellite surveillance on a large MacBook Pro.

Whelan knew from surveillance when the guards changed shifts. He and the other members of the unit waited until the morning shift had occurred before beginning their assault on the warehouse. He knew Levell was still alive because the ongoing thermographic surveillance indicated three heat producing entities inside. The guards appeared to work in pairs. The third person had to be Levell.

Following the latest change of shift, Whelan and the others watched the thermographic display as one of the guards appeared to rough up the third person inside the building for a few moments. Both guards then appeared to settle in at the small card table near the office section. Whelan was about to give the signal to commence the assault stage of the operation, when the MacBook showed a black Mercedes GL pulling up to the gate in front of the warehouse. The driver, a bulky man in an ill-fitting suit got out and opened the gate. He got back in, drove up to the front of the building and used a remote to activate the motor that began raising the large metal door. In a few minutes, the SUV pulled inside and the door was lowered back in place. Kirkland, sitting in the middle in the backseat, was operating the jamming device and monitoring the thermography imagery on another laptop. "Looks like two more unfriendlies just arrived," he said to Whelan who was riding shotgun in the front seat.

"Good," Whelan said. "There's no bag limit on these guys."

The man sitting on the passenger side of the SUV got out and walked over to Levell. He appeared to speak to him for a moment and made a gesture with his hand like a pistol, aiming it at Levell's head. After a moment, he turned and walked over to the table where the guards were seated. They immediately stood up, as if in the presence of a superior. The driver of the Mercedes slouched against the vehicle.

Whelan turned to face the others - Larsen seated next to him, Stensen in the driver's seat, Thomas and Almeida flanking Kirkland in the back. "Party time," he said and opened the right front door.

Kirkland used his cell phone to speed dial the man who had driven the mobile crane. He had moved from the truck cab to the crane cab. The outriggers previously had been extended from the chassis to level and stabilize the crane while stationary and hoisting. Almost immediately the hydraulics began extending the boom. Next, Kirkland activated the signal on the jammer. From this point, there would be no communication among any of them or with the world beyond the warehouse.

It was several minutes before one of the men inside the warehouse noticed that the video image from the surveillance cameras had failed. He walked over and began examining the monitor. He twisted some knobs, slapped it a few times then shrugged, signaling to the others that he didn't know what was causing the problem. They walked over to him and began adjusting and shaking the monitor.

Whelan led the others, except Kirkland who stayed with the monitoring and jamming equipment in the truck. The crane operator lowered a cable from the drum. It had a weighted ball on the end and came to rest on the ground near the Tundra. One by one the men scaled the cable, Larsen first, followed by Almeida. Thomas and Stensen were next. Whelan was the last one. When all men were on, the operator gently raised the boom and swung it over the high fence with enough height for the ball to clear it.

On the other side, the men, led by Whelan, descended the cable and dropped quietly to the ground. The operator rewound the cable, swung the boom back into position on the truck and retracted it. In moments he had scrambled back into the cab of the truck and driven away. He would take the mobile crane into a large warehouse a few blocks away where three other identical mobile cranes were waiting. Another driver would take over for him and all four cranes would depart simultaneously in separate directions. The original driver would drive a Jeep Wrangler into a parking garage in nearby mall and abandon it.

At the warehouse where Levell was being held, Stensen strategically placed C-4 explosive compound in gaps between the heavy entrance door and its frame. It had been specially made without the usually marker or odorizing taggant chemicals such as 2,3-dimethyl-2,3-dinitrobutane (DMDNB) that are used to help detect the explosive and identify its source. When he was finished, Stensen placed a detonator in it. He looked at Whelan and nodded. All of the men moved swiftly along the wall and away from the door. At Whelan's signal, Stensen detonated the charge with a remote signal. It blew the door completely off its hinges. The force of the blast sent chunks of bricks and metal shrapnel flying backwards into the warehouse. The man who had been driving the Mercedes was standing just inside the door. He was killed instantly.

Whelan and three of the others raced inside. Thomas remained on the outside in the event any of the unfriendlies managed to escape from the warehouse. The men who had been inside the warehouse were momentarily stunned by the noise and shockwave generated by the explosion. Even so, Levell was experienced enough to react on instinct. He threw himself sideways, tipping the wheelchair and sprawling on the hard, filthy concrete floor.

Whelan, the first man through the gaping hole where the door had been, saw the two guards reaching for their weapons. He shot one, the forty-caliber slug tearing through the man's left shoulder and spinning him to the floor. The other guard quickly raised his hands in surrender.

The third man, who had been the passenger in the Mercedes moved with incredible speed. He sprinted up a pile of crates and barrels stacked against the front wall of the warehouse and burst through a papered-over window at the top. On the other side, it was ten feet to the ground. The man spun gracefully in mid-air, feline-like, and landed on his feet almost on top of Thomas.

Caught by surprise, Thomas reached quickly out to grab the man. The man swatted Thomas' arm away with his left hand. In the same motion, and with shocking speed, he brought his right fist into the side of Thomas' head. Thomas was barely able to tuck his chin toward his shoulder or he would have caught the blow flush on his jaw, shattering it. As it was, he blacked out momentarily and fell to the ground.

The other man whipped a SIG SAUER P229 Enhanced Elite forty-caliber pistol from the waistband of his trousers and aimed it at the helpless Thomas. Simultaneously, Almeida burst through the opening where the door had been and squeezed off several shots with his weapon. One of them grazed the man's right arm, tearing out a chunk of flesh and causing him reflexively to drop the SIG. The man spun around and raced toward the fence behind him. Just before he reached it, Whelan and Larsen ran from the warehouse, having left Stensen to guard the prisoners.

They each fired at the man as he raced for the fence. One of the rounds tore through his shirt narrowly missing his flesh. He realized he would not make it to safety and froze, slowly raising his arms to the side.

"You all right?" Whelan said to Almeida.

"Yeah."

Whelan and Larsen sprinted toward Thomas, who was struggling to get to his feet, holding onto the side of his head where he'd been slugged.

"Cuff that sonofabitch and drag him back inside," he yelled to Larsen and Almeida. "And be very careful. He's a hellova lot quicker than he looks."

"The way he came out of that window and then slugged Quentin, he sure ain't your average bear," Almeida said, as he and Larsen bound the man's wrists behind him with double loop EZ Cuff nylon restraints. They spun him around and shoved him toward the blown out entrance to the warehouse. Each stayed just out of kicking range slightly to the side and behind him. The muzzles of their weapons never strayed from a direct line to the middle of the man's muscular back.

Larsen and Almeida had shackled the man's ankles together then bound the ankle cuffs to the ones binding his wrists. They shoved him into one of the folding chairs at the rickety card table. The cuffs made his position awkward and uncomfortable.

"That motherfucker hits about as quick and hard as you do," Thomas said to Larsen.

Whelan steadied Thomas and helped him walk slowly back inside the warehouse.

"Man," Thomas said through teeth clinched in pain. "I've never been hit that hard except when I've spared with you or Larsen in training."

Whelan eased Thomas down onto a crate and then went to assist Levell who was struggling to get back into his wheelchair.

"You sure took your sweet-assed time getting here," Levell said.

"We knew you had it under control," Whelan said.

"Nobody likes a smartass."

"All small talk aside, do you know who these guys are?"

"Yeah," Levell said. His eyes had narrowed and his upper lip was curled back in a snarl. "I know exactly who these bastards are."

"Who's the guy who performed the self-defenestration?"

"He's the guy who was sent to kill me. Says his name's Maksym."

"Guess our timing was pretty good after all."

Levell glared at him. "You know, you *really* are a fucking smartass." He continued to glare at Whelan for a few moments then said, "And where the hell is McCoy in all of this?"

"Don't be too hard on the General. He's the one who orchestrated the efforts that figured out where you were being held."

"Great. I'll buy him a beer," Levell said dryly. "Where is he now?"

"Negotiating for your release."

"Yeah? What's the tradeoff?"

"We are," Whelan said and looked around at Larsen and the others.

Levell gazed intently at him for a few moments. "It's beginning to make sense."

"Care to share that with us?" Whelan said.

"A Russian, guy named Federov, was here earlier and shared some information with me." Using an acronym common in government circles for president of the United States, Levell said "POTUS has become a pain in the Left's collective ass. They want him removed."

"I thought he was an odds on favorite to lose his bid for reelection," Kirkland said.

"Apparently they aren't willing to wait until next year. They want him removed now. And permanently."

Whelan said, "I think I'm beginning to get the picture. The puppet masters of the Far Left want POTUS assassinated. But they want it to appear as if it was done by right wing zealots."

Levell smiled and nodded.

"And," Whelan continued, "we would be those zealots."

"Yes," Levell said. "And, by logical extension based on what Harold Case uncovered, so would the rest of us. It would set the Team's efforts to restore this country's individual freedoms back a full generation. By then, it will be far too late."

"Where is this Russian, Federov, now?" Kirkland said.

"I suspect he's the one who's negotiating with McCoy," Whelan said.

Larsen looked at Whelan and motioned with his head toward their three captives. "What do you want to do with these guys?"

"First, let's see whether they have anything of value to tell us."

He looked at the two guards, both large, burley men, and said, "We're short on time. You're gonna tell us who's behind all this," he waved his hand that was holding the HK P30L pistol at them. "And you're gonna do it quickly. Otherwise, I'll shoot all of you on the spot and let the police clean it up."

Maksym sat calmly, although clearly uncomfortably, and looked at the two guards. They, on the other hand, tried to avoid eye contact with him.

After a few moments of silence, Whelan brought the muzzle of the HK around and shot the wounded guard between the eyes. His lifeless corpse hit the floor with a dull thud. The other guard's eyes opened very wide in fear. As Whelan brought the weapon slowly around and aimed it at the man's forehead, his eyes opened even wider.

With a thick Eastern European accent that Whelan suspected was Ukrainian, the frightened guard said, "Please, if I am speaking to you, he is killing me." He nodded toward Maksym, who was staring impassively at the man.

"You're afraid of this guy?" Thomas said and slammed the barrel of his weapon into the left side of Maksym's face. The blow split open the skin over his eyebrow and cheekbone. Maksym turned his head slowly, as blood began to flow down his face. He smiled at Thomas, but the look in his eyes was chilling.

"Drag that sonofabitch to the far side of the building and stuff a rag in his mouth. If he blinks, kill him," Whelan said to Larsen and Stensen. He turned back to the surviving guard and said "Maksym's not going to live long enough to be a threat to you." He paused for effect and said, slowly and emphasizing each word, "I'm the one you need to fear."

With Maksym no longer in his immediate presence, the guard loosened up and told Whelan and Levell as much as he knew. It wasn't much, but combined with what Whelan already knew and what Levell had learned from Federov and by observing the activities at the warehouse, a picture began to emerge.

A Russian agent, Federov, was orchestrating a plan to assassinate the president of the United States, and probably others as well. It was designed to create the impression that a right wing cabal was responsible. The guards at the warehouse were part of the large security detail that worked for Chaim Laski. All were Ukrainians. Maksym was their leader. All of the guards were tough and ruthless men whose backgrounds were more than unsavory. Still, they all feared Maksym, who was present at the warehouse for the purpose of killing Levell once he received the signal from someone else, presumably Federov.

When the guard had finished, Whelan turned to Levell. "What do you want to do about this situation?"

"Right now, we need to get out of this fucking warehouse. I have to talk with McCoy and some of the other leaders of the Team. We have work to do and time is short," Levell said. He looked at the remaining guard. "Kill him," he said.

61 WASHINGTON, D.C.

Major General Buster McCoy, the current commander of the United States Marine Corps Special Operations Command, or MARSOC, exited from the front passenger seat of a nondescript tan colored sedan. As he stepped up to the curb, the driver pulled back into traffic and drove away.

McCoy, wearing civilian clothes, but exhibiting the ramrod bearing of the lifelong Marine, turned and looked across Constitution Avenue at the Federal Reserve Building. He stared for a while at the Paul Philippe Cret designed structure. Its stark white marble exterior seemed cold and austere, even in the broiling late August sun of Foggy Bottom.

After a moment, he turned back, crossed the sidewalk and began walking into the National Mall. In a few minutes he found what he was seeking, a bench at just about the midpoint of the Reflecting Pond. A well-built man with the appearance of an athlete was sitting on the bench. He wore tan slacks with a Kelly green and navy blue horizontally stripped polo shirt, brown tassel loafers, sunglasses and a Washington Nationals baseball cap. There was a guidebook in his lap. To anyone who might notice him, the man seemed to be the quintessential tourist.

As McCoy paused in front of him, the man slid his sunglasses partway down his nose and peered out from under the bill of his cap. His eyes were very blue and cold. "General McCoy," he said. "Please sit down."

McCoy settled onto the bench and continued to look at the man. "So," he said, "you're Federov."

The man nodded.

On his way to this meeting, McCoy had received Whelan's coded message that Levell had been rescued. He was certain that Federov was not yet aware of that fact, or that the man assigned to kill Levell, Maksym, had

305

been captured. McCoy intended to play along with Federov's demands in order to learn what his end game was.

"What's Levell's status," he said.

"He's fine."

"I have no way of knowing that."

"Trust, General. It is a matter of trust." Federov smiled pleasantly as he said it.

McCoy cocked his head to one side as he regarded the Russian. In his gruff, raspy voice he said, "You expect me to deal on that basis?"

"Certainly. You have no other basis on which to negotiate."

Unctuous Russian prick, McCoy thought. If the Team and I didn't need to know what your endgame is, I'd knock that smile off your commie face and take my chances that you might have a sharpshooter or two somewhere nearby watching us. "Alright, then," he said. "What is it that you want in exchange for Levell?"

Federov's smile broadened. "I knew you would be a reasonable man, General."

"We'll see."

"Do you know the Hotel L'Orange?"

"On East Capitol Street? Used to be a group of old brownstones that had seen better days. What of it?"

"Room three thirty three is on the top floor, southwest corner. You will have these Sleeping Dogs of yours – all of them – there tomorrow morning at nine o'clock. They will be unarmed and will not be accompanied or supervised by anyone. Otherwise, your friend Mr. Levell will pay dearly for it. Do we understand each other?"

McCoy was pensive for a few moments. "If I'm right, there should be a good view down East Capitol Street to the steps of the Capital Building."

"Indeed."

"Tomorrow is Labor Day and the president and other dignitaries are scheduled to speak at that location around ten in the morning."

"You are very perceptive, General McCoy. No wonder you and your colleagues have been such a pain in the ass for us over the years."

"You'd do well to remember that it ain't over 'til it's over, you Marxist bastard."

Federov rose from the bench and gave McCoy a puzzled look. "I do not understand you Americans. That is the same expression your friend Levell used recently. I do not grasp the meaning of such foolishness...it is not over until it is over. That does not make sense."

"With any luck at all, you'll understand exactly what it means just as you are dying."

Clearly angry, Federov eyed the general balefully for a few moments. He spat on the ground in front of McCoy and said, "You Americans are naïve and too full of yourselves. You are finished as a superpower. Your people have lost the will to fight, to struggle. Just as we have trained them to do for all these years, they expect everything to be given to them, to be easy. Like the Western Europeans, you want your mommy, the state, to take care of every problem in your worthless, pathetic little lives. You are cowards, scarcely more than sniveling idiots. Your end is at hand. We have conquered the mighty United States of America!" He spit the final sentence out in undisguised contempt.

The general rose slowly from the bench. Although Federov was much younger and appeared to be in superb physical condition, McCoy stepped toward him until his face was six inches from the Russian's.

"The stupidity is all on your part," he said softly, but firmly. "You have done that which the great English poet Chaucer warned against. You have awakened sleeping dogs," McCoy paused momentarily for effect. "Or, more properly in this case, sleeping wolves. Killer wolves. Wolves from Hell, the likes of which you cannot imagine."

Federov stared at the general for a moment, shaking his head. "You are a fool. Americans are fools. They believe in fairy tales. No gods or demons can save you now." He turned and began to walk away. After a few steps, he stopped and turned around. "Tomorrow, nine in the morning, the Hotel L'Orange, room three thirty-three. If your men are not there, or if there is any trickery, I shall personally and with great pleasure kill Mr. Levell. It will be a hideously painful death." He spun on his heel and began rapidly striding toward Constitution Avenue and the car that was waiting to pick him up.

Once he was in the car, Federov pulled his cell phone from a trouser pocket and called Chaim Laski's personal number. When the other man was on the line, he said in Russian, "The transaction has been settled."

"Can the other side be trusted to fulfill their end of the bargain?"

"We have the resource they seek. They will not be so foolish as to jeopardize its safe delivery."

"And you are certain you can handle the resources to be delivered in exchange as well as that other matter that is to follow immediately?"

"Yes. With the assistance of your two employees who have been on site for sometime, this will be no problem. The resources to be received in the exchange will be destroyed as planned. The matter that follows will be made to appear as if it was occasioned by those resources."

"Very good. Call me when the transaction has been completed. At that time, I will advise Maksym to terminate that annoying resource being held in the warehouse."

"You will hear from me," Federov said, and disconnected the call at his end.

Laski, enjoying the warmth of the late summer weather from the pool deck of his home in Potomac, Maryland, smiled. Life was good. The plan was coming together beautifully. The surprisingly incompetent fool of a president that he, Federov and so many others had worked diligently and spent lavishly to get elected would soon be dead. The vice president was a team player. He would be easy to manipulate. He would finish out the term, then step aside so that Howard Morris could become the party's nominee. The sympathy vote for the slain president together with the widespread support the party had worked for decades to generate would propel Morris into the White House.

What was that expression from the old *A Team* series on television, he thought. 'I love it when a plan comes together'? Yes, that was it. Laski smiled again and repeated it to himself, 'I love when a plan comes together'. He reached for his phone again. It was time to call Maksym for a status report on Levell.

62 FREDERICKSBURG, VIRGINIA

Scarcely seventy miles from Laski's estate in Potomac, Maryland, in a large, stately manor home outside Fredericksburg, Virginia eight men were gathered around a huge table. Two centuries earlier a craftsman had patiently and skillfully made it from pieces of solid oak. Even so, it looked as if it had been crafted for this particular room, which resembled a refectory with its high vaulted ceiling and exterior wall of large stone blocks that had been perfectly fitted by highly skilled masons. The room was well lit by sunlight flooding through the tall, narrow casement windows.

Three open laptops sat on the table atop a myriad of aerial photographs, building plans, sketchpads and miscellaneous descriptive materials. Almost all of them had been gathered over the past few hours in anticipation of the operation planned for the Hotel L'Orange.

Levell was one of the men present. Whelan and his colleagues made up another six. The remaining man, short and rotund with curly red hair and a full beard that matched, was a professor of Slavic languages and literatures from the University of Virginia in Charlottesville. He had been flown the sixty-five miles to this meeting by private helicopter at the request of his old friend, Clifford Levell. Professor Nowicki was part of a plan Whelan and Levell had devised. They were concerned that if Maksym was expected to report in, and didn't, his handlers would try to find him. They likely would start with a call to his cell phone. If they couldn't raise him, they would suspect he had been compromised, abort their plans, and cover their tracks. This would be a substantial setback to the Team's long and diligent efforts to identify and neutralize their country's enemies.

To avoid this problem, Levell and Whelan planned to have Professor Nowicki, who was fluent in Polish, Russian, and Ukrainian, among other eastern European languages, answer Maksym's phone and pretend to be him.

It was something of a long shot, but Levell and Whelan had a few tricks designed to deflect suspicion.

Maksym's phone lay nearby on a corner of the table. Maksym and the other guard from the warehouse were still shackled and being confined in the rock chamber beneath the manor home. It was the same room in which Whelan had fought and killed the big Ukrainian who had tried to abduct Mitch Christie's family. Whelan and the others, especially Stensen, had favored killing Maksym and the guard at the warehouse. Levell, however, seemed intrigued by something about Maksym and wanted to learn more about him. He even had blood and DNA samples gathered from the man and sent for analysis at a lab in Alexandria that frequently did contract work for government agencies.

Whelan was running ideas by Larsen and Stensen for the following day's encounter with Federov and the planned assault on Laski's lavish and heavily guarded compound in Potomac, Maryland that would follow. Thomas sat at the far end of the table applying ice to his swollen jaw. Sitting in lotus position on the hard stone floor in one corner of the room, Kirkland meditated and practiced breathing exercises. Almeida was trying unsuccessfully to convince Levell that he worked harder than the others, and thus deserved more compensation when the mission was complete. Professor Nowicki was eating a very large sandwich. Much of it was clinging to the front of his shirt.

When Maksym's cell phone rang, it immediately refocused everyone's attention, including Kirkland's. He sprang effortlessly to his feet and switched on two devices on the table next to the phone. One was designed to produce an electromagnetic interference that would create static in the phone call, helping to disguise differences in Maksym's and Nowicki's voices. The other device was a beta version of the latest military and intelligence equipment for intercepting cell phone calls. In this case, the cell phone was Maksym's, which operated on the GSM standard serving about eighty percent of the world's population. Known as an International Mobile Subscriber Identity or IMSI catcher, the purpose of the device is to capture phone ID data and content.

The device masquerades as a base station and chooses the encryption mode, which can induce the mobile station to use no encryption at all without sending a warning message. The device essentially imitates a GSM tower and entices cell phones to send it data by emitting a signal that's stronger than legitimate towers in the area. With the help of a subscriber identification module, or SIM, it simultaneously logs into the GSM network as a mobile station. Hence, it can encrypt the plain text traffic from the mobile station and pass it to the base station.

In the earlier versions of IMSI-catchers, there was only an indirect connection from mobile station to the GSM network, essentially preventing incoming phone calls from being patched through to the mobile station. This current version, however, solved that issue and conversations between two cell phones could be intercepted and monitored by the IMSI-catcher. It simultaneously would transmit the intercepted calls to third parties using a complementary listen device.

The number of the phone from which the incoming call originated was not one that Levell or the others recognized. Levell shortly would send it to a Team member at the Bureau for identification.

Nowicki had put down his sandwich and waddled along the table to the spot where Maksym's phone was. Levell nodded at him and he picked it up and pressed the answer icon. "Yes?"

There was a momentary pause then Laski said in Russian, "Why is there so much static on the line?"

Nowicki glanced at Levell, then said, also in Russian, "It's this damn warehouse."

"You sound a little strange. Are you all right?"

Nowicki was beginning to sweat and his hand shook a bit. "Yes, I am having an allergic reaction to the dust and the chemicals that were stored here over the years." He coughed for effect.

"Really? I'm sorry to hear that, but I thought you were supposed to be all but invincible. Unfortunately, I need you to remain there until you receive Federov's call that the operation has been successful. Can you do that?"

"Yes."

Laski shifted the subject. "How is our guest doing?" He was referring to Levell, whom he supposed was still a captive.

"Fine."

"Excellent, but I trust you will not let him be too comfortable." Laski laughed at his own attempt at humor.

There was no response from the other end. "Well, Maksym, I have come to accept that it is not your nature to be much of a conversationalist. When you receive Federov's call, see that our guest departs." He paused. "And to be on the safe side, see that your two associates depart with him as well. I will see you back here tomorrow afternoon." Laski disconnected the call.

Professor Nowicki pressed the End button on Maksym's cell phone and placed it back on the table. All eyes turned toward Levell. He looked at Kirkland and said, "What was the calling number?"

Kirkland read it off the IMSI catcher.

Levell pulled his own cell phone from its holster clipped to his belt and dialed a number from memory. When the call was answered at the other end, he repeated the number and added, "I need that number immediately. And don't share this with anyone else just yet."

Moments later his phone rang. Levell listened for a few moments and hung up. Turning toward Nowicki, he said, "Thanks for your help, Doctor Nowicki. The chopper's standing by to return you to Charlottesville." The way it was said left no doubt in anyone's mind that the academic's services were finished and it was time for him to depart.

Nowicki said, "It was nice to see you again Cliff, and to be able to be of service." He took a step toward the door, where the chopper pilot awaited him, then turned and walked back to the end of the huge table. He picked up what was left of his sandwich with a fat, florid hand and waddled out of the room.

Larsen closed the heavy, ornate oak door behind him and all eyes swung once again to Levell.

He shook his cell phone a couple of times for emphasis and said, "That last call was from a colleague at the Bureau. He said the call to Maksym was made from a phone registered to someone employed and in residence at Chaim Laski's estate in Potomac, Maryland."

63 WASHINGTON, D.C.

Federov luxuriated in the soft, slate gray leather of the Lincoln's rear seat. The color was a pleasant monochromatic match for the well-tailored charcoal gray summer-weight suit he was wearing. The limousine was one of the Russian Federation Embassy's newest. It smelled new. He drew in a deep breath savoring the scent of the leather and exhaled slowly. The quality wasn't on a par with Chaim Laski's Bentley, which he had ridden in once or twice. Still, in his mind it was much more comfortable than the overpriced Russian Zil, even though that car was hand-built in limited production. He smiled to himself and thought, there is nothing wrong or criminal in luxury. It is only when fools like the nations of the West value luxury over power and control that the line is crossed. Encouraging the masses to seek careers in order to pursue luxuries like the Lincoln, that was the weakness that was destroying the West. Europe was lost and America was not far behind. Citizens should be forcefully guided by the State to engage in labor that was most beneficial and productive as determined by the State.

As he relaxed in the back of the chauffeur-driven limo, Federov felt confident, perhaps to the point of arrogance. He had Levell. Those weak fools known as the Team were desperate to get him back. They were nothing without him. Levell and McCoy were the ones who had formed the organization and made it effective, such as it was. Others, such as those ancient, but wealthy, Mueller brothers, merely provided resources. Even so, McCoy was not the real intellect behind the operation. Levell was. McCoy and the other members of the Team knew that and would do whatever was necessary to gain his return. They would even sacrifice their precious and recently resurrected special ops unit, the so-called Sleeping Dogs.

The Russian's near-reverie was interrupted as the limo driver pulled to the curb southbound on 4th Street NE about a half block north of its intersection with East Capitol Street. He exited the vehicle in a smooth, fluid motion and stepped back as the limo pulled away. Federov watched as the car paused briefly at the traffic light at East Capitol Street. When the signal changed, it moved on across the intersection and down 4th Street SE. As instructed, the driver would turn around and park at the curb on the one-way, northbound Third Street Northeast very near the Hotel L'Orange.

Federov walked the half block to the intersection and paused on the northwest corner. He looked around casually, as a tourist might do in order to get his bearings. In reality, he was looking for anything that didn't fit; anything that might alert him to danger. The gray painted Corner Market was to the east, across 4th Street from him. A sign in the window announced Cold Beer. He turned and looked across East Capitol Street. Traffic was thin on it and 4th Street. The Russian was surprised. He knew that the Capitol Hill district of Washington was the largest historic residential neighborhood in Washington D.C., and one of the oldest and most densely populated.

A fortyish man on a road bike passed through the intersection. He was wearing a neon green jersey covered with names and logos of bike equipment manufacturers, black cycling shorts, and shoes that clipped into his pedals. Across the street a young woman was walking west toward Capitol Hill. She was wearing a short black skirt that emphasized her long, shapely legs and slim hips. Her sleeveless dark red blouse was tight against her full breasts, and the low cut neckline displayed considerable cleavage. Federov admired her for a few moments, although he disapproved of her bare legs and low, black sandals. In Russia, no woman would go to her workplace without wearing pumps and pantyhose. He assumed she was a staffer for a member of the House or Senate. No wonder, he mused, that with such blatant sexuality and lack of modesty congressmen often seemed to become romantically involved with staffers.

He turned further to his right and looked back toward the north past Grubb's Pharmacy and up 4th Street NE. Satisfied that nothing seemed amiss, he began walking west along the tree-lined East Capitol Street. Little more than halfway down the block he turned to his right, and passed through an opening in a black wrought iron fence that was backed by a short, well-trimmed green hedge. He found himself on a short walkway lined with red brick pavers that led to a dark-stained oak door. A brass plate on the door said Hotel L'Orange. Federov climbed two short steps, opened the door and entered the building.

The Hotel L'Orange was located in the Capitol Hill district, which straddles both the Northeast and Southeast quadrants of the city. Development of the area began in the late 1700's when the fledgling government commenced work on two nearby locations, the Capitol Building and the Washington Navy Yard. It gained distinction as a community in the very early 1800's as the federal government became a major employer. Predominantly, its surviving buildings are row houses in a mix of Federal and Victorian architecture.

The hotel itself began life in the late 19th century as a series of individually owned common-wall row houses. Fire regulations in effect at the time required them to be constructed of pressed brick. Many of the grander homes were built with fine-textured, smooth-surfaced red, buff, or tan pressed brick with butter joints. They often were articulated with intricate and elaborate terra cotta panels. In 2005, a hotel company specializing in small boutique establishments acquired the titles to five of these classic row houses, converted them into a small hotel, and restored them to the glory they enjoyed in the Gilded Age.

Two of Federov's operatives, Ukrainians who spoke passable English, had been in residence in Room 333 for the past few weeks. What made that particular room special was its location on the top floor of what had been the westernmost row house. That particular section of the building jutted streetward from the rest of the hotel. It enjoyed an unobstructed, above-treetop view down East Capitol Street to the East Front of the Capitol Building.

Federov moved through the small lobby area of the hotel. His pace was not too fast, not too slow. He didn't want to draw attention to himself. The carpet was pale green and thick. The walls were painted in a matching shade above the chair rail. The lower part was papered with gold and brown vertical stripes. Portraits of long-dead Washingtonians in dark frames were spaced evenly about the room. There were two groups of three overstuffed chairs clustered around small coffee tables that held copies of avant-garde magazines focused on the cultural attractions of Washington. The chairs were upholstered in a plush, deep pile fabric. The western wall of the lobby featured a large Victorian landscape overmantle mirror with ornate crossed ribbon moulding and decorative corners. It was centered above a love seat covered in the same fabric as the chairs. Matching end tables paired with identical Tiffany lamps flanked the love seat.

Opposite the entrance from the street were an elevator door and a small registration area. The lobby area was empty except for the desk clerk and a man wearing cargo shorts, sandals, a sleeveless tee shirt and a white bucket hat. The man was seeking the clerk's advice regarding sightseeing tours. Hallways led away from the lobby to the west and east. Federov chose the hallway to his left that led toward the west. Partway down there was a narrow staircase. He climbed it to the top floor. Room 333 was at the very end of the hallway. On all floors, these end rooms actually were large suites. He paused in front of the door and knocked.

There were a few moments of near silence. The only sound was the soft hiss of air being forced through conduits by the HVAC equipment on the roof of the building. Federov imagined that the two Ukrainians were getting edgy and nervous at this late point in the operation. He sensed the presence of one of them on the other side of the door, peering at him through the fisheye lens of the glass peephole. A moment later a heavily accented, deep voice said, "Who is it?" It was the first test of a two-part pass code arrangement.

"Jefferson Smith," Federov said. A faint smile played swiftly across his lips. It was a play on a character portrayed by actor James Stewart in a 1939 film. Jefferson Smith was a naïve citizen appointed to fill a vacancy in the United States Senate. Being Russian, Federov was delighted by irony.

"Who sent you, Mr. Smith?" the voice said.

"The travel agency." This was the second part of the pass code.

A moment later Federov heard the security door chain being released from the track, and the door swung slowly open. He stepped inside into a small antechamber that separated the two major rooms of the suite. The suite's bathroom was straight ahead behind the antechamber. Without glancing at him, he brushed past the hulking man who had opened the door and entered the room to his left, the bedroom. It also was carpeted in a plush pile, but this time it was an eggshell color. A queen-size bed was on his right and beyond it an ornately carved armoire. The walls were paneled below the chair rail, and covered above it in wallpaper rife with pastoral scenes. A small, cut glass chandelier hung from the center of the room.

The far side of the room was in the part of the building that jutted out almost to the sidewalk, similar to a large oriel window. It had a large window facing East Capitol Street and two side windows. The curtains were drawn on each of the windows. Two side tables, borrowed from the sitting room of the suite, had been pushed together in the center of this space. Positioned on the tables and facing the western window was a Remington Model M24E1, the weapon of choice for the world's best snipers.

The other Ukrainian was hovering over the weapon making some minor adjustments. Federov shoved him out of the way and sat down in a chair facing the butt of the weapon at the end of the tables. He pulled a pair of thin gloves made of a synthetic material from his pants pocket, tugged them on and began examining the rifle. It had a ten-inch, titanium Titan-QD Fast Attach suppressor attached to the hammer-forged, stainless steel, Rem-Tough powder-coated barrel. The suppressor was designed to eliminate ninety-eight percent of muzzle flash and sixty percent of recoil, and reduce sound by thirty-two decibels. Federov knew that the barrel's unique 5-R rifling offered reduced bullet deformation, metallic fouling, and pressure curves, while providing higher bullet velocities.

A Leupold Mark 4 6.5–20×50-millimeter ER/T M5 Front Focal variable power telescopic sight was mounted on the barrel's Pitcatinny rail and secured with 30-millimeter mounting rings. It featured a 34-millimeter tube diameter, first focal plane Horus Vision grid system range estimation reticle and a .300 Winchester Magnum bullet-drop compensator. In daylight, in the hands of an expert marksman, it provided an effective range to twelve hundred meters, or almost four thousand feet. The distance from the room to the steps of the Capitol Building was six hundred and twenty meters, or just over two thousand feet.

The Remington was bolt-action operated and promoted a twenty-eight hundred feet-per-second muzzle velocity. It was chambered to fire .300 Winchester Magnum 190 grain hollow-point boat tail rounds from a five-round internal magazine.

The stock was made of a composite of Kevlar, graphite and fiberglass bound together with epoxy resins, featuring an aluminum bedding block and adjustable butt plate. A detachable bipod was mounted to the stock's fore-end for stability. All-in-all, Federov approved of the weapon and the job the Ukrainians had done in setting it up. For a lesser distance, he would have preferred to use a Barrett M107 that was chambered for a more destructive .50 caliber round. However, without an expert and strategically placed spotter following the target through his own scope and calling out adjustments in trajectory and windage as needed, the Remington was the better weapon for today's job.

When he was satisfied with the results of his close inspection of the M24E1, he glanced at his watch. It was fifteen minutes to nine. He turned and looked at the two Ukrainians. One was sitting on the bed and the other was standing by the door that he had locked and chained after Federov entered. Both men were large and unkempt looking with uncombed hair and day-old beards. The one by the door was wearing cowboy boots, faded jeans, a belt with a large western buckle and a short-sleeved, dull gray crew neck shirt. The one on the bed also wore jeans, well-used running shoes and a button-up shirt in a small green check pattern. Both of the men were staring at Federov.

Federov continued to sit in the chair by the rifle, occasionally glancing at his watch. Nine o'clock passed. He stared at the Ukrainians. The one on the bed quickly broke eye contact and stared at the floor, never raising his gaze beyond Federov's shiny black wingtips. The one by the door was another story. His face devoid of emotion, he returned the Russian's stare. This angered Federov. He always had considered Ukrainian's to be a lesser race. It was disrespectful for them to lock eyes with a superior Russian.

"Listen," he said, "the Americans will arrive very soon. You know what to do?"

Both men nodded.

"Where are your weapons?" he said.

Each man reached into the rear waistband of their jeans and retrieved a Sig Sauer P226 Tactical semi automatic pistol. Each had a SWR Trident L.C.D. suppressor attached. Federov carefully inspected each weapon to make certain the factory recoil spring had been replaced with a Nielsen device. In this case, it was a Wolff fourteen-pound spring designed to temporarily relieve the weight of the suppressor from the barrel, thus avoiding interference with its recoil action. He removed a fifteen round magazine from the butt of each pistol and determined that each was fully loaded with Alabama Ammo 147 grain "Special K" 9mm ammunition.

"Good," he said as he handed the weapons back. "When they are in the room, we will identify the one called Stensen, then shoot the other five at close range so as not to create a crossfire situation or send any errant shots through the walls. Stensen is to be spared. He will be our shooter. Once he has completed the task, shoot him too. His fingerprints will be on the rifle. Wipe your pistols down and place them in the hands of two of the others so it will appear that there was a falling out among them and they turned on each other. Understood?"

Again the two men nodded.

Time continued to pass without sign of Whelan and his colleagues. Federov felt his anger rising ever higher and looked at his watch several times. When the minute hand ticked around to nine-thirty, he pulled his cell phone from a trouser pocket and pressed the speed dial number for Maksym's phone. Voicemail was activated after several rings. This further angered the Russian. Where the hell was Maksym? The operation was at hand. He should be standing by for this call. It was just one more example of the worthlessness of Ukrainians.

Federov took a deep breath and released it slowly. "Maksym," he said into the recorder, "I trust you are still on the job." There was a mix of anger and sarcasm in his voice. "We have been deceived. It appears our expected guests are not coming." He paused then said through clenched teeth, "I will take care of things here myself. Complete the job at your end, and make sure it sends the proper message to his colleagues who have deceived us." He disconnected the call.

"What will we do now?" said the man sitting on the bed. He did not make eye contact with Federov when he said it.

"It is not your concern," Federov said. "I will take care of it myself."

The man standing by the door spoke. "But this is a very difficult shot and requires the skills on an expert marksman to be successful."

"Listen, you idiot," Federov said, "I competed for Russia in the 1996 Summer Olympics in Atlanta. As a shooter. I am one of the best marksmen in the entire Russian military. I will make this shot!"

The man on the bed nodded his head vigorously. The other man continued to stare impassively at the Russian.

"Come with me," Federov said. "I need you to wait in the other room so that you do not distract me."

He led them across the antechamber and into the sitting room. He turned to the man who had been sitting on the bed and said, "Let me see your weapon."

The man looked puzzled and shot a glance at his colleague who merely shrugged. After a moment's hesitation, he pulled his suppressed Sig from the waistband of his jeans and handed it to Federov. The Russian chambered a round, spun and shot the other Ukrainian in the middle of the forehead.

"What are you doing?" the remaining Ukrainian said and took a step backward. Federov closed the gap immediately and shoved the suppressor of the man's own gun under his chin. The man's eyes opened wide in terror. A nanosecond later he was dead, as a bullet tore upward through his tongue, the roof of his mouth and into his brain.

Federov bent down and removed the pistol from the waistband of his first victim's jeans. The large western belt buckle caught his eye. Fucking cowboy, he thought.

He stepped quickly over to the corpse of the second victim and went into the bathroom, grabbed a hand towel and wiped both weapons down. He placed a gun in the hand of the last man he killed. It was the same one he had used to kill both men. He manipulated the dead man's hand to fire another shot into the carcass of his late colleague. Now, when the police investigated the crime scene, they would assume it was a murder-suicide. Forensics would find traces of gunpowder on the presumed killer's hand. Ballistics would show that all slugs came from the same weapon. He placed the second pistol in the waistband of his own trousers.

Federov ripped the hand towel into four pieces and flushed them one-by-one down the toilet. He went to the door and stood there for a few moments listening for any sounds that might indicate the suppressed shots had been heard. After all, the suppressor only dampened the sound by about twenty-five percent. Satisfied that nothing was out of the ordinary, he returned to the bedroom and sat in the chair by the rifle.

When his watch told him it was few minutes before ten o'clock, he cracked the shades on the west-facing window. Using powerful binoculars that had been brought to the suite by the now-dead Ukrainians, Federov gazed down East Capitol Street toward the steps of the Capitol Building. He was careful not to get too close to the window lest he be spotted. The Secret Service and other local and federal agents were out in force, surveilling the area around the East Front of the Capitol Building. He was aware of the

319

presence of helicopters in the area, undoubtedly staffed with expert marksmen equipped with powerfully scoped rifles of their own.

Federov swept the glasses up the approach to the steps of the Capitol past the bollards designed to prevent motor vehicles from proceeding on beyond the foot of East Capitol Street. Jersey barriers had been temporarily placed for additional security and crowd control purposes. He noted the temporary wooden platform that had been built on the steps. A podium flanked by teleprompters had been centered on its front edge. Two rows of chairs for dignitaries were set up behind the podium. Most of the chairs already were occupied. A few hundred chairs had been placed on the brick pavers of the broad approach to the Capitol steps. These were for the general public and few of them remained unoccupied. Television crews had set up shop in the space between the front edge of the platform and the seating for members of the public.

He looked behind the dais and his gaze swept the front of the building. There were three sets of enormous bronze doors, one for the House entrance, one for the Senate and a central entrance to the Rotunda. Each consisted of two valves of panels. The bronze doors of the House and Senate are equal in size and motif. Their respective valves each contained three panels and a medallion depicting significant events in American history.

The bronze doors to the Rotunda, also known as the Columbus Doors, are almost seventeen feet high and weigh twenty thousand pounds. They also are divided into two valves but contain four panels each. The life of Columbus begins at the bottom of the left valve and continues in a clockwise progression. At the pinnacle is a bust of Columbus.

Federov noted the statues of War and Peace carved in Vermont marble and set into niches flanking the doors to the Capitol Rotunda. The sculptural pediment - a triangular space that forms the gable of a low-pitched roof usually filled with relief sculpture in classical architecture – was centered over the east central entrance of the Capitol. It is called *Genius of America*. The central figure represents America, who points to the figure of Justice, lifting scales in her left hand with a scroll in her right hand. To America's left are an eagle and the figure of Hope with her arm resting on an anchor. Federov was not impressed. In his opinion, this jumble of Greek, Roman, and other architectural styles could not hold a candle to the vastly more impressive Kremlin.

At precisely ten o'clock, the Secretary of Labor rose from his seat on the dais and walked to the podium. He spoke for approximately seven minutes then introduced the President of the United States. As the president approached the podium, the thought ran through Federov's head, party time.

He returned to the chair and placed his eye against the sniper scope. The interior of a scope is purged with nitrogen to create a humidity and fog-proof environment between the lenses, thus maintaining clarity of vision. The front lens usually is set back in the housing to provide a sunshade that casts a shadow and reduces glare. Beyond approximately five hundred and fifty meters, or six hundred yards, there are a number of variables that affect the bullet on its path to the intended target. Accordingly, where the sniper is aiming is not where the bullet will impact. Snipers must line up the point of aim with the point of impact by dialing a number of fine adjustments to the scope once range, heat and windage have been factored into the shot.

Federov didn't have the benefit of a spotter to advise him of these crucial data. He knew the range and could see the temperature on a small device the Ukrainians had placed on a ledge just outside the window. He had to estimate wind speed and direction from the flag flying from a pole located at the base of the dome on the East side of the Capitol dome. Using the scope's mil-dot reticle, Federov made the necessary calculations and dialed in the scope to line up the crosshairs. These were not the ideal conditions, complicated by the fact that he had only very limited practice with this particular weapon. Still, he was confident he could accomplish the mission.

He focused in on the president. The man had begun to deliver his prepared speech. Federov watched in disgust as the president's head, with its large, jug-like ears, constantly swiveled back and forth from the far left to the far right. He never looked to the center because there wasn't a teleprompter there. He can't utter an intelligible word without the damn prompter, Federov thought. The president was completely dependent on the display device that prompts the speaker with an electronic visual text of a speech or script. It was modern version of the old practice of using cue cards. Today's prompters were voice-activated, scrolling at the speed of the presenter's speech.

Federov watched as the president shook his finger at his audience as if berating its members. Although he couldn't hear the speech, he knew the man was speaking pedantically, as if lecturing small children. And the fools to whom he spoke couldn't get enough. He despised the man as a traitor, someone who had become a legend in his own mind, a self-involved rock star gone off the reservation to pursue his own agenda at the expense of those, including Federov, who had worked for decades to prepare the way. The man was the worst kind of fool. Blinded by his own sense of self-importance, infallibility and divine right of authority, he ignored the dictates of those who had put him in power. He deserved to die.

Federov struggled to get his anger under control. He regulated his breathing and, in a meditative fashion, forced his heartbeat to slow down. He felt calmness returning and refocused on the target. His goal was to strike right between the president's eyes, but the constant twisting of the man's head further complicated the situation. Leaning forward in the chair with the butt plate solidly against his right shoulder, his finger slowly squeezed, not pulled, the trigger. It was stiffer than Federov would have liked and he increased the pressure until it discharged.

He continued watching through the scope as the bullet missed its intended target, clipping off a small piece of the president's left ear. It traveled on and ripped into the throat of the attorney general who was sitting behind the president. The magnum slug nearly tore the man's head off his shoulders. It snapped forward and his body flipped over backwards landing in the bloodied lap to a middle-aged woman sitting behind him.

The Russian swore in anger and frustration. There was no opportunity for a second shot. The president had been swarmed under a crush of Secret Service agents like a running back under a pile of defenders. Other agents and law enforcement officers were pointing up East Capitol Street.

Federov strode quickly to the door and left the room. A moment later he exited onto Third Street Northeast through a side door on the ground floor of the hotel. The limousine was waiting for him. He slid in, pulling the hot, uncomfortable gloves off as soon as he settled into his seat. The driver immediately accelerated, heading north. The diplomatic plates on the vehicle would provide it with safe passage through the streets of the capitol.

After a few blocks, the driver turned left on Massachusetts Avenue and proceeded through Dupont Circle and around the United States Naval Observatory. Gazing out a side window, Federov's previous air of confidence had completely dissolved. His plan had been a brilliant one, but something had gone very wrong. This enraged Federov. Who was responsible, he wondered. Was it that damn Maksym? And, why hadn't he answered his phone? Under the circumstances, it should have been fully charged and in his immediate possession at all times. Then there was the matter of Whelan and his colleagues not showing up at the hotel. Had McCoy deceived him when he agreed to exchange the Sleeping Dogs for Levell?

The driver turned left on Edmunds Street Northwest then jogged south on Thirty-Sixth Street to Calvert Street.

Federov retrieved his cell phone from a trousers pocket and speed dialed Laski's personal cell phone number. After two rings, he heard the other man's raspy voice.

"The package was not properly delivered," Federov said.

"I am aware of that."

Federov swore vehemently and said, "What the hell happened to the deliverymen who were promised?"

"It was a deception from the very beginning. Somehow our customers discovered the whereabouts of the goods we offered in trade."

"And they knew this how?"

"It doesn't matter. They swept in and stole them."

"What of this formidable Maksym of yours? It was his task to safeguard these goods."

"True, unfortunately he was…ah, detained."

"Detained?"

"Yes, but he managed to free himself.

"How?"

"I do not know at this time. He is in the process of returning home."

"Home? Surely you are not referring to your residence."

"No, of course not," Laski said. "He's going to his original home."

Federov now understood Laski to mean The Ukraine, or possibly Russia. "And what of you?" he said.

"Me? I am perfectly safe." Laski said defensively. "There is nothing to associate me with any of these activities other than your testimony. And, you will not provide such testimony because you have diplomatic immunity. Nevertheless, I strongly suggest you cloister yourself in the embassy until you can safely travel home."

"Don't patronize me, you old fool," Federov said angrily. "I have no concerns for myself."

"Then perhaps you are the fool. Levell, McCoy and their operatives," Laski said in reference to Whelan and the others, "know about the location and timing of your recent activities. Even now they may be positioning themselves to capture you...or worse." Taking great pleasure at the discomfort that thought must be causing Federov, Laski smiled broadly.

Federov turned quickly and stared out the rear window of the limo then said to the driver, "Have you noticed anyone following us?"

The driver shook his head.

Federov removed the suppressed Sig from the waistband of his trousers and continued to scan the surroundings. "If these people wanted me, they would have tried to stop me from carrying out the mission."

"You are wrong. While they certainly have no admiration for the object of your mission, they would not visit harm to the individual. However, they would not interfere with someone else's efforts to do so." Laski hung up.

The driver crossed Wisconsin Avenue heading west on Calvert Street, and turned right on Tunlaw Road. The gated entrance to the compound where the Russian Embassy was located was a block and a half to the right on Tunlaw Road. It had taken twenty minutes to cover the five miles from the Hotel L'Orange.

Federov had always enjoyed roaming the sprawling Russian compound. In it, he was treated with great deference because of the nature of his work as well as his rank and reputation. The compound contained a number of buildings. Many people lived and worked there. Almost all of them regarded him with fear, and he enjoyed the sense of power it gave him. Now, however, as the limo eased through the gates at the entrance to the compound, he felt more like a prisoner within its walls.

64 POTOMAC, MARYLAND

In the late afternoon of the day the attempt had been made on the life of the president, Chaim Laski's Potomac, Maryland residence had the look and activity of an armed camp. The fifteen thousand square foot, three-story home was positioned inside a ten-acre estate. It was protected twenty-four hours a day by a fortune in electronic surveillance equipment. Tonight every one of Laski's eighteen remaining Ukrainian security people was fully armed and on duty. Ordinarily, two guards accompanied by watchdogs patrolled the grounds round the clock. Now the number of guard patrols had been beefed up to four.

Laski was concerned, but not overly alarmed at the prospect of physical danger. After all, he had a small army of very nasty and brutal men protecting him. And, he was expecting Maksym to arrive at any moment. He was in his library sipping a glass of one of the most rare and expensive Scotch whiskies in the world. He slowly savored each sip of the Chivas Regal 50-year Royal Salute, released in 2003 as a special edition to celebrate Queen Elizabeth II's fifty years on the throne. Only two hundred and fifty-five bottles were produced and each featured a hand-engraved 24-carat gold plaque. Laski had paid forty thousand dollars for the bottle, and had been saving it for a special occasion. He had expected to open the Scotch in celebration of the successful removal of the president. While it didn't turn out that way, he was not going to let Federov's incompetence cause him to postpone this pleasure.

He rose slowly from his seat, a classic wing chair in dark brown, tufted aniline leather. Holding the tumbler of precious Scotch almost lovingly, he walked to the window, pulled aside the heavy tapestry of the drape and looked out. The moon was in the new phase of the lunar cycle, positioning it between the earth and sun. It would be a very dark night.

Laski was aware of movement and turned toward the door to the library and saw the powerful frame of Maksym standing there. The other man glanced at the impressive bottle of Scotch on the library table. Laski smiled, but did not offer him a drink. Maksym was perhaps his most valuable employee, but this Scotch was not for sharing. He waved him to a chair and returned to his own seat.

"So, Maksym," he said in heavily accented Ukrainian, "tell me about your misadventure."

Knowing that Laski was much more comfortable in Russian, Maksym responded in that tongue. "Levell's comrades surprised us at the warehouse."

"How were they able to locate him?"

Maksym shrugged his thick shoulders. "It appears we underestimated their resourcefulness."

Laski nodded. "That was foolish of us. And how is it you managed to free yourself?"

Maksym smiled. It was a mean smile, and reflected a strong measure of self-satisfaction. "I too am resourceful."

"Tell me about it."

Settling back into his chair, Maksym said, "When we were captured, the one called Whelan shot and killed one of our guards in cold blood. It was designed to frighten the remaining guard into talking."

"My, my, such savage behavior," Laski said in mock condemnation. "We would never do such a thing."

Maksym ignored the cynicism. "The other guard and I were bound with nylon restraints, hooded, driven somewhere and thrown into a cellar of some sort."

Laski looked thoughtfully at the other man for a few moments. "And where exactly was this place?"

Maksym shrugged again. "I don't know the exact location, but it's near Fredericksburg, Virginia. It was a large and, except for the cellar, a luxurious country estate."

"Interesting. We were not aware of this place. Can you describe it further?"

"No. In my haste to escape, I was in no position to reconnoiter the premises."

"That's understandable. So, how did you manage to free yourself?"

"I ordered the other guard to chew through my restraints."

"And he did this?" Laski seemed surprised.

"I told him that if he did not, I would find some other means and then I would kill him."

325

"I suppose you killed him anyway."

"Of course."

"But you remained locked in the cellar. How did you escape?"

Maksym smiled again. "I arranged the dead man's body to appear as if he was sleeping. Then I feigned sleep myself with my hands behind my back as though still bound. When their jailer came to check on us during his next round, I sprang upon him and snapped his neck."

Laski nodded approvingly.

"I took his keys and his cell phone, locked the cellar door behind me and slipped out of the house. Using the remote on the dead guard's keys, I located his vehicle parked behind the building and drove back here. Along the way I used his cell phone to let our men know I was coming."

Laski's eyes widened in alarm. "Do you still have the phone with you?"

"No. I am familiar with how these things can be traced. I threw it and the jailer's keys into a farm pond."

"And what of the automobile?"

"When I called to let our men know I was coming, I told one of them to pick me up in Tyson's corner. I left the car in a shopping mall parking lot. Wiped clean."

Laski took another sip of the Scotch and rolled it around slowly on his tongue. As he did so, he regarded Maksym, the extremely muscular build, the pale blue eyes that never displayed concern or fear. He knew the man to be strong almost to the point of super human. His quickness defied logic. He also was brilliant, with the rare ability to connect the dots as fast as Laski himself could. Maybe faster.

All in all, Laski knew the younger man to be an extraordinary human being. He prided himself on having found him in the slums of Kiev after hearing rumors about him from others in his employ. Recruiting him had not been difficult. He simply offered him wealth and a lifestyle beyond his imagination. It had proven to be a wise move. Maksym ran all aspects of security and kept the brutish Ukrainian thugs under control, meting out discipline as required. Laski often confided in Maksym on the affairs he was involved in for the Russians. He had high regard for the other man's observations.

As he poured another two fingers of the Scotch into the tumbler, Laski said, "The government, as usual, knows nothing of our involvement in today's affair."

Maksym sat impassively, gazing unwaveringly at the older man.

"The Team, however, is a different matter. They have long known of my involvement in political affairs and the management of the funding for those activities."

Maksym's nod was almost imperceptible. He was not a man to waste motion or emotion.

"They may suspect our involvement today, but, thanks to Federov's conversations with McCoy and Levell, and Levell's subsequent survival, they mostly will blame our Russian friends."

He paused to savor another sip. "Nevertheless, I have placed all security personnel on high alert and doubled the patrols on the grounds. That, and a fortune in electronic surveillance equipment, will have to suffice. What is your opinion?"

Maksym shrugged slightly. "It is possible Levell will send his pet attack dogs," he said. "From what I saw of them in the warehouse, they are highly overrated."

"Perhaps so," Laski said. "But we are down to eighteen men, not including the two of us. Three were killed with Harold Case. We lost two in the botched attempt to abduct Agent Christie's family, two more at the hands of Federov this morning, the two who were with you and Levell at the warehouse, and one at that nightclub your men frequent in their off hours."

Maksym smiled darkly. "I hope Levell's people do come. I will enjoy killing them myself."

65 ARLINGTON, VIRGINIA

The war room was in a dingy office area in an older section of Arlington, Virginia. The building was what the real estate industry euphemistically refers to as flex space, a structure that has been converted to office space from what originally had been light industrial or warehouse usage. The place looked tired and neglected. An acoustical ceiling and drywall had been installed in what had been bare bones warehouse space. Several ceiling panels sagged from their gridwork of metal strips. The wallboard was deeply gouged in several places and badly scuffed. A few of the florescent light fixtures had gone out. The linoleum flooring had been laid directly on the concrete slab and was scarred and cracked from years of foot traffic.

There was a heavily barred door in the rear wall that opened onto the alley behind the building. A cheap, hollow core wooden door on the opposite wall led to what had once been a small reception area. Someone had smeared a coat of white paint over the door's original varnished surface. It hadn't improved its appearance.

Under Levell's direction, a mass of maps, aerials, building plans, satellite imagery and other data had been gathered hastily. Some of it was pinned to the walls and some was spread out on jury-rigged tables made of sawhorses and planks quickly acquired at a nearby Home Depot. In the center of the room, two three-foot square card tables had been pushed together to form a poor-man's conference table. They were made of gray metal legs and frames with cheap, brown vinyl tops. There were ten gray metal folding chairs scattered around the tables.

Brendon Whalen sat in one of the chairs near the middle of the combined tables. He was alone in the room, waiting for Cliff Levell to arrive. Gazing slowly around the room, he was reminded of the old saw, beggars can't be choosers. They had quickly vacated the country manor outside Fredericksburg when Maksym's escape had been noticed. It seemed a sure bet that he would report back to his comrades and they would place the estate under one or more modes of surveillance, particularly by Russian satellite. Levell and Whelan knew the Bureau and possibly others had the lodge in Tidewater Virginia under surveillance. Through a retired CIA colleague who had acquired various real estate investments, Levell was able to secure the use of the flex space in short order.

The attempt on the president and Maksym's escape had occurred earlier that morning. Now, it was late afternoon. Whelan knew that Levell had a plan. They had spent much of the day reviewing materials gathered for them by various contacts Levell had in government and the private sector. They were all Team members or sympathizers. The materials related mostly to Chaim Laski's estate in Potomac, Maryland.

The cheap wooden door to the reception area opened and Levell wheeled himself across the room to the table near Whelan. Despite the whirlwind activities of the day, he looked relaxed and pleased. He actually had a rare smile on his face. Whelan knew the old Cold Warrior was in his natural element – intrigue, retribution and violence.

"This isn't exactly the way the mission we planned for you boys was supposed to go, but we can salvage a part of it," Levell said.

"Laski?" Whelan said.

"Yeah, that sonofabitch."

"Is he more important than other parts of the planned mission?"

"Important enough. He's the money manager for those Russian bastards and their leftwing comrades who have infiltrated damn near every corner of this country and its institutions."

"Cut off the head and the rest of the snake dies?"

"Usually, but this fucking snake will just grow another head."

"But," Whelan said, "it won't grow it overnight."

"No, it definitely will suffer for a while. And, in the meantime, this will buy time for our side to regroup and replan."

"What about your Russian buddy, Federov? We knew where he was going to be and what he was going to do. Why didn't you let us intercept and kill him at the hotel?"

Levell's eyes flashed. "He's not my goddam buddy." He took a deep breath and said, "Frankly, I was hoping the sonofabitch would succeed. What a candy ass. He's supposed to be an expert fucking marksman. He nicks the president's ugly, fucking jug handle of an ear." He paused very briefly then said, "At least he took out that trouble-making AG."

"Must be a hell of a thing," Whelan said with a slight smile. "The president's own handlers want him dead and so does the loyal opposition."

"His people want him dead because he went off their reservation. Became full of himself. Believed his own press clippings like some asshole rock star. Decided he could ignore the Constitution and shove his own Marxist agenda down the throats of America's unwilling citizenry instead of following his handlers' game plan."

"So, did the original mission call for us to take the president out?"

"No. That sonofabitch is the worst thing to happen to this country in its almost two hundred and fifty year history. But that doesn't give us the right to ignore constitutional protocols and assassinate him."

"Then what was our mission to have been?"

"That's on a need to know basis and, under the circumstances, you no longer need to know."

Whelan regarded his old friend and mentor for a few moments. "Okay," he said, "after Laski, then what?"

Levell reached over and gave Whelan a good-natured clap on the shoulder. "After that, you go home to that beautiful wife of yours and those two spittin'-image boys."

Whelan smiled at the thought. "Fair enough, but I assume that, in time, the mission or something approximating it will be resurrected."

"You never know about these things," Levell said with a sly smile. "God willing and the crick don't rise, who can say what might transpire."

"I'm going back to ground in Ireland where I'll resume a normal life. But what about the other guys?"

"We'll take care of them, just like we did the last time."

"Meaning?"

"Meaning they'll be set up with new identities and jobs."

"Like witness protection?"

"Yeah. Something along those lines."

"And if any of them object to the new routines?"

Levell's eyes flashed again. "Goddammit stop with all these questions. The boys really don't have much say in the matter. They'll take what we offer or take their chances on their own. That would be a very bad decision if survival is high on their list of priorities."

A smile curled up the corners of Whelan's mouth, but it didn't spread to his icy blue eyes. "One more question," he said.

Levell sighed deeply and shook his head. "What is it?"

"That Bureau agent, Christie, what was the real reason you wanted us to protect his wife and children?"

Levell took a few moments before he answered. "I told you before, it was to keep the other side from kidnapping them and using that as pressure on her husband. As Supervisory Special Agent of the Harold Case situation, it could have drawn more unwanted attention to that investigation."

Whelan regarded the other man with a bemused smile. "Okay, that's the official reason. But it has a slight odor. What's the real reason?"

Levell gazed at Whalen with a look that might have caused psychological damage to a lesser man. After a long moment, he said, "Alright, goddammit. Sometimes you're too fucking smart for your own good. Debbie Christie, the agent's wife, is the daughter of a dear friend, a man who saved my life during the Tet Offensive in 'sixty-eight."

"That's right, you were a Marine before you joined the Agency."

"Damn right I was! Anyway, we were counterattacking north of the Perfume River in Hue. Charlie was dug in tight. It was house-to-house combat. I took a sniper round and was bleeding out when her dad stepped up and plugged the hole, tossed me over a shoulder and carried me back to a med post. Otherwise, I would have died on that filthy fucking street. Lord knows, enough of us did."

For just a moment, Whelan thought he detected a trace of moistness in Levell's eyes.

"Years later, on his deathbed – cancer was eating him up, I promised him I would look after Debbie."

Whelan looked at the older man and smiled. "You're a good man, Cliff."

"Aw, goddammit, don't go getting all sentimental on me." Levell seemed genuinely embarrassed by the compliment.

The door to the reception area opened again and Larsen, Thomas, Kirkland, Stensen and Almeida entered the room. Almeida was carrying a six-pack of beer in each hand. He placed one in the middle of each table. He started pulling bottles out and handed one to each of the other men. Although they were not twist-off caps, none of the men had any trouble popping them off their respective bottles. Whelan easily pulled the caps off two bottles and handed one to Levell.

"Go easy, boys," Levell said. There's a lot of wet work to be done tonight."

PART FIVE

DEAD DOGS

66 J. EDGAR HOOVER BUILDING

In his career with the Federal Bureau of Investigation, Mitch Christie had endured countless meetings. Some were better than others. This one clearly fell into the category of others. He had joined the Bureau fresh out of Georgetown law school at age twenty-four. He had moved up the career ladder from Probationary Agent to Special Agent to his current rank, Supervisory Special Agent. Until the Harold Case affair had been assigned to him, he had expected to be promoted to Special Agent in Charge of one of the Bureau's smaller Field Offices, or perhaps Assistant Special Agent in Charge of one of the larger offices. He might even have made it to Division Chief and eventually been able to retire on a comfortable pension.

Unfortunately, the Case investigation looked more and more like his career Waterloo. He had been heading it up for more than nine months with very little progress. Worse, he had been taunted by the principal suspect, Brendan Whelan, on the flight from Atlanta to San Francisco. And the Irishman had managed to stay a step ahead of him ever since. The man had even made a fool of him by abducting his own family. This crossed the threshold. This was personal.

Now, when he wanted to devote every second of each day and every ounce of his energy to finding the bastard, this new situation comes along. He and every other federal law enforcement officer and a lot of civilian ones were being mobilized in light of this morning's attempt on the life of the president. His boss's boss, the Chief of the Criminal Investigative Division had called this meeting at Bureau HQ in the J. Edgar Hoover Building, a massive, multistoried structure on the north side of Pennsylvania Avenue between 9th and 10th Streets Northwest in Washington, D.C. The auditorium was packed, standing room only, and it was being streamed live to all FBI field offices and installations around the country.

333

The chief rambled on about the horror, the ignominy, the shame that such an event could occur and not have been foiled by the Bureau. Worse yet, he reminded his audience, their ultimate boss, the attorney general had been killed. He did take pains to point out that the ultimate responsibility for security had been with the Secret Service. It was a statement that was lost on few of those listening.

Christie looked around him and noted that most of the other agents seemed to be dutifully hanging on the chief's words. Many had notebooks or iPads in their laps and were taking down some of what the chief was saying. He knew he should have been doing the same. But he was too distracted to be able to focus on the chief's words. Hell, he thought, I'm more than distracted. I'm flat out rattled. My ability to concentrate is shot.

In fact, the only thing he could think about was his wife. She and their children had returned home two days ago. It appeared they had been enjoying quite the life of luxury in captivity. They seemed jaded by it. While he truly was relieved to have them back safe and sound, something definitely was different. The kids seemed disappointed by their old, familiar surroundings. They talked about living in a mansion, being waited on by servants, enjoying gourmet meals at every sitting. And they spoke almost with hero worship about the men who had "saved them from bad people". His daughter had a crush on several of the men. Brett, his son, held them in the same high esteem he usually reserved for soccer superstars.

What ate at him the most, however, was the change that had come over his wife. She clearly seemed distant where he was concerned. While he knew she had grown unhappy with his chosen career, this was more than that. It was as if her experience with the abduction had driven her to an unspoken ultimatum: either we make radical changes in our life together or I move on without you.

Christie was frightened by this change in his wife and afraid he might be losing her. He also was seething with anger. He was angry at his wife's family friend, Cliff Levell, who had honored a pledge he had made to Debbie's father as he lay dying. And he was especially enraged at Whelan. When Debbie spoke about Whelan, it was clear from her words and body English that she was enamored with the man. Clearly, she was comparing her husband to that Irish bastard, and Whelan was winning.

His wife was an attractive woman, trim and voluptuous. What had gone on during her period of captivity, he wondered. Had Whelan seduced her? Had she been unfaithful to him? Did she want to leave him for Whelan? God, he hated Whelan.

An acute pain like a slash from a white-hot scalpel shot through his stomach. Even his own digestive organ had no love or respect for him. All this personal trauma caused the Mount St. Helens that his stomach had become to erupt continuously in all its fury. He was going through two large bottles of Mylanta per day and it seemed to make little difference.

He had tried convincing Debbie that she undoubtedly was experiencing Stockholm Syndrome. He explained to her that it was a psychological phenomenon where captives begin to express empathy and have positive feelings for their captors. The victims mistake a lack of abuse from their captors as an act of kindness. Christie knew the Bureau's Hostage Barricade Database System indicated that 27% of victims in situations similar to the one she had experienced show evidence of Stockholm Syndrome. He knew it was closely related in evolutionary terms to capture-bonding. That was a concept based on the theory that human ancestors, especially female ones, learned to adapt to the constant threat of being abducted by other tribes. Survival of the species was paramount, and women were fair game. Women who resisted capture and mating with their captors risked being killed. Christie also was aware of at least one Bureau report that cast doubt on the theory, but he desperately needed to believe in its validity.

He seemed alone in that regard. Debbie clearly rejected the theory and became incensed when he tried to bring it up. He felt he was losing her. She was talking about a trial separation. The thought sent an icy chill through his chest. He didn't know what to do. If he acquiesced to her wishes and left the Bureau, his pension would not be sufficient to support them in later years. She insisted he could find a better job with normal working hours in the private sector. He wasn't so sure.

The economy was staggering and many well-qualified people were out of work and had been for a long time. Companies were cutting back, not expanding. Most of the issues could be laid at the feet of the current administration. But, he thought, even if this morning's would-be assassin had succeeded in killing the president, it would have created a greater disaster. The vice president was a certifiable idiot who often came close to needing surgery to have his foot removed from his mouth. Although Christie was no supporter of the president, it was better to have sacrificed a highly expendable and incompetent AG.

The chief was droning on about the assassination attempt. Efforts were afoot to trace the weapon and ammunition used in the attempt. Forensics was all but disassembling the hotel room. The deaths of the two men found in the room appeared to be the result of a murder-suicide. The hotel staff had said that the men had been in residence for three weeks. Reportedly they both spoke with heavy Eastern European accents, but had used identification indicating they were British tourists.

This last bit of information jogged Christie's memory. He remembered his phone conversations with the man who called himself Maksym. He too had had a slight trace of an Eastern European accent. And what was it Maksym had told him? Something about evil men were going to do a bad thing. Assassinating the president was a bad thing. Could he have been talking about this morning's attempt? Maksym had gone on to say that he would tell Christie when and where to find these evil men. Yet he had heard nothing from the man.

Right now, he didn't want to hear from anyone. He just wanted to save his marriage. And, if there was a God, get his hands around the throat of Brendan Whelan.

67 POTOMAC, MARYLAND

It was just past nine o'clock on Labor Day evening. Petro Petrovich had just finished a quick meal and returned to his shift on guard duty. He and three others had been patrolling the grounds of Chaim Laski's estate in Potomac, Maryland. They had been at this for more than ten hours and were tired and bored. Yet, they had been instructed by their boss, Maksym, to continue through the night. As much as they might hate it, no one refused Maksym. Someone had done that once, a few years ago. Maksym, using his bare hands, had beaten the man to death swiftly and cruelly. The message had been clear and unmistakable: do not argue with Maksym.

The men on external guard duty had not been told why the usual shift of two men had been increased to four. Petrovich did not complain. Now he was responsible for patrolling only a quarter of the estate's grounds, not half. Nor did any of the men know why they were working double shifts without relief. Only Maksym knew the answers, and his volatile temper was a sufficient barrier to prevent anyone from asking.

Each of the four patrolling guards was teamed with a large, ill-tempered Boerboel. Originally bred in South Africa, it is the only breed of dog bred specifically to defend specific territory, such as a homestead. As a result, they are extremely powerful, brave and protective with a high degree of intelligence and resistance to pain. All of the Boerboels being utilized at Laski's estate were males. Each stood twenty-eight inches at the shoulder and weighed very close to two hundred pounds. No normal human being could survive an encounter with an angry Boerboel.

Petrovich and the other men on patrol were armed with the HK UMP45, a submachine gun chambering a .45 ACP cartridge from a straight, polymer magazine holding thirty rounds of Federal Premium 230 grain hollow-point ammunition. These weapons were supposed to be accessible

337

only to the military and law enforcement agencies. Maksym, however, had been able to acquire them. It had only been a matter of money. Each weapon had been fitted with Advanced Armament's Defender sound suppressor to which five cubic centimeters of water had been added. Firing the weapon with the wet suppressor further reduced the noise level over firing with a dry one by approximately thirty-nine additional decibels. As a result, the noise factor upon discharging the weapon was similar to that of an air pistol. Audible to be sure, but not sufficient to attract the interest or concern of neighbors on their own walled, multi-acre plots.

Petrovich's animal was called Moordenaar, the Dutch word for killer. The guard tentatively reached over and gently scratched Moordenaar behind its right ear. The dog turned and licked the man's wrist. Petrovich felt a great deal more than respect for the animal. There also was a strong presence of fear. He was certain the jaws of the huge beast could easily snap his hand cleanly off his wrist if it was inclined to do so. Petrovich marveled at the sheer muscularity of the animal. It had the huge head typical of mastiffs, as well as the deep chest and powerful shoulders. In a certain way, the beast reminded him of Maksym. He straightened up and wearily said to the animal in Ukrainian, "Come, my friend, it is time to go back to work." As he tugged gently on the leash to start the dog in the right direction, he wondered why it tolerated the restraint. Together they began to patrol their share of the grounds of the ten-acre estate.

Twelve miles to the northwest of Laski's estate in Potomac, a very substantially modified, black Eurocopter EC155 helicopter rose slowly from an isolated farm field. Tonight it carried two pilots and six passengers and was powered by two six hundred thirty-five kilowatt turboshaft Turbomeca Arriel 2C2 engines. At cruising speed, it would reach Laski's home in less than fifteen minutes.

Noise generated by the bird was damped by the use of additional main and tail rotor blades, which cut the speed of the rotor in half, particularly in forward flight below maximum speed. This greatly reduced the helicopter's classic whop-whop signature. The bird also had an elaborate system of exhaust ducts and fresh-air mixers in its tailboom. The tips of the main blades had been changed to a variation on Eurocopter's Blue-Edge rotor blades. It also had an engine exhaust muffler, lead-vinyl pads to deaden skin noise, and a baffle to block noise slipping out the air intake. In addition, it had a modified tail boom and a noise reducing covering on the rear rotors.

While similar in many respects to the top-secret stealth choppers that carried the Navy SEALs on the bin Laden mission, it was a civilian craft. The stealth modifications had been made to the Eurocopter EC155 by technicians and aeronautical engineers working for a company controlled by the Mueller brothers. The extensive modifications would not render the bird completely silent, but they damped the kinds of noise typically associated with a helicopter.

The passengers sat in jump seats, three on either side of the aircraft behind the pilots. The six men all were dressed black battledress uniforms from head to toe. Their jump boots were black, as were the watch caps they wore. All means of identifying the source of the clothing had been removed. None of the men carried any identification. The exposed areas of their hands and faces had been covered with camouflage face paint.

One of the men, Brendan Whelan, raised a secure satphone to his ear and said, "We're airborne, eta the Snake Pit in ten minutes."

Levell, who had chosen the code name for Laski's estate, said, "As we've discussed, make it quick and make it complete."

"Roger that."

There was a pause at Levell's end then he said, "You are aware that Laski's man, Maksym, is on the loose."

"Yes." Now it was Whelan's turn to pause. After a few moments, he said, "So what is your concern regarding Maksym?"

"He's unusual. Very dangerous. And I suspect he may be back at Laski's place by now."

"Anyone with a gun in his hand is dangerous."

"Yes. But you need to be particularly careful with this guy. I suspect he's different than anyone you and the boys have gone up against in the past."

"Are you suggesting that this Maksym character will outgun us?"

"No. Just be extra cautious where this sonofabitch is concerned."

"Cliff, have I, or any of us, ever fucked up a mission before?"

"Never. But this guy is dangerous. No doubt he's as strong and as quick as you are. And as clever. Watch yourselves." Levell paused then said, "If possible, we'd like to take this guy alive." With that, he terminated the call.

Whelan pondered what Levell had said. Was he suggesting that Maksym was genetically gifted, as he and the others were? If so, it should make for a very interesting encounter.

68 POTOMAC, MARYLAND

Maksym methodically made the rounds of the security stations. In one room on the first floor of the three-story structure, two men sat carefully watching monitors. One man was tracking the feed from video cameras that were strategically placed around the perimeters of the property. They were equipped with special night vision lenses. The second man monitored infrared sensors designed to pick up heat signals from living creatures on the estate's grounds. The twelve remaining Ukrainians were spread around the house, four on each floor. All security personnel were equipped with wireless headsets so that Maksym could be in communication with them, individually and collectively. Each was a fierce fighter, tough and ruthless; and they were well armed. Maksym had no concerns about the ability of himself and the others to protect the house and Laski from everything short of a full-strength Marine Company.

When he had finished his latest rounds, he strolled with a confident air back to Laski's library. The man had been joined by a guest, Senator Howard Morris. The senator held a tall glass of straight vodka in both hands and slurped greedily at it. A good bit of it was sloshing over the rim because his hands shook so badly. Laski was still sitting at the head of the table where Maksym had last seen him. He was continuing to nurse the precious bottle of Chivas Regal 50-year Royal Salute. Morris sat on his right.

Laski frowned disapprovingly at the small puddle of vodka forming on the gleaming finish of the library table. "Zenator," he said to Morris, "you act like frightened little girl. Iss boogie mans after you?"

Morris' head bobbed up and down. "I'm not a little girl. I'm a United States senator. But any prudent person would be somewhat apprehensive given the circumstances."

"Und vere iss our friend, Mr. Zhepard Jenkins? He iss usually viss you."

Morris shook his head rapidly back and forth. "I don't know where he is. The sonofabitch dropped out of sight. Like he fell off the face of the earth."

Both men looked up as Maksym entered the room. Laski waved him to a chair at the far end of the table. "You are seeing this man, Maksym, yes?"

Morris nodded and his hands shook a little faster. When he looked at Maksym he saw immense strength in his body, unspeakable cruelty on his face, and death in his eyes. In essence, the man terrified him. He reached for the bottle of Grey Goose and shakily splashed more into his glass.

"Diss iss my friend Maksym, chief of my zecurity force. Vee could not be zafer in middle of fucking Pentagon. So stop ziss qvaking and be still."

Morris shrugged and looked at the tabletop. He didn't want to look at Maksym. He had removed his finely tailored suit coat and dabbed at the spilled vodka with one of his shirtsleeves. There was so much starch in the shirt that he only succeeded in pushing the liquid around in widening circles. "The Pentagon is not so safe. Al-Quada crashed a plane into it, remember. Given what's happened today, Chaim, and the role we played in that activity, I believe it's wise to be concerned."

Laski slowly wagged his head back and forth. "Vee haff been vise from beginning. There iss no vay to connect us to attempt on life of president. Only person who could be connected iss Federov. Und he has departed country already."

"What about Levell and McCoy? That damn Russian certainly gave them enough information for them to deduce what was going to happen."

"Federov iss arrogant fool, yes. But, again, vhere iss connection to you und me?"

Morris took a big gulp of the vodka then shook his head. "I'd like to be as confident as you are, Chaim, but Levell is one smart son of a bitch. He might have connected the dots. He could be siccing those fucking hellhounds of his on us right now."

"Zmart? Yes, truly a vorthy adverzary," Laski said and smiled. "But, even if he is knowing of our inwolvment, how many of zees hellhounds, as you call zem, does he haff? Zix?"

He shook his head and made a sweeping gesture with his right hand. "Vee are surrounded by small army of heavily armed men. Wery nasty men who are completely loyal to me. Und vee haff latest in surveillance eqvipment. Nozzing iss on grounds zat we are not knowing. Und vun more zing," he gestured toward Maksym. "He iss baddest ass on planet."

Almost as if punctuating the comment, there was a sudden burst of noise, like gunshots. Laski's and Morris' eyes opened wide and their heads each swiveled as they stared at Maksym.

The security chief shouted into the mouthpiece of his headset in Ukrainian, "Pavel, what is happening?"

The man operating the camera monitors said, "One of the fucking neighbors is shooting off fireworks."

"Fireworks?"

"Yes, maybe because it's Labor Day."

"Maybe," Maksym said thoughtfully. "Maybe. But it also could be some kind of diversion tactic. Tell the men to be extra attentive."

He turned back to the other two men and said in English, "One of your neighbors is using fireworks."

Laski shook his head as if in disgust. "Zat vould be Michelsen who lives to za east of us. He is fucking poster boy for capitalism, supporter of right ving causes. Maybe he vill blow fucking hand off."

69 POTOMAC, MARYLAND

Petro Petrovich paused on his rounds of Laski's estate. Moordenaar, his massive Boerboel, swiveled its big head on a thick neck, looked at Petrovich and barked once. A moment later the fireworks started. Petrovich marveled at how the animal had been able to sense it. Moordenaar looked up into the dark night sky and a low rumble began deep in his chest. Petrovich followed the dog's lead and looked up. He saw nothing at first. Then he thought he saw a small red flash, but it was only for a fraction of a second. Almost immediately, just as Moordenaar was about to let loose a loud series of barks signaling alarm, Petrovich heard a splatting sound. The huge beast fell dead at his feet, a hole in the top of his head oozing blood. More blood flowed from a much larger exit hole in its chest.

Petrovich snapped his head up and thought he saw another brief red flash. An instant later a hollow-point slug from a 220 grain Remington .300 Ultra Mag bullet tore through his forehead and blew out the back of his skull. Within seconds all four patrolling guards and their Boerboels lay dead. Death had come from the inky sky above.

It was a relatively still summer night except for the fireworks display underway at a neighboring estate. Four dark colored parachutes drifted earthward. Two of them were larger tandem chutes. Whalen and Stensen were harnessed in one, with Whalen deploying the drogue chute. Because they had jumped from the chopper at low altitude, Whalen quickly deployed the main chute and maneuvered it through the descent to provide stability for Stensen. It was Stensen's job to take out two of the patrolling guards along with their dogs. Larsen maneuvered the other tandem chute harnessed to Thomas, whose job was to terminate the other two guards and their animals.

The two shooters, Stensen and Thomas, each used a Remington Model M24E1/XM2010 rifle equipped with an AN/PVS-22 Universal Night

Sight mounted on a Picatinny rail along with an in-line 10x42 Leupold Ultra M3A telescopic sight. Their weapons were of the same type that Federov had used earlier that morning. Stensen and Thomas were better shots.

As Whalen maneuvered the chute for maximum stability, he heard Stensen softly singing "The Ballad of the Green Berets".

"Fighting soldiers from the sky"

He knew Stensen was doing it out of sense of irony. That was Stensen.

"Fearless men who jump and die"

He nudged Stensen with his knee and the singing stopped. Looking at the movement of the guards and their dogs on the ground below, he said, "What kind of dogs are those?"

"Big, ugly ones. And dead too." Stensen squeezed off his first round.

Almost instantly, one of the dogs slammed face first into the ground. Whalen was glad the dogs weren't German Shepherds. Other than wolves, they were the smartest animals he had ever seen. Smarter than most of the humans he knew. And more reliable.

Whalen and Larsen each wore enhanced night vision goggles (ENVG) mounted on their helmets. The devices incorporate image intensification and long wave infrared sensors designed for optimal night operations. They were obtained for them by McCoy from a military colleague who supervised an experimental weaponry lab. The devices were necessary because night jumps typically finish in the Dark Zone, the last one hundred feet or so. The closer the jumper gets to the ground, the darker the ground becomes. This makes it difficult, if not impossible, to judge the distance and anticipate impact. Below the hundred-foot mark it's similar to landing in a black hole. The goggles make it possible to eliminate this problem.

Almeida and Kirkland jumped individually. None of the others had confidence in Almeida's ability to maintain stability while maneuvering a tandem chute with a sniper harnessed to him. He also was not the same caliber of marksman that Thomas and Stensen were. He was to land near the separate caretaker's bungalow and additional guest quarters located on the other side of a small lake across from the main house. His job was to neutralize anyone occupying either structure.

Kirkland, the team's resident technology expert, again had responsibility for jamming cell phone operations, just as he had during the rescue of Levell from the Warehouse in Richmond. Equally important, he also was to cripple the generator that supplied Laski's home with auxiliary power.

He jumped slightly ahead of the other five and dropped in very close to a wall of the main house. This enabled him to take out the power supply before the others reached the effective range of the infrared heat sensors. Kirkland's specially designed clothing would protect him. It was constructed similarly to the ghillie suits he and the others had worn in their training exercise with the Army Rangers in North Carolina.

Levell, with the assistance of certain other members of the Team, had arranged for the electrical power to the estate to be shut off at Zero Hour plus five. By that point in time, Whelan and the others would be on the ground and in position to begin the assault. And Kirkland would have jammed the phone signals and destroyed the power feed from the generator.

The fireworks began on the neighboring property at precisely Zero Hour. Their sounds would drown out gunfire. Within five minutes, Whelan, Larsen, Thomas and Stensen were deployed at entrances to the main house. Almeida was positioned at the guest cottage. On the east side of the main structure, Kirkland had strategically placed a small charge of C-4 explosive compound between the conduit that was affixed to the wall of the house and the wall itself. The conduit acted as a protective cover for the electrical wires that ran from the generator buried in a concrete vault to the main switchbox in the house. When he was finished, Kirkland placed a detonator in the C-4. He moved swiftly along the wall and took refuge behind the thick trunk of a tree. At precisely Zero plus five, the outside electrical supply to the estate was shut down and Kirkland detonated the C-4 charge with a remote signal and activated the jamming device. The entire ten-acre estate was plunged into darkness. Without electricity, the landlines were inoperative. All cell phone signals were being jammed.

The interior of the house exploded in chaos. Some of the Ukrainian guards began firing indiscriminately at doors and windows. Maksym grabbed Laski and Morris and, despite the pitch-black environment, shoved them into the panic room that was connected to the library. He shouted at Laski in Russian, "Do not open the door for anyone but me."

Maksym moved swiftly by feel and memory to the library entrance off the hallway. "Use your NVGs!" he screamed in Ukrainian at the guards. The random gunfire stopped as the guards slipped on the night vision goggles that had been provided to them and powered them up.

The house became very still for a few moments. Maksym's mind was racing to connect the dots. What had happened to the power? Why hadn't the auxiliary generator kicked in? Why had the patrolling guards and their dogs not raised an alarm if someone was on the grounds? Why had the men monitoring the cameras and infrared sensors not reported security breaches? When his NVGs had powered up, he slipped his head around the corner of the library doorway and checked out the hallway.

The guard posted just inside the front entrance turned and looked at Maksym, He started to give a thumbs up sign to indicate he saw or heard nothing. At that moment, the massive front door blew inward off its hinges striking the man. He was killed instantly. Smoke and dust swirled around the opening where the door had been. Maksym pointed the muzzle of his HK

UMP45 submachine gun at the former doorway and emptied a thirty round clip.

A small object sailed through the smoke that appeared to have a greenish hue, made so by the NVGs. The goggles purposely turned the scenery into shades of green, as the human eye can detect more variations of that color than any other. The object, an M84 flashbang or stun grenade, detonated, emitting an enormous bang in the 170 to 180 decibel range. It was accompanied by a blinding flash equal to more than the power of one million candles. When detonated close enough to a human being, it causes brief flash blindness, confusion and loss of coordination and balance by disturbing the fluid in the inner ear.

The M84 is an ideal weapon for close quarters combat. It also produces concussion effects in enclosed areas, disabling occupants of those areas and temporarily preventing resistance to attackers entering the room.

Maksym was far enough away from the blast that it only had a modest and very temporary effect on him. He slipped back into the library and replaced the spent magazine in his weapon. He looked for a moment at the library window. The thought occurred to him that maybe the game was up. Perhaps he should leap through the window and try to make his escape. On the other hand, he admitted that he had no idea how large the assault force was. Perhaps it *was* an entire company of Marines or Rangers. He could be jumping from the frying pan into the fire. Better to see how strong the assault force was, he thought. The window was always an option.

He heard the sounds of glass breaking in other parts of the house. He suspected more flashbang grenades had been thrown through various windows. This quickly was confirmed when he heard the concussions and saw brief, but brilliant, flashes in doorways and stairwells. He knew the enemy, whoever it was, would be storming into the house through doors and windows under cover of the flashbangs. He peered around the jamb of the library door again. The NVGs made the movement awkward.

Someone in the blown out entranceway, shielded by the smoke and dust of the explosion, laid down a field of fire with an automatic weapon. Deadly slugs snapped past Maksym's ear like a swarm of bloodthirsty hornets. He stuck the muzzle of his HK around the corner and emptied the new magazine in the direction of the entranceway. He doubted firing blindly would have much effect.

He heard two loud blasts in rapid succession and recognized the sound of shotguns being fired. Maksym dropped to the floor and sneaked a quick look around the doorjamb. The two men who had been operating the monitors in a room between the library and the entranceway lay motionless in the hallway. He could tell by the positions their bodies had assumed that they were dead.

The two men had run into the hallway, weapons at the ready, to repel invaders. At the same moment, Brendan Whelan had burst through the entranceway with cover fire from Larsen's MP5 SD. With Whelan's genetic makeup, he was much quicker to react than Maksym's two men. He put a blast into each man's chest at close range with his Kel-Tec KSG shotgun. It was the weapon of choice for Whelan and most of his colleagues for close quarters combat. The downward ejecting KSG weighs just less than seven pounds with a 26.1-inch overall length and an 18.5-inch cylinder bore barrel. The feature they most appreciated about the weapon was the internal dual tube magazine capable of holding seven rounds of 12 gauge 2-3/4-inch shells in each tube. It had a total capacity of fifteen shells including one in the chamber.

The sounds of flashbang grenades mixed with the chatter of HK UMP45s and the responding roars of KSGs came from other parts of the huge home. Like he and Larsen, Whalen knew that Thomas, Stensen and Kirkland were moving from room to room, killing everyone who resisted and everyone who didn't. The ENVGs, stun grenades and Kel-Tecs, along with their genetically superior quickness and intelligence gave them an advantage over Laski's security force. In the small space of the rooms they occupied, the disorienting effect of the flashbangs left the Ukrainians temporarily helpless. Before they could recover, they were gunned down by the Kel-Tecs.

Whelan saw a head wearing NVGs glance around a doorjamb down the hall. He snapped off a round from his shotgun, but the head disappeared in time to avoid the blast. The pellets did chew a chunk out of the fine-grain wood case molding. Whelan noted the quickness with which his intended victim had moved. Was it Maksym, he wondered. Expecting whomever it was to slip his weapon around the jamb and fire blindly down the hall, Whelan pumped another shell into the chamber and fired at the same spot he had seen the head. It ripped off another piece of the molding along with a chunk of the adjoining wall.

He ducked into the room where the monitors were located and chambered another round. Larsen slipped in right behind him.

"We've got an unfriendly down the hall. The room on the left, two doors down." He paused and sneaked a quick glance down the hallway. "I think it might be Maksym."

Larsen nodded and a tight little smile played across his lips. It was his sinister smile, known to cause sphincter failure in lesser men. "Plan?" he said.

"Go around to the library window and put several rounds through it. High, just so he knows he can't get out that way." Whelan glanced around the jamb and began firing rounds down the hall to discourage anyone from exiting the library, and to provide cover for Larsen. He stepped back into the room, reached over with his left hand and switched to the second magazine.

Moments later he heard Larsen's MP5 SD spitting bullets through the library window. He edged cautiously down the hall with the thick recoil pad pressed firmly against his right shoulder, sighting over the barrel through the folding iron sights. He stopped about a foot short of the doorway, reached around and tossed a flashbang into the room. For good measure, he waited a couple of seconds after the blast and followed it up with a second grenade.

He slid down the wall. Then, quickly spinning around what was left of the doorjamb, he swept the room with the muzzle of his KSG. Maksym was sprawled beneath the large library table. His powerful body was jerking spasmodically. Blood was oozing from his nose and ears. A Norm, Whelan thought, would have been killed by the blasts. What did this say about Maksym? He remembered Levell's comments made earlier that evening.

Larsen leapt over the jagged windowsill and landed deftly on the balls of both feet. "Kill him?" he said, motioning at Maksym's writhing form with the muzzle of his MP5 SD.

Whalen shook his head. "Not yet."

He handed his Kel-Tec to Larsen, reached under the table and grabbed Maksym by the collar, dragging him out. A woozy Maksym swung a clumsy roundhouse right at Whelan, who easily blocked it with his left forearm and crashed a hard right hook into the left side of the man's jaw. Maksym's knees buckled. Whelan tossed him several feet into a portion of the bookshelves. Maksym slid slowly to the floor, as tomes rained down on him. He just sat there, slumped against a bookshelf with a stunned look on his face. Larsen stepped closer to him. He had slung the MP 5 over his left shoulder and had his SIG SAUER P226 Tactical Operations pistol in his right hand. He loved the heft and feel of the black, hard-anodized frame of lightweight alloy and its polymer Magwell grips. The fifteen round super capacity magazines also were a plus. He pointed the weapon at the middle of Maksym's broad chest and smiled his bad smile.

Thomas, Stensen, and Kirkland entered the room together. "The target has been secured," Kirkland said. "No more unfriendlies. Jamming has been terminated. Power will be back on any moment." He looked at Maksym. "We going to kill him too?"

"Not yet," Whalen said. He looked around. "What's Rafe's status?"

The three newcomers looked at each other and shrugged. As they did, the power was restored and the library lights came up.

"Shit," Whalen said. He pressed the push-to-talk or PTT button of his lightweight tactical headset and spoke into its noise canceling adjustable boom microphone. "This is Alpha Dog One. What's your status Alpha Dog Six?" There was no response. He tried several more times, but the results were the same.

He turned to Stensen and Kirkland. "Find the little bastard. And do it quickly." He paused then said, "If he's been terminated, bring the body back. We'll take it with us in the extraction."

The two men nodded and left. Whalen pulled the secure satcom from a cargo pocket and spoke into it. "Kennel One, this is Alpha Dog One. The Snake Pit is secure."

There was a slight crackling sound on the receiver then Levell said, "Roger that, Alpha Dog One. We can see that via satellite feed. What's the casualty situation?"

"Unfriendlies have been neutralized. Your friend from the warehouse is in custody."

"What about your unit?"

"Jury's out on Alpha Dog Six. He's MIA. Alpha Dogs Three and Five are searching for him."

There was a brief pause at Levell's end then he said, "You haven't mentioned the status of the priority target."

"No sign of the priority target yet. As we suspected, he's probably in the panic room."

"What is your position now?"

"The library."

"Good. As you know from the plans we reviewed, the entrance to the panic room is behind the bookshelf in the far right corner of the library."

"Roger that."

"Get his worthless ass out of there asap. The chopper with the extraction team is on schedule." With that, Levell hung up.

Whelan stuck the satcom back into a cargo pocket of his battle dress uniform and glanced at his watch. They had less than ten minutes until extraction time. He turned to Maksym who was still sitting on the floor surrounded by fallen books. "We gotta job for you," he said.

"Fuck you. I do not fear any of you." He sneered as he said it.

"Wouldn't expect you to fear us. That's not what people in your line of work are about." Whelan paused for effect. "But there is a finite point somewhere between life and death that's almost too difficult for the mind to conjure."

"What, you are scaring me now with tales of boogie man? You are wasting your breath."

"You're the one who needs to be concerned about his breath. You may not have much left."

For a few moments, Maksym stared sullenly at Whalen then Whalen said, "You have options. There are some people who would like to have you kept alive, for interrogation purposes."

Larsen said, "And then there are people like me, who would love to jack a round through your miserable skull."

Maksym shrugged to indicate his indifference.

"Or, there is Alpha Dog Three," Larsen said, in reference to Stensen, "who lives for the thrill of killing people he despises, people like you. He'll take days to kill you, inflicting indescribable pain and horror. You'll be begging him to kill you long before he ever takes a mind to do it."

Maksym's head swiveled on his thick neck and he looked up at Larsen. "You are talking about the one called Stensen. We know of him. He is insane. The devil is in him."

"Probably worse than that," Whelan said.

"Laski is not alone in the panic room," Maksym said. "Senator Howard Morris is with him."

Whelan and Larsen exchanged quick glances. Each man thought the same thing: two birds with one stone.

"If I help you get them from the room, my reward is to spend my life in a maximum security prison being subjected to torture and round the clock interrogation techniques, yes?" He did not sound enthused.

"It's a life," Larsen said.

"And if I refuse to be of assistance to you, you will let your insane comrade butcher me."

"No," Whelan said. "We don't have time for that. Instead, I will shoot you in both knees and both elbows. You won't be able to run or to drag yourself out of the way."

"The way of what?"

"The door to the panic room is made of steel reinforced concrete. It's behind those books." He pointed to the far right corner of the room. "We have C-4. We'll prop your sorry, shot-up ass against the door and blow it open. If the explosion doesn't kill you, the door falling on you will."

Maksym's eyes narrowed in thought. He had escaped the clutches of the Team once before. Perhaps he could do it again. What he needed to do now was buy time and wait for the right opportunity.

Whelan said, "Time is short. What's it gonna be, Slick, the lady or the tiger?"

"I will help you," Maksym said.

Stensen and Kirkland returned. Almeida was slung over one of Stensen's thick shoulders. His right pant leg was drenched in blood.

"He alive?" Whelan said.

"Yes, I'm fuckin' alive," Almeida said with a grunt. The pain in his voice was clear.

"What's his status?" Whalen said to Kirkland.

"Gunshot wound to the upper right leg. He's losing blood, but he'll make it if the extraction is on time."

He looked at Almeida and said, "What happened?"

Through clenched teeth, the other man said, "The guest quarters were empty, but the fuckin' caretaker was at home in his place. He must have seen me crossing over from the guest house, grabbed a weapon and fired at me." He paused for a moment than said, "He ain't ever gonna do that again. I was happy to kill that sonofabitch. 'Nother inch over and his slug woulda' blown off most of my world famous python. Women everywhere woulda' cried for months."

"Python? Is that what you call that little twinkie?" Stensen said, as he unloaded Almeida on the library table none too gently.

"Sounds to me like he's hallucinating. Must be post traumatic shock," Kirkland said.

"Fuck you fuckin' wiseasses. At least *I* got a battle souvenir." Behind the pain, there was a definite sense of triumph in his voice.

"Only because you're too slow to avoid getting shot," Stensen said.

"Alright, that's enough banter, girls," Whelan said. "We have a precise timetable to meet if we want to get out of here ahead of the excitement that's sure to ensue."

He turned to Maksym and pulled him to his feet then shoved him to the area of the bookshelf that disguised the door to the panic room. "Work your magic, Merlin. And, just so you know, several of us enjoy some degree of fluency in Russian."

Covered by several weapons, Maksym pulled on a section of the bookshelf. It swung outward on carefully hidden hinges to reveal a door set flush with the concrete wall. To the right of the door there was a callbox built into the wall. Maksym held down the PPT button and said in Russian, "Chaim, it is me, Maksym. All is clear now. We have repelled the attackers."

Laski's voice, sounding metallic, came through the speaker in the callbox. "Are you zure it is zafe to emerge? What if there are others?"

Maksym sighed. "There are no others. We have checked. This place is secure now. Do not act like little girl; come out."

There was a long pause followed by an audible click, and the door began to move inward along a slow arc. Larsen grabbed Maksym and pulled him back so that he no longer was in front of the door. He did not want him to leap through the door and reshut it. While they could use the C-4 to blow it, it would take too much time. The timing of the extraction was very precise.

When the door had opened far enough, Whelan nodded at Thomas and Kirkland. They burst through the doorway into the vault. Moments later they emerged, dragging Laski and Morris. When they saw what their situation was, both men stared at their captors in shock.

Laski looked around the badly damaged room and said in his accented English, "What haff you done to my house, my beautiful house?" He sounded as if he was about to cry. Then he saw Maksym, bruised and bloodied. "You haff betrayed me," he said incredulously. "After all I haff done for you? How could you do ziss to me?" Maksym smiled at the old man, but his eyes were cold and devoid of emotion.

Whelan looked at Thomas and Kirkland and motioned toward the library door with his head. The two men began shoving Laski and Morris out of the room and down the hallway following Whalen. Stensen slung a loudly complaining Almeida over a shoulder and brought up the rear. At the end of the hallway was Laski's glassed-in sunroom. Most of the glass had been blown out when Kirkland had preceded his entrance with a flashbang grenade. Parts of the carpet and upholstered furniture had been charred.

Kirkland shoved Laski roughly into one of the chairs. A moment later Thomas did likewise with Morris, pushing him into a badly damaged loveseat facing Laski. Stensen deposited Almeida in a comfortable looking chair near the entrance from the hallway. Thomas and Larsen focused their weapons on Maksym. The look on Thomas' face left no doubt about his thoughts. Maksym had gotten the drop on him at the warehouse and had injured him. He felt humiliated by it and longed for the opportunity for vengeance. His finger was tight on the trigger, his body tense. If Maksym so much as belched, Thomas would feed him several loads from his KSG.

Whelan glanced at Kirkland and Stensen and nodded. As they left the room, he turned back to Laski, whose eyes were opened wide with fear in a face grown very pale.

"I zink I know who you are," Laski said. "You are zose people Harold Case knew, za vuns dey call za Sleeping Dogs, yes?"

Whelan nodded. "Thanks principally to you, Case, and the senator we're no longer sleeping. We're wide-awake. And there's a price to be paid for that."

Laski seemed to perk up. He detected that the conversation had entered an area he knew very well. "Price? I can pay price. I am vealthy man. I haff billions. Name your price. I can pay," he said, hope rising in his voice.

Whelan shook his head. "There is no price. This time your wealth can't help you."

Laski's voice took on a pleading tone. "But zere iss alvays a price. Und I can pay it." He paused then said, "Und vee vill forget all about ziss affair. Even za zenator." He looked at Morris and said, "Yes, Zenator?"

Morris just stared at Laski, his face contorted in fear. A large wet spot was spreading across the crotch of his trousers. The smell of fecal matter began to waft through the room.

"The senator is having sphincter issues. I don't think he'll be of much help to you."

"Bu...but," Laski stuttered, "he iss zenator of United Ztates. Surely you vould not harm him."

"He isn't our objective. You are."

Laski sagged back into his chair, seemingly defeated for the first time in his life. He looked over at Maksym. The other man again smiled his cold, empty smile. Then Laski thought of something that raised his spirits. There were eighteen Ukrainians in Maksym's security force. It seemed illogical to assume Maksym would be so calm under the circumstances, unless he was confident that some of his men survived. Laski knew Maksym was brilliant; therefore, he must have had a plan for a situation like this. Surely, his men would counterattack at any moment and kill these invaders. They just needed a little more time.

A crafty look came over Laski's wrinkled face. "Zo, tell me, my friend, who it vass zat zent you."

"You're a very smart man, Laski. You can figure it out."

Laski tipped his head to one side and said, "No doubt it vass our old adverzary, Clifford Levell."

Whelan gave no response, either verbal or physical.

"Yes, of course it vass him. Und his fellow compatriots vith zo-called Team."

It was playing out just as Levell had said it would. Laski would stall for time in hopes that some members of his security force still survived. He would expect them to storm into the room at any minute, guns blazing. Whelan remembered Levell's words: "Laski has been a major player in deceiving the majority of Americans into settling for the path of least resistance; to foolishly trade personal freedoms for a promise of endless largesse from the central government. He has helped to raise their hopes for a pain free life of ease, when the reality of it is that they've made a pact with the devil. In the final act, it's only fitting that we allow his hopes to rise before we terminate him."

Kirkland and Stensen reentered the room. Entwined in the fingers of their hands were long greasy strands of hair attached to the severed heads of Maksym's security men. They dropped the heads in front of Laski.

He shrank back in his chair in horror. After a few moments, he leaned slowly forward and looked at the heads, silently counting them. Sixteen. Two men must still be alive, he thought. He glanced hopefully at Maksym. The same empty smile returned to the other man's face, but his head slowly moved back and forth.

Kirkland again left the room momentarily. He returned with two additional heads. "Looking for these?" he said and dropped them at Laski's feet.

It was the final blow. All hope now was gone. Laski collapsed back into his seat and began to sob. "Plees, I am an old man. I never intended to harm any vun. I vas only following orders."

"Free will," Whelan said.

"Vhat?"

"You always had the option not to work for the Russians. It might have been more difficult and taken longer, but with your intelligence and prowess in the world of finance, you would have succeeded eventually. Maybe you wouldn't have accumulated quite as much wealth, but it would have been more than enough."

Laski stared at him. "Don't kill me, plees. I can help you. I know who zee Russians are. Zey are led by a man named...."

"Federov," Whelan said.

Laski looked stunned.

"He's nothing more than a handler. There are many others above his pay grade."

"But I vill use my vealth to counter zeir efforts." He looked at Whelan hopefully

"It doesn't work like that. Their efforts have been underway for decades. The disease has penetrated the cells of this county's vital organs. It will take more than a generation to exorcise it. If, in fact, it can be exorcised."

Whelan looked at Stensen and said, "It's time."

The red areas in the other man's eyes were dilated well beyond mere dots. He stepped up to Laski and said, "Open wide."

Laski, paralyzed by fear, just looked at him. Stensen swiftly jammed the barrel of his Kel-Tec shotgun into Laski's mouth, breaking teeth and wedging the man's tongue back into his throat.

Thomas purposely kept his gaze focused on Maksym.

Stensen squeezed the trigger and most of Laski's head disappeared in a shower of blood, bone splinters and brain goo. Thomas never looked away from Maksym. The captive winced. It was the first time he had experienced emotion in a very long while. Morris fainted and fell out of the loveseat. Kirkland picked him up and threw him back into it. He slapped the senator until he regained consciousness.

Stensen pumped a new round into the chamber, shoved the barrel down the stump of Laski's throat and fired another load. He grabbed a charred section of drapery and wiped blood and goo off the barrel.

Whelan turned to Morris who was curled in a fetal position.

In a quavering, high-pitched voice he just kept repeating, "Oh my God, oh my God."

"Give it a rest, Senator. It's not your time...yet. Without Laski funneling money to you and the organizations that support you and others like you, you're finished. Even more, what you've experienced here will haunt you for the rest of your life. You'll never stop looking over your shoulder, and you'll never be the same cocky little bastard again." Whelan paused then said, "You won't even win reelection to the Senate."

Through the broken out glass panes, they could hear the very quiet sound of the stealth chopper approaching for the extraction.

"Time to move." Whalen said. "The train is pulling into the station."

70 GUAM

The island of Guam rises out of the western Pacific south of Japan and east of the Philippines, or about three-quarters of the way from Hawaii to the Philippines. At two hundred twelve square miles it is the largest island in the Mariana island chain as well as all of Micronesia. It is the southernmost and oldest island, at thirty million years, in the Marianas chain. The first European to discover the islands was Ferdinand Magellan on March 6, 1521, during the course of the historic circumnavigation of the earth.

The islands are part of an arc-shaped archipelago consisting of the tops of fifteen volcanic mountains. They are part of a geologic structure known as the Izu-Bonin-Mariana Arc system, which forms the boundary between two tectonic plates. As the edge of the oceanic Pacific Plate, the largest of all the tectonic plates on Earth, continues its inexorable journey west, it encounters the eastern edge of the continental Mariana Plate. The heavier oceanic crust is subducted, or pushed to the bottom and the lighter continental crust is pushed upward.

Among other things, this results in two geological developments. The combination of the upward thrust of the Mariana Plate and volcanism resulting from subduction of water trapped in minerals created a submerged mountain range that extends more than one thousand five hundred miles from Guam to a point near Tokyo. The tips of these mountains form the Marianas. The subducted oceanic crust, in turn, created the Mariana Trench just east of the island chain. This is the deepest part of the Earth's oceans and lowest part of its crust. Despite its depth, the trench is relatively narrow at forty-three miles, but overall is one hundred twenty times the size of the Grand Canyon. At thirty-six thousand feet, the deepest point in the Mariana Trench is Challenger Deep, which is approximately two hundred and fifteen miles southwest of Guam. It was named after the HMS Challenger II, which discovered it in 1948.

The United State's Andersen Air Force Base occupies much of the northern portion of Guam. The central portion of the island is the most developed with Hagåtña, the capital, and the tourist areas around Tumon Bay. It is the southerly part that many people believe is the most scenic territory on the island; a rural kaleidoscope of small, ancient settlements, breathtaking waterfalls and unspoiled beaches.

Whelan and his five colleagues had arrived on Guam three days after the events on Labor Day. The stealth chopper had whisked them to a private airfield near Morgantown, West Virginia. From there, a civilian cargo plane had flown them to San Francisco. While aboard the flight, each man had been carefully disguised by professionals. They also had been provided with assumed identities as members of a delegation representing an electronics manufacturer. From San Francisco, they had flown commercial to Antonio B. Won Pat International Airport on Guam. Because of the connecting flight originated in Honolulu, they easily passed through customs.

A battered, plain vanilla motor coach had taken them from the airport to a tired and cramped bungalow in the village of Santa Rita. The men didn't care. The lengthy nonstop travel, combined with their activities leading up to and including Labor Day, had left all of them exhausted. They each had experienced far worse hardships and were glad just to have a place where they could pause for a few days.

They spent their time relaxing and taking turns protecting the native Chamorro women from Almeida's predatory intentions. And they ate. A local Chamorro woman came by three times a day and prepared meals for them. For the most part, they found the native cuisine to be very much to their liking, especially the chicken *kelaguen* - shredded chicken marinated in a sauce of lemon juice, fresh coconut, green onions, salt and hot red chilies. It was served at room temperature and eaten over red rice or wrapped in a warm tortilla or *titiyas*. It typically was served with *finadene,* a salty, spicy, sour condiment made of soy sauce, vinegar or lemon juice, chopped white onion, and fresh chilies used in Chamorro cuisine.

Guam is a territory administered by the United States government. It's divided into nineteen areas commonly referred to as villages. The modest bungalow they were staying in was located in an area known as Santa Rita, on the southwest coast of the island with hills overlooking Apra Harbor. It was a peaceful, quiet area. Whelan and Thomas had engaged in a philosophical discussion about the possible reasons why the village was named after the patron saint of abused wives. The topic of wives caused him to think about Caitlin and his sons in Ireland. It was early September and he had been home the previous month. Not even thirty days had passed, but it seemed like years.

On the morning of the third day of their sojourn in Santa Rita, the battered motor coach returned. This time it carried scuba gear, as well as highly sophisticated and exotic communications equipment. The six men boarded the coach leaving behind just about everything they had brought with them, which wasn't much.

The coach rattled and bumped over the spine of the mountainous interior then south along the coast road through Inarajan, the best preserved of the Spanish era villages. The scenery was stunningly beautiful. The mountains formed magnificent verdant backdrops for the little coastal towns interspersed between long stretches of pristine beaches.

Ultimately, they reached their objective. Merizo is a modest village located on the coast beneath the ancient volcanic hills of southern Guam. It is the southernmost village in Guam. The coach stopped at the Merizo Pier. It was a spot from which tourists could catch ferries to Cocos Island. Moored at the end of the pier, an old commercial fishing boat rocked gently in the warm Pacific waters. It looked as if it had seen far better days. The reality was that it had a new and powerful engine and was capable of cruising at more than twenty knots.

The men piled out of the coach and began loading the diving and communications gear aboard the vessel. When they were finished, they all climbed aboard the sixty-foot ship. Larsen took the wheel and powered the vessel up. Stensen and Thomas cast off the bow and stern lines, and they headed out to sea and assumed a southwesterly bearing. The sea was calm as they cruised through the long, full Pacific rollers, but ahead of them the sky was darkening. Whelan wondered if it was an omen of things to come.

Sixty minutes later, he picked up a secure satcom and spoke to Levell. "We're under way, about an hour out."

"Roger that. Maintain your course as planned."

"Is the rancher after the wolves?" This was a coded reference to any entity that might be pursuing them.

"Yes. If our timing is right, the interception should occur as planned."

"What's this 'if' shit? The timing had better be right. We won't get a second chance."

"Relax. Everything is right on schedule." There was a pause at Levell's end then he said, "Regarding our friend Maksym, something's come up that you should know."

"Does this have something to do with the DNA tests you ordered run on his blood samples from the warehouse in Richmond?"

"You do connect the dots very quickly."

"It wasn't so difficult. I knew you wanted us to take him alive. So what is it you think I need to know, that he's genetically advanced like we are?"

"Yes. But it's more complicated than that."

"How complicated?"

Again there was a long pause before Levell responded. "I know you remember what motivated your family to emigrate to this country from Ireland."

"Yes. I was less than a year old. My parents lost their only other child, my older brother."

"And your mother was having a great deal of difficulty dealing with it."

"Yes, they both had relatives who had immigrated to the States. My father thought they could be a positive influence, and that a complete change of environment also might help the healing process."

"Have you ever thought about what might have happened to that brother?"

"Given that he most likely was abducted by a pedophile, sexually abused and murdered, why would I want to think about it?"

Another pause at Levell's end then he said, "Because he wasn't killed. Maksym is your brother."

The statement so stunned Whelan that it took a moment for him to respond. "What!" He spit the word out like it was burning a hole through his tongue.

"The DNA report is preliminary, but the evidence doesn't lie. He's your long lost brother."

Whelan was too shocked and confused to respond.

"Look," Levell said, "I've been worrying on this like a dog on a bone, debating whether I should tell you or not."

"So why didn't you tell me sooner?"

"I didn't want to risk compromising your effectiveness during the mission at the Snake Pit. I was concerned that such knowledge might affect your judgment, your reaction time in a face-to-face confrontation. It could even have adversely affected the mission overall."

Whelan was quiet for a few moments. "What do you plan to do with him?"

Now it was Levell who didn't respond immediately. "We had planned to interrogate him then terminate him…with extreme prejudice."

Whelan thought about this for a moment. "What do you mean 'had planned'?"

Levell cleared his throat. "It seems the man has escaped once again."

"Great," Whelan said with sarcasm. "Now I find out I've got a brother who is diametrically opposed to, and hell bent on destroying, the things I hold dear. Then to top it off, I learn that he's still on the loose."

"We're using all resources available to try to locate him. I don't want him out there anymore than you do."

359

"Yeah? Well there is a small difference. He's not your brother."

"What's your point? You think he'll come after you?"

"I don't know what *he'll* do, but if I were in his shoes, I'd hunt him down and kill him…and his family."

Levell's voice sounded sincere and calm. "But he's *not* you. I don't know anyone else who is. Sometimes you scare the shit out of me, and I've seen just about everything."

"He and I have the same genes, the same blood. Think about it."

71 WASHINGTON, D.C.

Mitch Christie stood looking out the sliver of window in his office at FBI headquarters in Washington. It was about eight o'clock in the morning and he had spent another restless, lonely night. He and his wife were seeing a marriage counselor now, but they still were not living in the same house. The kids seemed to be adjusting to the situation, and Debbie had yet to indicate that things were improving between them. He, on the other hand, was a physical and emotional wreck. He had switched from the over-the-counter Mylanta to a powerful drug, lansoprazole. It had been prescribed for him by his physician along with an antibiotic regimen and an anti-anxiety drug. It seemed to be helping his stomach, but he felt that he was losing his ability to focus. Was it a side effect of the drugs, or was it something much more sinister? Christie feared that on top of everything else he could lose his job for inability to perform.

Outside his minimal window the mugginess was almost palpable. The window was still partially misted from the effect of the heavily saturated air outside making contact with the glass surface, which was cooled by the building's overly efficient air conditioning system. The chilled exterior surface of the window drew moisture from the humid outside air, forming tiny droplets. Although it was early, not quite eight o'clock in the morning, the dog days of summer had embraced Foggy Bottom in a mean grip. The combination of heat and humidity had pushed the heat index above the one hundred mark for the past several days. You couldn't even walk across the street without your shirt sticking to you like a second layer of skin.

Washington is in the Eastern Daylight Time zone in early September. The sun rises shortly before 7 a.m. Christie watched the light of a new day softly filling the landscape beyond his window. After several quiet moments, he turned and slowly settled into his desk chair.

Where to begin, he thought. He idly shuffled some papers around on his desk, stared at them for a few moments, and then, dissatisfied, readjusted them. Thoughts were tumbling through his head. His marriage. His future with the Bureau. Life after the Bureau. His future no longer seemed promising. And it all seemed to begin less than a year ago. With the Harold Case shooting and the arrival on the scene of Brendan Whelan. That damn Whelan.

He leaned back in his chair and tilted his head back against the headrest. Staring at the ceiling of his office, he tried to focus on the recent events that seemed to have involved Whelan. He thought about the strange calls he had received from the man who called himself Maksym. What had the man promised? That "evil men" were going to do a "bad thing". Were Whelan and his associates the evil men? Was the attempted assassination of the president the bad thing?

Forensics was positive that the two dead men in Room 333 of the Hotel L'Orange had not fired the sniper weapon found there. Their deaths appeared to be the result of a murder/suicide. Ballistics had positively identified the sniper rifle as the weapon that wounded the president and killed the attorney general. Despite an almost immediate shut down of the area, no suspects had been apprehended. Hell, the Bureau, working with the Metropolitan PD and the Secret Service, hadn't even been able to identify possible suspects. The act clearly had been done by a person or persons who were very skilled in this type of work. In Christie's mind, Whelan and his colleagues certainly had received the training and experience for something like this. But that was twenty years ago. Would they still have that same level of skills?

And then there was the matter of the slaughter and destruction at Chaim Laski's estate in Potomac. That certainly had the look of a project that Whelan and the others could have pulled off. But why the severed heads? Why the mutilation of Laski's body? And what was the connection between the Ukrainians at Laski's and the two dead men at the Hotel L'Orange? The common thread was that they all were undocumented Ukrainian aliens.

As for Whelan, it appeared that the Bureau had gotten lucky for a change where he was concerned. Anonymous tips from several sources had been received over the past twenty-four hours. It appeared that the Irishman and his colleagues had managed to escape the country. Their elusiveness didn't surprise Christie. The tips were continuing to come in. Hopefully they were reliable and would lead to the fugitives' location.

The joint Bureau, Secret Service and Police Task Force investigating the assassination attempt had issued a standing order to terminate them on sight with extreme prejudice. Internally, the task force members realized that they might never find or prove who really was behind the attempt on the president. Nevertheless they needed to pin the deed on someone, and they needed to do it very quickly. Whelan and the others were ideal targets. They had been under a similar shoot on sight edict two decades earlier and had escaped, and that order was still in effect. It didn't appear that they had any political or economic standing that would mitigate their situation. In other words, they were ideal candidates for framing.

Christie had not been included as a member of the task force. He interpreted this as a sign that his superiors had lost confidence in his abilities. Even though he was the Bureau's foremost expert on Whelan and the others, he had chased the man for almost a year and never gotten close to catching him. There was a price to be paid for that failure.

His musings were interrupted suddenly as Aaron Rickover burst into his office and stood before his desk. Christie fixed him with a stern have-you-forgotten-how-to-knock look.

It didn't phase Rickover. He was excited almost to the point of breathlessness. Christie looked at him and thought, if Rickover was a little boy right now he'd be wetting his pants.

"Mitch, Mitch," Rickover said. His face was aglow with excitement.

"What has you so damn excited, kid? You and the wife expecting your first child?"

Rickover puzzled over that one for a second then stammered. "No, no. He…he's dead! We got 'em."

Christie's eyes narrowed and he leaned slightly forward in his chair as he looked at Rickover. "Slow down, kid. Who's dead?"

"That Whelan guy…and all his buddies. Isn't that great!"

Rickover's words momentarily stunned Christie. His jaw dropped and he quickly leaned forward in his chair, palms of his hands on the desktop. After a moment he said, "What the hell are you talking about? How? Where? When?"

Grinning broadly, the younger man said, "In Guam, they were in Guam."

"Guam? How did we find them in Guam?"

"The Joint Task Force received an anonymous tip. It wasn't traceable, but the caller said they were leaving Guam on an old fishing trawler."

"When was this?"

"Not more than an hour ago."

Christie's father had been an Air Force officer and Guam had been one of his duty posts when Christie was a youth. He knew there was a fourteen-hour time differential between the Eastern Daylight time zone, where Washington was located, and the Chamorro Standard time on Guam. He glanced at his watch. It was exactly eight o'clock. He did a fast mental calculation and realized it was ten o'clock in the evening on the island. That meant that the event that had Rickover so excited must have occurred at about nine o'clock at night on Guam.

"Give me the details," he said. "Was there a gunfight? Do they have bodies?"

Rickover's grin broadened. "It's even better than that. They blew them up."

Christie stared at Rickover, a puzzled look spreading across his face. "Blew them up where? How did they blow them up? And who in the hell is 'they'?"

"It was the Air Force. The Joint Task Force had the base on Guam scramble a couple of fighters. They found the boat about two hundred and twenty miles southwest of the island."

"And they just blew it up?"

"Yeah, something like that. The people on the boat fired a SAM. It was defective and flew off target. Then the jets returned ordnance and blew the boat to hell and back. Isn't that great!"

"Bodies? Any fucking bodies?" Christie's voice was almost a shout.

The grin faded from Rickover's face. "Well...not yet. The boat sank very quickly." He brightened again. "But they'll find some."

Christie sighed and leaned slowly back in his chair.

"What's wrong, Mitch? I thought you'd be excited about this. You've been after those bastards for a long time. And, and...they kidnapped your wife and kids."

Christie stared at the ceiling of his office for a few moments then looked at Rickover. "You're a well educated guy. Do you know what's approximately two hundred and twenty-five miles southwest of Guam?"

Rickover thought about it for a few moments than shook his head. "A lot of ocean?"

"You have no idea. It's the Challenger Deep, the deepest part of the Marianas Trench. That just happens to be the deepest part of any ocean anywhere on earth. Thirty-six thousand feet deep. You could stick Mount Everest in that hole and its peak would still be seven thousand feet from the surface of the Pacific."

Rickover gave him a puzzled look and shrugged. "Yeah, so? What are you getting at, Mitch?"

"Do you know what happened to Whelan and the others about twenty years ago?"

Rickover shrugged. "Not really."

"Do you know much about baseball, Aaron?"

After a moment, Rickover's face brightened. "Yeah, I know a little bit about it. My uncle Herb used to be a big fan. Talked about it a lot. Why?"

"Do you know who Yogi Berra is?"

Rickover thought about the question for a few moments then said, "Yeah, the cartoon bear in Jellystone Park. Right?" He was smiling like someone who had just aced an exam.

Christie just stared at Rickover for several seconds, shaking his head. Then he slowly turned his chair one hundred eighty degrees and looked out his misted sliver of a window.

He said softly to himself, "Déjà vu all over again."

72 NEW ORLEANS, LOUISIANA

New Orleans is not much of a tourist town in January once the Sugar Bowl game is over. It's cold, wet, and windy. The town doesn't come back to life until Mardi Gras, or Fat Tuesday. The earliest it rolls around is February 3, depending on the date of Easter Sunday in any given year. Large portions of the town are below sea level. Generations of the dead are buried in aboveground crypts because the water table is barely below the surface. A pernicious dampness permeates everything, contributing at times to a malodorous stench that hangs over the oldest parts of the town. Mildew, rot and mold thrive in the environment. It's a popular background for tales of vampires and other gothic horrors. The FBI's Uniform Crime Report for 2010 reported the murder rate in New Orleans was 10 times the national average. According to the report, the city had 175 murders that year, or 50 victims per 100,000 residents. Given those statistics, the local gentry found some measure of relief that the attempt on the president four months earlier had not happened in the Big Easy.

Daylight hours in New Orleans are in short supply in January while the sun vacations south of the equator. Business is slower in the bars and clubs along Bourbon Street. The old city seems to hold its fetid breath, as if saving its energies for the coming madness of Mardi Gras.

It was about nine o'clock on a cold, soggy night in early January. A dark haired, attractive woman smoking a cigarette rounded the corner from Bienville Street and strolled purposefully north in the three hundred block of Bourbon Street. The sidewalk was littered and uneven, paved with red bricks. The ancient and narrow street was lined with tired three and four story buildings adorned with ornate wrought iron balconies. The ground floors of the buildings were occupied by seedy-looking bars and lounges.

The woman's walk was provocative, as was her attire. She wore a very short black skirt and tight ivory colored sweater with a steeply plunging neckline. Her breasts were large and a lot of cleavage was on display. Fishnet stockings, a black leather purse slung over one shoulder on a long strap, and black shoes with six-inch stiletto heels completed her dress. The casual observer might assume she was a hooker trolling for her next john. That would be a false assumption, although in the same general ballpark.

Mid-block, the woman entered a bar. She smiled at the bouncer and ran her hand across the front of his pants on her way inside. He shook his head and said, "Nice to see you too, Leonie."

Inside, the bar was purposely kept very dark to hide its indiscretions as well as those of its patrons. It stank of decades of cheap whisky, tobacco, rot, and human smells. The woman took a seat at the midway point of the scarred, dark wood bar that spanned most of the back of the room. It was her favorite spot. From it, she could survey the entire room. She looked around and saw that business was very slow tonight. There was a young couple at a table, obviously tourists visiting the city during one of the cheapest times of the year. Two old men sat at another table, nursing their drinks and ogling the young waitresses. The women's full breasts seemed on the verge of bursting free from the very skimpy bra-like tops they wore. A chanteuse with a worn out voice was trying to sound enthusiastic about the rock songs she was bruising. Not only had her voice seen better days, but so had her body and the low-cut, short shimmery cocktail dress that stretched over it.

The bartender, a thin, dark man with bad teeth and a receding hairline walked up and leaned toward her over the bar. "'Evenin', Leonie." He looked her up and down, his eyes coming to rest on her cleavage. "You're looking good tonight. I get off at two. Wanna get together?"

She hid her disinterest well. "No thanks, Sugah. I plan to get off well before then." She smiled slyly.

The bartender nodded. "Well, if things don't go the way you planned, keep my offer in mind. I'll show you a real good time." He rubbed his crotch suggestively. She was unresponsive. Finally, he said, "The usual?" She nodded and he wandered down the bar to make her drink.

Leonie was aware of movement beside her. She turned to her right and smiled provocatively at the man taking a seat on the stool next to hers. He returned her smile.

"Hi, Sugah, I'm Leonie." She held her hand out coyly. The stranger had a powerful build and was handsome in a rugged way. She turned up the wattage in her smile.

The man took her hand, squeezed it gently and held it for a moment longer than usual. She liked it. Their eyes locked and he said, "I'm Tom."

Tom appeared to be about forty with short, darkish blond hair and long sideburns and a mustache. He was wearing jeans, running shoes and a gray sweatshirt. He also was wearing sunglasses.

"I haven't seen y'all in he'ah before, Tom. Where y'all from?"

The bartender returned with Leonie's Bourbon and Branch and set it on a small cocktail napkin in front of her. He stared sullenly at Tom. "What's it gonna be, pal?"

"A Restoration ale," Tom said.

The bartended moved off at a slow pace to get the Abita product.

Tom turned on his stool and faced Leonie, his right arm resting on the bar. She reached over and put her hand on top of his and began gently stroking it.

"So, Tom," she said, "are y'all wearin' them sunglasses 'cause you got an eye problem or you jes' tryin' to be cool?" She was smiling when she said it.

He laughed easily and said, "A little bit of both I guess."

The bartender returned and put the bottle of beer down in front of Tom hard enough to slop a small amount on the bar. He didn't offer a glass or a cocktail napkin. "You payin' for hers too?" He nodded at Leonie.

"Yeah, I'll take care of it."

"Twelve bucks," the bartender said.

Tom peeled off a ten and a five from a roll in his pocket and laid them on the bar. "Use the change to buy yourself a better attitude."

"You sonofa…," the bartender started to say. He cut it short when he saw the look on Tom's face. It frightened him. He scooped up the bills and retreated to the far end of the bar.

"You're funny," Leonie said. "I like that in a man." She drank the remaining swallow in her glass and said, "This place is kinda' expensive. Why don't we go back to my place and get to know each other better?"

"Stole the words right out of my mouth," Tom said.

They left the bar and strolled hand in hand on their way to Leonie's apartment a few blocks away.

"Tell me about yourself, Leonie. Where are you from? What brought you to the Big Easy? You know, the whole life story thing." Tom said.

She tilted her head back and ran her free hand through her thick, dark hair. "There's not much to tell. Ah' grew up over in Houma, 'bout fifty miles from he'ah. Shitty little hick town. Nothing much for a girl to do there but find her a guy, get married and have a shit load of screamin' little kids."

"Sounds pretty bad. How much of all that did you do?"

"I got to the married part, but it wasn't for me. God put me on this earth to have fun." She looked at him. "Fun means men. God, I love men!"

"So you're saying you weren't exactly faithful to your husband."

"Sugah, I managed to be cool for most of the first year, but after that I tried not to miss a single opportunity."

"Did your husband catch you?"

"Naw, he always kinda suspected, but he didn't really want to know. Funny thing is, he was the prize catch of that little hick town. Marine war hero in the Gulf War. Good lookin'. Smart. Pretty much everything most girls would want."

"But not you?"

Her voice took on a tinge of a whine. "He didn't pay 'nuff attention to me. Spent all his time teaching martial arts in that *dojo* of his." She paused and said, "That's one of them karate places."

"I know. Did you ever talk to him about your needs, Leonie?"

"Shit, a lot of good that woulda done. He was always worn out from that *dojo*. And besides, I was gettin' all the lovin' I could handle from jes' about everyone else in town."

"I take it he wasn't the one who wanted the divorce."

"No, Sugah, that was my idea. I needed out of that damn town. I needed to enjoy life to the fullest." She paused then said, almost wistfully, "He shore was a hellova guy, though. A nicer, gentler, kindhearted man than you could find anywhere."

"How do you suppose this affected him?"

"How do ya think, Sugah? The poor man was devastated. Sold his *dojo* for a song and went to work up north somewhere for an old Marine Corps friend. It was probably a good thing, 'else he woulda killed himself."

They reached her place, a small apartment on a corner above a boarded up former grocery store. The building was faced with rough red bricks. A rather plain wrought iron railed balcony ran along the two street sides of the building.

As she was unlocking the door, Tom said, "Do you ever hear from him?"

"Who?"

"Your former husband."

"No. He's dead. Got hisself killed playin' bodyguard." She opened the door lock, looked at him and said, "I don't wanna talk about Paul, my ex. I jes' wanna get to know *you*, Sugah,...real intimate. You know what I mean?"

When they were inside, she said, "Wanna drink or somethin', Sugah?"

"No, Leonie. Right now all I want is you."

"That's mah man," she said with a squeal of delight. She gently removed his sunglasses. "You won't need these in here." She looked at his eyes. There was something unusual about them; there were tiny red dots in their centers. The unusual excited her, and this was no exception.

In moments they were undressed and standing at the foot of her bed. She pressed her large breasts against his chest and tried to kiss him, but he moved his head away. "Plenty of time for that in the afterglow," he said. "Right now I just really want you."

Leonie admired his erection then turned and rested her elbows on her bed. She spread her feet wide apart on the scuffed hardwood, and waited

369

excitedly for him to enter her. Instead, he put his left hand on the back of her head and his right hand around her chin. With a sudden powerful twist, he snapped her neck. Her lifeless body collapsed in a loose heap. Like her muscles and tendons no longer were working her bones in concert.

For the next hour, he carefully scrubbed the scene. In his bare feet, he vacuumed the areas where he had been and wiped down the few places he'd touched. He had been careful not to exchange saliva, semen or other body fluids with her. When he was through, he put the disposable vacuum bag in a plastic grocery sack that he withdrew from one of his pockets. He would take it with him.

Before leaving, he stood over Leonie's corpse. "Paul was a friend of mine; a good man. He deserved a lot better."

He carefully slipped on his socks before he stepped off the carpet at the top of the stairs. He put his shoes on at the bottom. Using the rag he had wiped the place down with, he opened the door and stepped out onto the still deserted street. He took the rag and the plastic bag that held the vacuumed hairs and fibers with him.

Closing the door softly behind him, he strolled casually off into the night. Within seconds, Nick Stensen had vanished into the darkness.

###

ACKNOWLEDGMENTS

A great many people have contributed to the experiences that have shaped me as an individual, and developed the perspectives that influence my writing. I'm grateful to all of them, even the ones who were involved in the not so pleasant experiences. Each of us, after all, is the product of the sum total of our life experiences.

There are some people to whom I am especially grateful. Most important is my wife, "Annie". She has been my most ardent supporter in this effort. She is a lady of refinement and sensitivity, and I take it as a very good sign that, after reading this novel, she wasn't upset by the dialogue or gore.

My dad, a self-described (tongue-in-cheek) "fine Irish bastard", played a major role in my desire to write. He encouraged my thirst for adventure stories as a youngster. More importantly, he totally freaked out when, at about age ten, I announced that I wanted to be a writer when I grew up. I remember the salient bits and pieces of his diatribe: "freeze to death...bare, unheated attic...starvation...no friends...no money". It was a blessing in disguise. I spent years moving in other directions and gained much valuable experience and insight, which, hopefully, has made me a better chronicler of the human condition.

At a very early age, my mother taught me to read and took to the local library where I was introduced to a vast treasure trove of adventure. She also instilled in me toughness in the face of challenges, an unwillingness to take the path of least resistance.

My sons, Jack and Ryan, both articulate, intelligent men, spent many hours proofreading my efforts and offering valuable comments and suggestions, including cover art and layout. Do not be surprised to see their names on bestseller lists one day.

Suzanne Anderson, a friend, former student of mine, and published author (*Mrs. Tuesday's Departure*), was very generous in taking time to review this novel.

There are two general categories of writers who have influenced me. The first are the classical chroniclers of heroic deeds and writers of adventurous tales, such as Herodotus' *Histories*, Xenophon's *Anabasis*, *One Thousand and One Nights*, the *Song of Roland*, and others.

The second category includes more modern writers from Raphael Sabatini to Dashiell Hammett, Raymond Chandler, John D. MacDonald, and Robert B. Parker. Current writers in the thriller genre who I greatly admire include Lee Child, Brad Thor, David Baldacci, Vince Flynn, and Alex Berenson.

ABOUT THE AUTHOR

John Wayne Falbey has worn many hats: attorney, martial artist, real estate developer, triathlete, university professor, competitive cyclist, lecturer, downhill skier, author and adventurer. He has published numerous works of nonfiction on law, real estate development, and finance; but his first love has always been fiction, particularly the thriller genre. He wrote his first novel in his "spare time" as a student at Vanderbilt University in order to counter the creativity-stifling regimentation of law school. This novel, Sleeping Dogs: The Awakening, is the first in a planned trilogy. When not travelling for business or pleasure, he and his wife live in Naples, Florida, and have a vacation home in Beaver Creek, Colorado.

Connect with Me Online:
http://Twitter.com/jwfalbey

13367997R00218

Made in the USA
Charleston, SC
05 July 2012